THE
PARIS
WIFE

THE
PARIS
WIFE

Paula McLain

virago

VIRAGO

First published in Great Britain in 2010 by Virago Press

Copyright © Paula McLain 2010

The permissions on pages 391–392 constitute an
extension of this copyright page.

The moral right of the author has been asserted.

A CIP catalogue record for this book
is available from the British Library.

Hbk ISBN: 978-1-84408-666-5
C-format ISBN: 978-1-84408-667-2

Typeset in Centaur by M Rules
Printed and bound in Great Britain by
Clays Ltd, St Ives plc

Papers used by Virago are natural, renewable and
recyclable products sourced from well-managed forests and certified
in accordance with the rules of the Forest Stewardship Council.

Mixed Sources
Product group from well-managed
forests and other controlled sources
www.fsc.org Cert no. SGS-COC-004081
© 1996 Forest Stewardship Council
FSC

Virago Press
An imprint of
Little, Brown Book Group
100 Victoria Embankment
London EC4Y 0DY

An Hachette UK Company
www.hachette.co.uk

www.virago.co.uk

'It is not what France gave you but what it did not take from you that was important.'

GERTRUDE STEIN

'There's no *one* thing that's true. It's all true.'

ERNEST HEMINGWAY

PROLOGUE

Though I often looked for one, I finally had to admit that there could be no cure for Paris. Part of it was the war. The world had ended once already and could again at any moment. The war had come and changed us by happening when everyone said it couldn't. No one knew how many had died, but when you heard the numbers — nine million or fourteen million — you thought *impossible*. Paris was full of ghosts and the walking wounded. Many came back to Rouen or Oak Park, Illinois shot through and carrying little pieces of what they'd seen behind their kneecaps, full of an emptiness they could never dislodge. They'd carried bodies on stretchers, stepping over other bodies to do it; they'd been on stretchers themselves, on slow-moving trains full of flies and the floating voice of someone saying he wanted to be remembered to his girl back home.

There was no back home any more, not in the essential way, and that was part of Paris too. Why we couldn't stop drinking or talking or kissing the wrong people no matter what it ruined. Some of us had looked into the faces of the dead and tried not to remember anything in particular. Ernest was one of these. He often said he'd died in the war, just for a moment; that his soul had left his body like a silk handkerchief, slipping out and levitating over his chest. It had returned without being called back, and I often wondered if writing for him was a way of knowing his soul was there after all, back in its place. Of saying to himself, if not to anyone else, that he had seen what he'd seen and felt those terrible things and lived anyway. That he had died but wasn't dead any more.

One of the best things about Paris was coming back after we'd gone away. In 1923 we moved to Toronto for a year to have our son, Bumby, and when we returned, everything was the same but more somehow. It was filthy and gorgeous, full of rats and horse chestnut blossoms and poetry. With the baby our needs seemed to double, but we had less to spend. Pound helped us find an apartment on the second floor of a white stucco building on a tight curving street near the Luxembourg Gardens. The flat had no hot water, no bathtub, no electric lighting — but it wasn't the worst place we'd lived. Not by a long shot. Across the courtyard, a sawmill buzzed steadily from seven in the morning until five at night, and there was always the smell of fresh-cut wood, and sawdust filtered in under the windowsills and doorframes and got in our clothes and made us cough. Inside, there was the steady report of Ernest's Corona in the small room upstairs. He was working on stories — there were always stories or sketches to write — but also a new novel about the fiesta in Pamplona that he'd started in the summer.

I wasn't reading the pages then but I trusted his feeling about them and trusted the rhythm of every day. Each morning, he'd wake early and dress and then head upstairs to his room and begin the day's writing. If things weren't hitting for him there, he'd take the notebooks and several well-sharpened pencils and walk to the Closerie des Lilas for a café crème at the marble table he liked best, while Bumby and I breakfasted alone, and then dressed for a walk or went out to see friends. In the late afternoon, I'd head home and if the day had gone well, Ernest would be there at the dining table looking satisfied with some nice cold Sauternes or brandy and seltzer, and ready to talk about anything. Or we would go out together, leaving Bumby with our landlady, Madame Chautard, and find a plate of fat oysters and good talk at the Select or the Dôme or the Deux Magots.

Interesting people were everywhere just then. The cafés of Montparnasse breathed them in and out; French painters and Russian dancers and American writers. On any given night, you could see Picasso walking from Saint-Germain to his apartment in the rue des Grands-Augustins, always exactly the same route and always looking quietly at everyone and everything. Nearly anyone might feel like a painter walking the streets of Paris then, because the light brought it out in you, and the shadows alongside the buildings, and the bridges which seemed to want to break your heart, and the sculpturally beautiful women in Chanel's black sheath dresses, smoking and throwing back their heads to laugh. We could walk into any café and feel the wonderful chaos of it, ordering Pernod or Rhum St James until we were beautifully blurred and happy to be there together.

'Listen,' Don Stewart said one night when we were all very jolly and drunk as fishes at the Select. 'What you and Hem have is perfect. No, no,' he was slurring now, and his face contorted with feeling. 'It's *holy*. That's what I meant to say.'

'That's swell of you, Don. You're all right too, you know.' I cupped his shoulder lightly, afraid he might cry. He was a humorist, and everyone knew the funny writers were the most serious sort under their skins. He also wasn't married yet, but there were prospects on the horizon, and it was all very important to him to see that marriage could be done gracefully and well.

Not everyone believed in marriage then. To marry was to say you believed in the future and in the past, too – that history and tradition and hope could stay knitted together to hold you up. But the war had come and stolen all the fine young men and our faith too. There was only today to throw yourself into without thinking about tomorrow, let alone forever. To keep you from thinking there was liquor, an ocean's worth at least, all the usual vices and plenty of rope to hang yourself with. But some of us, a very few in the end, bet on marriage against the odds. And though I didn't feel holy, exactly, I did feel that what we had was rare and true – and that we were safe in the marriage we had built and were building every day.

This isn't a detective story – not hardly. I don't want to say, *Keep watch for the girl who will come along and ruin everything*, but she's coming anyway, set on her course in a gorgeous chipmunk coat and fine shoes, her sleek brown hair bobbed so close to her well-made head she'll seem like a pretty otter in my kitchen. Her easy smile. Her fast, smart talk – while in the bedroom, scruffy and unshaven and laid flat out on the bed like a despot king, Ernest will read his book and care nothing for her. Not at first. And the tea will boil in the teapot, and I'll tell a story about a girl she and I both knew a hundred years ago in St Louis, and we'll feel like quick and natural friends while across the yard, in the sawmill, a dog will start barking and keep barking and he won't stop for anything.

ONE

The very first thing he does is fix me with those wonderfully brown eyes and say, 'It's possible I'm too drunk to judge, but you might have something there.'

It's October 1920 and jazz is everywhere. I don't know any jazz, so I'm playing Rachmaninoff. I can feel a flush beginning in my cheeks from the hard cider my dear pal Kate Smith has stuffed down me so I'll relax. I'm getting there, second by second. It starts in my fingers, warm and loose, and moves along my nerves, rounding through me. I haven't been drunk in over a year – not since my mother fell seriously ill – and I've missed the way it comes with its own perfect glove of fog, settling snugly and beautifully over my brain. I don't want to think and I don't want to feel, either, unless it's as simple as this beautiful boy's knee inches from mine.

The knee is nearly enough on its own, but there's a whole package of a man attached, tall and lean, with a lot of very dark hair and a dimple in his left cheek you could fall into. His friends call him Hemingstein, Oinbones, Bird, Nesto, Wemedge, anything they can dream up on the spot. He calls

Kate Stut or Butstein (not very flattering!), and another fellow Little Fever, and yet another Horney or The Great Horned Article. He seems to know everyone, and everyone seems to know the same jokes and stories. They telegraph punch lines back and forth in code, lightning fast and wise-cracking. I can't keep up, but I don't mind really. Being near these happy strangers is like a powerful transfusion of good cheer.

When Kate wanders over from the vicinity of the kitchen, he points his perfect chin at me and says, 'What should we name our new friend?'

'Hash,' Kate says.

'Hashedad's better,' he says. 'Hasovitch.'

'And you're Bird?' I ask.

'Wem,' Kate says.

'I'm the fellow who thinks someone should be dancing.' He smiles with everything he's got, and in very short order, Kate's brother Kenley has kicked the living room carpet to one side and is manning the Victrola. We throw ourselves into it, danc-ing our way through a stack of records. This boy is not a natural, but his arms and legs are free in their joints, and I can tell that he likes being in his body. He's not the least shy about moving in on me either. In no time at all our hands are damp and clenched, our cheeks close enough that I can feel the very real heat of him. And that's when he finally tells me his name is Ernest.

'I'm thinking of giving it away, though. Ernest is so dull, and Hemingway? Who wants a Hemingway?'

Probably every girl between here and Michigan Avenue, I think, look-ing at my feet to hide my blushing. When I look up again, he has his brown eyes locked on me.

'Well? What do you think? Should I toss it out?'

6

'Maybe not just yet. You never know. A name like that could catch on, and where would you be if you'd ditched it?'

'Good point. I'll take it under consideration.'

A slow number starts and without asking, he reaches for my waist and scoops me toward his body, which is even better up close. His chest is solid and so are his arms. I rest my hands on them lightly as he backs me around the room, past Kenley cranking the Victrola with glee, past Kate giving us a long, curious look. I close my eyes and lean into Ernest, smelling bourbon and soap, tobacco and damp cotton – and everything about this moment is so sharp and lovely, I do something completely out of character and just let myself have it.

Two

There was a song from that time by Nora Bayes called 'Make Believe', which might have been the most lilting and persuasive treatise on self-delusion I'd ever heard. Nora Bayes was beautiful, and she sang with a trembling voice that told you she knew things about love. When she advised you to throw off all the old pain and worry and heartache and *smile* — well, you believed she'd done this herself. It wasn't a suggestion but a prescription. The song must have been a favorite of Kenley's, too. He played it three times the night I arrived in Chicago, and each time I felt it speaking directly to me: *Make believe you are glad when you're sorry. Sunshine will follow the rain.*

I'd had my share of rain. My mother's illness and death had weighed on me, but the years before had been heavy, too. I was only twenty-eight, and yet I'd been living like a spinster on the second floor of my older sister Fonnie's house, while she and her husband Roland and their four dear beasts lived down-stairs. I hadn't meant for things to stay this way. I had assumed I'd get married or find a career like my schoolfriends. They were harried young mothers now, schoolteachers or secretaries or aspiring ad writers, like Kate. Whatever they were, they were living their lives, out there doing it, making their mistakes. Somehow I'd gotten stuck along the way – long before my mother's illness – and I didn't know how to free myself exactly.

After playing an hour of passable Chopin, I'd collapse onto the sofa or the carpet, feeling whatever energy I'd had while playing leave my body. It was terrible to feel so empty, as if I were nothing. Why couldn't I be happy? And just what was happiness anyway? Could you fake it, as Nora Bayes insisted? Could you force it like a spring bulb in your kitchen, or rub up against it at a party in Chicago and catch it like a cold?

Ernest Hemingway was still very much a stranger to me, but he seemed to do happiness all the way up and through. There wasn't any fear in him that I could see, just intensity and aliveness. His eyes sparked all over everything, all over me as he leaned back on his heel and spun me toward him. He tucked me fast against his chest, his breath warm on my neck and hair.

'How long have you known Stut?' he asked.

'We went to grade school together in St Louis, at Mary Institute. What about you?'

'You want my whole educational pedigree? It's not much.'

'No,' I laughed. 'Tell me about Kate.'

'That would fill a book, and I'm not sure I'm the fellow to write it.' His voice was light, still teasing, but he'd stopped smiling.

'What do you mean?'

'Nothing,' he said. 'The short and sweet part is our families both have summer cottages up near Petosky. That's Michigan to a southerner like you.'

'Funny that we both grew up with Kate.'

'I was ten to her eighteen. Let's just say I was happy to grow up *alongside* her. With a nice view of the scenery.'

'You had a crush in other words.'

'No, those are the right words,' he said, then looked away.

I'd obviously touched some kind of nerve in him and I didn't want to do it again. I liked him smiling and laughing and loose. In fact, my response to him was so powerful that I already knew I would do a lot to keep him happy. I changed the subject fast.

'Are you from Chicago?'

'Oak Park. That's right up the street.'

'For a southerner like me.'

'Precisely.'

'Well, you're a bang-up dancer, Oak Park.'

'You too, St Louis.'

The song ended and we parted to catch our breath. I moved to one side of Kenley's long living room while Ernest was quickly swallowed up by admirers – women, naturally. They seemed awfully young and sure of themselves with their bobbed hair and brightly rouged cheeks. I was closer to a Victorian holdout than a flapper. My hair was still long, knotted at the nape of my neck, but it was a good rich auburn color, and though my dress wasn't up to the minute, my figure made up for that, I thought. In fact, I'd been feeling very good about the way I looked the whole time Ernest and I were dancing – he was so appreciative with those eyes! – but now that he was surrounded by vivacious women, my confidence was waning.

'You seemed awfully friendly with Nesto,' Kate said, appearing at my elbow.

'Maybe. Can I have the rest of that?' I pointed to her drink.

'It's rather volcanic.' She grimaced and passed it over.

'What is it?' I put my face to the rim of the glass, which was close enough. It smelled like rancid gasoline.

'Something homemade. Little Fever handed it to me in the kitchen. I'm not sure he didn't cook it up in his shoe.'

Over against a long row of windows, Ernest began parading back and forth in a dark blue military cape someone had dug up. When he turned, the cape lifted and flared dramatically.

'That's quite a costume.' I said.

'He's a war hero, didn't he tell you?'

I shook my head.

'I'm sure he'll get to it eventually.' Her face didn't give anything away, but her voice had an edge.

'He told me he used to pine for you.'

'Really?' There was the tone again. 'He's clearly over it now.'

I didn't know what had come between these two old friends, but whatever it was, it was obviously complicated and well under wraps. I let it drop.

'I like to think I'm the kind of girl who'll drink anything,' I said, 'but maybe not from a shoe.'

'Right. Let's hunt something up.' She smiled and flashed her green eyes at me, and became my Kate again, not grim at all, and off we went to get very drunk and very merry.

I found myself watching for Ernest the rest of the night, waiting for him to appear and stir things up, but he didn't. He must have slipped away at some point. One by one nearly everyone did, so that by three in the morning the party had been reduced to dregs, with Little Fever as the tragic centerpiece. He was passed out on the davenport with long dark wool socks stretched over his face and his hat perched on his crossed feet.

'To bed, to bed,' Kate said with a yawn.

'Is that Shakespeare?'

'I don't know. Is it?' She hiccupped, and then laughed. 'I'm off to my own little hovel now. Will you be all right here?'

'Of course. Kenley's made up a lovely room for me.' I walked her to the door, and as she sidled into her coat, we made a date for lunch the next day.

'You'll have to tell me all about things at home. We haven't had a moment to talk about your mother. It must have been awful for you, poor creatch.'

'Talking about it will only make me sad again,' I said. 'But this is perfect. Thanks for begging me to come.'

'I worried you wouldn't.'

'Me too. Fonnie said it was too soon.'

'Yes, well, she would say that. Your sister can be smart about some things, Hash, but about you, nearly never.'

I gave her a grateful smile and said goodnight. Kenley's apartment was warren-like and full of boarders, but he'd given me a large and very clean room, with a four-poster bed and a bureau. I changed into my nightdress then took down my hair and brushed it, sorting through the highlights of the evening. No matter how much fun I'd had with Kate or how good it was to see her after all these years, I had to admit that number one on my list of memorable events was dancing with Ernest Hemingway. I could still feel his brown eyes and his electric, electrifying energy – but what had his attentions meant? Was he babysitting me, as Kate's old friend? Was he still gone on Kate? Was she in love with him? Would I even see him again?

My mind was suddenly such a hive of unanswerable questions that I had to smile at myself. Wasn't this exactly what I had wanted coming to Chicago, something new to think about? I turned to face the mirror over the bureau. Hadley

Richardson was still there, with her auburn waves and thin lips and pale round eyes — but there was something new too, a glimmer of potential. It was just possible the sun was on its way. In the meantime, I would hum Nora Bayes and do my damnedest to make believe.

THREE

The next morning, I walked into the kitchen to find Ernest leaning lazily against the refrigerator, reading the morning newspaper and devouring half a loaf of bread.

'Did you sleep here?' I asked, unable to mask my surprise at seeing him.

'I'm boarding here. Just for a while, until things take off for me.'

'What do you mean to do?'

'Make literary history, I guess.'

'Gee,' I said, impressed all over again by his confidence and conviction. You couldn't fake that. 'What are you working on now?'

He pulled a face. 'Now I'm writing trash copy for *Firestone Tires*, but I mean to write important stories or a novel. Maybe a book of poetry.'

That threw me. 'I thought poets were quiet and shrinking and afraid of sunlight,' I said, sitting down.

'Not this one.' He came over to join me at the table, turning his chair around to straddle it. 'Who's your favorite writer?'

'Henry James, I suppose. I seem to read him over and over.'

'Well, aren't you sweetly square?'

'Am I? Who's your favorite writer?'

'Ernest Hemingway.' He grinned. 'Anyway, there're lots of writers in Chicago. Kenley knows Sherwood Anderson. Heard of him?'

'Sure. He wrote *Winesburg, Ohio*.'

'That's the one.'

'Well, with your nerve, you can probably do anything at all.'

He looked at me seriously, as if he were trying to gauge whether I was teasing or placating him. I wasn't. 'How do you take your coffee, Hasovitch?' he finally said.

'Hot,' I said, and he grinned his grin, that began in his eyes and went everywhere at once. It was devastating.

When Kate arrived for our lunch date, Ernest and I were still in the kitchen talking away. I hadn't yet changed out of my dressing gown, and there she was, sharp and fresh in a red wool hat and coat.

'I'm sorry,' I said, 'I won't be a minute.'

'Take your time, you deserve a little indolence,' she said, but seemed impatient with me just the same.

I went off to dress, and when I came back, Kate was alone in the room.

'Where did Nesto run off to?'

'I haven't the faintest,' Kate said. And then, because she clearly read disappointment in my face, 'Should I have invited him along?'

'Don't be silly. This is our day.'

In the end, we had a lovely afternoon. Out of all the girls in my class at Mary Institute, Kate was the boldest and most fearless, able to talk to anyone and make fun out of nothing at all. She was still that way and I felt bolder, too, walking along Michigan Avenue with her, and years younger. We had lunch at a restaurant across from the marble vastness of the Art Institute, where two regal lions presided over traffic and an ever-shifting sea of dark coats and hats. It was a chilly day, and after lunch, we huddled arm in arm along State Street, tucking into every interesting shop we came to. She tried to urge me to open up about things at home, but I didn't want to lose my good mood. Instead, I got Kate talking about her summer up in Michigan, the fishing and swimming parties and general rambunctiousness. All of her stories seemed to involve rowboats and ukuleles, full moons and campfires and grog. I was desperately jealous.

'Why do you get all the young men?'

'They're not mine, I'm just borrowing them.' She smiled. 'It's having brothers, I guess. And anyway, sometimes it's a nuisance. I spent half the summer trying to encourage this one and discourage that one and all the signals got mixed and in the end no one even kissed anyone else. So there, see? Nothing to be envious of.'

'Is Carl Edgar still proposing to you regularly?'

'Ugh, I'm afraid so. Poor old Odgar. Sometimes I wonder what would happen if I actually said yes – as an experiment.'

'He'd fall over.'

'Or run away in terror, maybe. Some men seem to only want the girls beating a path in the other direction.'

'What about Ernest?'

'What about him?' Her eyes snapped to attention.

'Does he like his women on the run?'

'I wouldn't know.'

'How young is he, anyway? Twenty-five?'

She smirked. 'Twenty-one. A boy-o. I know you're more sensible than that.'

'What do you mean?'

'I thought I saw some interest.' She gazed at me with intensity.

'I'm just bored,' I said. But I'd always been a terrible liar.

'How about a new hat instead?' she said, and pointed to something towering and feathery I couldn't see myself standing beneath in a million years.

By the time we made it back to the apartment late that afternoon, the place was chock full again. Kenley and his brother Bill, the youngest of the Smith clan were trying to get together a card game. A fellow named Brummy was playing a ragtime tune on the piano, while Ernest and another cohort, Don Wright, circled each other on the carpet in a spontaneous boxing match. They were stripped to the waist, bobbing and weaving with their fists up, while a group stood around egging them on. Everyone was laughing, and it looked like great fun until Ernest lit out with a right hook. Don managed to dodge most of it and the match went on good-naturedly, but I'd seen the killer look on Ernest's face when he threw the punch and knew it was all very serious to him. He wanted to win.

Kate seemed unfazed by the boxing and everything else going on in the apartment. Apparently the place was always this crazy in the evenings, a good time Grand Central. Prohibition had been underway for the better part of a year, and that 'noble experiment' had spurred the popping up, nearly overnight, of speakeasies in cities everywhere. There were supposed to be thousands of these in Chicago alone, but who needed a speakeasy when Kenley, like many resourceful young men, had stockpiled enough hooch to pickle a herd of elephants? That night, there was plenty of open wine in the kitchen, so Kate and I had some of that, and then some more. As dusk fell, purpling and softening the room, I found myself on the davenport squeezed in between Ernest and Horney while they talked over me in Pig Latin. I couldn't stop collapsing into fits of giggles – and when was the last time I giggled anyway? It was surprisingly, intoxicatingly easy now.

When Horney got up to join Kate on the improvised dance floor, Ernest turned to me and said, 'I've been thinking all day about how to ask you something.'

'Really?' I didn't know if I was more surprised or flattered.

He nodded. 'Would you want to read something of mine? It's not a story yet, more like a sketch.' He tucked his chin nervously and I almost laughed with relief. Ernest Hemingway was nervous and I wasn't, suddenly. Not in the least.

'Sure,' I said. 'But I'm no literary critic. I'm not certain I can help you.'

'It's all right. I'd just like to get your take on it.'

'Okay, then. Yes,' I said.

'I'll be right back,' he said, and bolted half-way across the carpet before turning around. 'Don't go away, all right?'

'Where would I go?'

'You'd be surprised,' he said, mysteriously, and then ran off to fetch the pages.

Essentially, the story wasn't a story, he was right. It was a darkly funny sketch called 'Wolves and Donuts' set in an Italian restaurant on Wabash Avenue. But even unfinished, the voice was acid-sharp and hilarious. We went into the kitchen for better light and a little quiet, and as I read, Ernest paced the room, his arms swinging and pawing the air as he waited for me to answer the question he couldn't bring himself to ask: *is it good?*

When I'd turned the last page, he sat in the chair opposite me with an expectant look.

'You're very talented,' I said, meeting his eyes. 'I've probably spent too much time on Henry James. Your stuff isn't that.'

'No.'

'I'm not sure I get it completely, but I can tell you're a writer. Whatever that thing is, you have it.'

'God that's good to hear. Sometimes I think all I really need is one person telling me that I'm not knocking my fool head against the bricks. That I have a shot at it.'

'You do. Even I can see that.'

He looked at me intently, boring a small hole with those eyes. 'I like you, you know. You're a good clear sort.'

'I like you too,' I said back, and it struck me how comfortable I felt with him, as if we were old friends or had already done this many times over, him handing me pages with his heart on his sleeve – he couldn't pretend this work didn't mean everything to him – me reading his words, quietly amazed by what he could do.

'Will you let me take you to dinner?' he said.

'Now?'

'What's stopping us?'

Kate, I thought. *Kate and Kenley and the whole drunken throng in the living room.*

'No one will even notice we're gone,' he said, reading my hesitation.

'All right,' I said, but slunk off like a thief to get my coat anyway. I wanted to go with him. I was dying to go, but he was wrong about no one noticing. As we ducked out the door together, I felt Kate's green eyes moving hotly over my back and heard her silent shout, *Hadley, be sensible!*

I was tired of being sensible. I didn't turn around.

It was a sheer pleasure to walk the chilly Chicago streets with Ernest at my side, talking and talking, his cheeks flushed, his eyes beaming. We went to a Greek restaurant on Jefferson Street where we had roasted lamb and a cucumber salad with lemon and olives.

'I suppose it's embarrassing, but I've never had olives before,' I said when the waiter arrived with our order.

'That should be illegal. Here, open.'

He put the olive on my tongue and as I closed my mouth around it, oily and warm with salt, I found myself flushing from the deliciousness but also the intimacy, his fork in my mouth. It was the most sensual thing that had happened to me in ages.

'Well?' he prodded.

'I love it,' I said. 'Though it's a little dangerous, isn't it?'

He smiled and looked at me appreciatively. 'A little, yes.' And then he ate a dozen himself, one after the other.

After dinner we walked under the elevated train and headed toward the Municipal Pier. The whole time he talked fast about his plans, all the things he wanted for himself, the poems, stories and sketches he was burning to write. I'd never met anyone so vibrant or alive. He moved like light. He never *stopped* moving – or thinking, or dreaming, apparently.

When we reached the pier, we walked along it all the way out to the end of the streetcar line.

'Did you know they had barracks and Red Cross Units out here during the war? I worked for the Red Cross over in Italy, as an ambulance driver.'

'The war seems very far away now, doesn't it?'

'Sometimes.' A line of worry or doubt appeared on his forehead. 'What were you doing in those days?'

'Hiding out, mostly. I sorted books in the basement of the public library. I'm told they eventually went to soldiers overseas.'

'That's funny. I hand-delivered those books. Chocolate bars, too. Letters, cigarettes, candy. We had a canteen set up, but sometimes I went out to the line at night, on a bicycle. Can you picture it?'

'I can. It's a wobbly red bicycle, right?'

'The boy was wobbly too after he got blown all to hell.'

I stopped walking. 'Oh, Ernest, I'm sorry. I didn't know.'

'Don't worry. I was a hero for a day or two.' He leaned against the railing and looked out at the lake, gray on gray, with just a ghost of white. 'You know what I think about now?'

I shook my head. **GALWAY COUNTY LIBRARIES**

'Silkworms. I spent a night in San Pedro Norello, a village on the front. Horney was there — that's where I met him — and our cots were set up on the floor of this building, right? It was a silkworm factory. They were up over our heads, in the eaves, chewing away in racks full of mulberry leaves. That's the only thing you could hear. No shellfire, no nothing. It was terrible.'

'I've never thought of silkworms that way. Maybe I've never thought of silkworms at all, but I can hear them now, the way you did.'

'Sometimes when I can't sleep, I think I hear them chewing. I have to get up and turn the lights on and look up at the ceiling.'

'Are they ever there?' I smiled, trying to lighten the mood.

'Not yet.'

We headed away from the brightly lit shops and turned toward home – and I was struck by how rare it was to hear a near-stranger share something so essential about himself. He told it beautifully, too, with real feeling. I think I was a little dumbstruck. Just who was this Ernest Hemingway?

Suddenly he stopped walking and faced me on the sidewalk. 'Listen, Hash. You're not going to run off on me are you?'

'I'm not much of an athlete,' I said.

'I like your spine. Did I tell you that?'

'You did.'

'I like it more than that, then,' he said. Then he gave me a winning smile and started to walk again, tucking my gloved hand under his arm.

The next morning Kate came into my room without knocking. I wasn't even dressed yet.

'I waited past midnight. Where were you?'

'I'm sorry. Ernest invited me to dinner. I wasn't sure how I could say no.'

'No is the easiest word there is. *Children* learn to talk by saying no.'

I pulled my robe more tightly around my waist and sat down on the bed. 'All right. I didn't want to say no. It was just dinner, Kate. There's no harm done.'

'Of course,' she said, obviously still flustered. 'I just feel protective of you and don't want to see you get tangled up in something awful.'

'Why awful? He doesn't seem like a bad fellow.'

'He's not bad, exactly.' I could see she was trying to choose her words carefully. 'He's just young. He likes women – *all* women, apparently. And I see you throwing yourself at him, blindly trusting him, and it worries me.'

'I'm not throwing myself at anyone,' I said, suddenly angry. 'I had dinner with the man. Honestly, Kate.'

'You're right, you're right,' she said. 'I'm getting carried away.' She sat down beside me on the bed and reached for my hand. 'Forget I said anything, okay? You're a level-headed girl. You'll know what to do.'

'*Nothing* happened.'

'I know. I'm terrible.' She rubbed my hand with hers and I let her, but my head was fairly spinning.

'This is all too much to think about before breakfast,' I said.

'You poor thing.' She stood, smoothing her skirt, and then she smoothed her expression too, while I watched; righting and simplifying everything. It was a good trick. I wished I could do it.

The rest of that morning passed in a daze as I brooded over Kate's words and her concern for me. Was Ernest really someone to watch out for? He seemed so sincere and forthcoming. He'd confessed to writing poetry, for goodness' sake, and those stories about being wounded at the front – and the silkworms! Was this all part of some elaborate ploy to take advantage of me? If so then Kate was right, I was falling for it, heaving myself at him like a dumb country mouse – likely one of dozens. I could barely stand to think about it.

'Maybe we should hightail it out of here before anyone stirs,' Kate said when we'd finished our coffee. 'I don't have to be at work at all today. What shall we do? The sky's the limit.'

'You decide,' I said. 'I don't much care.' And I didn't.

Another kind of girl might have suspected Kate of jealousy, but I was very simple and trusting, then. More than this, I was inexperienced. At twenty-eight I'd had a handful of beaux, but had only been in love once, and that had been awful enough to make me doubt men, and myself, for a good long while.

His name was Harrison Williams and he was my piano teacher when I was twenty and just returned home to St Louis after a single year at Bryn Mawr. Although he was only a few months older than I was, he seemed much older and more sophisticated to me. I found it both appealing and intimidating that he'd studied overseas with famous composers and knew loads about European art and culture. I could listen to him talk about anything, and I suppose that's how it started, with admiration and envy. Then I found myself watching his hands and his eyes and his mouth. He wasn't an obvious Casanova, but he was handsome in his way, tall and slender, with dark thinning hair. Most appealing of all was his impression of me as exceptional. He thought I could make it as a concert pianist and I thought so too, at least for the hours I sat at his piano bench working through finger-cramping etudes.

I worried a lot about my hair and dress those afternoons at Harrison's. As he paced and corrected and occasionally praised me, I did my best to decode him. Did the tapping of his fingertip on his temple mean he had or hadn't noticed my new stockings?

'You have a lovely alignment at the bench,' he said to me one afternoon, and that's about all it took to send me spiraling into a fantasy of my alignment in white lace, his alignment in morning tails and gorgeous white gloves. I played terribly that day, distracted by my own swooning.

I loved him for a full year and then, in one night, all my wishing came apart. We were both at a neighbor's evening party, where I forced myself to tip back two glasses of too-sweet wine so I could be braver near him. The day before we'd gone for a walk together in the woods just outside of town. It was fall; crisp and windless, with the clouds overhead looking like perfect cutouts of themselves. He lit my cigarette. I stamped at some yellow leaves with the toe of my lace-up shoes, and then, in the middle of a very nice silence he said, 'You're such a dear person, Hadley. One of the best I've known, really.'

It was hardly a declaration of love, but I told myself he did care for me and believed it — long enough for the gulping of the wine in any case. I waited for the room to pitch just that much off its center then walked up to Harrison, picking each foot up and putting it back down again, getting closer. I was wearing my black lace. It was my hands-down favorite dress because it never failed to make me feel a bit like Carmen. And maybe it was the dress as much as the wine that lifted my hand toward Harrison's coat sleeve. I'd never touched him before, so it was probably clean surprise that stopped him still. We stood there, locked and lovely as statues in a garden — and for several dozen heartbeats I was his wife. I had already borne his children and secured his loyalty, and was well beyond the thorny rim of my own mind, that place where hope got itself snagged and swallowed over and over. I could have this. It was already mine.

'Hadley,' he said quietly.

I looked up. Harrison's eyes were the pale blue of drowned stars, and they were saying no — simply and quietly. Just *no*.

What did I say? Maybe nothing. I don't remember. The music lurched, candlelight blurred, my hand dropped to the lace of my skirt. A minute before it had been a gypsy's dress, now it was funereal.

'I have a terrible headache,' I said to my mother, trying to explain why I needed to go home that instant.

'Of course you do,' she said, and her expression softened. 'Let's get our girl to bed.'

Once home, I let her lead me up the stairs and help me into my muslin nightgown. She tucked me into layers of quilting and put a cool hand on my forehead, smoothing my hair. 'Get some rest now.'

'Yes,' I said, because I couldn't begin to explain that I'd *been* resting for twenty-one years, but that tonight I'd tried for something else.

That was my one brush with love. Was it love? It felt awful enough. I spent another two years crawling around in the skin of it, smoking too much and growing too thin and having stray thoughts of jumping from my balcony like a tortured heroine in a Russian novel. After a time, though more slowly than I wanted, I came to see that Harrison wasn't my failed prince and I wasn't his victim. He hadn't led me on at all; I'd led *myself* on. The thought of love could still make me queasy and pale, though, more than half a decade later. I was still gullible, clearly, and needed someone's guidance – Kate's for instance.

We tramped all over Chicago that day looking first for world-class corned beef and then for new gloves. I let Kate chatter away and distract me, and felt grateful that she had warned me about Ernest. Even if his intentions were entirely above suspicion, I was far too susceptible just then. I'd come to Chicago wanting escape and I'd gotten it, but too much dreaming was dangerous. I wasn't happy at home, and yet drowning myself in fanciful notions about Ernest Hemingway wasn't going to solve anything for me. My life was my life; I would have to stare it down, somehow, and make it work for me.

✽

I spent another full week in Chicago, and every day of that time brought some new excitement. We went to a football game; saw a matinee showing of *Madama Butterfly*; roamed the city by day and by night. Whenever I saw Ernest, which was often, I strove to keep my head clear and just enjoy his company without conjuring up any drama in one direction or another. I might have been a little more reserved with him than I'd been before, but he didn't say anything and didn't force any intimacy until my last evening in town.

It was freezing that night – too cold to be out, really – but a group of us grabbed armfuls of wool blankets, poured rum into flasks and then piled into Kenley's Ford and headed out to Lake Michigan. The dunes were steep and pale in moonlight, and we invented a game around them, climbing to the top of one – drunkenly, of course – and then rolling down like a log. Kate went first because she loved to be the first at anything, and then Kenley went, singing his way down. When my turn came, I crawled up the dune as the sand shifted under my feet and hands. At the top, I looked around and everything was bright frosted stars and distances.

'C'mon, then, coward!' Ernest yelled up at me.

I closed my eyes and let myself fall, barreling down over the hard bumps. I'd had so much to drink I couldn't feel a thing – nothing but a thrilling sense of wildness and freedom. It was a kind of euphoria, really, and fear was a key part of it. For the first time since I was a girl, I felt the heady rush of being afraid, and liked the sensation. At the bottom, I'd barely come to a stop when Ernest whirled me up out of the dark and kissed me hard. I felt his tongue for a hot instant against my lips.

'Oh,' was all I could say. I couldn't think about whether anyone was watching. I couldn't think at all. His face was inches from mine, more charged and convincing and altogether awake than anything I'd ever seen.

'Oh,' I said again, and he let me go.

The next day I packed my bags for my return trip to St Louis feeling a bit lost. I'd been so swept away by living for two weeks, I couldn't really imagine going back home. I didn't want to.

Kate was working that day and we'd already said our good-byes. Kenley had to be at work as well, but had been kind enough to offer to drive me to the station on his lunch break and save me the cab fare. After everything was stowed and ready, I put on my coat and hat and went to wait for him in the living room. But when a body appeared in the hall to fetch me, it was Ernest's.

'Kenley couldn't get away after all?' I asked.

'No. I wanted to do it.'

I nodded dumbly and collected my things.

It wasn't much of a distance to Union Station and we passed it mostly in silence. He wore wool trousers and a gray wool jacket, with a dark cap pulled down nearly to his eyebrows. His cheeks were pink with cold and he looked very beautiful. *Beautiful* was exactly the right word for him, too. His looks weren't feminine but they were perfect and unmarred and sort of heroic, as if he'd stepped out of a Greek poem about love and battle.

'You can let me out here,' I said as we neared the station.

'Would it kill you to give a guy a break?' he said, finding a place to park.

'No. Probably not.'

A few minutes later, we stood together on the platform. I clutched my ticket and my pocket book. He held my suitcase, shifting it from hand to gloved hand – but as soon as my train appeared, its silver-brown body trailing smoke and soot, he set it down at his feet. Suddenly he was holding me tight against his chest.

My heart beat fast. I wondered if he could feel it. 'I don't think I've ever met anyone like you,' I said.

He didn't say anything at all, just kissed me, and through that kiss I could feel all of him radiating warmth and life. There was so much I didn't know about Ernest, and even more I wouldn't let myself ask or even imagine, but I found myself surrendering anyway, second by second. We were surrounded by people on the platform, but we were entirely alone. And when I finally boarded my train a few minutes later, my legs were shaking.

I found a seat and looked out my window into the crowd, scanning the dark suits and hats and coats. And then there he was, pushing closer to the train, smiling at me like a maniac and waving. I waved back, and then he held up one hand like a sheet of notebook paper, and the other like a pencil, panto-miming.

'I'll write to you,' he mouthed. Or maybe it was, 'I'll write *you.*'

I closed my eyes against hot, sudden tears, and then leaned into the plush seat as my train carried me home.

Four

In 1904, the year I turned thirteen, St Louis was host to the Louisiana Purchase Exposition, better known as the World's Fair. The fair grounds covered twelve hundred acres in and around Forest Park and Washington University, with seventy-five miles of paths and roads connecting the buildings and barns, theaters and palaces. Many of these structures were plaster of Paris over wooden framing, built to last only a few months, but they looked like opulent neo-classical palaces. Our crown jewel, the Palace of Fine Arts, boasted a sculpture garden fashioned after the Roman Baths of Caracalla. There were lagoons you could paddle along; enormous manmade waterfalls and sunken gardens; exotic animal zoos and human zoos with pygmies and primitives, bearded girls and pinheaded boys. All along the Pike, hundreds of amusements and games and food stalls enthralled the passersby. I had my very first ice-cream cone there, and couldn't stop marveling at how the sugary cylinder wasn't cold in my hand. The strawberry ice cream inside it seemed different too. Better. It might have been the best thing I'd ever tasted.

Fonnie was with me on the Pike that day, but she didn't want ice cream. She didn't want cotton candy or puffed wheat or iced tea or any of the other novel offerings either, she wanted to go home where our mother was preparing to host her weekly suffragette meeting.

I'd never understood why Fonnie was drawn to Mother's group. The women always seemed so unhappy to me. To hear them talk, you would think that marriage was the most terrible thing to happen to a woman. My mother was always the loudest and most emphatic one in the room, nodding sharply while Fonnie passed plates of teacakes and watercress sandwiches, trying very hard to please everyone.

'Another half-hour,' I said, attempting to bargain with Fonnie. 'Don't you want to see the Palace of Electricity?'

'Stay if you like. I'm surprised you can enjoy yourself.' And then she flounced imperiously off into the crowd.

I *was* enjoying myself, or had been until she reminded me I was supposed to be sad. It was probably very selfish of me to want to stay and smell the salt on the popcorn, and hear the braying from the barns. But it was April and the cherry trees around the lagoons were flowering. I could close my eyes and hear fountains. I could open them and imagine I was in Rome or Versailles. Fonnie grew smaller in the crowd, her dark skirt blotted by riotous color. I wanted to let her go without caring what she thought of me or said to our mother, but I couldn't. I took a last dejected look at my ice-cream cone, and then dropped it into a trash barrel as I trotted off after my sister toward home, where the curtains were drawn and the lights were banked, and had been for some time. We were in mourning. My father had been dead two months.

*

Ours was the quintessentially good family, with Pilgrim lineage on both sides and lots of Victorian manners keeping everything safe and reliable. My father's father founded the St Louis Public Library, and the Richardson Drug Company, which became the largest pharmaceutical house west of the Mississippi. My mother's father was a teacher who started the Hillsboro Academy in Illinois and later a private high school in St Louis called the City University. Fonnie and I went to the best schools wearing navy-blue skirts with knife-sharp pleats. We sat for private lessons at one of our two Steinway Grand pianos, and spent summers in Ipswich, Massachusetts at our beach cottage. And everything was very good and fine until it wasn't.

My father, James Richardson, was an executive at the family drug company. He'd go off in the mornings in his bowler hat and black string tie smelling of shaving cream and coffee and, just underneath, a ghost of whiskey. He kept a flask in his dressing gown. We all knew another lay tucked in his desk drawer in the study, which he locked with a tiny silver key. Still another waited behind stacked jars of stewed fruit in the pantry where our cook, Martha, pretended not to see it. He tried not to be home very often and when he was, he was quiet and distracted. But he was kind, too. My mother, Florence, was his perfect opposite – all sharp creases and pins, full of advice and judgements. It's possible my father was too soft and too cowardly around her, inclined to back away into his study or out the door rather than face up to her about anything, but I didn't fault him for this.

My mother always preferred Fonnie, who was twenty-two months older than me. We had an older brother, Jamie, who was off to college before I started kindergarten, and there was Dorothea, eleven years older but very dear to me just the same, who married young and lived nearby with her husband Dudley.

Because of the closeness in our ages, Fonnie was my primary companion as a girl, but we couldn't have been more different. She was obedient and bendable and good in a way my mother could easily understand and praise. I was impulsive and talkative and curious about everything – far too curious for my mother's taste. I loved to sit at the end of our driveway, my elbows on my knees, and watch the streetcar trundle along the center of the boulevard, wondering about the men and women inside, where they were headed, what they were thinking, and if they noticed me there, noticing them. My mother would call me back to the house and send me up to the nursery, but I'd simply stare out the window, dreaming and musing.

'What could you possibly be fit for?' she often said. 'You can't keep your head out of the clouds.'

It was a legitimate enough question, I suppose. She worried about me because she didn't understand me in the least. And then something terrible happened. When I was six years old, I managed to dream myself right out the window.

It was a spring day, and I was home sick from school. When I grew bored with the nursery, which generally happened quickly, I began to watch our handyman, Mike, pushing a wheelbarrow across our yard. I was crazy about Mike and found him infinitely more interesting than anyone in my family. His fingernails were square and nicked. He whistled and carried a bright blue handkerchief in his pocket.

'What're you up to, Mike?' I said, shouting out the nursery window, craning over the sill to better see him.

He looked up just as I lost my balance and fell crashing to the paving stones below.

For months I lay flat in bed while the doctors wondered if I would walk again. I recovered slowly, and as I did, my mother had a baby carriage specially adapted for me. She liked to push me around the neighborhood, stopping at each of our neighbors' houses so they could exclaim about the wonder of my survival.

'Poor Hadley,' my mother said. 'Poor hen.' She said it over and over, until her words became stitched onto my brain, replacing any other description of me, as well as every other possible outcome.

It didn't matter that I healed completely, and learned to walk again without a limp. My constitution was a great worry in the house and stayed that way. Even the slightest sniffle, it was thought, would damage me further. I didn't learn to swim, didn't run and play in the park as my friends did. I read books instead, tucked into the window seat in the parlor, surrounded by swirls of stained glass and claret-colored drapes. And after a time, I stopped struggling even internally against the prescribed quietness. Books could be an incredible adventure. I stayed under my blanket and barely moved, and no one would have guessed how my mind raced and my heart soared with stories. I could fall into any world and go without notice, while my mother barked orders at the servants or entertained her disagreeable friends in the front room.

When my father was alive, I often watched him come home while the women were still gathered. Hearing them, he'd freeze and then retrace his steps, slinking back out the door. Where did he go? I wondered. How far did he have to walk and how much whiskey did it take to quiet my mother's voice in his head? Did he remember the way he used to love his bicycle? I did. There was a time when he would happily ride anywhere in St Louis, choosing his bicycle over any other mode of transportation, probably because of the freedom it offered. Once he hitched a cart to the back and took Fonnie and me along the paths in Forest Park, singing 'Waltzing Matilda.' He had the most beautiful baritone, and as threads of song floated back to us in the cart that day, his happiness seemed so real and so strange to me, I was afraid to move in case I might startle it away.

It was a cold morning in February when a single shot rang through the house. My mother heard it first and knew instantly what had happened. She hadn't let herself think the word *suicide*, that would be too terrible and too common, but she'd been half expecting it just the same. Downstairs, behind the locked doors of his study, she found my father lying on the carpet in a pool of blood, his skull shattered.

For weeks after, the noise of my father's death rang through the house. We learned he'd lost tens of thousands of dollars on the stock market, that he'd borrowed more and lost that too. We already knew he drank but not that he did little else in his last weeks, plagued by throbbing headaches that made sleep impossible.

After he was gone, my mother stayed in her room, crying and confused and staring at the drawn curtains while the servants took over. I'd never seen this kind of chaos in my house, and didn't know what to do with it but play Chopin's nocturnes and cry for my father, wishing I had known him better.

The door to my father's study stayed closed for a time, but not locked. The carpets had been cleaned but not replaced; the revolver had been emptied and polished and placed back in his desk. These details were so terrible I couldn't help but be magnetized by them. Again and again, I imagined the last moments of his life. How alone he must have felt. How deadened and how hopeless, or else he couldn't have done it, lifting the muzzle and tripping the trigger.

My mood grew so low that my family began to worry I might hurt myself. Everyone knew that children of suicides stood a greater risk of taking that route. Was I like him? I didn't know, but I had inherited his migraine headaches. Each one was like a dreadful visitation, pressure and nausea and a dull but constant thrumming from the base of my skull while I lay absolutely still in my airless room. If I stayed there long enough, my mother would come in and pat my hand and tuck the covers around my feet, saying, 'You're a good girl, Hadley.'

I couldn't help but notice my mother responded to me more warmly when I was ill, so it's no surprise that I often was or thought I was. I missed so much school as a junior and senior that I was forced to stay another year as all my girlfriends went away to college without me. It was like watching a train leave the station for some far-off and exciting place, with no ticket myself and no means to purchase one. When letters began to arrive from Barnard and Smith and Mount Holyoke, I suddenly felt sick with jealousy of my friends' excitement and promise.

'I want to apply to Bryn Mawr,' I told my mother. Her sister Mary lived in Philadelphia, and I thought having a relative nearby would put my mother at ease.

'Oh, Hadley. Why do you insist on overreaching yourself? Be realistic.'

Fonnie came into the room and sat near Mother. 'What about your headaches?' she said.

'I'll be perfectly fine.'

Fonnie's brow furrowed skeptically.

'Mary can care for me if something happens. You know how competent she is.' I put particular stress on the word *competent* because my mother loved and was often persuaded by it. For the moment, however, she only sighed and said she would give it serious thought, which meant that she would take the matter up with our neighbor Mrs Curran and the Ouija board.

Mother had long been interested in matters of the occult. There were séances in our house occasionally, but many more of them down the street at Mrs Curran's. According to my mother, she was a savant of the supernatural and had a very familiar and persuasive way with the board. I wasn't invited to attend the session, but when Mother returned home from Mrs Curran's she reported that I could go to Bryn Mawr the following year after all, and that everything would be well.

Later I had to wonder about Mrs Curran's prophecy because it seemed blatantly false to me. I did go away, in 1911, but the whole venture was doomed before it even began. The summer before I left for Bryn Mawr, my older sister Dorothea was badly burned in a fire. Though she was well out of the house during the years I was growing up, Dorothea had always been the kindest and most supportive member of my family, and I felt she understood me in a way no one else did or wanted to. When things at home grew too stifling and restrained, I'd walk to her house and watch her two young boys wrestling around her, feeling calmed and restored.

Dorothea was heavily pregnant that summer. She was home alone with the boys a great deal, and one afternoon the three were out on the front porch when Dorothea saw that a fire had started in a pile of rubber tires in the empty lot next door. The boys were curious about it but Dorothea was afraid it might spread to her own yard. She ran over and tried to stamp out the flames with her feet, but her long summer kimono quickly caught fire. Her stockings did too, badly burning her all the way to the waist before she fell to the ground and rolled, snuffing out the flames.

When her husband Dudley called us with the news, we

were at our vacation cottage on Ipswich Bay. We were all worried sick about Dorothea, but Dudley reassured us she was in the hospital getting the best of care. She had no fever, and the doctors believed she would recover fully. The next day, she delivered a stillborn baby girl. Dorothea and Dudley were both devastated, but the doctors were still saying she'd live. They kept saying that until she died, eight days after the fire. Mother got on a train for the funeral but the rest of us stayed in Ipswich, heartbroken and numb.

I remember feeling that I might not survive Dorothea's loss, and maybe that I didn't want to. Mother came back from St Louis, bringing Dudley and the boys with her. They stepped off the train looking wretched, and what comfort could I offer? *They have no mother*, I found myself saying over and over.

One afternoon shortly after the funeral there was a terrible storm in Ipswich Bay and I talked one of the boys from a neighboring cottage into taking me out in it, in a rowboat. Waves slashed at the bow and came stinging over the sides and into our faces. I couldn't even swim, but he didn't turn back, even when the lighthouse captain signaled us to come in. The clouds were low and terrible and the air was drenched and salty. I felt as I if was drowning the whole time, over and over again. And even when we made it back to shore that day, the feeling that I was still out in the bay, sinking deeper and deeper, stayed with me through the rest of that summer and long afterward.

In September I boarded the train and went off to Bryn Mawr as planned, but my classmates seemed to be running on a different frequency. The girls in my dorm spent their afternoons in the salon drinking tea and frothy hot chocolate, talking about dance mixers and potential conquests. I felt well removed. As a girl I knew I was pretty, with bright red hair, nice eyes and fair skin – but now I couldn't seem to care whether boys noticed me or not. I stopped taking an interest in my clothes and my coursework too. I began to fail exams, which was difficult and surprising to me since, aside from my appalling pile of absences, I'd been a good student all of my life. Now I found I couldn't summon any focus or attention or even interest.

The next fall, I let Fonnie and my mother persuade me to stay home. I can't say it was any better for me there than at school. There was nowhere to go in the house to escape my dark thoughts. I couldn't sleep and when I could, I had terrible, obsessive dreams about Dorothea and my father, replaying the last awful moments of their lives. I'd wake to a panicked feeling and the promise of more joyless days and nights. And if I said that I remained in this kind of coma for eight more years, then you'd understand just how ready I was to live just as my mother began to die.

My mother was sick with Bright's disease for years, but things got quickly worse in the summer of 1920. Throughout the hottest weeks of July and August, I hardly ever left the upstairs apartment, and when I did leave, she worried endlessly.

'Elizabeth? Is that you?' she called out weakly as soon as she heard me on the stairs. I wasn't sure why she was using my given name after all these years, but much about her baffled me just then. She didn't resemble the steel-spined and difficult woman who had always been able to dissolve me with a single look. She was frail and anxious, calling out again as I hurried up the stairs: *'Elizabeth?'*

'I'm here, Mother.' I came into the main room where she rested on the worn pink velvet settee. I put down my shopping bags and unpinned my hat. 'Are you too warm? Can I open a window?'

'Is it warm?' Her hands kneaded the afghan in her lap. 'I'm chilled to the bone.'

I pulled a chair over to the settee and took up her hands, rubbing them to bring blood to the surface, but wherever I touched, the impressions of my fingertips became set, as if her skin had become bread dough. I let her go and she started to whimper.

'What can I do?'

'Bring your sister. I need Fonnie with me now.'

I nodded and stood to leave, but her eyes opened wider. 'Don't go, please don't leave me.' So I sat again, and this is how it went, all that long night. She took a little broth and slept lightly for a few hours. Then, near midnight, she became suddenly calm.

'I worry greatly for you, Elizabeth,' she said. 'What will become of you when I'm gone?'

'I'm a grown woman, Mother. I'll be fine. I promise.'

'No.' She shook her head. 'Years ago Mrs Curran and I spoke to Dorothea about you.' Her breath was labored, and I didn't want to see her struggle this way.

'Shh. It doesn't matter.'

'It does. We asked her about you several times and she rebuffed us. She had nothing to say.'

I'd always been skeptical of the occult – the board, the hushed, candlelit séances and automatic writing sessions with red scarves on the lamps – but now I felt a rush of cold through me. Was it possible that Mother *had* been in touch with Dorothea? And if so, why had my sister, dead for nine years, turned her back on me? Did she know something hard and sad about my fate? The idea terrified me and yet there was no way to be certain. I couldn't ask my mother to elaborate on the session; she was exhausted and more anxious than ever. I also wasn't entirely sure I wanted to know. What if the future was worse than the present? What if it didn't exist at all?

All that August night I stayed in the straight-backed chair next to the settee. I swabbed Mother's forehead and neck with a damp cloth and looked out the window at the summer night, the dark sky and darker trees, everything as remote as exhibits in a museum. And I knew that I too could die in this room. This was one way my life's wheel could turn.

Hours later, near dawn, my mother died without a sigh or rattle or ragged breath. How very different from the way my father had gone — the crack of his revolver shaking the doors in their jambs — but no less final. While everyone else was downstairs sleeping, I looked at the face I'd hated sometimes and felt sorry for at others. Her hands were curled to each side of her thin body, and I traced one with my fingertips, feeling a terrible and complex love for her. Then I went downstairs to wake Fonnie and Roland and call the doctor. I made breakfast and had a bath, and then sat with Fonnie in the parlor to see about the funeral arrangements. Mother's body was still upstairs waiting for the coroner, and I could feel her there, still pressing on me. She'd always seemed to take pleasure in the quietness of my life, as if I'd become what she thought I would, which was not much of anything at all. This tugging was very old and powerful, and I knew I could easily give into it, into nothingness. Or I could push with everything I had the other way.

FIVE

'Everything all right, miss?' the cab driver asked. 'It will have to be,' I said, and opened the door.

I was back in St Louis after a long day on the train, a day that had been stretched further by the feeling that I'd failed at something in Chicago. Now here I was again, back at Fonnie and Roland's house on Cates Avenue. It was all I could do to pay the man and get out of the car.

Outside, the air was crisp and chill. The driver walked behind me, delivering my bags to the porch; our footfalls rang hollowly on the flagstones. Inside, I dropped my luggage at the bottom of the steps and went up to my apartment, which felt cold and unlived-in. Though it was late and I was exhausted, I lit the lamps and built a fire to warm myself. I sat on the pink settee and wrapped my arms around my shoulders, and wondered if some part of my mother was still there in the room, swaddled in an afghan maybe, and looking at me pitifully: *Poor Hadley. Poor hen.*

The next morning I slept later than usual, and when I came downstairs, Fonnie was waiting for me in the dining room.

'Well? I want to hear everything. What did you do? What kind of people did you meet?'

I told her all about the parties and games and the interesting people who moved through Kenley's apartment in swells – but I didn't tell her about Ernest. What was there to tell? I wasn't sure where we stood at all, even as friends.

As Fonnie and I talked, Roland came into the room, fastening his cuffs, moving in a cloud of soap and piney hair tonic. He sat down and Fonnie eased her chair ever so subtly away from his so that she didn't have to see him eat. That's how they were at this point. Their marriage was a disaster and always had been, and it made me feel badly for them both.

'Well,' Roland said. 'Was Chi-town everything you imagined?'

I nodded, spreading marmalade on toast.

'And did you conquer dozens of new beaux?'

Fonnie made an almost inaudible huffing noise, but said nothing.

'I wouldn't say dozens,' I said.

'You must have made at least one conquest. This letter just arrived for you.' He pulled a crumpled looking artifact from his suit pocket. 'Special delivery,' he said. 'It must be serious.' He smiled and handed over the letter.

'What's that?' Fonnie said.

'Special delivery,' I repeated in a kind of trance. Ernest's name was on the envelope, scrawled but clear enough. He must have mailed it just after he put me on the train, paying the extra ten cents to make sure it arrived first thing. *I'll write to you. I'll write you.* I fingered the envelope, half afraid to open it.

'What's your fellow's name?' Roland asked.

'I wouldn't call him my fellow, but his name is Ernest Hemingway.'

'Hemingway?' Fonnie said. 'What kind of name is that?'

'I have no idea,' I said, and carried the letter out of the room to open it. It was as clutched and creased as if it had spent days in his pocket – and I already loved that, no matter what the letter held. I found a quiet corner in the sitting room near my piano and discovered that inside the pages were rumpled too, and scratched at with dark ink. *Dear Hasovich* – it began – *You on the train and me here and everything emptier now you're gone. Tell me, are you real?*

I put the letter down because I almost couldn't bear the feeling that he'd crawled into my head. *Are you real?* I wondered exactly the same about him – and had more right too, I thought, particularly after Kate's warning. I was as solid as the ground he walked on, too solid probably. But what about him? His attentions to me had never faltered during my visit, but that didn't mean he was reliable, only that for the time being he thought I was worth pursuing. The truth was I didn't know what to think about him, and so I kept reading, devouring the rest of his letter very quickly, all he had to say about what he was doing and wanted to do, his work, his thoughts. He said there might be a job for him at a monthly magazine called the *Cooperative Commonwealth* if he'd give in to doing the whole thing himself – as writer, reporter, editor, the whole ball of wax. *Not crazy about the terms but will probably take it,* he wrote. Though there was a good deal of unquiet chatter in my mind about him, I couldn't help liking his voice and vibrancy, and how his words on paper sounded like the Ernest who invented reasons to pop into my room in Chicago. His letter was doing that now, bringing Ernest into the sitting room that had been dark and airless a moment before.

'Well?' Fonnie said, coming through the door with a swish of her somber wool skirt. 'What does he have to say?'

'Nothing out of the ordinary,' I said, but of course that wasn't true. Everything about Ernest Hemingway was out of the ordinary.

'Well, it's nice to have new friends, anyway. I'm happy you've found a pleasant distraction.' She sat and took up her lacework.

'Are you?'

'Of course. I want you to be happy.'

That was probably true, but only if *happy* meant I was locked upstairs for the rest of my life, the lonely maiden aunt.

'Thank you, Fonnie,' I said, and then excused myself to my room, where I started in on my answer. I didn't want to be too enthusiastic. I didn't want to make my reply mean more than it did – but I found that I liked writing to him. I made my letter last all day, putting things down as they happened, wanting to be sure he could picture me moving from room to room, practicing the piano, sitting down to a perfect cup of ginger tea with my friend Alice Hunt, watching our gardener prune the rosebushes and swaddle them in burlap for winter. *I miss the lake tonight*, I wrote. *Lots of other things too. Do you want to meet me in the kitchen for a smoke?*

My mother had kept a snapshot of me in a bathing suit, splashing knee-deep in the Meramec River with Alice, both of us happy and washed over with sunshine. This version of Hadley hardly ever made an appearance these days, it was true, but I thought Ernest would like her open face and any-thing-goes smile. I tucked the photo into an envelope with my letter, and then, before I could have second thoughts about anything, I walked down the street to the letterbox on the corner. It was dark out and as I walked, I looked into houses as if they were glowing bowls. Everything glowed faintly – and for a moment I could imagine light speeding over all the knobby cornfields and sleeping barns between St Louis and Chicago. When I arrived at the box, I gripped my letter, kissed it on impulse, and then pushed it into the slot and let it go.

Six

I have so many schemes about writing — so much I want to see and feel and do. Say, do you remember playing the piano with your hair glinting full on, and how you got up and came over to me on the davenport and said, 'Do you gather me, Begonia?'

Do you gather me, Hash?

Will you come up here already and give me some of that dead-sure stuff that's you?

His letters came crushed and strangled, full of deliciousness, sometimes two or three a day. I tried to be more reserved at first, vowing to write only once a week, but that fell apart immediately. Before long I found myself in a real bind. The letters were flying back and forth, but what did they mean? Kate's voice often filled my head — *he likes women* — all *women, apparently* — and I debated over whether or not I should tell her about our quickly progressing friendship. I couldn't imagine her not feeling hurt and angry; I was blatantly, willfully disregarding her advice after all. But if I confessed everything, she might give me *more* advice, and then I'd have to listen and perhaps act on it.

I was torn between wanting to know if I could trust Ernest, and wishing I could stay blind enough to keep things exactly as they were. His words already meant so much – too much. Each of his letters was a perfect tonic and writing him, too, was a tonic, and before long I learned I could hear the mail boy on his bicycle from several blocks away even if he didn't ring his bell. I told myself that Kate didn't know *every-thing* about Ernest. Who knew everything about anyone? There were qualities coming through in his letters – tender-ness, for instance, and palpable warmth – that she might never have seen in all those summers in Michigan. It was possible. It had to be, because the happiness that grew out of Ernest's interest in me was seeping over into the rest of my life. I was suddenly busier and more content at home than I'd ever been. Two friends, Bertha Doan and Ruth Bradfield, had moved into the upstairs apartment with me as boarders, and for the first time in almost a decade, I wasn't lonely in my own house. I also had young men interested in me, and even if they weren't anything extraordinary, they were a nice diversion. I let them take me dancing or to the theater, and even let a few of them kiss me goodnight. Not one of them had Ernest's great big square head or padding feet and hands; not one asked his wonderful questions or made me want to say, *Do you gather me, Begonia?*

I kept up with it, though, going out with nearly anyone who asked because Ernest, dear soul that he was, was theo-retical – a lovely hypothesis – and hundreds of miles away. In St Louis, where I was fated to live my actual life, there was Dick Pierce, the brother of a good friend. I liked his company and knew that if I encouraged him at all, he'd fall in love with me and perhaps even propose, but I felt little or nothing for him. There was also Pere Rowland, a pleasantly rumpled boy who knew a lot about books and music, but romantic dates didn't appeal to me as much as when a group of us would jam into someone's car and go to a movie in town or the dance-hall where everyone was happy and free. Afterwards, Ruth and Bertha and I would sit up in our nightgowns with tea and talk through the events of the night.

I was on the verge of my twenty-ninth birthday, but in a way I felt younger and more carefree than I did my first year at Bryn Mawr, when I couldn't enjoy the smallest happiness or intimacy. It was as if I was experiencing a long-delayed coming out, and I was grateful for every minute of it.

And then there were the letters arriving every day, always beautifully crumpled and full of busy news. Ernest told me all about his articles for the *Commonwealth*, his ideas for sketches and novels. But more and more he was also sharing stories about his growing up — about the long summers in Michigan when his father Ed, who was a practicing obstetrician and natural outdoorsman, had taught him how to build a fire and cook in the open; how to use an axe; land and dress a fish; hunt squirrel and partridge and pheasant.

Whenever I think of my father, he wrote, *he's in the woods flushing jacksnipe or walking through short dead grass or shocks of corn, or splitting wood, with frost in his beard.* I read these sentences with tears in my eyes because I had so few warm memories of my own father. When I did think about him, the first image that came to me was his revolver, and then the noise it made ringing through the house. Remembering his death and the way I used to painfully fixate on it disturbed me so much I had to walk twice around the block in a stinging wind before I was calm enough to return to Ernest's letter.

But if I was jealous of his relationship with his father, his mother was troubling in other ways. Nearly every time he mentioned her in a letter, she was 'that bitch.' He described her as utterly dominant in the household, quick to criticize and full of unbendable ideas about how life should proceed, down to every detail. Before he could read, she'd taught Ernest to memorize Latin and German phrases and lines of 'essential' poetry. Although he tried to respect her creative spirit — she sang opera and painted a little and wrote poetry — Ernest ultimately believed she was a selfish mother and wife, intent on her own needs at the risk of destroying everyone around her, particularly her husband. She forced Dr Hemingway into giving into every one of her demands, and seeing this made Ernest despise her.

Though Ernest's passionate rejection of his mother gave me chills, I couldn't help but recognize it. Learning just how alike our parents' relationships were was eerie, and yet what struck me hardest was how, even though I'd often detested my mother's indomitable will and even blamed her for my father's suicide, I'd never expressed this hatred to a soul. It had seethed and roiled inside me. On the occasions it forced its way to the surface, I took up my feather pillow and screamed my feelings into it, choking them off at the root. Ernest spat out his rage freely. Whose response was the most terrifying?

Ultimately, I felt a growing respect for the way he could express even the worst bits of himself, and was drawn in by his confidences. I looked forward to Ernest's letters as I did little else. But his candor, I soon learned, applied to everything equally. In early December, not long after my birthday, he wrote that he'd been attracted the night before by a girl in a flashing green dress at a party. It made me sick to read this. I had no flashing green dress, and even if I did, he wouldn't see it. He was hundreds of miles away, absorbed by the details of his days and nights there. We were friends and confidants, yes, but he didn't owe me anything, had not made me a single promise, not even a false one. He could follow that green dress like a siren into the lake if he wanted. I had no hold on him.

No one seemed to have any hold on anyone, in fact. That was a sign of the times. We were all on the verge now, bursting with youth and promise and little trills of jazz. The year before, Olive Thomas had starred in *The Flapper* and the word suddenly meant jazz and moved like it too. Girls everywhere stepped out of their corsets and shortened their dresses and darkened their lips and eyes. We said, 'cat's pajamas' and 'I'll say,' and 'that's so jake.' Youth, in 1921, was everything, but that was just the thing that could worry me sick. I was twenty-nine, feeling almost obsolete but Ernest was twenty-one and white-hot with life. What was I thinking?

'Maybe I'm not up to this game,' I told Ruth after I'd gotten Ernest's siren letter. Bertha was out and Ruth and I were making dinner together; moving easily around each other in the small kitchen, snapping beans and boiling water for spaghetti, as if we were two maiden aunts who'd done this for decades.

'I'm not sure any of us are,' she replied, measuring salt and tossing some over her shoulder for luck. She had wonderfully strong hands, and I found myself watching them and wishing I could be more like her. She turned to face me and gave me a wry smile. 'But what else is there? If we give up now, we're done for.'

'I might just crawl under my bed and not come out until I'm old and doddering and can't remember feeling anything for anyone at all.'

She nodded. 'You want to, but you won't.'

'I won't.' I moved around the small table, setting the plates and second-best silver, smoothing our two napkins. 'I'll try very hard not to.'

I was desperate to get to Chicago again and see the big old room at Kenley's – the piano, the Victrola, the knobbly rug pushed aside for two people to dance. I wanted look into a pair of impossibly clear brown eyes and know what that beautiful boy was thinking. I wanted to kiss him and feel him kiss me back.

In the middle of January, my friend Leticia Parker and I cooked a plan to get me there. I'd be her guest for a week. We'd stay at a hotel and go shopping, and I could see Ernest as much as I wanted. But then, two days before our scheduled departure, Leticia phoned to cancel. Her mother was ill, and she simply couldn't be away for so long. I told her I understood; of course I did. My own mother had been ill for months, and I knew those demands well, but I was also crushed. Everything had been set for weeks. Ernest would meet the train, and that moment alone I'd worked through in my imagination a hundred times or more.

'Now what?' I railed to Ruth later that day.

'Go,' she said.

'Alone?'

'Why not? These aren't the dark ages, you know. Didn't you go alone last time?'

'I wasn't attached then. Fonnie would hate it.'

'All the more reason to go,' Ruth said, smiling.

The evening I left for Chicago, Roland drove me to the train station on the north side of St Louis in his new Peugeot, a bottle-green coupe that made him feel proud and more masculine, I think, while sending Fonnie into near-apoplectic levels of anxiety. I liked Roland but also felt sorry for him. His situation was very like my father's. He peeped only when Fonnie gave him leave to; it was pathetic, and yet he could also be very charming, in a bookish, infinitely apologetic way. I felt we were allies in the house, and hoped he felt so too. Though he could easily have left me at the curb, Roland parked and walked me to the platform where he handed my suitcases to the porter. Then, as he was saying goodbye, he cocked his head to one side, one of his most annoying and endearing tics, and said, 'You look beautiful, Hadley.'

'I do?' I felt suddenly shy with him and smoothed the skirt of my pale gray traveling suit.

'You do. It just occurred to me you might not know this about yourself.'

'Thank you.' I leaned in to kiss him on the cheek, and then boarded my train, taking new pleasure in my traveling clothes – my soft wool hat and buttery gloves, my tan suede t-strap shoes. The seats and couches were plush and inviting, and Fonnie's puritanical voice, telling me I shouldn't enjoy it, was suddenly very far off. This was the Midnight Special, and I tucked myself into my Pullman berth, behind deep green curtains.

When I arrived at Union Station the next morning, I was well rested and only slightly nervous until I saw Ernest on the platform, almost exactly where I'd left him in November – and then my mouth was dry as cotton, my stomach full of bees. He was gorgeous in a charcoal pea coat and muffler, and his eyes were bright with cold. As I came off the train, he picked me up off my feet with a squeeze.

'Nice to see you too,' I said when he'd put me down, and we both grinned, embarrassed to be together suddenly. Our eyes met and fell away. So many thousands of words had thrummed between us. Where were they now?

'Are you hungry?' he asked.

'Sure,' I said.

We rubbed noses and then walked off through the icy morning to find breakfast. There was a place he liked off of State Street where you could get steak and eggs for sixty cents. We ordered and then sat in the booth, our knees just touching under the table.

'*The Saturday Evening Post* just rejected another story,' he said as we waited for our meals to arrive. 'That's the third time. If this doesn't take off, I could spend my whole life writing junk copy or someone else's story for magazines. I won't do it.'

'You're going to see your stuff in print,' I said. 'It has to happen. It *will*.'

He looked at me levelly, and then raised the toe of his shoe to press it firmly against the inside of my calf. Holding it there, warm and insistent, he said, 'Did you think you wouldn't see me again?'

'Maybe.' I felt my smile fade. 'I could be a real fool for you, Nesto.'

'I'd like it if you could love me for a little while at least.'

'Why a little while? Are you worried that you can't stick it out for very long yourself?'

He shrugged, looking nervous. 'You remember my talking about Jim Gamble, my Red Cross buddy? He thinks I should follow him to Rome. It's cheap there, and if I saved enough beforehand, I could just write fiction for five or six months. This sort of shot might not come around again.'

Rome. I felt my chest contract. I'd just found him, and he was going to run off overseas? My head was spinning, but I knew with absolute certainty that to even *try* to hold him back would be a mistake. I swallowed hard and set each word down carefully. 'If your work's the thing that matters most, you should go.' I tried to meet his eyes squarely over the table. 'But a girl would miss you.'

He nodded seriously but didn't say anything.

The rest of my visit was filled with concerts, plays and parties, every evening finishing up in Kenley's long living room with wine and cigarettes and heated conversations about great books and paintings. Everything was very much as it was in the fall, except that Kate was persistently absent.

Just before I left St Louis, I put a letter in the mail to her. I wasn't sure it would reach her before we ran into each other in Chicago, as we inevitably would, but I couldn't not write and at least try to gently pave the way. *Nesto and I have become quite close,* I wrote. *We're truly good friends and you're my good friend too, and I hate to think this could come between us. Please don't be angry for long. Your lovingest, Hash.*

Kenley insisted she was simply busy with work, saying, 'You know Kate. She takes on too much and then can't get free. I'm sure we'll see her before too long.'

But we didn't see her, and as the days passed, I wished more and more that I could talk about the situation with Ernest. It wasn't like me to be duplicitous, but I'd painted myself into a corner by not ever divulging how Kate had warned me away from him. I had plenty of reasons not to. I didn't want to hurt his feelings, for one, and also didn't feel it was my place to step between them and create bad blood. As my visit drew to a close and Kate's silence grew thicker, I wondered if any element of this lopsided triangle could end well. It was entirely possible she'd stop trusting me altogether. It was possible – even *probable* – that Ernest would go off to Rome to work on his fiction, leaving me in the lurch on two counts.

It was dangerous to keep my heart on the line with Ernest, but what real choice did I have? I was falling in love with him, and even if I didn't feel at all brave about the future, my life had unquestionably changed for the better since I'd met him. I felt it at home in St Louis and at Kenley's too. At the beginning of each evening, I was nervous and shy, worried that I had nothing to contribute to the group, but then I'd settle into my skin and my voice. By midnight, I would be part of things, ready to drink like a sailor and talk until morning. It was like being born over each night, the same process again and again, finding myself, losing myself, finding myself again.

'It wasn't so long ago that I didn't have the energy for more than half an hour at the piano,' I said to Ernest over breakfast one morning. 'We were up until three last night, and here I am bright-eyed and chipper at eight. I used to be so tired – and not a little sad too. What's happened to me?'

'I don't know,' he said, 'but I can vouch for the bright eyes.'

'I'm serious,' I said. 'We're talking about a *major* transformation.'

'Don't you believe in change?'

'I do. But sometimes I don't even recognize myself. It's like those stories where the elves come and take one body away and leave another – a changeling.'

'For what it's worth, I like you this way, Hash.'

'Thanks. I like me this way too.'

The next evening was my last and I was determined to enjoy every minute of it. I wasn't sure when or if Ernest and I would see each other again. He hadn't mentioned Jim Gamble or Italy after that first day, but he also wasn't spinning any other story about the future. When I asked if he might visit me sometime in St Louis, he said, 'Sure I will, kid,' light as air, with no prom-ise attached, no hint of intention. I didn't bring it up again. Clutching and clawing wasn't the way to hold a man like Ernest – if there was a way. I would simply have to wait it out, and see my hand through.

The night went characteristically, with buckets of drink and plenty of song, all of us smoking like paper mills. Ernest asked me to play Rachmaninoff and I was happy to oblige. He came and sat on the bench, like the night of our first meeting, and I felt more than a twinge of nostalgia as my fingers flew over the keys. But in the middle of the piece, he got up and circled the room, rocking back and forth on his heels, jumpy as a thor-oughbred at the gate. By the time I finished he'd left the room. When I finally found him, he was out on the stoop smoking a cigarette.

'Was I that bad?' I said.

'I'm sorry. It's not you.' He cleared his throat and looked up into the cold night sky, which was dizzy with stars. 'I've been wanting to tell you about a girl.'

'Uh-oh.' I sat down on the chilly stone steps, trying to con-trol my dread. If Kate had been right about Ernest, I didn't know if I could bear it.

'Not that kind of girl. Ancient history. I told you about being wounded at Fossalta?'

I nodded.

'When they sent me to Milan to recover, I fell in love with my night nurse there. Isn't that a gas? Me and ten thousand other poor saps.'

It wasn't a new story, but I could tell by watching his face that it was the only story for him.

'Her name was Agnes. We were all set to marry when they shipped me back to the States. If I'd had money then, I would have stayed and made her marry me. She wanted to wait. Women are always so damned sensible. Why is that?'

I didn't half know what to say. 'You were just eighteen then?'

'Eighteen or a hundred,' he said. 'My legs were full of metal. They took twenty-eight pieces of shrapnel out of me. Hundreds more were too deep to reach, and none of that was as bad as the letter that finally came from Ag. She fell in love with someone else, a dashing Italian lieutenant.' He sneered, his face contorting. 'She said she hoped I'd forgive her some-day.'

'You haven't.'

'No. Not really.

After we'd passed several minutes in silence, I said, 'You shouldn't get married for a long while. That kind of blow is like a long illness. You need time to recuperate or you'll never be one hundred per cent.'

'Is that your prescription, then, doctor? A rest cure?' He had gradually moved toward me as he spoke, and now he reached for one of my gloved hands. Rubbing the wool pile first one way then the other, he seemed calmer. 'I like your directness,' he said after a while. 'You listen to me and tell me just what you're thinking.'

'I suppose I do,' I said, but in truth I was thrown. He had obviously been hopelessly in love with this woman, and likely still was. How could I ever compete with a ghost – me, who knew so very little and nothing good about love?

'Do you think we can ever leave the past behind?' he said.

'I don't know. I hope so.'

'Sometimes I think if Agnes vanished, this could too.'

I nodded. I'd had the very same anxiety.

'Maybe she didn't vanish at all. Maybe she never loved me.'

He lit another cigarette and inhaled deeply, the tip flaring an angry red. 'Isn't love a beautiful goddamn liar?'

His voice was so charged with bitterness, I had a hard time meeting his eyes, but he peered at me closely and intensely saying, 'Now I've scared you.'

'Only a little.' I tried to smile for him.

'I think we should go back upstairs and dance until morning.'

'Oh, Nesto. I'm awfully tired. Maybe we should just turn in.'

'Please,' he said. 'I think it would help.'

'All right then.' I gave him my hand.

Back upstairs the party had mostly dispersed. Ernest slowly rolled the rug to one side and cranked the Victrola. Nora Bayes' voice quavered into the room – *Make believe you are glad when you're sorry.*

'That's my favourite song,' I said to Ernest. 'Are you clairvoyant?'

'No, just smart about how to get a girl to stand closer.'

I don't know how long we danced that night, back and forth across the living room in a long slow ellipse. Every time the recording ended, Ernest shuffled away from me briefly to start it again. Back in my arms, he buried his face in my neck, his hands clasped low on my back. Three minutes of magic, suspended and restrung. Maybe happiness was an hour glass already running out, the grains tipping, sifting past each other. Maybe it was a state of mind – as Nora Bayes insisted – a country you could sculpt out of air and then dance into.

'I'll never lie to you,' I said.

He nodded into my hair. 'Let's always tell each other the truth. We can choose that, can't we?'

He swept me around and around, slow and strong. The song ended, the needle clicked, whispered, shushed into silence. And we kept dancing, rocking past the window and back again.

SEVEN

When I returned home to St Louis, Fonnie had a long string of questions and warnings. Just who was this Ernest Hemingway, anyway? What were his prospects? What could he offer me? She'd no sooner finish this line of questioning then begin her rant about my own shortcomings. Did Hemingway know about my nervous attacks and general ill health? My history with weakness? You'd have thought she was talking about a lame horse, but I wasn't over-troubled. I knew Fonnie's tactics by heart and could turn her voice off almost entirely. My own voice was harder to control, unfortunately. When I was with Ernest in Chicago I'd felt strong and capable of weathering uncertainty about the future. But outside the circle of his arms, well beyond his range and powerful physical effect on me, I was struggling.

It didn't help that the stream of letters from him were growing moodier and more intermittent. He hated his job and was fighting with Kenley about an increase in his room and board. *Kenley knows full well how I'm trying to save every last seed for Rome but insists on twisting my arm anyway*, he wrote. *Some friend*. I wanted to commiserate, but was selfishly grateful for any delay in his plans.

I had quite a cache of letters by that point, well over a hundred, which I kept squirreled neatly away on a shelf in my closet upstairs. I took the box down and reread them on days I got no beautifully crumpled *special*, which happened more and more. They cost a dime in postage and he was saving those dimes for lire. It disturbed me to know he was prioritizing Jim Gamble, adventure, and his work. I also couldn't forget how much younger he was than me. Nine years might not feel like much if we ever got to middle age together, but Ernest could be so very youthful and exuberant and full of plans I had a hard time imagining him in middle age at all. He was a light-foot lad on a Grecian urn chasing truth and beauty. Where did I fit in exactly?

'I think I'm too old to fall in love sometimes,' I said to Ruth one afternoon. We sat in my room on the bed, a plate of tea biscuits between us, while outside it snowed like it might never stop.

'You're too old – or he's too young?'

'Both,' I said. 'In a way he's lived more than I have, and he's certainly had more excitement. But he can be awfully romantic and naïve too. Like this business with Agnes. She did break his heart, I believe that full well, but he carries it around like a wounded child.'

'That's not very fair, Hadley. You suffered over Harrison Williams, didn't you?'

'I did. Oh, Ruth,' I put my head in my hands. 'I don't know what's gotten into me. I think I'm just afraid.'

'Of course you are,' she said gently. 'If you honestly think he's too young for you, all right then, make your decision and stick to it.'

'Do you think I'll stop worrying when I know he loves me for sure?'

'Just listen to yourself.'

'There's so much to lose.'

'There always is,' she said.

I sighed and reached for another biscuit. 'Are you always this wise, Ruth?'

'Only when it comes to other people's lives.'

The next day there was no letter from Ernest, and the next day also none, and the next as well. It seemed clearer and clearer that he was either forgetting me or consciously pushing me to the side, choosing Rome and the hope of making a go with his writing instead. I was hurt, but also terribly jealous. He had something real to pin his hopes on, something to apply his life to. My dreams were plainer and, quite frankly, more and more tied to him. I wanted a simple house somewhere with Ernest coming up the walk whistling, his hat in his hand. Nothing he'd ever done or said suggested any such thing could ever happen. So just who was naïve and romantic?

'If it's over, I can be brave,' I told Ruth and Bertha on the evening of the third day, feeling a heavy knot clench and dissolve at the back of my throat. 'I'll roll up my sleeves and find someone else.'

'Oh, kid,' Ruth said. 'You're down for the count, aren't you?'

After we went to bed, I tossed and turned for hours before falling into a light sleep sometime after two. The next morning, still feeling foggy-headed and quite low, I checked the letterbox. It was too early for the mail to have arrived but I did it anyway – I couldn't help myself. There in the box was not one letter but two, both of them fat and promising.

Rationally, I knew the mail boy must have come by with them the evening before, catching me unawares, but part of me wanted to believe that I conjured the letters there with my longing. Either way, Ernest's silence had finally broken. I leaned against the doorjamb, my eyes blurring with tears of relief.

Back upstairs, I tore open the letters greedily. The first spilled the usual news of work and fun at Kenley's place, lately referred to as 'the Domicile.' There had been a boxing match in the living room the night before, with Ernest playing the role of John L. Sullivan, ducking and weaving in long underwear and a brown silk sash. I laughed to think of him this way and was still laughing when I began reading the second letter. *Still thinking about Rome,* it began, *but what if you came along — as wife?*

Wife. The word stopped me cold. I hadn't met his mother or any of his family. He hadn't even been to St Louis to sit in the front parlor and bear Fonnie's disapproving gaze. Still, he might be serious. It was just the way he'd propose, off the cuff, following a joke about boxing. I wrote back later that morning: *If you're ready to make the mad dash, I'm game.*

Rome. Together. It was an extraordinary thought. When I let myself fantasize about marrying Ernest, we lived in St Louis or Chicago, in a place very like the Domicile, full of fun and good talk at any hour. Living with Ernest in Italy was a thrilling and terrifying and completely revolutionary idea. When I was seventeen, I took a trip to Florence and Rome with my mother and two sisters. The whole thing went miserably, and I remembered very little beauty — only heat and fainting spells and mosquitoes. Being in Rome with Ernest had to be different. *I* would be different there. How could I not be? I could see us walking the Tiber, arm in arm, crossing all the bridges one by one. *Let's go*, I wrote blithely, flushed with anticipation. *I'm already packed.*

Then I walked outside without coat or scarf. The sky was low and gray, spilling fat wide flakes. I looked up into it and opened my mouth, tasting the snow.

EIGHT

Two weeks after Ernest's proposal, I made the necessary trip to Chicago to greet an entire contingent of Hemingways. I was so nervous I drank the better part of a bottle of wine first, pacing the living room at the Domicile, while Ernest tried to reassure me as best he could. It didn't help that Kate had finally turned up that afternoon. Ernest was at work and she found me at Kenley's alone.

'You're not really going to *marry* Wem? That's ridiculous.' Her voice was shrill. She had stomped in without taking off her hat and coat.

'Kate, please sit down and be reasonable.'

'You're going to regret this. You know you will. He's so young and impulsive.'

'And I'm what? A sedate little spinster?'

'No, just naïve. You give him too much credit.'

'Honestly, Kate. You're supposed to be his friend. What did he do to turn you against him?'

She stopped ranting suddenly and sat down heavily on the davenport. 'Nothing.'

'Then why all this?' I lowered my voice and moved to sit near her. 'Please tell me what's going on.'

'I can't.' She shook her head slowly. Her eyes were clear and sad. 'I don't want things to get any uglier, and neither do you. I'll be happy for you, I swear I will.'

I felt a roaring in my ears then that wouldn't quiet for the rest of the afternoon. When Ernest came home from work, I was still so upset I nearly ambushed him at the door. 'Is there anything you want to tell me about Kate? I think she's quite in love with you.' I was surprised to hear myself say it out loud, but Ernest took it with a strange calmness.

'Maybe,' he said. 'But it's no fault of mine. I didn't encourage her.'

'Didn't you? I think she's very hurt by something.'

'Listen. Kate is Kate. That's all behind us now. Do you really want to know everything?'

'I do. I want to know all of it. Everyone you've ever kissed or imagined yourself in love with for even two minutes.'

'That's crazy. Why?'

'So you can tell me how much they don't matter and how you love me more.'

'That's what I am telling you. Aren't you listening at all?'

'How can we get married if there are secrets between us?'

'You don't want to get married?'

'Do you?'

'Of course. You're making much too much of this, Hash. Please be reasonable.'

'That's what Kate said.'

He looked at me with such exasperation I couldn't help bursting into tears.

'Oh, come here, little cat. Everything's going to be fine. You'll see.'

I nodded, and then dried my eyes. And then asked for a drink.

We borrowed Kenley's car to drive out to the big family house in Oak Park. The closer we got to Kenilworth Avenue, the more agitated Ernest became.

'Don't you think they'll like me?' I asked.

'They'll adore you. They're not crazy about me is the thing.'

'They love you. They have to.'

'They love me like a pack of wolves,' he said bitterly. 'Why do you suppose I board with Kenley when my family's just fifteen miles away?'

'Oh, dear. I never thought of it like that. Is it too late to turn around?'

'Much too late,' he said, and we pulled into the long, circular drive.

Ernest's mother Grace met us at the door herself, literally pushing the servants to the side to do it. She was plump and plush, with a sheaf of graying hair piled on her head. I was barely over the threshold when she charged at me, swallowing my hand in hers, and even as I smiled and did my best to charm her, I could see why Ernest fought against her. She was bigger and louder than anything else around her, like my own mother. She changed the gravity in the room; she made everything happen.

In the parlor, there were fine sandwiches on finer plates, and pink champagne. Ernest's older sister, Marcelline, sat near me on a chaise, and although she seemed a pleasant enough girl, it was a bit unsettling that she looked so much like her brother. Ursula, too, had his looks, his smile to the letter, and his dimple. Sunny was sixteen and sweetly turned out in pale yellow chiffon. Little Leicester, only six, trailed Ernest like a puppy until he submitted to a round of shadow-boxing in the dining room. Meanwhile, Grace had me pinned in the parlor, talking about the superiority of European lace, while Dr Hemingway hovered with a plate of cheeses and beets he'd preserved himself, from his garden at Walloon Lake.

After dinner, Grace asked me to play the piano as she stood by it and sang an aria. Ernest was clearly mortified. Greater mortification arrived when Grace insisted on showing me a photo in an obviously much-cherished album of Marcelline and Ernest dressed alike, both in pink gingham dresses and wide-brimmed straw hats trimmed with flowers.

'Hadley doesn't want to see any of that, Mother,' Ernest said from across the room.

'Of course she does.' Grace patted my hand. 'Don't you dear?' She fingered the photograph in a proprietary way. 'Wasn't he a beautiful baby? I suppose it was silly of me to dress him like a girl, but I was indulging a whim. It didn't hurt anyone.'

Ernest rolled his eyes. 'That's right, Mother. Nothing ever hurts anyone.'

She ignored him. 'He always loved to tell stories, you know. About his rocking horse, Prince, and his nurse Lillie Bear. And he was a terrible card, even as a baby. If he didn't like something you'd done, he'd slap you hard, right where you stood, then come around for kisses later.'

'Mind you don't do that with Hadley,' Marcelline said, arching an eyebrow at Ernest.

'She might go in for that,' Ursula flashed a smile.

'Ursula!' Dr Hemingway snapped.

'Put the book away, Mother,' said Ernest, looking entirely miserable.

'Oh, pooh,' Grace replied, and flipped the page. 'Here's one of the cottage at Windemere. Beautiful Walloona.' And she was off again, rhapsodizing.

The evening went on and on. There was coffee and little thimblefuls of brandy and delicate cakes, and then more coffee. When we finally had permission to leave, Grace called out after us, inviting us to Sunday dinner.

'Fat chance,' Ernest said under his breath as he led me down the walk.

Once we were safely back in the car and on our way to Kenley's, I said, 'They were awfully civil to me, but I can see why you'd want to distance yourself.'

'I'm still a child to them, even to my father, and when I strain against that, I'm selfish or thoughtless or an ass, and they can't trust me.'

'It wasn't so different for me when my mother was alive. Our mothers are so alike. Do you suppose that's why we're attracted to each other?'

'Good god, I hope not,' he said.

With the onset of our engagement, new rules applied to our living situation at Kenley's. I was still invited to stay in my usual room, but Ernest was asked to impose on other friends for the duration of my visit.

'I don't know why Kenley's acting so square suddenly,' Ernest said when he delivered the news. 'He's hardly pure as the driven snow.'

'It's my reputation he's protecting, not his own,' I said. 'It's rather gallant if you think about it.'

'It's a pain in the neck. I want to see you first thing, just after your eyes open for the day. Is that too much to ask?'

'Only for now. As soon as we're married, you can see me any way you like.'

'What a nice thought.' He smiled.

'The very nicest.'

It wasn't any great secret that I was a virgin. Aside from a passionate kiss here and there from various suitors, my experience as a lover was nil. Ernest liked to hint that he'd known lots of girls. I assumed he'd been with Agnes in Italy – they were going to marry after all – but any more than that, I tried not to think about. It made me too anxious to wonder if I could satisfy him, so I pushed that thought aside and focused on how making love would be a way of knowing him, in all the ways that were possible, with no obstacles or barriers. It wouldn't matter that I was inexperienced. He would feel me loving all of him and holding nothing back. How could he not?

Ernest seemed prepared to wait for our wedding night – he'd certainly never pushed me in any way – but on the night of our visit to Oak Park, after a lingering kiss goodnight at Kenley's door, he told me he wasn't heading off to Don Wright's place to sleep that night after all. 'I'm camping out.'

'What?'

'C'mon. I'll show you.'

I followed him up the fire escape to the rooftop, expecting it to be freezing up there – it *was* March, and weeks away from true spring in Chicago – but tucked into a sheltered corner, Ernest had piled up quilts and blankets to cozy effect.

'You've made quite a little kingdom here, haven't you?'

'That's the idea. Do you want some wine?' He reached into his nest and pulled out a corked bottle and a teacup.

'What else have you got hidden in there?'

'Come in and find out.' His voice was light and teasing, but when I was lying beside him on the quilt and he reached to wrap a blanket around my shoulders, I felt his hands shaking.

'You're nervous,' I said.

'I don't know why.'

'You've been with plenty of girls, haven't you?'

'None like you.'

'Well *that's* the perfect thing to say.'

We tented the blankets around us and kissed for a long while, cocooned and warm and separate from the rest of the world. And then, without even knowing that I was going to do it beforehand, I took off my jacket and blouse, then lay down beside him, not minding the scratching of his wool jacket on my bare skin, or the way he pulled back to look at me.

I didn't feel as shy or exposed as I thought I might. His eyes were soft and his hands were too. They moved over my breasts and I was surprised at the charge his touch sent running through me. I arched automatically into his body and everything happened very quickly after that, my hands searching for his urgently, his mouth on my eyelids, my neck, everywhere at once. It was all new, but natural and right feeling somehow, even when there was pain.

When I was a teenager, my mother published an article in *The New Republic* saying that a wife who enjoyed sexual activity wasn't any better than a prostitute. Submission was required for children, of course, but the final goal for women could only be a strict and blissful celibacy. I didn't know what to think about sex or what to expect but discomfort. As I grew older and more curious, I scanned excerpts of Havelock Ellis' *The Psychology of Sex* in Roland's *Literary Digest* for much-needed information. But there were things I had a hard time thinking too specifically about – such as where our bodies would meet, and how that would actually *feel*. I don't know if I was repressed or just dense, but in my fantasies about our wedding night, Ernest carried me across some flower-strewn threshold and my white dress dissolved. Then, after some sweetly vague tussling, I was a woman.

On the rooftop, all the veils fell away, and when there wasn't a diaphanous scrap of fantasy left, I think I was most surprised by my own desire, how ready I was to have him, the absolute reality of skin and heat. I wanted him, and nothing – not the awkward jarring of knees and elbows as we struggled to get closer, not the sharp jolting sensation when he moved into me – could change that. When his weight was on me fully, and I could feel every bump and contour of the roof against my shoulders and hips through the blankets, there were moments of pure crushing happiness I knew I'd never forget. It was as if we'd pressed ourselves together until his bones passed through mine and we were the same person, ever so briefly.

Afterwards, we lay back on the blankets and watched the stars, which were very bright everywhere above us.

'I feel like I'm your pet,' he said, his voice warm and soft. 'You're mine too, my small perfect cat.'

'Did you ever think it could be like this? The way we're happening to each other?'

'I can do anything if I have you with me,' he said. 'I think I can write a book. I mean, I want to, but the thing is it could all be stupid or useless.'

'Of course you can do it, and it will be wonderful. I'm sure of it. Young and fresh and strong just like you are. It will be you.'

'I want my characters to be like us, just people trying to live simply and say what they really mean.'

'We say what we mean, but it's hard, isn't it?'

'Kenley says we're rushing things. He doesn't understand why I'd want to move in the marriage direction when single life suits me so well.'

'That's his prerogative.'

'Yes, but it's not just him. Horney's worried I'm going to gum up my career. Jim Gamble thinks I'm going to forget the whole point of Italy once we're hitched. Kate's not speaking to either of us.'

'Let's don't bring her up, please. Not now.'

'All right,' he said. 'I'm just saying that no one seems to get that I *need* this. I need you.' He sat up and looked into my face until I thought I might dissolve from it. 'I hope we'll get lucky enough to grow old together. You can see them on the street, those couples who've been married so long you can't tell them apart. How'd that be?'

'I'd love to look like you,' I said. 'I'd love to be you.'

I'd never said anything truer. I would gladly have climbed out of my skin and into his that night, because I believed that was what love meant. Hadn't I just felt us collapsing into another, until there was no difference between us?

It would be the hardest lesson of my marriage, discovering the flaw in this thinking. I couldn't reach into every part of Ernest and he didn't want me to. He needed me to make him feel safe and backed up, yes, the same way I needed him. But he also liked that he could disappear into his work, away from me. And come back when he wanted to.

NINE

Ernest pushed off, suspending his body over the lake before he punched through. Coming to the surface again, he treaded water and faced the dock where Dutch and Luman sat and passed a bottle of rotgut back and forth, their voices carrying clearly over the water.

'Good form, Wem,' Dutch called out. 'Can you teach me to dive like that?'

'No,' he called back. 'I can't teach anyone anything.'

'Do you have to be so stingy about it?' Dutch said with a snort, but Ernest didn't feel like answering, so he balled himself up like a rock and let himself sink, falling through the lake until he bumped the mossy bottom and drifted there, the moss cool and strange against his toes.

Was it just last summer that Kate and Edgar had been on the dock eating stolen cherries and spitting the meaty pits at him as he bobbed nearby? Kate. Dear old Katy with the cat-green eyes and the smooth strong legs all the way to her ribcage. One night she had said, 'You're the doctor, examine me,' and he'd done it, counting each of her ribs with his hands, following the curve all the way around from her spine. She didn't flinch or even laugh. When he reached her breast, she pushed the top of her bathing suit down while looking at him. He stopped moving his hands and tried to breathe.

'What are you thinking, Wemedge?'

75

'Nothing,' he said, working to keep his voice steady. Her nipple was perfect and he wanted to put his hand on it and then his mouth. He wanted to fall through Kate the way he liked to fall through the lake, but there were voices coming down the sandy path toward them. Kate straightened her suit. He stood up quickly and plunged into the water, feeling it burn him all over.

Now Kate was little more than a mile up the road in her Aunt Charles' cottage with Hadley, both of them in the same room in little beds that smelled of mildew. He knew that room well and all the rooms in the house, but found it hard to picture Hadley there or in any of the places he knew best. When he was a little boy, he'd learned to walk on the slope of patchy grass in front of Windemere. And that was just the beginning. He'd learned everything worth learning here, how to catch and scale and gut a fish, how to hold an animal living or dead, and flint a fire and move quietly through the woods. How to listen. How to remember everything that mattered so he could keep it with him and use it when he needed to.

This place had never once let him down, but he felt slightly outside of it tonight. Tomorrow, at four o'clock in the afternoon, he and Hadley would be married in the white Methodist church on Lake Street. He felt a surge of panic about it, as if he were a fish thrashing in a taut net, fighting it instinctively. It wasn't Hadley's fault. Getting married had been all his idea, but he hadn't told her how very afraid of it he was. He seemed to need to force his way through it anyway, as he did with everything that scared him terribly. He was afraid of marriage and he was afraid of being alone, too.

Rising up from the cool bottom of the lake on the night before his wedding, he found it hard not to turn away from Hadley or grow confused. He loved her. She didn't scare him like Kate did or challenge him to touch her with green eyes in the dark, saying, 'Go on then, what are you afraid of, Wemedge?' With Hadley, things felt right almost all of the time. She was good and strong and true, and he could count on her. They had as good a shot at making it as anyone did, but what if marriage didn't solve anything and didn't save anyone even a little bit? What then?

Now that he was on the surface, he could hear Dutch and Luman again, *talking of stupid things, not understanding anything at all. The water felt flat and cool against his skin, holding him and letting him go at the same time. He looked up into the black whorl of the sky and took a single deep breath into his lungs, and then he kicked hard for the dock.*

TEN

September 3, 1921 dawned clear and balmy and windless — a perfect day. The leaves were just beginning to turn on the trees, but you wouldn't have known it to feel the lake, which was still warm as bathwater. Ernest had arrived in Horton Bay that morning in a stormy mood after three days of fishing with bachelor friends. He was sunburned along the bridge of his nose and his eyes were lined with exhaustion or anxiety or both.

'Are you ready for this?' I asked when I saw him.

'Damned straight,' he said. He was bluffing, but wasn't I bluffing too? Wasn't everyone dead terrified on their wedding day?

While Ernest spent his last hours as a free man in a cottage on Main Street in Horton Bay, passing a whiskey bottle back and forth with his groomsmen, I took a long swim after lunch with Ruth and Kate, my bridesmaids.

It hadn't been an easy road getting Kate to agree to even come to the wedding. There'd been a string of strained and difficult letters, nearly all of them going her way at first. But after many weeks, she finally confessed: *I'm afraid I was very in love with Ernest at one time. Not sure why I haven't been able to say this, except it's been painful to see him fall for you instead, and terribly embarrassing to think the two of you might have laughed at my expense.*

I felt a sharp sympathetic twinge reading her words. I knew well how low someone could be driven by unrequited love, and yet here was Kate, showing what a very good friend she was. She had loved Ernest and lost him to me, and was still willing to stand up for us both in front of our family and friends.

I was full of admiration for her that afternoon and couldn't help swimming over to where she splashed in the shallows, saying, 'You're a good guy, Kate.'

'You too, Hash,' she said. Her eyes brimmed with tears.

If we had only known then that nine years ahead of us, in a Paris we hadn't begun to imagine, John Dos Passos would fall victim to Kate's sparkle and pursue her with force until she agreed to marry him. That Dos was a figure nearly as dashing and important to American letters as Ernest was would have softened this moment ever so much – but we never know what waits for us, good or bad. The future stayed hidden as Kate gave me a wan smile and paddled away into the reeds.

The water was so warm and ideal that afternoon, we swam until three when I realized with a kind of panic that my hair would never dry before the service. We rushed back to the cottage where I tied it back with ribbons and then stepped into the ivory lace dress, which fit me so perfectly I thought it made up for the damp hair. There were creamy silk slippers for my feet, a garland of flowers and a veil to trail down my back. I carried a spray of baby's breath.

At quarter past four, we entered the little church, which

Kate and Ruth had decorated with swamp lilies and balsam and goldenrod picked from a nearby field. Ribs of sunlight pierced the window and scaled the wall. Ernest and his ushers stood at the altar, all of them flush and gorgeous in white trousers and dark blue jackets. Someone sneezed. The pianist began playing Wagner's wedding march, and I began to walk, led down the aisle by George Breaker, a family friend. I had hoped my brother Jamie could come out from California to give me away, but he was very ill with tuberculosis. My mother's brother, Arthur Wyman was my second choice, but he was also too unwell to attend. I felt sad that more of my family couldn't be there with me, but wasn't I getting new family that very day?

On my way toward the pulpit, I passed Fonnie, stiffly dressed with a small, tight navy hat. Roland stood beside her and gave me a dear smile, and then my niece Dodie grinned and pointed to Ernest's knees, which were shaking slightly in his white flannel trousers. Was this just more evidence of cold feet, or something else? I honestly didn't know, but it was too late to be asking these questions anyway – too late to stop or take anything back, even if I wanted to. And I didn't want to.

The ceremony was quiet and beautiful and went off without a hitch. We walked out of the little church into the last of the day's sunshine. Later, after a chicken dinner and sticky chocolate cake and too many pictures in the yard with everyone squinting into the sun, Horney offered to drive us out to nearby Walloon Lake, where we would be honeymooning at Windemere, the Hemingway family's summer cottage. Grace and Dr Hemingway had offered to put us up for two weeks as a wedding gift. It was dusk when we stepped into the rowboat and began our journey across the lake. Our luggage bumped around our knees, and a sweet nervousness fell between us now that the business of the day was over.

'Are you happy?' he said softly.

'You know I am. Do you need to ask?'

'I like asking,' he said. 'I like to hear it, even knowing what I'm going to hear.'

'Maybe especially then,' I said. 'Are you happy?'

'Do you need to ask?'

We laughed lightly at one another. The air was damp and still and filled with night birds and feeding bats. By the time we beached the boat in the shallow cove at Windemere, it was fully dark out. Ernest helped me scramble onto the sandy shore, and then we walked up the hill holding each other close. We opened the door and lit the lamps and looked into the cottage. Ernest's mother had taken it upon herself to wax everything within an inch of its life, but though the rooms were clean, they were chilly. Ernest opened a bottle of wine that Grace had left in the icebox for us, and then we lit a fire in the parlor and dragged mattresses down from a few of the beds to make a nest in front of it.

'Fonnie was on rare form today,' he said after awhile. 'A perfect tank.'

'Poor Fonnie,' I said. 'Her own marriage has been one big bust. It's not surprising she's so stingy with us.'

'Aren't you a good egg?' he said, stroking my hair. And I was reminded of my afternoon swim.

'Kate behaved awfully bravely, don't you think?'

'Yes she did, but I'm glad that's all behind us now.' He got up and crossed the room to turn on the lamp. 'I should have mentioned this before, but I always need to sleep with some light. Will that be all right?'

'I think so. What happens if you leave it off?'

'You don't want to know.' He climbed back into our nest and squeezed me tight. 'After I was shot, when my head was still in pretty bad shape, a very wise Italian officer told me the only thing to really do for that kind of fear was get married.'

'So your wife would take care of you? That's an interesting way to think about marriage.'

'I actually took it to mean that if I could take care of her – you, that is – I'd worry less about myself. But maybe it works both ways.'

'I'm counting on that,' I said.

ELEVEN

Three traveling clocks
Tick
On the mantelpiece
Comma
But the young man is starving.

E.H., 1921

'We're hardly starving,' I said to Ernest when he showed me his newest poem.

'Maybe not, but you couldn't call us flush,' he said.

Our first apartment was a cramped and dingy two-floor walk-up on North Dearborn Street, a dodgy neighborhood on Chicago's North Side. I hated it there, but it was all we could afford. We were living on about two thousand dollars a year — money from a trust fund that had been set up for me by my grandfather. There was, or would be, a little more money coming from my mother's estate, though that was still tied up with various lawyers. Ernest had been making almost fifty a week writing for the *Cooperative Commonwealth*, but he resigned just a few weeks after we returned from our honeymoon, when gossip began circulating that the paper was involved in crooked financial dealings and was quickly going bankrupt. Ernest didn't want to be caught up in any of that ugliness, and I understood why, particularly if he was going to be a famous writer, but our plans to travel to Italy seemed more and more impossible.

The squalor of our living situation didn't bother Ernest as much as it did me because he was gone all day, writing in restaurants and coffee shops. I was stuck in the apartment — two rooms, the bath down the hall — and had very few ways to keep myself busy. At another time it might have occurred to me to find work, but I'd only ever volunteered and the idea, at least, of throwing myself into domesticity was appealing. I missed the energy of the Domicile, but Kate had gone off to journalism school in Buffalo, and things were strained between Ernest and Kenley. He still owed Kenley back rent from well before the wedding, but as time passed, Ernest only dug in more stubbornly, saying that Kenley was trying to gouge him. He wasn't paying, and Kenley was livid, finally sending a letter saying that Ernest could come get his things from storage.

Ernest sent a brutal reply back, sacrificing the friendship as if it meant nothing. I knew he was hurting over the loss and his own mistakes, but he wouldn't admit it. His mood was pretty low during this time. He'd gotten several more rejections on stories he'd sent to magazines, and it hurt his pride. It was one thing when he was writing part time and having no success. But now he was devoted to his craft, working every day, and still failing. What did that mean for the future?

Certainly there'd been moments in our courtship when Ernest's spirits flagged and he got down on himself. A dark letter from him could seem pretty ominous, but then a few days would pass and his tone would grow more buoyant and positive. Seeing his mood turn at close range was more trying, to be sure. In fact the first time, which came shortly after we were married, disturbed me more than I could comfortably confess.

He'd come home from working in a coffee shop one day looking simply terrible. His face was flat and drawn, his eyes were pink with exhaustion. I thought he might be ill, but he shrugged off this concern. 'I've just been too much in my head. Why don't we take a walk?'

It was November and quite chilly, but we bundled up and trudged along for a good while, moving toward the lake. Ernest was quiet and I didn't force the issue. By the time we reached the shore, it was growing dark and the water was rough with chop. Still we could see some brave or stupid soul, maybe half a mile out, in a small rowboat that tipped ominously, taking in water.

'What would Darwin think of this rube?' Ernest said, cracking a wry smile.

'Aha,' I said. 'I was worried I wouldn't see those lovely teeth at all.'

'I'm sorry. I don't know what's wrong with me.' He put his head in his hands and sighed. 'Goddamn it,' he whispered fiercely, and then struck his forehead sharply with his fists.

'Ernest!' I said, and then he did it again.

He began to cry, or at least I think he was crying; he hid his face in his hands.

'Please tell me what's wrong,' I said. 'You can tell me anything.'

'I don't even know. I'm a wreck. I didn't sleep at all last night.'

'Are you having regrets about getting married?' I tried to meet his eyes. 'If you are, I can take it.'

'I don't know. I'm just so lost.' He rubbed his eyes hard against the sleeves of his wool jacket. 'I have these nightmares and they're so real. I can hear mortar fire, feel the blood in my shoes. I wake up in a sweat. I'm afraid to sleep.'

I felt a wave of maternal love for him, wanting to wrap him tightly in my arms until the cold feeling in his heart went away. 'Let's go home,' I said.

We walked back to our apartment in silence. When we got there, I steered Ernest straight to the bedroom and undressed him the way my mother always did for me when I was sick. I pulled the blankets tightly around his shoulders, and then rubbed his shoulders and arms. After several minutes, he fell asleep. I found a blanket and went to a corner chair to watch over him. It was only then that I let myself feel the whole weight of my own anxiety. *So lost*, he'd said, and I could see it in his eyes, which reminded me of my father's. What did it all mean? Was this crisis related to his experiences in the war? Did those memories descend to plague him from time to time, or was this more personal? Did this sadness belong to Ernest in the fatal way my father's belonged to him?

From across the room, Ernest made a small animal noise and turned to face the wall. I pulled my blanket more tightly around my shoulders and looked out our bedroom window at the stormy November sky. It had started to rain hard, and I hoped that poor soul in the rowboat had found his way to shore. But not everyone out in a storm wants to be saved. I knew that myself from the summer Dorothea died. My summer friend and I had made it safely out of Ipswich Bay, but that was happenstance. If the raging waters had reached out to swallow me, I would have let them. I wanted to die that day – I did – and there'd been other times too. Not many, but they were there, and as I watched Ernest twitch in an uneasy sleep, I couldn't help wondering if we all had them. And if so, *if* we survived them, was it by chance alone?

Hours later, Ernest woke up and called out for me through the darkened room.

'I'm here,' I said, going to him.

'I'm so sorry,' he said. 'I get like this sometimes, but I don't want you to think you're getting a bum horse in the deal.'

'What sets it off?'

He shrugged. 'I don't know, it just comes.'

I lay down quietly next to him and stroked his forehead lightly as he talked.

'When I got shot up, I had it pretty rough for a while. If it was daytime and I was doing something, fishing or working, anything, I was okay. Or at night, if I had a light on and could think about something else until I fell asleep. If I could name all the rivers I'd ever seen. Or I'd map out a city I'd lived in before, and try to remember all the streets and the good bars and people I met there and things they'd said. But other times it was too dark and too quiet, and I'd start to remember things I didn't want in my head at all. Do you know how that is?'

'I do a little, yes.' I held him tightly. 'It scares me, though. I never knew my father was so unhappy, but then he was gone. It all got to be too much for him.' I paused, trying to get this part right. 'Do you think you'll know when it's too much for you? Before it's too late, I mean.'

'Do you want a promise?'

'Can you?'

'I think so. I can try.'

How unbelievably naïve we both were that night. We clung hard to each other, making vows we couldn't keep and should never have spoken aloud. That's how love is sometimes. I already loved him more than I'd ever loved anything or anyone. I knew he needed me absolutely, and I wanted him to go on needing me forever.

I tried to be strong for Ernest's sake, but things weren't easy for me in Chicago. His preoccupation with his work made me sharply aware that I had no passion of my own. I still practiced at the piano because I always had, but it was a rented upright, not the graceful Steinway of my childhood, and the draftiness of the apartment wreaked havoc on the tuning. Because I no longer had any friends in Chicago, there were whole weeks when I didn't talk to anyone but Ernest and Mr Minello, the grocer down the street. Every afternoon, I'd walk the three blocks to the market and sit and chat with him. Sometimes he'd make us a cup of tea – a strong leaf that tasted of mushroom and ashes – and we'd chat like fishwives. He was a widower, a sweet man who knew a lonely woman when he saw one.

It was Mr Minello who helped me plan my first dinner party as a married woman, for Sherwood Anderson and his wife Tennessee. Kenley had introduced Ernest to Anderson in the spring, before their falling out. *Winesburg, Ohio* was still fairly big news, and Ernest could hardly believe Anderson would meet with him, let alone ask to see some of his stories. Anderson had seen promise in Ernest's work and offered to help launch his career if he could, but he and Tennessee had promptly left the States after that, for a long European tour. They were just back in town when Ernest sought him out and invited the couple over to dinner. I was excited to meet them but also panicked. Our flat was so terrible, how could I possibly manage to pull it off?

'Low light,' Mr Minello said, trying to calm my nerves. 'Spare the candles but not the wine. And serve something in a cream sauce.'

I wasn't much of a cook, but the evening went off smoothly anyway. Anderson and his wife both had perfect manners and pretended not to notice how awful our living situation was. I liked them both immediately, particularly Anderson, who had an interesting face. Sometimes it seemed blank and completely without feature — squishy and ordinary and Midwestern. At other times he had a kind of dramatic intensity that lent everything a lovely hardness and charge. He was just short of magnificent when he began to talk about Paris over dinner.

'What about Rome?' Ernest asked, filling him in on our long-standing plans to move to Italy.

'Rome certainly has its appeal,' Anderson said, blowing smoke away from his empty plate, '*la dolce vita* and all that. What's not to like about Italy? But if you want to do any serious work, Paris is the place to be. That's where the real writers are now. The rate of exchange is good. There are things to do at any hour. Everything's interesting and everyone has something to contribute. Paris, Hem. Give it some thought.'

After we climbed into our cold little bed that night, snuggling closer to warm our feet and hands, Ernest asked me what I thought of the idea.

'Can we just switch so quickly? We've done so much planning.'

'Rome will be there whenever we want it — but Paris. I want to follow the current. Anderson knows his stuff, and if he says Paris is where we want to be, we should at least seriously consider it.'

We were still so broke the whole thing would have been a moot point, but then I got news that my uncle, Arthur Wyman, had died and left me an inheritance of eight thousand dollars. He'd been ill for some time, but the gift was completely unexpected. That amount of money – a fortune to us – guaranteed our trip abroad overnight. As soon as we heard, Ernest went to see Sherwood in his office downtown and told him we were keen on Paris. Was there anything he could do to pave the way? Where should we go? What neighborhood? What was the right way to go about things?

Anderson answered all of his questions in turn. Montparnasse was the best quarter for artists and writers. Until we found a place, we should stay at the Hôtel Jacob off the rue Bonaparte. It was clean and affordable and there were lots of American intellectuals to be found there and nearby. Finally Anderson sat down at his desk and wrote Ernest letters of introduction to several of the famous expatriates he'd recently met and gotten friendly with, including Gertrude Stein, James Joyce, Ezra Pound and Sylvia Beach. All were or would soon become giants in the field of arts and letters, but we weren't aware of this at the time, only that having Anderson's letter as a calling card was essential. Ernest thanked him for everything he'd done and hurried home to read his words aloud to me in our dim kitchen, each of the letters saying essentially the same thing, that this Ernest Hemingway was an untried but very fine young newspaperman whose 'extraordinary talent' would take him well beyond the scope of journalism.

In bed that night as we talked and dreamed about Paris, I whispered into Ernest's ear, 'Are you this fine young writer I've been hearing about?'

'God, I hope so.' He squeezed me hard.

On 8 December 1921 when the *Leopoldina* set sail for Europe, we were on board. Our life together had finally begun. We held onto to each other and looked out at the sea. It was impossibly large and full of beauty and danger in equal parts – and we wanted it all.

TWELVE

Our first apartment in Paris was at 74 Cardinal Lemoine, two oddly shaped rooms on the fourth floor of a building next door to a public dancehall, a *bal musette*, where at any time of day you could buy a ticket to shuffle around the floor as the accordion wheezed a lively tune. Anderson had said Montparnasse, but we couldn't afford it, or any of the other more fashionable areas. This was old Paris, the Fifth Arrondissement, far away from the good cafés and restaurants and teeming not with tourists but working-class Parisians with their carts and goats and fruit baskets and open begging palms. So many husbands and sons had been lost in the war, these were mostly women and children and old men, and that was as sobering as anything else about the place. The cobblestone street climbed and wound up from the Seine near Pont Sully and ended at the Place de la Contrescarpe, a square that stank of the drunks spilling out of the bistros or sleeping in doorways. You'd see an enormous clump of rags and then the clump would move and you'd realize this was some poor soul sleeping it off. Up and down the narrow streets around the square, the coal peddlers sang and shouldered their filthy sacks of *boulets*. Ernest loved the place at first sight; I was homesick and disappointed.

The apartment came furnished, with an ugly oak dining set and an enormous false-mahogany bed with gilt trimmings. The mattress was good, as it would be in France, where apparently everyone did everything in bed – eat, work, sleep, make lots of love. That agreed with us, as little else in the apartment did, except maybe the lovely black mantlepiece over the fireplace in the bedroom.

Right away we began to rearrange the furniture, moving the dining table into the bedroom, and a rented upright piano into the dining room. Once we had that done, Ernest sat down at the table and began to write a letter to his family, who were anxious for news of us, while I unpacked our wedding china and the few nice things we'd brought along, like the pretty tea set that had been a gift from Fonnie and Roland, with its pattern of salmon-colored roses and leaf-work. Cradling the round teapot in my hands and thinking about where it might belong in my tiny, medieval kitchen, I suddenly had such a pang for home that I began to cry. It wasn't St Louis I longed for exactly, but some larger and more vague idea of home – known, loved people and things. I thought of the wide front porch of my family's house on Cabanné Place, where we lived until just after my father's suicide: the swing that made a cricket's noise when I lay in it, my head on a pillow, my eyes fixed on the perfectly straight varnished bead-boarding above. Within minutes I was so soggy with longing I had to set down the teapot.

'Is that whimpering from my Feather Kitty?' Ernest said from the bedroom.

'I'm afraid so,' I said. I went to him, wrapping my arms around his neck and pressing my damp face into his collar.

'Poor wet cat,' he said. 'I'm feeling it too.'

The table was propped against a narrow window and through it we could see the rough sides of neighboring buildings and shops and little else. In five days it would be Christmas.

'When I was a little girl my mother strung holly boughs along the red glass windows in the parlor. In sunlight or candle-light everything glowed. That was Christmas.'

'Let's not talk about it,' he said, and stood to hold me. He guided my head into his chest, to that spot where he knew I felt safest. Through the floorboards and walls, we could hear the accordion from the dance hall and we began to move to it, rocking lightly.

'We'll settle in,' he said. 'You'll see.'

I nodded against his shirt.

'Maybe we should go out now and shop for our Christmas stockings. That'll cheer up the cat.'

I nodded again and we left the apartment. At the landing of every floor of the building, there was a basin and a communal toilet, which you used while standing on two pedals. The smells were terrible.

'It's barbaric,' I said. 'There must be a better system.'

'Better than pissing out the window I suppose,' he said.

Out on the street, we turned left to go down the hill, and stopped to peek into the doorway of the dancehall, where two sailors rocked bawdily against a pair of girls, both painfully skinny and heavily rouged. Above the bodies, strings of lanterns threw spangled shadows that made the room seem to swim and reel queasily.

'It's a bit like a carnival in there,' I said.

'I imagine it improves when you're drunk,' he said, and we quickly agreed everything would be much cheerier if we got drunk ourselves.

We'd yet to fully get our bearings, but we took a winding route in the general direction of the Seine, passing the Sorbonne and the Odéon Théâter, until we found the Pré aux Clercs, a café on the rue des Saints-Pères that looked welcoming. We went in, taking a table near some British medical students who were talking dryly about the effects of alcohol on the liver. Apparently they'd recently been intimate with cadavers.

'You can have my liver when I'm done with it,' Ernest joked with them. 'But not tonight.'

Prohibition had been in full swing when we left the States, and though we'd never stopped drinking – who had? – it was a relief to be able to buy and enjoy liquor openly. We ordered Pernod, which was green and ghoulish looking once you added the water and sugar, and tried to concentrate on that instead of our dinner, which was a disappointing *coq au vin* with grayish coins of carrot floating in the broth.

'It doesn't feel right to be so far from home at Christmas. We should have a proper tree and holly and a fat turkey roasting in the oven,' I said.

'Maybe,' he said. 'But we have Paris, instead. It's what we wanted.'

'Yes,' I said. 'But we'll go home again someday, won't we?'

'Of course we will,' he said, but his eyes had darkened with something – recollection or anxiety. 'First we have to find a way to make it here. Do you think we can?'

'Of course,' I bluffed.

Out the café window, the streets were dim and the only passing thing was a horse pulling a tank wagon full of sewage, the cart's wheels throwing spliced shadows.

He signalled the waiter over to order us two more Pernods, and we got down to serious drinking. By the time the café closed, we were so tight we had to hold onto one another for balance as we walked. Uphill was infinitely harder than down, particularly in our state, but we managed in our slow way, stopping to rest in doorways, sometimes sharing a sloppy kiss. This was something you could do in Paris without drawing much attention.

At home, we were both sick, one after another, in the chamber pot. The dancehall was still roaring with drunks when we went to bed; the accordion had risen to a fever pitch. We nuzzled forehead to forehead, damp and nauseous, keeping our eyes open so the world wouldn't spin too wildly. And just as we were falling asleep, I said, 'We'll remember this. Someday we'll say this accordion was the sound of our first year in Paris.'

'The accordion and the whores and the retching,' he said. 'That's our music.'

It rained for much of January, and once that passed, the rest of winter in Paris was stingingly cold and clear. Ernest had believed he could write anywhere, but after a few weeks of working in the cramped apartment, always aware of me, he found and rented a single room, very nearby, on rue Descartes. For sixty francs a month, he had a garret not much bigger than a water closet, but it was perfect for his needs. He didn't want distractions and didn't have any there. His desk overlooked the unlovely rooftops and chimney pots of Paris. It was cold, but cold could keep you focused, and there was a small brazier where he could burn bundles of twigs and warm his hands.

We fell into a routine, rising together each morning and washing without talking, because the work had already begun in his head. After breakfast, he'd go off in his worn jacket and the sneakers with the hole at the heel. He'd walk to his room and struggle all day with his sentences. When it was too cold to work or his thoughts grew too murky, he'd walk for long hours on the streets or along the prettily ordered paths of the Luxembourg Gardens. Along the Boulevard Montparnasse there was a string of cafés – the Dôme, the Rotonde, the Select – where expatriate artists preened and talked rot and drank themselves sick. Ernest felt disgusted by them.

'Why is it every other person you meet says they're an artist? A real artist doesn't need to gas on about it, he doesn't have time. He does his work and sweats it out in silence, and no one can help him at all.'

I could certainly see how hanging around cafés all day wasn't work, but I also wondered if everyone was as serious and inflexible about their craft as Ernest was. I imagined there were lots of other writers who worked in their own houses and could tolerate conversation at breakfast, for instance. Those who managed to sleep through any given night without stewing or pacing or scratching at a notebook while a single candle smoked and wavered. I missed Ernest's company all day, but he didn't seem to miss mine; not while there was work to do. When he craved contact, he stopped in to visit the Cezannes and the Monets at the Musée du Luxembourg, believing these painters had already done what he was striving for – distilling places and people and objects to their essential qualities. Cezanne's river was thick and brown and realer for it. That's what Ernest was after – and sometimes the going was achingly slow. Many days he came home looking exhausted, defeated, as if he'd been struggling with sacks of coal all day instead of with one sentence at a time.

When Ernest worked, I kept house for us, making the bed, sweeping and dusting and washing up the breakfast dishes. In the late morning, I'd take a market basket into the street and do our shopping, hunting for the best bargains. Even though it was on the right bank of the Seine and nowhere near our apartment, I liked to walk to Les Halles, the open-air market that was known as 'the stomach of Paris.' I loved the maze of stalls and stands with offerings more exotic than anything I'd ever seen back home. There was all manner of game; venison and boar and pyramids of soft, limp hares. Everything was displayed naturally, hooves and tusks and fur left intact so you knew just what you were looking at. Although it was disconcerting to know these creatures had recently been up and running in the nearby fields and farms, there was something almost beautiful in the sheer volume and variety of things on display, all edible in some form. I didn't half know what to do with most of it – unplucked pheasant and goose, or the baskets of small dun-coloured birds I couldn't even identify – but I loved to look before gravitating toward the vegetable and fruit stalls. I always stayed much longer than I needed to, walking and admiring the baskets of leeks and parsnips, oranges and figs and thick-skinned apples.

But in the alleyways behind the marketplace, fruit and meat rotted in crates. Rats crawled, pigeons crowded and pecked each other savagely, trailing feathers and lice. This was reality, and though living with Ernest was giving me more tolerance for the real than ever before, it made me feel sick even so. It was like looking into the gutters at the place de la Contrescarpe, where colored dyes ran freely from the flower vendors' carts: brief false lushness, and ugliness underneath. What had Ernest said way back when in Chicago? *Love is a beautiful liar?* Beauty was a liar too. When I saw the rats the first time, I wanted to drop my basket and run away, but we weren't rich enough for symbolic gestures. So I walked.

From the wasted alleyways threading out from Les Halles, I walked toward the Seine. At the edge of the Pont Neuf, the quay was harsh and imposing. A cold wind sliced through my thin coat, but just beyond was the Île St Louis with the beautifully preserved houses and elegant streets that made it an oasis. I walked all the way along the island until I found a park at the tip, thick with bare chestnut trees, and then followed a little staircase down to the river. Fishermen were stringing their lines for *goujon* and frying them up on the spot. I bought a handful wrapped in newspaper and sat on the wall watching the barges move under Pont Sully. The nest of fish was crisp under a coarse snow of salt and smelled so simple and good I thought they might save my life. Just a little. Just for that moment.

Thirteen

'It's so beautiful here it hurts,' Ernest said one evening as we walked to take our evening meal at the Pré aux Clercs, which had quickly become our routine. 'Aren't you in love with it?'

I wasn't, not yet — but I was in awe of it. To walk the best streets in Paris just then was like having the curtained doors of a surreal circus standing open so you could watch the oddity and the splendor at any hour. After the enforced austerity of the war, when the textile industry collapsed and the great couturiers nailed their doors shut, brightly colored silks now ran through the streets of Paris like water — Persian blues and greens, startling oranges and golds. Inspired by the orientalism of the Ballet Russes, Paul Poiret dressed women in culotte harem pants and fringed turbans, and ropes and ropes of pearls. In sharp contrast, Chanel was also beginning to make her mark, and you saw splashes of sharp, geometric black amid all that color. More and more, *chic* meant a shingle-bob and deeply lacquered nails and impossibly long ivory cigarette holders. It also meant lean and hungry looking — but that wasn't me. Even when I was hungry, I never lost my round face and my plump arms. I also didn't care enough about clothes to do any thinking about what would suit me. I wore what was easiest and required the least maintenance; long wool skirts and shapeless sweaters and wool cloche hats. Ernest didn't seem to mind. If anything, he thought highly costumed women were ridiculous. It was part of the way he favored everything simple – good straightforward food; rustic, almost chewy wine; peasant people with uncomplicated values and language.

'I want to write one true sentence,' he said. 'If I can write one sentence, simple and true every day, I'll be satisfied.'

He had been working well since we'd come to Paris, chinking away at a story he'd begun on our honeymoon at Windemere called 'Up in Michigan.' It was about a blacksmith and a maid in Horton Bay who meet and discover each other sexually. He'd read some of it to me, from the beginning, where he described the town and the houses and the lake and the sandy road, trying to keep everything simple and pure and as he remembered it, and I couldn't help but be struck by how raw and real it was.

His ambitions for his writing were fierce and all encompassing. He had writing the way other people had religion – and still he was reluctant to send Sherwood Anderson's letters of introduction to any of the famous American expatriates. I guessed he was afraid they'd reject him out of hand. He was more comfortable making friends with the working class of Paris. The language I had was stiff, schoolgirl French, but his was picked up here and there during the war; rough-and-tumble common speech suited to conversations started on street corners with cooks and porters and garage mechanics. Around them he could be himself without feeling defensive.

That night, though, after dinner, we were set to meet Lewis Galantière, a writer friend of Sherwood's. Lewis was originally from Chicago and now worked for the International Chamber of Commerce. He had a reputation for having wonderful taste, and when Ernest finally met him at his apartment in the rue de Jean Goujon, it was full of expensive looking antiques and engravings that he described in detail when he came home to me. 'All the tables and chairs had slender, spindly feet. A little fastidious for my liking, but you could see the man knows style.'

I was anxious about meeting Galantière because I wasn't remotely elegant and didn't feel I belonged in Paris at all. If the women in Paris were peacocks, I was a garden-variety hen. I'd recently given in to pressure and bobbed my hair – maybe the last American woman to do so – and hated it. It made me look like an apple-faced boy, and even though Ernest said he loved the way I looked, every time I caught a glimpse of myself in the mirror, I felt like crying. It may have been dowdy and Victorian before, but my hair had been mine – me. What was I now?

Lewis had offered to treat us to dinner at Michaud's, a fashionable restaurant I'd only stopped at to peer in the window. When we arrived, I paused at the door and fussed hopelessly with my clothes, but Ernest didn't seem at all aware of my self-consciousness. He held me firmly by the elbow and gave me a small but insistent shove toward Lewis, saying, 'Here's the swell, smart girl I told you about.'

'Hadley. I'm honored and pleased,' Lewis said as I blushed furiously. I still felt embarrassed, but loved knowing that Ernest was proud of me.

Lewis was twenty-six, dark and slim and endlessly charming. He did very funny impressions, but when he showed us his best James Joyce he had to explain it for us. We'd glimpsed Joyce a few times on the streets of Montparnasse, with his neatly combed hair and rimless glasses and shapeless coat, but we'd never heard him speak.

'He *does* speak,' Lewis insisted, 'but only under some duress. He has several hundred children, I'm told.'

'I've seen two girls,' I said.

'Two or two hundred, it's all the same in Paris, isn't it? He can barely afford to feed them, they say, but if you come here to Michaud's any night of the week at five o'clock sharp, you can see the whole brood consuming buckets of oysters.'

'Everyone says *Ulysses* is great,' Ernest said. 'I've read a few serialized chapters. It's not what I'm used to, but you know, something important is happening in it just the same.'

'It's dead brilliant,' Lewis said. 'Joyce will change everything if you believe Pound. Have you been round to Pound's studio?'

'Soon,' Ernest said, though he hadn't sent that letter of introduction yet either.

'Good man, you have to go. Not everyone can tolerate Pound, but meeting him is compulsory.'

'What's difficult about Pound?' I asked.

'He himself, actually.' Lewis laughed. 'You'll see. If Joyce is the very quiet professor with his shabby coat and walking stick, Pound is the devil, bumptious and half-crazed with talk of books and art.'

'I've met the devil,' Ernest said, finishing his glass of wine, 'and he doesn't give a damn about art.'

By the end of the evening, we were all drunk and back at our flat, where Ernest was trying to get Lewis to box with him. 'Half a round, just for laughs,' he coaxed, stripping to the waist.

'I've never been a fighting man,' Lewis said, backing away —

but after a few more cocktails, he finally submitted. I should have done something to warn him that no matter what Ernest said, sport was never a laughing matter for him. I'd seen the look in his eye in Chicago, when he'd nearly laid Don Wright flat out on Kenley's floor. This match went the same way, to the letter. For the first few minutes, it was all a pleasant enough cartoon, with both men hunkered into position, knees bent, fists out and curled. It was so obvious that Lewis wasn't athletic I thought Ernest would give up altogether, but then, without any provocation, he threw a live punch, dead center, from his shoulder.

His fist landed hard. Lewis's head whipped back and forward again, his glasses flying into a corner. They were shattered, and his face was nicked in several places.

I ran and tried to help him recover himself, but found he was laughing. Ernest began laughing too – and it was fine, after all. But I couldn't help thinking how close we'd come to losing our only friend in Paris.

It was Lewis who helped bolster Ernest's courage enough to send the rest of the letters of introduction, and soon enough an invitation came from Ezra Pound. Pound wasn't terribly well known in the States yet, unless you knew something about poetry and read literary magazines like the *Dial* and the *Little Review*, but in Paris he had a great reputation as a poet and critic who was helping to revolutionize modern art. I didn't know more than a scrap about what was modern – I was still reading the terribly square Henry James, as Ernest liked to remind me – but Lewis had also said nice things about Pound's English wife Dorothy. I was keen to make new friends, and was happy to go along when Pound invited Ernest to tea.

Dorothy met us at the door and led us into the studio, an

enormous draughty room filled with Japanese paintings and scrolls and scattered pyramids of books. She was very beautiful, with a lovely high forehead and skin like a China doll. Her hands were pale and finely tapered, and she talked in whispers as we walked to where Pound sat in a blood-red damask chair surrounded by shelves stacked high with dusty volumes and stained teacups, sheaves of paper and exotic-looking figurines.

'You're a redhead,' Pound said to me once Dorothy had made the introductions.

'So are you. Is that auspicious?'

'No one holds a grudge like a redhead,' he said gruffly and with all seriousness. 'Mind that young Mr Hemingway.'

'Yes, sir,' Ernest said like a good pupil.

Ernest *was* Pound's pupil, too, from the first moment they clapped eyes on one another. Pound could evidently spot a man hungry for knowledge and obliged Ernest by talking non-stop while Dorothy ushered me over to another corner of the studio, well away from the men. Under a long window streaming sunlight, she poured me tea and told me about her famous lineage.

'My given name's Shakespear, though without the "e" at the end. My father was a descendant of the great man himself.'

'Why no "e"?'

'I have no idea, actually. It's more Bohemian-feeling that way. Not that I need help in that regard. My mother was mildly notorious for a time as the mistress of William Butler Yeats. That's how I met Ezra, when he was Yeats's assistant. I suppose I should have been a poet with all this history, but I married one instead.'

'We were reading Yeats a little in school, sprinkled in with the Robert Browning and Oliver Wendell Holmes. Ernest showed me "The Second Coming" in a magazine. We were both very struck by it.'

"'The best lack all conviction, while the worst are full of passionate intensity,'" she said. And then added, 'I wonder how Uncle Willy would feel about all the passionate intensity around here?'

Over in their shadowy corner of the studio, Ernest was literally crouched at Pound's feet while the older man lectured, waving a teapot around as he talked. His ginger-colored hair was growing wilder all the while, and I could see why Lewis Galantière would compare him to Satan — not just because of the hair and his satyr-like wiry goatee, but also because of his natural vehemence. I couldn't hear individual words, but he ranted in a volcanic stream, gesturing all the while, rarely sitting down.

I thought the two were a funny match, with Dorothy so elegant and reserved, and Pound so vociferous, but she claimed he'd been very important in her work. She was a painter, and as we talked that afternoon she pointed out some of her canvases to me. I thought they were lovely, with colors and forms as soft and gauzy as Dorothy's own voice and hands, but when I began to ask her questions about them, she quickly said, 'They're not to be shown.'

'Oh. Well, you're showing them here, aren't you?'

'Only incidentally,' she said, and smiled a beautiful smile, looking like something out of a painting herself.

At the end of our visit, after Ernest and I said our farewells, we made our way down the narrow staircase and out onto the street.

'I want to know everything,' I said.

'He's very noisy,' Ernest said. 'But he has some fine ideas. Big ideas, really. He wants to start movements, shape literature, change lives.'

'Then he should be a good person to know,' I said. 'Watch that you don't aggravate him, though. You've been warned about redheads.'

We laughed and walked to the nearest café, where Ernest told me more over squat glasses of brandy and water. 'He's got some funny ideas about women's brains.'

'What? That they haven't got any?'

'Something like that.'

'What about Dorothy? How's he feel about her brains?'

'Hard to say — though he did tell me they both have leave to take lovers.'

'How forward-thinking,' I said. 'Do you suppose this is how all artists' marriages go in Paris?'

'I couldn't say.'

'It's hardly something you could force on someone. You'd have to agree, wouldn't you?'

'Are you feeling sorry for her? What if she likes it? What if it was all her idea?'

'Maybe, but more likely the other way around.' I drank from my brandy, eyeing him over my glass.

'In any case, he's going to send some of my poems to Scofield Thayer at the *Dial*.'

'Not stories?'

'I don't have anything good enough yet, but Pound said I should write some articles for them about American magazines.'

'Well, that's flattering.'

'This has to be the beginning of something,' Ernest said. 'Pound says he'll teach me how to write if I teach him how to box.'

'Oh, God help us,' I said laughing.

⁕

Our next major introduction came a few weeks later, when Gertrude Stein invited us to tea. Strangely, it went much the same way our encounter with Pound and Dorothy had. There were two corners here too, one for the men – in this case, Ernest and Stein – and one for the women, with no crossover whatsoever.

When we arrived at the door, a proper French maid met us and took our coats, then led us into the room – *the* room, we knew by now, the most important salon in Paris. The walls were covered with paintings by heroes of cubism and post-impressionism and the otherwise highly modern – Henri Matisse, André Derain, Paul Gauguin, Juan Gris and Paul Cézanne. One striking example was a portrait of Stein done by Picasso, who had long been in her social circle and often attended her salon. It was done in dark browns and grays, and the face seemed slightly detached from the body, heavier and blockier, with thickly lidded eyes.

Gertrude seemed to be somewhere between forty-five and fifty, with an old-world look to her dark dress and shawl, and to her hair, which was piled in great skeins onto her beautiful head. She had a voice like rich velvet and brown eyes that took in everything at once. Later, when I had time to study her, I was struck with just how like Ernest's her eyes were – the deepest and most opaque shade of brown, critical and accepting, curious and amused.

Her companion Alice Toklas looked like a tight string of wires in comparison. She was dark in coloring with a sharply hooked nose and eyes that made you want to look away. After a few minutes of general conversation, she took my hand and off we went to the 'wives corner.' I felt a twinge of regret that I wasn't a writer or painter, someone special enough to be invited to talk with Gertrude, to sit near her in front of the fire, as Ernest did now, and speak of important things. I loved to be around interesting and creative people, to be part of that swell, but for the time being I was removed to the corner and interrogated by Miss Toklas on current affairs, about which I knew nothing. I felt like an idiot, and all the while we had tea and more tea and tiny, artfully arranged cakes. She did needle-point, her fingers moving endlessly and efficiently. She never looked down and never stopped talking.

Meanwhile, Ernest was sharing a glass of some sort of gracefully tinted liquor with Gertrude. I think I half fell in love with her that day, from a distance, and Ernest did too. When we walked home he had much to say about her taste, which was forward-thinking and impeccable. He also admired her breasts.

'What do you think they weigh?' he asked. He seemed to seriously want to know.

I laughed. 'I couldn't even wager a guess.'

'How about them living together? Women, I mean.'

'I don't know. They have such a life.'

'The paintings alone. It's like a museum in there.'

'Better,' I said. 'There are cakes.'

'And eau-de-vie. Still, it's strange. Women together. I'm not sure I buy it.'

'What do you mean? You don't believe they can get anything substantial from one another? That they love each other? Or is it the sex you don't buy?'

'I don't know.' He bristled defensively. 'She said women together are the most natural thing in the world, that nothing is ugly to them or between them, but men together are full of disgust for the act.'

'She said this?'

'In broad daylight.'

'I suppose it's flattering she was so open with you.'

'Should I give her an earful about our sex life next time?'

'You wouldn't.'

'I wouldn't,' he smiled. 'She might want to come watch.'

'You're horrible!'

'Yes, but you love me for it.'

'Oh, do I?' I said, and he swatted me on the hip.

Two weeks later, Gertrude and Alice accepted our invitation to come to tea in our dreary flat. What they thought as they climbed the dim and ramshackle stairwell, past the *pissoir* and the ghastly smells, I could hardly bear to guess – and yet they were gracious and accommodating, behaving as if they came to this quarter of Paris all the time. They drank our tea out of the wedding-gift china teapot – *that* at least was nice – and sat on the mahogany bed.

At the last visit, Gertrude had offered to look at some of Ernest's work and now she asked for it, reading quickly through the poems, a few stories, and part of a novel set in Michigan. Just as he'd done in Chicago, when I read his work for the first time, Ernest paced and twitched and seemed to be in pain.

'The poems are very good,' Stein said finally. 'Simple and quite clear. You're not posing at anything.'

'And the novel?'

I thought he was very brave to ask or even show her the pages, because he was newly in love with it. So protective was he, he had shown me next to nothing.

'It's not the kind of writing that interests me,' she said finally. 'Three sentences about the color of the sky. The sky is the sky and that's all. Strong declarative sentences, that's what you do best. Stick to that.'

As Gertrude spoke Ernest's face fell for a moment, but then he recovered himself. She'd hit on something he'd recently begun to realize about directness, about stripping language all the way down.

'When you begin over, leave only what's truly needed.'

He nodded, lightly flushed, and I could almost hear his mind closing in on her advice and adding it to Pound's. 'Cut everything superfluous,' Pound had said. 'Go in fear of abstractions. Don't tell readers what to think. Let the action speak for itself.'

'What do you think about Pound's theory about symbolism?' he asked her. 'You know, that a hawk should first and foremost be a hawk?'

'That's obvious, isn't it?' she said. 'A hawk is always a hawk, except' – and here she raised one heavy eyebrow and gave a mysterious smile – 'except when the hawk is a cabbage.'

'What?' Ernest said, grinning and game and clearly perplexed.

'Exactly,' Gertrude said.

FOURTEEN

Over the coming weeks, Ernest took Gertrude's advice and pitched out most of the novel to begin from scratch. During this time, he came home whistling and famished and eager to show me what he'd done. The new pages crackled with energy. It was all adventure, hunting and fishing and rutting. His character's name was Nick Adams and he was Ernest but bolder and purer – as Ernest would be if he followed every instinct. I loved the material and knew he did too.

In the meantime, he'd discovered Sylvia Beach's famous Shakespeare and Company on the Left Bank, and was surprised to find she'd lend him books on credit. He came home with his arms loaded down with volumes of Turgenev and Ovid, Homer, Catullus, Dante, Flaubert and Stendhal. Pound had given him a long reading list that was sending him back to the masters and also pointing him forward, toward T. S. Eliot and James Joyce. Ernest was a good student. He devoured everything, working his way through eight or ten books at once, putting one down and picking up another, leaving tented spines all over the apartment. He'd also borrowed *Three Lives* and *Tender Buttons*, two books Gertrude had published to a very small audience. It seemed most of the literary world didn't know what to make of her strangeness, and neither did Ernest. He read one of the poems from *Tender Buttons* aloud to me: 'A carafe, that is a blind glass. A kind in glass and a cousin, a spectacle and nothing strange a single hurt color and an arrangement in a system to pointing.'

He put the book down, shaking his head. '"A single hurt color" is nice, but the rest just goes right through me.'

'It's interesting,' I said.

'Yes. But what does it mean?'

'I don't know. Maybe it doesn't *mean* anything.'

'Maybe,' he said, and picked up Turgenev again.

It was April by this time, our first spring in Paris, and the rains fell soft and warm. Since we'd first arrived, Ernest had been supplementing our small income by writing editorials for the *Toronto Star*. One day he received notification from his editor John Bone that they wanted him in Genoa for an international economic conference. They would pay him seventy-five dollars a week plus expenses, but there wasn't any allowance made for wives. I would stay in Paris, the first separation in our seven months of marriage.

'Don't worry, Cat,' he said as he packed up his beloved Corona. 'I'll be back before you know it.'

For the first few days, I enjoyed my solitude. Ernest was such a *big* person, metaphorically speaking. He took up all the air in a room and magnetized and drew everyone to him; men and women and children and dogs. For the first time in many months, I could wake to quiet and hear my own thoughts and follow my own impulses. But soon enough there was a shift. I don't know how to describe it, but after the blush of my own company wore off, I became so aware of Ernest's absence it was as if the *lack of him* had moved into the apartment with me. His shadow was there at breakfast and at bedtime. It hung from the curtains in the bedroom where the accordion music pushed in and out like a bellows.

Ernest had suggested I go to Sylvia's bookshop for tea, and though I did go once, I couldn't help but think she was just being polite by engaging me in conversation. She liked writers and artists, and I was neither. I went to dinner at Gertrude and Alice's, and although I felt they were truly becoming friends, I missed Ernest. His was the company I liked best. It was almost embarrassing to admit how dependent on him I'd become. I tried to stave off depression by going everywhere I was invited and staying out of the apartment as much as possible. I haunted the Louvre and the cafés. I practiced for hours at a new Haydn piece to perform for Ernest when he returned. I thought playing would make me feel better, but in truth it only reminded me of the worst times in St Louis, when I was lonely and cut off from the world.

Ernest was gone for three weeks, and by the end of that time I was sleeping so badly in our bed I'd often move in the middle of the night to an upright wingback chair and try to rest there, huddled in blankets. I couldn't enjoy much of anything except walking to the Île St Louis to the park I'd come to love and rely on. The trees were flowering now, and there was the thick smell of horse-chestnut blossoms. I also liked to look around at the houses surrounding the park, and wonder about the people who filled them, what kind of marriages they had and how they loved or hurt each other on any given day, and if they were happy, and whether they thought happiness was a sustainable thing. I'd stay in the park as long as I could, and then walk home through sunshine I couldn't quite feel.

When Ernest finally came home in May, I squeezed him hard, my eyes filling with tears of relief.

'What's this now? Did you miss me, Feather Cat?'

'Too much.'

'Good. I like to be missed.'

I nodded into his shoulder, but part of me couldn't help wondering if it *was* good to rely on him so utterly. He admired my strength and resilience, and counted on it; more than this, *I* liked feeling strong and was uncomfortable knowing that had vanished when he left. Was my happiness so completely tied to him now that I could only feel like myself when he was near? I had no idea. All I could do was undress him slowly while in the dancehall below us, the accordion wrenched away at a melancholy tune.

We had two hundred dollars from the *Toronto Star* burning with possibility when Ernest came back, and decided to splurge on a trip to Switzerland. He was feeling good about nearly everything just then. Scofield Thayer at the *Dial* had recently sent back the poems Pound had recommended with a stingingly impersonal rejection letter, but Ernest had made a lot of new connections in Genoa, other correspondents he'd worked closely with such as Max Eastman, an American editor who wanted Ernest to send along some of his prose sketches, and Lincoln Steffens, the famous muckraking journalist who impressed Ernest to no end with his bold politics. Steffens had recently traveled to the Soviet Union and come back with an enthusiasm for Communism, telling the press and anyone else who would listen, 'I've been over into the future, and it works.' Ernest was thrilled to have Steffens take notice of him and, bolstered by a new sense of community and ambition, he'd just sent off fifteen poems to Harriet Monroe at *Poetry*.

'Why the hell not?' he said. 'Maybe the door won't open unless I bang on it loud and long.'

'It's all going to happen for you,' I said. 'I feel it coming.'

'Maybe,' he said, 'but let's not jinx it by talking about it.'

We bought third-class tickets to Montreux, and then took the electric tram straight up the mountainside to Chamby, which overlooked Lake Geneva. Our chalet was large and rough, and the mountain air was wonderfully clear. We spent hours a day hiking on densely forested mountain trails and came back to a lunch of perfectly roasted meat, winter squash and parsnips and stewed fruit with heavy cream. At night, we read by the fire and drank mulled wine with lemon and smoky spices. We slept as much as we wanted, made love twice a day, read and wrote letters and played cards.

'You're so tan and strong and healthy,' Ernest said to me as we hiked one day. 'Everything seems to agree with you here.'

I liked to hear any praise from him, but those weeks alone in Paris were still on my mind. They'd scared me and had me thinking about what it meant to be really strong, on my own terms – not just fit and brown from the sun, not just flexible and accommodating.

After the first week, Ernest's old war friend Chink Dorman-Smith joined us. The two had met in Schio, at the Italian front, before Ernest was wounded. Chink was Irish, as tall as Ernest but much fairer, with ruddy cheeks and a red-blond mustache. I liked him immediately. He had the most beautiful manners, much more suited to someone who'd spent time at court than the professional soldier he was. Every morning he came to breakfast humming merrily and calling me Mrs Popplethwaite. Ernest loved Chink like a brother and had endless respect for him. He wasn't competitive with him as he could be with many of his writer or reporter friends, and so the time was easy going, day after day. The Rhone Valley was on top form just then, with narcissus blooming in every bare patch of meadow and in the jagged crevices of rock. The first time I saw narcissus pushing through ice and thriving, I thought it was perfect and wanted that kind of determination for myself.

Every day we tramped well into the mountains to find nice inns and promising fishing spots. The Stockalper, a stream near the junction of Lake Geneva and the Rhone was Ernest's favorite place this side of Northern Michigan. He spent hours there happily hooking trout while Chink and I lounged in the grass and read or talked.

'It's wonderful to see the two of you in love this way,' Chink said one afternoon as we lounged in the shade of a blossoming pear tree. 'There were times I wondered if Hem would ever get over Milan.'

'Milan or his beautiful nurse?'

'Both, I guess,' he said. 'That whole time hardly brought out the best in him. But you do.' Chink crossed his arms behind his head and closed his eyes. 'Good old Hem,' he said, and then promptly fell asleep.

I liked that Chink saw and understood what was good in us. He also knew things about Ernest I didn't. They shared a history, oceans of beer, late-night confessions. Sometimes they talked about the war in the long cool evenings on the chalet's wide porch, and it gave me a new appreciation for what they'd both seen and endured.

Chink was and would always be a soldier. When Ernest went home to his life in the States, Chink stayed on with the British Army. For the past several years he'd been stationed in Ireland with a British occupying force that was trying to control violence in the Irish fight for independence. It was a difficult post, and he'd seen a good bit of death, which you could feel him trying to throw off a little more every day he was with us.

'It must be so strange,' I said to him one evening, 'with terrible fighting going on there, and you boarding a ship to take a holiday from it. Just buying a ticket and stepping away.'

Chink laughed darkly. 'In our war,' he paused to nod to Ernest, 'when the front ran all the way to the English Channel, there were men who got short furlough to go home for tea. They'd come back again and pick up their bayonets and gas masks and get to it, still tasting biscuit crumbs on their tongues.'

'Your mind can't survive that, though,' Ernest said. 'You can't keep up with that jump. You get stuck one place or the other, or somewhere between. And that's when the crack-up starts.'

'That's right,' Chink said.

'Sometimes, though, once you've been to war and have that in you, you can go back there. And that's sort of like what you were saying, Tiny.' He nodded to me over the table, meeting my eyes. 'Like buying a ticket and going there, and then climbing out of it again when you snap to or wake up.'

'That's not always so pleasant, is it?' Chink said, because he knew about Ernest's nightmares of the front, and the way he still woke in the middle of the night, sweating and screaming with his eyes wild and terrified. The two friends nodded at one another and lifted their glasses.

It was on one of these evenings full of drink and talk that Chink brought up the idea of crossing the Great St Bernard Pass into Italy.

'It was good enough for Napoléon and Charlemagne,' he said, sweeping beer foam from his mustache.

'How far do you think it is?' I asked.

'Maybe fifty kilometers?'

'Let's do it,' Ernest said. 'From Aosta, we can take the train to Milan.'

'Or Schio,' Chink said. 'Return to the scene of the crime.'

'I'd love to show you Schio,' Ernest said to me. 'It's one of the finest places on earth.'

'There's an old mill we made into a barracks and called the Schio Country Club,' Chink said smiling. 'I couldn't tell you how often we swam in the stream there in the heat of the day. And the wisteria!'

'And the trattoria with the little garden where we drank beer under a full moon,' Ernest said. 'There's a charming hotel in Schio, the Due Spadi. We'll stay there for a night or two, and then head on to Fossalta. I could even write the whole trip up for the *Star*. Wounded soldier returns to front.'

'Brilliant,' Chink agreed, and it was settled.

The next morning we left the chalet with heavily loaded rucksacks. Ernest had come into the room when I was packing and seen me trying to find space for my bottles of face cream and toilet water. 'Do you have any room in yours?' I asked, holding out the bottles.

'Fat chance,' he said. 'Are you hoping to smell nice for the trout?'

'Give a girl a break,' I said, but he wouldn't budge. Finally I asked Chink to carry them, which he did, grudgingly. But the vanity of wanting toilet water nearby while crossing a treacherous mountain pass was nothing in comparison to my shoe choice — slim tan Oxfords instead of proper boots. I don't know what I was thinking except that my legs looked better in the Oxfords. A lot of good swell-looking legs did me. We hadn't gone five miles before my feet were soaked through. In my defense, we didn't know what we were in for. The pass was crossable in spring, but it hadn't been opened that year. No one had yet gone through and the snow was still thigh-deep in some places. We trudged on anyway, through valleys and thickly forested pine trails and wide meadows dotted with wild flowers. The scenery was extraordinary, but Ernest and I were both in pretty bad form. My feet throbbed and my legs ached. He'd developed some sort of altitude sickness – nausea and a headache – and as we climbed, the symptoms worsened. His head swam, and every mile or so, he leaned over and retched into the snow. In a way, Chink had it worst of all since he had to take up our slack, often carrying two packs several hundred yards at a time, then dropping them and returning for the third. As we walked I started to fantasize about being rescued by one of the famous St Bernard dogs that would tug us, all three, up the rest of the mountain on a comfy sled.

Half-way up, we stopped at Bourg St Pierre and ate lunch in a patch of sun. My feet were so swollen I was afraid to take off my shoes thinking I might never get them on again. Good for nothing but a nap, I curled up on a wooden bench while Ernest and Chink wandered around the town sampling the beer.

'You missed a great little cemetery,' Chink said when they came to wake me later.

'There are rows and rows of tombstones for the poor bastards taken down by the mountain,' Ernest said.

'*This* mountain?' I said with alarm. 'Are we really in danger?'

'Do you want to cash it in and stay here?' Ernest said.

'And miss the monks?' Chink said. 'How would we forgive ourselves?'

The Hospice of St Bernard sat at the highest point of the pass, where an order of devotees had been aiding travelers for a thousand years or more. Anyone knocking at their door would be given bread and soup, a cup of wine and a straw bed to pass the night on. And so it was we came to them, late that evening, thirty kilometers up the mountain and a little drunk from the cognac we'd been sipping every twenty minutes to get us there from Bourg St Pierre. It was a clear night. The moon loomed up behind the hospice and lit it eerily.

'Looks like a barracks, doesn't it?' Chink said, stepping forward to rap at the imposing wooden door.

'You'd make a barracks of any old thing,' Ernest said before the door swung wide to reveal a taut bald head.

The monk asked no questions, just led us in and through the dark hushed corridors to our rooms. They were simple, as advertised, with straw mattresses for sleeping, but there was good reading light and a nice fire. While Chink and Ernest rested before dinner, I went exploring, thinking I might find a kitchen and a basin to soak my poor feet. But every corridor looked like every other. I tried to follow voices, but there were none. Finally, I took a chance on a long, dark passageway only to find that I'd stumbled on the monks' private quarters. Several doors opened all at once, shaved head after shaved head popping out like moles. I was horrified, and returned to the room where I collapsed and spat out my story. The boys just laughed, of course, and then Ernest told me he thought I'd likely been the first woman to tread these halls in a thousand years! He promptly put it in a letter to Gertrude and Alice: *Mrs Hemingway trying to seduce monks, here. Please advise.*

The next morning we headed out for Aosta feeling more ready to tackle the rest of the pass – or so I thought until my right Oxford split open at the seam.

'Serves you right, Miss Vanity,' Ernest barked. Frankly, he wasn't in much better shape. Still nauseous from the altitude, it took everything he had to go the remaining leg of the journey. Only Chink was still in good form. He took a knife and cut open my other shoe for me, and this was the way we hobbled into Aosta the next day, stepping out of a snow-throttled pass into full-on spring, pale green hills with glorious vineyards to every side. I joked in a letter home to Ruth that the boys all but had to carry me into town, but the truth was I'd surprised myself by my stamina. It hadn't been pretty by any stretch, but I'd shown more endurance than I thought was even possible. If it hadn't been for those terrible shoes, I might have run the last hundred yards to Aosta.

FIFTEEN

On the train to Milan, I slept like the dead and woke to hear Ernest and Chink talking about Benito Mussolini. The new fascist leader was in town, and Ernest wanted to use his press card to arrange an interview. He thought Mussolini was the biggest bluff in Europe just then, and was dying to meet him. Meanwhile, Chink had to get back to his post, and so he left us there with kisses and promises that we'd meet again soon.

Ernest was happy to be in Milan again. After finding me new shoes, our first stop was the gorgeous and imposing stone mansion in the Via Manzoni that had been converted into the Red Cross hospital where Ernest and Chink had both recovered. We stood at the gates and looked up at the balconies and terraces, the striped awnings and wicker furniture and fat potted palms.

'It looks like a fine hotel,' I said to Ernest.

'It was good living, all right. Too bad we had to get shot to get inside.'

'I'm sorry I can't really know what it was like for you.'

'It's all right. I'm glad you're here to hold my hand for it.'

'That I can do,' I said, and reached for him. We walked to the Duomo next and then to Biffi's at the Galleria where we drank sparkling wine floating with fresh strawberries, and although Ernest didn't often speak about his time at the front, talking and being with Chink had primed the pump and he was full of it now. Stepping into Milan had completed the process. The whole trip had become a time machine, and he was back.

'It's funny,' he said, 'but sometimes what I remember most about the night I was shot is the mosquitoes. They got in your ears and into the corners of your eyes and you couldn't sleep for them. Not that we were sleeping much anyway. Then the sky went up in flames. I was blasted right off my feet. We all were. I couldn't feel anything at first, and then there was just a pressure in my chest like I couldn't breathe and a jangling in my head.'

'Do you really want to say all this?' I asked gently. 'You don't need to.'

'I guess I do,' he said, and then fell quiet for a few minutes. 'My hearing was all off, but someone was yelling for help. Somehow I got over there, and lifted him up and carried him to the command post. I don't even know how. I hardly remember that part, just feeling my legs going to pieces under me. I heard the machine gun afterwards, as if it had nothing to do with me. I went on running and put the bastard down and then I was down too. Then nothing. I don't know what else.'

'Then the field hospital,' I said. 'And the train to Milan.'

'Yes,' he said. 'Every time that train stopped, flies streamed through the open windows and covered my bloody bandages. I was two days on that train.'

I nodded. It wasn't years behind him at all, but right there in his face and in his eyes, the way he'd come to Milan like a broken doll. Not a hero, but a boy who might never truly recover from what he'd felt and seen. It gave me a sharp kind of sadness to think that no matter how much I loved him and tried to put him back together again, he might stay broken forever.

'You must be thinking about Agnes today,' I said after a while.

'Only a little.' He covered my hand with his. 'I'm glad we can do this together.'

'Me too.' I knew he was telling me the truth, but I also knew that if it were possible, he would have preferred to have me and Agnes there both – his past and his present, each of us loving him without question – and the strawberries too. The wine and the sunshine and the warm stones under our feet. He wanted everything there was to have, and more than that.

I slept and read at our hotel the next afternoon while Ernest arranged for an interview with Mussolini. He'd recently been elected to the Italian Chamber of Deputies, and this fascinated Ernest. The man seemed to be a mass of contradictions. He was strongly Nationalist, and wanted to bring Italy back to its former glory by reaching into its Roman past. He seemed genuinely invested in the plight of the working class and of women, all of which he'd laid out in *The Manifesto of the Fascist Struggle*. And yet he also managed to endear himself to the aristocracy and the bourgeoisie, guaranteeing their continued existence. He seemed to want to be all things to all people, traditional and revolutionary, loved by the military, the business class and the liberals. There was no National Fascist Party, not yet, but the ranks of fascism were growing so quickly it all seemed terribly inevitable.

'Are you nervous?' I asked as he was organising his note-books and preparing to leave.

'Of what? He's just a big bully, isn't he?'

'I don't know. Some say he's a monster.'

'Maybe, but monsters don't always look that way. They have clean fingernails and use a knife and fork and speak the King's English.'

I buttoned his coat and brushed the fabric over his shoulders with my hands.

'You're fussing, wife. Take a nap, and don't worry.'

He was gone for two hours, and when he came back to the hotel to type up his notes, he seemed all too pleased to tell me he'd been right. 'The man's up to here with bluff,' he said, gesturing to his neck, 'and nothing on top.'

'Was he wearing his black shirt?' I asked, very much relieved.

'He was, they all were.' He sat down at the desk and put fresh paper in his Corona. 'He's bigger than you'd guess, too, with a wide brown face and very pretty hands. A woman's hands, really.'

'I wouldn't write that if I were you.'

He laughed and began to type rapid fire in his usual way, his fingers stabbing quickly with very little breaking or breathing. 'I'll tell you what else,' he said without looking up, 'there was a beautiful wolfhound pup with him in the room.'

'So the fascist monster is a dog lover.'

'Maybe he planned to eat it later,' he said grinning.

'You're terrible.'

'Yes,' he said, his index fingers poised for another violent attack on his machine. 'That was a fine dog.'

The next day we boarded a bus to Schio, where Ernest wanted to show me the mill and the wisteria and every part of the town that had managed to stay so fine in his memory, no matter what else had happened around it. But on the way, the sky dimmed and grew gray. It began to rain and didn't stop. When we finally arrived at the town, Ernest seemed surprised. 'It's so much smaller,' he said.

'Maybe it's shrunk in the rain,' I said, trying to lighten the mood, but quickly realizing that it wasn't going to be possible. For the whole visit, Ernest wrestled with memory. Everything had changed and grown dingy in the four years since he'd last been here. The woolen mill – closed down during the war – spewed black muck into the swimming hole where Ernest and Chink had bathed on so many hot afternoons. We walked up and down the winding streets in the rain, but everything looked dull and lonely, the shop windows full of cheap dishes and tablecloths and postcards. The taverns were empty. We went into a wine shop where a girl sat carding wool.

'I can barely recognize the town,' Ernest said to her in English. 'So much is new.'

She nodded and continued with her work, drawing the paddles back and forth, the white fibers becoming long and smooth.

'Do you think she understands you?' I said to Ernest quietly.

'She understands me.'

'My husband was here during the war,' I said.

'The war is over,' she answered without looking up.

Deflated, we gave up on sightseeing, and went to check in at the Two Spades, but it had changed too. The bed creaked, the linens were sad looking, and the light bulbs were filmed over with dust.

In the middle of a tasteless dinner, Ernest said, 'Maybe none of it happened.'

'Of course it did,' I said. 'I wish Chink were here. He'd find a way to cheer us up.'

'No. He wouldn't be able to take it either.'

We slept badly that night, and when morning came the rain went on and on. Ernest was still determined to show me Fossalta, where he'd been wounded, and so we found a driver who would take us as far as Verona, and then boarded a train to Mestre, where we had to find another car and driver. On and on, all day, and for the whole of the trip, Ernest studied maps and tried to match up what he saw in the countryside to what he remembered seeing years before. But nothing was the same. Fossalta, when we finally arrived, was worse than Schio because there wasn't a single sign of ravage. The trenches and dugouts had vanished. The bombed houses and buildings had been changed out for new. When Ernest found the slope where he'd been wounded, it was green and unscarred and completely lovely. Nothing felt honest. Thousands of men had died here just a few years earlier, Ernest himself had bled here, shot full of shrapnel, and yet everything was clean and shiny, as if the land itself had forgotten everything.

Before we left, Ernest combed the hedgerows, and finally came away with a single rusted shell fragment, not much larger than a button.

'Chasing your past is a lousy, rotten game, isn't it?' He looked at me. 'Why did I come?'

'You know why,' I said.

He turned the fragment over in his hand a few times and I guessed he was thinking about our talk with Chink, and how the war in his head couldn't be counted on any longer. Memory couldn't be counted on. Time was unreliable and everything dissolved and died – even or especially when it *looked* like life. All around us, the grass grew. Birds made a living racket in the trees. The sun beat down with promise. From that moment forward, Ernest would always hate the spring.

Sixteen

We didn't return to Paris until late in June, and before long the Bastille Day celebrations had begun, and there was dancing and singing in the street at all hours. It was hot and noisy, and we shouldn't even have tried to sleep. I could see Ernest's restless outline in the dark, one arm over his eyes.

'It will be our anniversary soon,' I said.

'Should we go away?'

'Where would we go?'

'To Germany, or maybe to Spain.'

'We wouldn't have to,' I said. 'We could stay home and get very drunk and make love.'

'We could do that now,' he laughed.

'We could,' I said.

The clarinetist outside our window played a series of low notes, waiting for accompaniment, then fell silent again. Ernest turned on his side and reached to stroke my bare shoulder. His touch gave me a delicious run of chills, and then he pulled me toward him and onto my stomach without saying anything, covering my body with his. He was heavy and warm, and I could feel his lips and forehead against my neck.

'Don't move,' he said.

'I'm hardly breathing.'

'Good.'

'It like it slow this way.'

'Yes.' His arms were bent to each side of me so he wouldn't crush me completely, but I wanted to be crushed a little.

Afterward, as we lay in the dark, the same laughter rose from the street, and the music was louder, if anything, and more chaotic. Ernest grew very quiet again, and I wondered if he was thinking about Schio and all that wouldn't be found there, and of the sadness he'd carried home with him afterward.

'Should I get up and shut the window?'

'It's too hot, and it won't help anyway. Just go to sleep.'

'Something's on your mind. Do you want to tell me?'

'Talking won't do a lick of good either.'

I could hear that he'd fallen into a very low place, but I believed, naïvely, that I could help if I could get him to talk about it. I continued to gently press and finally he said, 'If you really want to know, it's making love. There's something about it that makes me feel emptied out afterwards, and lonely too.'

'How awful,' I said, feeling the sting of his words. We'd just been so very much with each other, or at least I'd felt that way.

'I'm sorry. It's nothing you've done.'

'The hell it's not. Let's not ever do it again. We won't have to. I won't care.'

'We do, though. You see that. I know you do.'

'No.'

He pulled me closer then. 'Please don't worry, just tell me you love me.'

'I love you,' I said, and kissed his hands and eyelids and tried to forget what he'd said. But I couldn't. I couldn't forget anything he'd ever said to me. That's how it was.

'Go to sleep now.'

'All right,' I said.

He rose and dressed. It must have been three o'clock in the morning, or maybe four.

'You're not going to work now?'

'Maybe not,' he said. 'But I'm going to try.'

I heard him leave, his steps on the stairs, all the way down, and then fell asleep for a few hours. When I woke up he was still away working, and it was already hot and close in the apartment. I kicked the bed sheet away and put my robe on, and went into the kitchen to make the coffee. Musicians from the night before were still in the street and it made me feel tired just to hear them. I didn't know how they managed to keep playing. Did they sleep standing up in doorways? Did they sleep at all?

After breakfast, I washed and dressed and sat at the piano for a few hours, but it wasn't satisfying work. The day was too hot and I was too distracted by the night before. I lay down again, and then heard Marie Cocotte in the kitchen, clearing dishes from the night before. We'd gotten her name from the concierge in our building, and now she came in every morning as our *femme de ménage*, taking care of all the washing and cooking for two francs an hour. Marie was childless and nearing middle age, petite and sturdy, with quick and competent hands. She'd earned her nickname, *cocotte*, which was French slang for wench, from a dish she made often and beautifully for us, *poulet en cocotte*. Several days a week, she returned in the late afternoon to prepare our dinner, and because she made everything so well, I'd asked her to teach me French cooking. But now that it was high summer, I didn't want to be in the kitchen at all, and was happy to eat fruit or nothing until Ernest was finished with his work. Then we'd go to a café for an aperitif when it was dark and much cooler and felt right again to eat and be hungry.

'Good morning, Madame,' Marie Cocotte said, coming into the bedroom where the curtains were still open from the night before. We'd never closed them.

'Will the music ever stop?' I asked in my still-graceless French, pointing to the window.

'Not today,' she said, laughing.

'I think Bastille Day will last forever,' I said, and she laughed again.

'That is how we like it,' she said.

The summer stretched on this way, becoming several summers in a row, with time not moving at all. The days grew harder to fill. I felt my headaches coming back, and though I knew I shouldn't resent Ernest's working or try to keep him from it, I was always happiest when he woke up and said he wasn't going to try to write at all that day, and that we should go to the boxing matches, instead, or drive out to the country to see the bicycle races.

One afternoon Gertrude and Alice invited us to lunch at their country house in Meaux. We went out all together, in Gertrude's Model-T, and had a picnic feast with two kinds of eggs and potatoes and roast chicken. We drank several bottles of chilled wine and then three-star Hennessy, and everything was beautiful – the valleys and bridges, the charming house and its flowering trees. After lunch, we lay in the grass and talked and felt free.

Ernest had taken to showing Gertrude all of his work, and reading hers as well. Though he'd felt put off by the difficulty of her writing at the beginning of their friendship, he'd grown to appreciate the strangeness of it and was becoming more and more interested in what she was doing. She even began to influence his style, particularly the habit she had of naming and repeating concrete objects, places and people, not trying to find variation, but reveling in how any word took on a striking power when you used it again and again. In some of the new Nick Adams passages, I saw how he was doing this too with the simplest language and things – lake, trout, log, boat – and how it gave the work a very distilled and almost mythic feel.

Ernest's connection to Gertrude was obviously very important to them both, and I loved that we were all becoming good, easy friends with one another, though there was still a persistent pairing off when we met. Ernest and Gertrude were the artists, and when they talked, their heads close together, they seemed almost like siblings. Alice and I were the wives, even without the four walls of the salon to define us, and she seemed content with this. Was I? Ernest was utterly supportive of my playing, and often referred to the piano as my 'work', as if I were an artist too. I loved to play and felt it was very much a part of my life, but I wasn't at all convinced I was special, as Ernest was. He was inside the creative sphere and I was outside, and I didn't know if anything would ever change that. Alice seemed to feel easier in her role as an artist's wife, throwing herself wholly behind Gertrude's ambition, but maybe she'd just been doing it longer and could hide her jealousy better. I gazed into my glass of brandy – at the kaleidoscope it made on the pale blanket cloth, which was some kind of Irish wool. We were here together now, I told myself. Everything was lovely and fine. I should just know it and hold onto it and be happy. I would. I would try.

*

The next day we woke late and I still felt the Hennessy. Ernest must have been feeling it too, because we weren't even out of bed yet before he said, 'The work won't be any good at all today. I shouldn't bother.'

'You could go and try anyway, just for a few hours,' I said, feeling a small sting because I didn't mean it.

'No,' he said. 'It won't come to anything. I already know.'

We rose and had our breakfast, and then decided we would go out to Auteuil, to the horse races. It would be cooler out of the city. Marie Cocotte would pack a basket with sandwiches and wine, and then we'd get the racing forms and read them on the train. As soon as it was settled, I felt the pressure in my head leave, whooshing out quickly like a ghost being exorcised from a house. I felt guilty for how happy it made me not to share him – guilty and happy, all at the same time.

Ernest and I both loved Auteuil. We always went over the racing form together and then visited the paddocks to see the animals. I loved the deep smell of the horses and the track itself, and the noises of the happy crowd taking their luck as it came. Ernest was fascinated by everything – the beautiful rippling of horse flesh, the stumpy-looking jockeys in their silks, the trainers standing at the rails and seeming to know something mysterious, the slang of the boys in the stable and the smell of horse piss. We never had a lot to spend at the races, but we always had something, and it felt good to be out together in the sun. Ernest would spread his coat in the grass and we'd lunch there, and then I'd nap or just watch the clouds and wait for the next race. When we won, we had champagne, and sometimes when we lost too, because we were happy to be there and be together, and what was money to us anyway? We never had enough to make a difference if we lost it.

That day, the favorite was a shiny dark beauty, a good

jumper with a quick way. He had tight sharp lines on the jump, making you think you'd barely seen it at all. We didn't bet on the favorite, but on another, lighter horse called Chèvre d'Or that was running a hundred and twenty to one. Sometimes we picked the horses together, after walking the paddock, or standing at the rails and seeing how the horses moved, and waiting for a feeling. Sometimes Ernest found someone he knew who'd give him a name or two, good odds. That day I followed my own hunches and found the horse myself. I could be lucky for us that way. It had happened before, and that day I felt sure it would happen again. Chèvre d'Or wasn't quick and dark but moved like brandy in a glass. I watched his smooth legs and told Ernest he was the one.

'Let's really bet on him,' I said. 'Do we have enough?'

'Maybe we do,' he said.

'Let's spend it anyway, even if we don't.'

He laughed and went off to place the bet, still smiling at me. He loved it when I was bold.

'Are you still stuck on this horse?' he asked when he came back.

'I am.'

'Good. He's got six months of living expenses on him.'

'You don't mean it.'

'I do,' he said, and we crowded up to the rail with the rest, both of us tingling with risk.

My horse took the lead from the start. By the second hurdle, nothing could touch him. He was four lengths ahead by the fourth hurdle, a brandy-colored blur.

'He's doing it,' I said, feeling flushed. My stomach was taut and knotted.

'He's doing it all right,' Ernest said, watching the other horses break. But it was too late for any of them because

Chèvre d'Or was too fast and too far ahead – too good as he was, ten lengths ahead, then more. The favorite gained and took the others, his jockey's whip slicing, but my horse was in his own race.

He was twenty lengths ahead and twenty paces from the finish when it happened. As beautiful as the rest had been, that's how ugly it was when he fell at the last jump. If he was brandy before, now he was a busted wheelbarrow. He was sticks and string, a child's toy breaking with a crack. It was so terrible, I couldn't watch. I buried my face in Ernest's shoulder and didn't see the end of the race, the other horses parting around the fallen animal, the favorite taking everything he hadn't earned.

I cried half the way home on the train, through the gloomy neighborhoods with the clotheslines and the garbage and the children dressed in rags, trying to forget the day and what we'd seen.

SEVENTEEN

When our first anniversary came, we decided to spend it with Chink, in Cologne, and took a boat down the Rhine to meet him. The weather was still very warm then, and the days were lovely and long, and when we met up with Chink we were all very happy to be together. He was good for us, and we were good for him and Cologne was beautiful.

One afternoon I was lying back on the grass watching Ernest and Chink fish. Ernest reached into the duffel bag on the bank next to him and pulled out a bottle of cold white wine that he uncorked with his teeth. In his other hand he held the rod, its line well out, the water moving around it in gentle eddies. There was a nice breeze and yellow pollen blew by in small clouds and sifted down on us from the trees.

'You boys look like something out of a painting,' I said, squinting up at them.

'We have an admirer,' Ernest said to Chink.

I got up out of the grass and walked over to Ernest and watched him closely for several minutes. 'Show me how it's done,' I said.

'Tired of admiring already?'

'No,' I smiled. 'But I'd like to give it a try.'

'All right, then.' He stood behind me on the soft, grassy bank and showed me how to point the rod. I swung my arm back and forward again in a smooth arc, just as he said, and managed to release the reel perfectly. It sailed out into the current like a dream.

'That felt good,' I said.

'That's how you know you've done it right,' Chink said.

'What now?'

'Now you wait,' Ernest said, and walked over to the rod case. Before he'd even reached it I felt a small tug at the line, then another stronger tug. On instinct, I pulled up and the hook struck. I could feel the fish working against it.

'Hey,' Chink said, watching. 'She's a ringer.'

Ernest rushed back and helped me land the trout, and then the fish was on the grass, pale brown and spotted.

'I feel a little sorry for him,' I said.

'You can throw him back if you like,' Chink said.

'Like hell she will,' Ernest said, laughing.

'No, I want to eat him. I want to know if it tastes different when you catch it yourself.'

'Good girl,' Ernest said. 'It does, you know.'

'I thought so.'

'This one's got the killer instinct,' Chink said, and we all laughed.

'You might as well know it all,' Ernest said later when I had landed three trout, one after the other. He showed me how to clean and gut the fish and rinse the body well in the stream for cooking.

'I'm not disgusted,' I said as we worked.

'I know it. I can tell.'

We roasted my three over the fire on sticks, as well as the other half-dozen Chink and Ernest had caught between them.

'I like mine best,' I said, licking salt off my fingertips.

'I like yours best too,' Ernest said, and opened another bottle of wine as the sky softened and evening came on.

In Cologne itself, the mood was more troubled. At the British Occupation Garrison, where Chink had recently been stationed, an angry mob had defaced a statue of Wilhelm II on horseback, wrenching down the huge iron sword and shattering off the spurs. Other rioters had murdered a German policeman, chasing him into the river and then severing his fingers when he tried to hold onto a bridge to save himself. From a distance, the city looked like something out of a fairytale, with red-roofed houses and villagers dressed in lederhosen, but like the rest of Allied-occupied Germany, it was in a state of supreme unrest.

A few days later, on 14 September, we were in a café catching up on our newspapers when we learned that the Turkish port city of Smyrna was burning. The Greco-Turkish war had been raging for three years, since the repartitioning of the Ottoman Empire that came out of the war, but the conflict had finally broken with this fire. No one knew who was responsible. The Greeks blamed the Turks and vice versa, and the only clear thing was the tragic results. The harbor and had been set alight with petroleum, as had many of the Greek and Armenian quarters in the town. People were driven out of their houses and into the streets. Scores drowned in the harbor, and others were slaughtered where they stood. Refugees were fleeing into the hills. We felt very chastened where we sat in the café, having our fine lunch, for not having been more aware of the conflict.

'I imagine I'll be there soon enough,' Chink said. His expression was stern.

'Maybe I will too,' Ernest said, and I felt a cold rush go through me.

'You don't really think so,' I said.

'I don't know. It's possible.'

'I've always wanted to see Istanbul,' Chink said.

'Constantinople's a better word, though,' Ernest said. 'Or Byzantium.'

'Right,' Chink said. 'Well, either way, it's in the crapper now, isn't it?'

Back in Paris, we hadn't even unpacked before a telegram came for Ernest from the *Star*. John Bone was sending him to Turkey to report on the conflict, just as he'd suspected. He would leave in three days' time. He'd just read the news, the torn envelope still in his hands, when I felt myself come crashing down.

'What is it?' Ernest said, watching my face fall. 'I won't be long. It will be like Genoa, the same as that. And then I'll be home and we'll be together again.'

But I had never told him about how low I'd been when he was away in Genoa, how every day without him had been a struggle against myself.

'I don't want you to go,' I said.

'What?'

'Tell them you can't, that I'm ill.'

'You're not making any sense.'

'But I am, don't you see? I'm telling the truth for once.'

'No, you're being childish. This is a tantrum, and I want you to stop it now.'

That's when I began to cry, which was worst of all; he hated tears.

'Please stop,' he said. 'We've just had a wonderful time in Cologne, haven't we? Why can't we simply be happy?'

'That's all I want,' I said, but the tears still came. I opened my suitcase, then closed it again and went into the kitchen to boil water for tea. I thought maybe he'd gone into the bedroom, but he was there, just behind me, pacing.

'It's too far away,' I finally said.

'That's the point, isn't it? You don't want a war breathing down your neck.'

'Can't we just pretend the telegram never came?'

'No, we can't.' His face grew suddenly hard then, because I was asking him to choose me over his work. 'To hell with the tea,' he said, but I kept at it, measuring leaves for the pot and pouring water through the porcelain sieve. He strode back and forth behind me in the tiny kitchen, waiting for me to apologize. When I didn't and didn't even turn around, he finally stormed out of the apartment.

I knew he'd gone to a café. I could have found him easily and it might have been fine, then, if I had. We could have had a brandy and water and agreed to put it behind us. Or asked the waiter to bring the absinthe and let it erase everything beautifully. But I stayed where I was and drank the damn tea, though I didn't even want it.

By the time Ernest came home, I was drunk and pretending to sleep. I'd abandoned the tea and taken up a bottle of whiskey instead. I'd eaten nothing, and just drank the whiskey, several glasses, warm without water. When I was drunk enough to do it, I took up the lovely china teapot which had come so far with us and let it drop to the floor with a crash. I meant to leave the pieces there for him to see but once I'd done it, it was too small and childish – the act of a tantrum, like he'd said. I hated feeling so desperate and out of control, but couldn't seem to rein it in either. I picked up the mess, one wet ruined shard at a time, and put it in a small paper sack. Then I went to bed. My head swam viciously on the pillow, but I closed my eyes and tried to slow my breathing. Much later, I heard him on the stairs, then in the room.

'Hadley,' he said, sitting next to me on the bed. He touched my face and neck lightly, but I didn't move. 'Let's don't do this, Feather Cat.'

I pinched my eyes tight to keep the tears from coming, and tried to appear as if I were sleeping. But he knew I wasn't.

'Damn you,' he said, when I wouldn't open my eyes or answer him. He gave my shoulder a rough shove. 'It's the job. You know I have to go.'

'You don't have to. You want to go.'

'To hell with you anyway,' he said, and left to sleep elsewhere.

Maybe he went back to his room on the rue Descartes that night, or slept on the long bench downstairs in the dancehall. I don't know. He stayed out until after noon the next day, and then came in to pack and make arrangements. He moved around the apartment, throwing things into a bag, getting his notebooks together.

'Is this how it's going to be then?'

I stared out the window at nothing.

'You said you'd never do this, you know.'

He was right. Over and over I'd sworn I'd never stand in the way of his work, particularly when we were just beginning, when I saw his career as my own and believed it was my role or even my fate to help him carve a way. But more and more I understood that I didn't know what those promises really meant. Part of me wanted him to be as unhappy as I was. Maybe then he'd give in and stay.

But he didn't. We didn't speak or touch for three days, and when he left, on 25 September, he was so hurt and angry I could barely stand to look at him. I stood at the door and watched him struggle with his bags on the stairs. Toward the bottom, he dropped the valise holding his Corona. It fell hard, bounced with a sickening clatter, and then fell again. He kicked it angrily before he picked it up. When he got to the door at the bottom of the stairs, he kicked that too, and then I heard nothing.

EIGHTEEN

It might be malaria breaking through the quinine, but everything is strangely yellow. The long road is a tamped and stark ochre color and the mountains in the distance are darker. There's a river, the Maritza, and it's running high and fast because it's been raining for five days and the rain, too, is yellow.

He hasn't slept well since he left Paris, and this makes the rain harder to walk through. There isn't an end to any of it, the rain or the walking. Columns of refugees surge and spill onto the Karagatch Road. They've loaded their carts with everything they can't bear to leave behind, the ones who have carts, and the rest are strapped to bundles and carry other bundles or carry children. The children carry what they can and cry when they get too tired or scared. Everyone's scared and wet and the rain keeps coming.

He is here to bear witness, he understands that, and so makes himself see everything and not look away from any of it, though much he sees gives him a sick feeling in his stomach. It's his first taste of war since he was inside the war, and that alone started a terrible shaking in him the first two days. The shaking is gone now. He's forced it back and now can do what he came to do.

Along the Karagatch Road, he talks with many who've come from Smyrna and seen the fires there and worse. A man with a bright red face watched his sister run down to the quay screaming and alight to the tips of her hair.

Another man is bandaged from his hand to his shoulder, the cloth filthy and sodden, and even in the rain you can smell the gangrene, a sweet smell like roasting almonds. The man speaks through an interpreter and says he hid under the pier at Smyrna for almost a day and a night, the water up to his chest sometimes. It was the mussels on the footings of the pier that cut his hand and arm when the tide came in and pushed him against the hard shells.

'There were searchlights in the harbor,' the man says. 'And you didn't want to see the things floating there, all around you.'

In the end he came out of the water and found his family and took to the road, like so many others. He was cut deep in several places but he wasn't bleeding. He had thought the salt would cure his wounds and that he'd be fine without a surgeon.

'You can see I'm not fine,' the man says through the interpreter, and keeps walking.

'Yes, anyone can see that,' Ernest says.

They walk next to a cart pulled by a single great ox streaming with rain, and in the cart the man's wife is in labor. The bedding in the cart is wet through, and there's another blanket, tented and dripping, that two of her children hold over her as she bears down. An old woman crouches between her knees while the children try to look away, and it makes Ernest sick to see this and to hear her screaming, which won't be helped until the child is born, and maybe not even then.

The man is still walking and looking ahead through the rain and says, 'My wife knows I'm a coward. I hid under the pier. I meant to leave them all.'

Ernest nods and looks up to see they're coming to a bridge over the river, a wooden structure that looks slick but sound for all the weight on it, carts and oxen and camels, the bodies packed in and no one moving forward or back.

In the distance, over the heads of the living, he sees the fine white spires of a mosque, minarets rising out of the yellow muck, detached from the very real things happening on the road, the mud and the screaming and the cowardice and the rain. In the pocket of his jacket there's a blue notebook folded in half, and two pencils. The paper's drenched through, he knows it without having to check, but he couldn't write any of this anyway. He'll send a dispatch tonight from the hotel, if it hasn't floated off in the rain. For now, all he can do is make himself see everything and not shake and not look away.

A week passes but it feels as if he's never been anywhere else. It's one of the things war does to you. Everything you see works to replace moments and people from your life before, until you can't remember why any of it mattered. It doesn't help if you're not a soldier. The effect is the same.

He sleeps on a cot in a hotel in Adrianople wrapped in a dirty blanket and covered with sores from the lice. He spends his days talking to refugees and writing and sending dispatches to the Star and to the INS under the name John Hadley. Sometimes he's too tired and sends the same story twice. He couldn't give a damn; let them fire him. They'll have to find him first and he's nowhere.

When night falls, he goes to a bar where a very dark Armenian girl with deep shadows under her eyes wears a colored dress that ties at the waist. He can see the shape of her breasts under the cloth and wants to touch her, and it all becomes very simple. Another man comes along, a British soldier, and puts his hands on the girl's waist and she smiles. That's when Ernest flares forward and punches the soldier. He hasn't meant to do it exactly. He just knows he needs to move if he wants the girl. They never come to you, and why would you want them to? He feels his fist connect with the soldier's jaw and the jaw springing loose. He doesn't feel anything yet himself. The soldier drops to one knee, and then comes up again fast, his eyes bright and very wide. He lunges, but isn't quick or low enough. Ernest hits him in the gut this time, and feels the man's breath collapsing around his hand.

The girl says something he doesn't understand but it sounds like, 'Enough.' He takes her hand and they leave. There's a taxi outside and they go to her room without saying anything. Behind the door, she unties the dress, and then reaches for his belt. He pushes her hands away. He'll do it all himself, though his right hand is bleeding. He sits on a small wooden chair and pulls her down

147

on top of him and feels how rough and silky she is straddling him. He is the one moving her, as if she's a doll, and he knows it has to be this way because it makes him feel that he won't die, at least for tonight. He groans when it's over, and it's over quickly the first time. He stays with her in her filthy bed, and in the morning, he leaves the address of his hotel on a sheet of notebook paper and also two American dollars. He thinks he probably won't see her again, but that it would be all right if he did. He has more money to spend, and maybe if he saw her again, he wouldn't feel so sick, like he does now, and maybe it will be better and maybe it will fix something.

He goes into the street, where it's still very early and cool and hasn't yet started to rain again. He walks back to his hotel thinking, You've done it now, haven't you? It's too late to take anything back and you wouldn't anyway. You need to remember that later, when you see your wife and want to die for hurting her. Remember no one made you do anything. It's never anyone but you who does anything, and for that reason alone you shouldn't be sorry.

Now it is raining again, a very fine drizzle that seeps into the fabric of his shirt and trousers. He feels the small buildings push toward him along the muddy road, and there is the very real thought, again, that there isn't any other world. What does it matter if you know your being with another will kill your wife, if you have no wife? You don't have Paris, either, or anything else. You might as well see the dark girl again. You might as well bring your-self down and make yourself stinking sick with all you do because this is the only world there is.

Nineteen

W/hen he was gone, I felt sad and guilty; hating myself
instantly. I looked at the whiskey bottle on the shelf
and even held it for a moment before putting it back. Not
before lunch. I would never make it through that way. So I
made some coffee instead and peeled an orange, and tried not
to think about him on the train. He would be two days traveling, at least, and then he'd be in another world, and a
dangerous one. All I could do was hope that he'd be safe, and
that the thread that bound us was strong enough to weather
the damage done.

Except for two scribbled postcards sent before he was over
the border into Turkey, I didn't hear from Ernest when he was
gone and I blamed the cable service for it because I didn't want
to think what else his silence might mean. I read his first story
in the *Star* when it arrived two weeks later, but thinking too
specifically about what was happening there — not just violence
but disease too, apparently, cholera and malaria in epidemic
proportions — only made things worse, so I burned the paper
and went for a walk.

Marie Cocotte came every afternoon. 'You need to get out of your bed,' she said, and brought me an apron to tie around my robe. Together we made *bœuf bourguignon* and *blanquette de veau* and *cassoulet*, and it was all lovely, though I couldn't make myself eat it.

Lewis Galantière came by and sat at the terrible dining table and tried to drag me out to Michaud's.

'James Joyce has apparently fathered six more children just this week. They're all there, eating an enormous mutton and spouting milk out their nostrils. Tell me you don't need to see it for yourself.'

I made myself smile and then dressed, putting on my coat and my least unfashionable shoes. 'Let's go around the corner, though,' I said. 'Not Michaud's tonight, all right?'

'I'm your humble servant, Madame.'

I didn't tell Lewis or anyone else how bad things had gotten between us. I was too embarrassed. In the mornings I wrote letters and lied, telling Grace and Dr Hemingway that all was fine and well. I explained how smoothly Ernest's work had been going for the *Star*, how promising his career looked. I didn't say he'd recently decided to break his exclusive contract with them and file stories under a pseudonym for the International News Service. All of this had been negotiated in secret, and meant lying and stickiness when something for INS hit the wire before his 'exclusives' for the *Star* did, but he'd claimed it was worth it for the money. He'd work it out with his own conscience. I had a harder time with this dishonesty, because it seemed to speak of something larger. The way he was always out for himself, whatever the cost.

But thinking this way got me nowhere. Nowhere but back to the whiskey, that is, so I put my thinking down with the stack of letters and walked to the Musée du Luxembourg instead, to visit the Monets. I stood and looked into the brightest patches of his lilies and the lovely purpling in the water and tried not to see anything else at all.

At the end of October, in the very early morning, Ernest stepped off his train at the Gare de Lyon looking as if he'd been in a terrible battle and lost. He was weak and exhausted and feverish with malaria. He'd shed twenty pounds or more, and I hardly recognized him. He moved into my arms and collapsed there, and then we went home where he leaned over the basin and let me shampoo his head, which was crawling with lice.

'I'm so sorry for everything, Tatie,' I said when his eyes were closed.

'Let's not say anything about it. It doesn't matter now.'

I took up the scissors and cut his hair very close to his head and picked the rest of the lice out one by one, bringing the lamp over so I could see everything. Then I rubbed his body all over with cream and helped him into fresh clean sheets where he slept for twenty-four hours. When he woke up, I brought him eggs and toast and ham and mustard, and he ate this all gratefully, and then he slept again.

He didn't leave the bed for a week, and sometimes I just watched him sleep and knew by the look of him that he'd suffered in ways he wouldn't be able to talk about, not for a long time. The breach between us had been terrible and the silence too, but his time in Turkey had come in to out-shadow all of that. And maybe he was right that it didn't matter. He was home now, and we were together again, and maybe it would all be all right as long as we didn't think about it or give it any room or air.

After a week, he could get out of bed and bathe and dress,

and was almost ready to see friends. He went to his duffel bag and moved the notebooks aside to bring out presents rolled in newspaper and layers of cloth. He'd brought me a bottle of attar of roses and also a heavy amber necklace with big, rough beads that were threaded with black coral and silver.

'It's as beautiful as anything ever,' I said, holding up the necklace.

'It belonged to an extremely important Russian diplomat who's now a waiter.'

'I hope you paid him well for it.'

'I did, and got him drunk to boot,' Ernest said, nearly himself now.

I waited for him to say more about it all, but he just sat at the table and drank his coffee and asked after the newspapers.

I knew he loved me again; I could see that. No matter what each of us had felt or thought about the other in our weeks apart, that time was over now. I opened the bottle of attar of roses, which was a deep yellow and smelled like pure rose, the absolute thing. Somehow, without finding or fixing any words to it, the next part of our story had begun.

TWENTY

'Careful now,' Ernest said. 'You know you're inviting the devil in.'

'Am I?'

'You know you are.'

'He can come then, as long as he comes this way, all in green vapor.'

We were at the Select with Pound and Dorothy, who we'd taken to calling Shakespear. Pound had just taken on the editorship of a new literary press called Three Mountains, and was keen to publish something of Ernest's. We were all in high spirits that night, and I'd only meant to have the one glass of absinthe, to celebrate.

'You must go more slowly,' Pound said.

'Must I?' I said, but he wasn't talking to me at all, but to the waiter pouring water over a sugar cube into the drink, which was going from a wickedly clear yellow-green to a cloudy white as the water dripped in. Absinthe was illegal in France and had been for years. So was opium, but you could find both everywhere in Paris if you knew where to look. I loved the delicate licorice taste and the way the ritual of the cube and specially perforated spoon made raindrops, sugar drops. Our waiter was doing it beautifully, I thought, but Pound grabbed the pitcher with force, taking over.

'You're drunk, darling,' Shakespear said to him in her civilized whisper.

'I'm trying to picture you drunk,' Ernest said to her. 'I'm betting you never spill a drop.'

She laughed. 'If I don't, it's because I won't touch absinthe.'

'It's licorice candy and smoke,' I said.

'You'll wish it were only that tomorrow,' Ernest said.

'Maybe, but it makes everything easier now, doesn't it?'

'Yes, it does,' Ernest said, touching my glass with his. 'So have it and to hell with tomorrow.'

'Hear, hear,' said Pound, leaning forward in his rumpled tweed jacket and putting his elbows on the table. I was growing to like him more all the time – but I was generally liking everyone. I thought I might be in love with our waiter. He had the prettiest mustache, unwaxed and pure and fresh as flowers. I wanted to touch it or eat it.

'You should grow your mustache like that,' I said to Ernest, pointing not at all subtly.

'I am, dear. It's just the same.'

I looked at him square. 'So it is,' I said. 'Where have you been?' And we all laughed.

Later, when we'd moved on to the Dôme, Pound started talking about the States.

'I'd never return to the middle-west,' he was saying, 'I renounce it, in fact. Indiana's full of prigs and idiots.'

'Oh, that old story,' Shakespear said in her low perfect whisper.

I looked into the long smoky mirror and touched my face,

then the glass. 'I can't feel anything,' I said to Ernest. 'Isn't it wonderful?'

'Have another, Tatie,' Ernest said. 'You're very beautiful.'

Shakespear smiled at us with her curved mouth and her eyes smiled too. 'Look at our pretty lovers,' she said to Pound.

'Indiana's always been an intellectual wasteland, mind you,' he said, and then blew a smoke ring that circled before being swallowed by the rest of it, the blue halo that was everywhere, blending and blurring. All of us breathing it in and out.

'All they have is the moral high ground,' he went on. 'There's nothing else within reach. I was useless teaching at Wabash. What did those young people with cornhusks between their ears want to hear me rant on about? Not Yeats, that's for certain. Not poetry.'

'The actress was a small bit of poetry,' Shakespear said.

'The most scrumptious knees I've ever seen on a woman,' Pound said.

'Do go on,' Ernest said. 'I'm getting hungry.'

'There was rain that night – it's always raining in Indiana, intellectually speaking, you understand – and the actress . . . what was her name?'

'Bertha,' Shakespear said.

'Not Camille?' Ernest said.

'No, no. She wasn't consumptive. Just didn't want to get her hair damp. She had lovely hair. I'd suggested we go out to dinner, but then there was the matter of dampness.'

'One of my favorite problems,' Ernest said.

Everyone laughed and then Pound said, 'When word got out I'd entertained her in my room, you'd think I'd have murdered the girl instead of roasted a chicken.'

'Poor Ezra,' Shakespear said. 'They fired him next day.'

'Poor Ezra nothing. I'd be in Indiana still, teaching poetry to stalks of corn.'

'And roasting the occasional chicken,' I said.

'Even chicken won't save you from Indiana,' Ezra said.

Late that evening, after we'd abandoned the Dôme for the Ritz, Ernest and Pound began heatedly discussing the merits of Tristan Tzara. Pound thought the Surrealists might be onto something, possibly, if they could stay asleep long enough. Ernest thought they were idiots and they might just as well wake up so we could all move on to something else.

'I'm dropping off just listening to you all,' Shakespear said, and the two of us moved to the other side of the room and sat at a small table.

'You and Hem really are beautiful together,' she said.

'Are we?' I'd been drinking only warm water for an hour, and could finally feel my tongue.

'I wonder how that happens. Love, I mean.' She touched the sweep of her hair, still smooth and perfect.

'Don't you and Pound have it?'

'Oh, no,' she laughed with a small puff of air. 'We have what we have, though.'

'I'm not sure I understand you.'

'I'm not sure I do either.' She laughed a dark laugh and then became quiet, stirring her drink.

The weather turned wonderful that fall, and although we knew the cold, damp season would be coming soon enough, we were living deep into what we had and feeling happy and strong. Ernest was working well on his Nick Adams novel and new stories, and saw so clearly the books they could be, it was almost as if they already fully existed. In our circle, everyone believed things would hit for him, and that it was only a matter of time.

'You're making something new,' Pound told him one day in his studio. 'Don't forget that when it starts to hurt.'

'It only hurts to wait.'

'The waiting helps you boil it down. That's essential, and the hurting helps everything along in its way.'

Ernest put this wisdom in his pocket the way he did everything Pound said.

Soon enough, the light began to change in the streets in the late afternoon, thinning and waning, and we started to wonder if we had it in us to face the long winter.

'I've been thinking about writing to Agnes,' Ernest said to me one evening. 'It's been on my mind since Milan. Do you mind?'

'I don't know. What do you want out of it?'

'Nothing. Just for her to know I'm happy and thinking of her.'

'And that your career is going just as you said it would.'

He smiled. 'That's the cherry on top, is all.'

'Send your letter.'

'Yes,' he said. 'I already have.'

I felt a flare of jealousy. 'You were so sure I wouldn't mind?'

'Maybe. But if you did, I knew I could make you see it was all right. It's just a letter, in any case, and we have each other.'

'That's what Shakespear said the other night.'

'Shakespear? What does she know about love?'

'Maybe more than we do, because she doesn't have it. She's not in the thick of it.'

'That's why I can't write about Paris now, because it's everywhere.'

'So you write about Michigan.'

'It feels so close. As if I could never lose it.' He'd been reading over the day's work from a notebook on the table in front of him. He rested his hand on the pages, his fingertips brushing over the boldly slanted sentences. 'But it's not just the real place. I'm inventing it too, and that's the best part.'

Over his writing desk he'd pinned a pale blue map of Northern Michigan, and all the essential places were there – Horton Bay, Petoskey, Walloon Lake, Charlevoix – the precise locations where important things had happened to him, Ernest, but also to Nick Adams. Ernest and Nick weren't the same guy, but they knew a lot of the same things, like where and when to look for bait hoppers heavy with dew, and how the water moved and what it told you about where the trout were. They knew about mortar shelling in the middle of a still night, and what it felt like to see a place you'd loved burned down and hollowed out and changed. Nick's mind wasn't altogether right and you could sense the pressure coming up inside him, in a story like 'Big Two-Hearted River,' though Ernest never had him look at it directly or name it.

'I love your Michigan stories,' I said.

He squinted at me through the lantern light, across the table. 'Is that true?'

'Yes, of course.'

'Sometimes I wonder if you want me writing at all. I think it makes you feel lonely.'

'It's not the writing that makes me lonely, it's your being gone. It's been so long since you've even tried to write here at home. Maybe it would work now and I could see you. I wouldn't have to talk or disturb you.'

'You know I need to go away to make anything happen.' He closed the notebook and put his pencil on top, rolling it back and forth with his fingertips. 'I have to be alone to get it started, but if I really was alone, that wouldn't work either. I need to leave that place and come back here and talk to you.

That makes it real and makes it stick. Do you get what I'm saying?'

'I think so.' I walked behind him and put my head on his shoulder, rubbing my face into his neck. But the truth was I didn't, not really. And he knew.

'Maybe no one can know how it is for anyone else.' I straightened and walked over to the window where the rain came down in streams and pooled on the sill. 'I'm trying.'

'Me too,' he said.

I sighed. 'I think it's going to rain all day.'

'Don't kid yourself. It's going to rain for a month.'

'Maybe it won't after all.'

He smiled at me. 'All right, Tiny. Maybe it won't.'

TWENTY-ONE

Near Thanksgiving, 1922, the *Star* sent Ernest to cover a peace conference in Lausanne that would decide the territorial dispute between Greece and Turkey, the thing that had started the terrible business at Smyrna and had generally kept them killing each other for the better part of three years. When the cable came, I saw Ernest's nervousness. He almost couldn't open it and I knew why. We couldn't take another fight like the last. We might not survive it.

'Lausanne,' he said finally. 'We have the money. You'll come too.'

'I needn't,' I said. 'I can be good.'

'No,' he said. 'I want you there.'

I was relieved he'd insisted and agreed to go – but by the time the trip was launched, I was sick in bed, my head stuffed and aching. I couldn't eat anything without retching. We decided he would go alone, and that I would join him when I could travel. My old friend Leticia Parker from St Louis happened to be coming through Paris just then, and she said she wanted to visit every day and take care of me when Ernest was gone. It wouldn't be like his time in Turkey at all, or even like Genoa.

By the time I felt well enough to join him, it was early December. I packed happily knowing that when the conference was over and the reporting done, we'd have a long skiing holiday at Chamby, and have Christmas there with Chink, and then go on to Italy and Spain. All in all, we wouldn't be back in Paris for four months, and I was ready for a nice long break from the cold and dampness. I hadn't been out of bed for a week and though I wasn't sure I'd have the energy for skiing, I was damned well going to try.

Along with the travel plans passing back and forth between us, Ernest had also cabled to say that Lincoln Steffens, one of the journalists he'd met in Genoa, was in Lausanne and highly impressed with his dispatches. He wanted to see everything Ernest had written so far, but he only had one thing with him, 'My Old Man,' a story about a boy and his ruined jockey father. Steffens thought the story was wonderful and compared it to Sherwood Anderson. Ernest didn't like being compared to anyone, and it seemed worse, somehow, that it was Anderson, a friend and champion, but it helped that Steffens had offered to send the story on to an editor friend at *Cosmopolitan* magazine. Ernest had one published piece at that point, in a small art magazine out of New Orleans called the *Double Dealer*. There was only that, and the promise from Pound about printing something for Three Mountains. This was much more promising, thrilling even.

As I packed my big suitcase, I thought about how long we'd be gone, and how anxious Ernest would be to return to his stories and the novel. It went without saying that he'd like to show more of his work to Steffens, so I headed for the dining room, to the cupboard where Ernest kept all his manuscripts.

I gathered everything together and packed it in a small valise. This was my surprise for him, and I felt buoyed by it as I left the apartment for the Gare de Lyon.

The station was busy, but I had never seen it any other way. Porters scrambled by in their red jackets — past the waxed wooden benches and the ornamental palms and the well-dressed travelers headed home or away with anticipation. By morning, I would be with Ernest again and all would be well, and this was my only thought as I moved through the station and handed my bags to a porter. He helped me onto the train, put the big suitcase with my clothes on the rack up high, and placed the small valise under my seat, where I could reach it. The train was nearly empty. We had half an hour before departure, so I went to stretch my legs and get a newspaper. I threaded through the station, past the vendors with their apples and cheese and Evian water, the rented blankets and pillows and warm wrapped sandwiches and little flasks of brandy. When the conductor called for boarding I hurried onto the train with the stream of passengers and found my compartment just as it was before. Except for the small valise.

It wasn't under my seat. I didn't see it anywhere.

In a panic, I called for the conductor.

'Is there something I can do?' my seatmate said while I waited for him to appear. She was a middle-aged American who seemed to be traveling alone. 'I can lend you something of mine to wear.'

'It isn't clothing!' I shrieked, and the poor woman turned away, understandably horrified. When the conductor finally arrived, he didn't seem to understand either. I couldn't stop crying long enough to find the right words in my terrible French. Finally he called over two French policemen, who led me outside the train and interrogated me while everyone stared. They asked for my identification cards, which one officer examined while the other asked me to describe the bag and my actions in detail.

'It was yours, this valise?'

'My husband's.'

'Is he on board?'

'No, he's in Switzerland. I was bringing it to him. It's his work. Three *years* worth of work,' and here I lost any remaining composure. I felt sick with rising dread. 'Why are you standing here questioning me?' My voice pitched shrilly. 'He's getting away! He's probably long gone by now!'

'Your husband, Madame?'

'The thief, you idiot!'

'We cannot help you if you're going to be hysterical, Madame.'

'Please.' I felt as if I might lose my mind. 'Please just search the train. Search the station.'

'What do you estimate is the value of the case and its contents?'

'I don't know,' I said in a fog. 'It's his *work*.'

'Yes, so you said. We'll do what we can.' And the two men walked off officiously.

The conductor agreed to hold the train for another ten minutes while the police performed their search. They walked from one end of the train to the other asking the passengers if they'd seen the bag. I didn't for a moment believe that whoever had stolen it was still on the train. It had obviously been a common pickpocket who'd seen an opportunity and taken it, hoping for valuables. Instead, it contained every thought and sentence Ernest had sweated over since we came to Paris and well before, the Chicago stories and sketches, every poem and fragment. He never threw anything away, and it was all there.

The two officers came off the train empty-handed. 'Nothing yet, Madame,' one of them said. 'We'll continue to look, but if you still intend on traveling to Switzerland, I suggest you take your seat.'

I gave them our address and the phone number for the dancehall, since there wasn't a phone in our apartment, but I didn't hold out much hope they'd succeed in their efforts. Paris was vast and too much time had passed. I imagined the thief hurrying to an empty alleyway, opening the case and then shutting it immediately. He'd have dropped it where he stood or pitched it into a rubbish pile. It could be in any alleyway or gutter or burning trash barrel in Paris. It could be listing, at that moment, toward the bottom of the Seine.

'I'm very sorry for your trouble,' my seatmate said when I'd finally made my way back to the compartment.

'No, I'm sorry,' I said, beginning to weep again. 'I'm not usually this discomposed.'

'Is it very dear, what you've lost?'

The train grumbled beneath us, then lurched away from the platform with finality. There was no stopping or changing anything now. No avoiding the truth of what had happened. I felt dread settle in to fill me completely and a new hard-won certainty. There was only one answer to her question. 'Priceless,' I said, and turned away.

Twenty-Two

What followed was the longest night of my life. The mountains closed in as we headed into Switzerland and blackness fell. I thought about how I would tell Ernest the work was gone, but I couldn't even think it. There were no words.

When we finally pulled into Lausanne the next morning, and I saw Ernest on the platform with Steffens right beside him, it was all I could do to stand and walk toward them. I was crying. Ernest looked at Steffens and shrugged as if to say, 'Who can understand a woman,' but I couldn't stop and Ernest knew something was very wrong then.

Still, it was ages before I could say the words. Steffens excused himself, telling Ernest he'd phone to arrange a meeting. When he was gone, Ernest made me sit down at a café table near the entrance of the station. All around us couples and families kissed goodbye or bade each other farewell, and they seemed so painfully untroubled to me. A fresh wave of tears came.

'What is it?' Ernest asked again and again, first worried and tender, then angry, then worried again. 'Whatever it is, we'll get through it. Nothing can be that bad.'

But it was. It was exactly that bad. I shook my head and cried harder, and it went on this way until finally I was able to tell him about packing the case and stowing it for the journey.

I didn't need to say more. His face grew pale and very serious. 'You lost it on the train.'

'It was stolen out from under me.'

He nodded, taking it all in, and I watched his eyes carefully, how they changed and steadied, changed and steadied. He was trying to be brave for me, I knew. Because he wasn't sure what I'd do.

'You couldn't have packed everything. Why would I need it all?'

'If you were going to be making changes in the originals, I thought you'd want the copies too, so that everything would be right.'

'You must have left something,' he said.

I shook my head and waited. Would he snap from the strain and fly into a rage? I'd certainly earned that. I'd taken what was his – what was most his in the world – without his asking me to, as if I had that right. And now it was gone.

'I have to go back. I need to know it for myself.'

'I'm so sorry, Tatie.' I shook with remorse and heartsickness.

'It's going to be all right. I made it. I can make it all again.'

I knew he was bluffing if not outright lying, but I held him tight and let him hold me and we said all the words people say to each other when they know the worst has come.

Late that night, he boarded a train back to Paris while I waited in Lausanne in a wet knot. Steffens took me to dinner and tried to calm my nerves, but even with several whiskies in me, I jangled.

He was gone for two days and sent no cable. But just as I could see myself reaching into the cupboard over and over, packing everything away in the valise, I could see him coming into the quiet apartment and discovering for himself that it was all really gone.

Turning on all the lights, he first looks at everything in plain sight, the table and the bed, the kitchen. He looks at the floor and walks between the two rooms slowly, saving the cupboard until he's seen everything else, because that's the last place, and there won't be anywhere to look after and no hope left at all. He has a drink first, then another, but finally he has to see it. He puts his hand on the knob and pulls the door open and then he knows everything. There isn't a page left in the cupboard. Not a note or a scrap. He looks and looks, standing there, wrenched out and hollow. As desolate as the cupboard is, that's how he is too because the pages belong to him and are him. It's like someone has taken a broom to his insides and swept it out until everything's clean and bright and hard and empty.

TWENTY-THREE

When Ernest came back from Paris, he was tender with me and kept saying over and over that all was forgiven, but his eyes were bruised-looking and changed. There was still work to do at the conference, and he did it as he always did, throwing himself into the day and coming home tired and glad for a drink. I passed my time walking through the town looking for gifts to send home for Christmas. Even more than our first year in France, I was desperate to see something that captured the holiday as I remembered it from childhood. I wandered for hours, peering in shop windows, but search as I might, nothing in Lausanne looked like Christmas to me.

At the end of the week, we readied our things for the trip to Chamby. 'It doesn't seem right to simply follow our plans through after all that's happened,' I said to Ernest as we packed.

'Maybe,' he said. His voice sounded tired. 'But what should we do instead?'

'Go back to Paris?'

'That would be worse, wouldn't it?'

'I don't think I can bear Christmas Day feeling like this.

Everything's such a bust. Maybe it's time we think about going home.'

'Stateside? And admit failure? Are you trying to kill me?'

'I'm sorry. It's just hard to know how to go on.'

'Yes,' he said. He picked up his Corona and carefully nestled it in its black case before snapping the case closed. 'It certainly is.'

When we arrived at Chamby, the town was the same. Our chalet was perfect and exactly as before, as were the snow-covered mountains and our proprietors, the Gangwisches, who greeted us as if we were long-lost family members. It was all so welcome after our heavy-hearted time in Lausanne that we surrendered completely. Before we'd even unpacked, we put on our skiing togs and caught the last train up the mountain to Les Avants. The sun was fading as we tied on our skis and flew down the powder-laced slope toward the village. With the wind roaring in our ears and stinging our cheeks, we raced along, Ernest just ahead of me, his bad knee bandaged with strong black cloth. He favored it a little, but looked lighter in his body than I'd seen in some time. I was grateful and relieved and sent a small prayer of thanks out to the snowy firs and the creamy sky turning every shade of pink, and Lake Geneva in the distance, flat and polished as glass.

The next day we slept late in our big soft four-poster bed and didn't even wake when the maid tiptoed in to start the fire. We roused ourselves later, when the room was warm and the porcelain stove purred with the blaze.

'We were right to come, Tatie,' I said and nestled behind him, kissing his neck and the buttons of his spine.

'Yes,' he said. 'Let's enjoy every minute and not think about anything else.'

'There isn't anything else,' I said. I rolled to cover him,

straddling his flat, strong belly. I pushed my nightgown over my hips and then reached to draw him inside of me.

He groaned and closed his eyes, giving himself over completely.

Chink arrived on Christmas Day and in the end, our holiday wasn't sad at all. We'd hung stockings for each other and for Chink, and we opened those, and then had a dinner fit for kings. It was only when we sat by the fire late that night, warm brandy in our bellies and more in our glasses, that Ernest brought up the terrible business of his lost manuscripts.

'Oh, kid,' Chink said when Ernest reached the end of the story. 'Can you really start over with nothing?'

'I don't know. I wrote the damned stuff once, didn't I?' Ernest said. 'I have to, in any case.'

Chink nodded seriously.

'I've been working like a dog for the *Star*,' Ernest went on, 'and now we have enough to live on for eight months. Eight months, and I'm going to give all of them to fiction. Only that.'

'That's my Tatie,' I said. Chink raised his glass, and we all toasted Christmas and each other.

But as the days passed, Ernest's notebooks and pencils stayed packed away. His Corona never left its black case. He said nothing about this and I didn't either; I knew better. Meanwhile, we skied all day and sometimes well into the evening, when the sun bled through the cloud line and seemed to be showing us something no one had seen before. We enjoyed every moment of Chink's good company and each other's too. We made love every day, sometimes twice a day – that is, until I told Ernest I'd left our usual precautions back in Paris.

We had always tracked my monthly cycles carefully. Ernest did this himself, the way he kept accounts of everything in our marriage. There was a notebook for recording expenses and incoming monies, another for correspondence, another for noting story ideas and how many words he'd written each day. And there was a notebook marked 'Hadley' devoted to the rising and falling of my fertility each month so we could have unprotected intercourse as often as possible. In the beginning, in the unsafe times, we used the withdrawal method the way most couples did. 'Not so very different from Russian roulette,' Ernest used to joke, and it wasn't. You could get condoms at the chemist's or the barbershop, but these were thick and coarse, made of rubber cement — uncomfortable at best and sometimes riddled with holes.

When we got to Paris, Gertrude, who could be wonderfully frank this way, asked if we knew about the diaphragm. Without too much trouble, we found a doctor and got me fitted for one, and this is what we'd used ever since. Ernest kept a count of the days and knew better than I did which were safe and which weren't. About a week into our time in Chamby, he reminded me we'd come to the end of our window.

'Could you make the necessary arrangements?' he said when we were in bed one night. This was his usual code. My role was to say, 'Yes sir,' as if I were his secretary, and he'd just asked me to make a lunch reservation or send a telegram. But this particular night, I didn't laugh and didn't get up to search my stocking drawer for the case. Instead, I said, 'Oh dear.'

'Don't tell me you've left it in Paris.'

I could only nod.

'Your timing stinks.' His face was red. I could tell he was very angry.

'I meant to tell you in Lausanne, as soon as I realized, but that was hardly the time either.'

'What else are you keeping from me?'

'Nothing. I'm sorry. I should have told you.'

'I'll say.' He threw back the bedclothes, then got up and began to pace the room in his underwear, fuming. 'Sometimes I wonder who I married exactly.'

'Please be fair, Tatie. It's not as if I meant to forget it.'

'No?'

'Of course not.' I crossed the room and stood near enough to see his face in the dim. 'I didn't. And yet I'd also be lying if I said I didn't think a baby would be a wonderful idea.'

'Now it comes out. I knew it. We've always said I'd get a really good start on things before we'd even talk about a baby. We agreed.'

'I know we did,' I said.

'I'm just finally getting going. Do you really want to ruin it for me?'

'Of course not,' I said. 'But I have worries too. I'm thirty-one.'

'Just. And you've never been crazy about children. You don't care at all for other people's.'

'It's different to want one of your own. I don't have all the time in the world.'

'I don't either. Life doesn't often give you more than one shot. I want to take mine now.' His eyes were clear and challenging, the way they always were when he was asking for loyalty. 'Are you for me?'

'Of course I am.' I put my arms around his neck and kissed him, but his lips didn't soften under mine. His eyes, just a few inches from mine, were open and questioning.

'I suppose you think I'm going to lie down with you now.'

'Ernest! I'm not trying to trap you!'

He said nothing.

'Tatie?'

'I need a drink.' He headed for the door, grabbing his robe as he went.

'Please stay so we can talk about this.'

'Go to sleep,' he said, and left the room.

I couldn't sleep though, for all my fretting. He didn't come to bed at all, and in the morning, I dressed and went down to look for him. He was in the dining room having his morning coffee, already wearing his skiing togs.

'Can we please make up, Tatie?' I said, going to him. 'I'm just sick about everything.'

'I know you are,' he said, and sighed. 'Listen. We have to be together on this. If we're not, then nothing's any good. You see that, don't you?'

I nodded and leaned into his shoulder.

'If you really want a baby, the time will be right some day.'

'But not now.'

'No, little cat. Not now.'

Chink came into the room, saying good morning. Then he stopped, eyeing us carefully for a moment. 'Is everything all right then?'

'Hadley's under the weather.'

'Poor Mrs Popplethwaite,' Chink said tenderly. 'You should be in bed.'

'Yes. Go and try to get some rest,' Ernest agreed. 'We'll be up to check on you at lunch.'

They went off to ski alone, while I did my best to find some peace. I put on some nice thick socks and my Alpine slippers and then curled up in a chair by the fire to read *The Beautiful and Damned*. 'Fitzgerald's a poet,' Shakespear had said

173

when she recommended it, just before she and Pound left for several months in Italy. The writing was exquisite, I had to admit, but it was making me sad to read about Gloria and Anthony. They talked prettily and had nice things, but their lives were hollow. I didn't have the stomach for such a dire picture of marriage, not just now.

I'd put the novel down and climbed in bed to try for a nap when Ernest came in. His hair was damp and crushed from his wool hat, and his face was pink from the cold. He sat on the bed near me and I saw that his eyes had softened considerably. Time away with Chink had done him some good.

'You look very warm,' he said. 'Do you mind if I share your cocoon?'

'Of course. If you think that's a good idea.'

'I stopped at the chemist's in the village,' he said, and took the little tin of condoms out of his trouser pocket.

'I'm surprised. You always say you hate them.'

'Not as much as being away from you.'

I looked at his trim belly and flanks as he undressed. 'You're very beautiful,' I said.

'So are you, Tatie.'

As he climbed into bed, his skin chilly against mine, it began to snow outside. We pressed ourselves together in a crush on the featherbed, his hands wonderfully rough, his hipbones sharp against my thighs. Later I would see plum-colored bruises there, and the skin on my face and breasts would be chapped and pink from where he hadn't shaved, but for now there was only wordless desire and a feeling of return. He'd left me for a time. He'd doubted me but now he was mine again and I wanted to keep him here in a tangle of limbs and bed sheets until I'd quieted every last voice and we were only right again.

✳

After three weeks at Chamby, when we were well fed and sun-chapped and had parted ways with Chink, we headed off to Rapallo, on the Italian Riviera, where the Pounds had a rented villa.

'Ezra thinks he's discovered the place,' Ernest said on the train. 'Though Wordsworth and Keats had a go at it before him.'

'Ezra thinks he's discovered trees and the sky.'

'You have to admire the guy anyway, though, don't you?'

'I don't have to, but I will, I guess. For you.'

After traveling south for a full day and more, we were finally near Genoa, where the countryside grew ever more spring-like and lovely.

'This is heaven,' I said. 'I had no idea it would be so beautiful.' Through our window I caught glimpses of the sea, quick bursts of frothed blue then dark rock again, then the sea. 'Aren't we lucky to be so happy, Tiny?' I said, just as we entered a mountain tunnel.

'Sure we are,' he said, and kissed me. The sound of the train bounced against black rock, roaring in our ears.

When we arrived at Rapallo, I thought the town was charming, with its pale pink and yellow hotels on the shoreline, its quiet empty harbor. Ernest disliked it on sight.

'There's no one here,' he said when we got to our hotel.

'Who should be?'

'I don't know. It just doesn't seem to have any life, this place.' He stood at the window in our room that faced the shore. 'Doesn't the sea seem a bit spineless to you?'

'It looks like the sea,' I said, and came up behind him and put my arms around him tightly. I knew it wasn't the place that was troubling him. During our last week at Chamby, I had woken several mornings to find him at the small desk in our room, the sharpened pencil lifeless next to his hand, his blue *cahier* open but empty. He still wasn't working, and the longer that went on, the harder it would be to start again. He was utterly determined to do it. He *would* do it. But how?

We played tennis every day in Rapallo and had long lunches with the Pounds in their terraced garden. Another couple arrived to join us on holiday, Mike Strater, a painter friend of Pound's, and his wife Maggie. They had a delicious-looking baby girl, with wisps of yellow hair and gray eyes. I liked to watch her exploring the world just beyond her blanket, plucking fistfuls of grass and staring at her hand intently, as if it held the secret to something. Meanwhile, Ernest and Mike ducked and lunged in a boxing match on the nearby flagstones. Aside from being a very good painter, Mike was athletic and game for a good deal, and I could tell Ernest liked him immediately. Mike was a much better physical match for Ernest than Pound, who tried very hard in his blustery way, but had a poet's delicate hands.

February was a changeable time in Italy. Some days were hung with mist, blotting out the hills behind the town until we felt very remote. The palm trees dripped and the swallows hid away somewhere. Sometimes the air was humid and drenched with sun. We could walk in the piazza or along the promenade to see fishermen on the concrete pier, dangling their poles out into the tide. The village was famous for its lace, and I liked to scan the shop windows looking for the best pieces to send home as gifts while Ernest took long walks into the rocky hillside with Ezra, talking about Italian troubadours and the questionable virtues of automatic writing. Ernest liked to say he didn't want his mind shut off when he was working because it was the only thing he had going for him. True enough, but

176

when he was through for the day, he couldn't turn his thoughts off without a glass of whiskey, and sometimes not even then. When he wasn't writing at all, like now, it was often more than he could take. This was hard to watch and I worried about him.

A week into our stay in Rapallo, I had something new to unsettle me, however. I woke feeling dizzy, with a strange buzzing in my head. I tried to eat breakfast but couldn't stomach it, and returned to bed.

'It must have been the mussels we had last night,' I said to Ernest, and stayed in our room until midday, when the feeling passed.

The next morning, when the same symptoms hit at precisely the same time, I forgave the mussels and began instead to count the days forward and back. We'd arrived in Chamby just before Christmas and a few days after my monthly bleeding. It was now 10 February, and I hadn't had another period. When Ernest left the room to meet Ezra, I found his cache of notebooks and studied the one in particular that could illuminate my situation. Sure enough, for the last year I'd never been late by more than a day or two. This was a week at least, maybe ten days. I felt a small thrill of excitement, but didn't say anything to Ernest. It wasn't a certainty yet, and I was too afraid of what he would say.

I couldn't keep my secret forever, though. I could hardly stand the sight of food and even the smell of whiskey or a cigarette turned me green. Ernest was thankfully content to blame the exotic food, but Shakespear was growing suspicious. One afternoon as we sat at a table in the garden watching Ernest and Mike practicing tennis serves at one another, she looked at me with her head cocked and said, 'There's something different about you these days, isn't there?'

'It's my newly revealed cheekbones,' I said. 'I've lost five pounds.'

'Maybe,' she said thoughtfully, but there was a strange clarity in her look that made me think she'd guessed the truth.

I tried to ignore it and said, 'You seem to be reducing too, my dear. You're fading away.'

'I know. It's this business with Olga Rudge,' she said with a sigh.

She'd long since told me about Olga, a concert violinist who'd been Pound's mistress for over a year. 'What's happened?' I asked. 'Has something changed?'

'Not really. I expect him to be in love with half a dozen women, that's simply who he is, but this one seems different. The affair's not waning for one thing. And she's appearing in the *Cantos*, well disguised in myth, of course. But I can see her.' She shook her pretty head as if to clear the image. 'She's dug in. I wonder if we'll ever be free of her now.'

'I'm so sorry,' I said. 'But it seems to me you're awfully tolerant of him. I don't understand marriage this way at all. I suppose I'm a Puritan.'

She shrugged gracefully, 'Mike Strater's in the middle of something now too. An actress, I hear.'

'Oh, God. Does Maggie know?'

'Everyone knows. He's gone off his head.'

'He doesn't look it.'

'No,' Shakespear said, 'but they never do. Men are stoics when it comes to matters of the heart.'

'You seem very stoic to me too.'

'Yes,' she said. 'But I work impossibly hard at it, darling.'

Ezra was famous for his roving affections; I expected nothing less from him. But the news about Mike Strater had thrown me, because he and Maggie looked so solid. I'd been watching and admiring them and their daughter, and stitching a fantasy about how our child – mine and Ernest's – could squeeze in naturally at ringside and change very little about our lives or Ernest's work. Now that dream was punctured. This baby was almost certainly coming, but into what?

Marriage could be such deadly terrain. In Paris, you couldn't really turn around without seeing the result of lovers' bad decisions. An artist given to sexual excess was almost a cliché, but no one seemed to mind. As long as you were making something good or interesting or sensational, you could have as many lovers as you wanted and ruin them all. What was really unacceptable were bourgeois values, wanting something small and staid and predictable, like one true love, or a child.

Later that afternoon, when we went back to our room at the Hotel Splendide, it began to rain hard and looked as if it wouldn't ever stop. I stood at the window and watched it, feeling a growing worry.

'Mike Strater's in love with some actress in Paris,' I said to Ernest from the window. 'Did you guess?'

He sat on top of the bedclothes reading W. H. Hudson's *Green Mansions* for the hundredth time. He barely looked up. 'I don't think it means anything. Ezra says he's quite the philanderer.'

'When *does* it mean something? When everyone finally gets smashed to bits?'

'Is this what's gotten into you today? It doesn't concern us in the least.'

'Doesn't it?'

'Of course not. You don't catch infidelity like the measles.'

'You like him, though.'

'I do. He's a good painter. He wants to come by here tomorrow and do my portrait. Yours too, maybe, so you'd better find a less troubled face by then.' He smiled lightly and went back to his book.

Outside the rain picked up and the wind canted it sideways, so that the boats in the harbor tipped dangerously.

'I'm hungry,' I said.

'Then eat something.' He didn't look up.

'If it would stop raining, we could eat in the garden on the flagstones.'

'It's going to rain all day. Just eat something already or be quiet.'

I walked over to the mirror and studied myself impatiently.

'I want to grow my hair out again. I'm tired of looking like a boy.'

'You don't,' he said to the book. 'You're perfect.'

'A perfect boy. I'm sick of it.'

'You're just hungry. Have a pear.'

I watched him with his head bent over into his book. He'd been letting his hair grow and now it was nearly the same length as mine. We had begun to look a bit alike, in fact, just as Ernest had said he wished we might, long ago on a star-hung rooftop in Chicago. But we wouldn't look this way for long. In a few months I would feel and see the roundness at my waist. It was unavoidable.

'If I had long lovely hair, I'd tie it up at my neck and it would be silky and wonderful and I wouldn't care about anything else.'

'Hmmm?' he said. 'So do it.'

'I will. I'm going to.'

There was a pair of tiny nail scissors on the bureau under

the mirror. On impulse, I took them up and trimmed a little hair under one ear, and then the other.

He watched me and laughed curiously. 'You've lost your mind, you know.'

'Maybe. Now you.' I went over and straddled his waist and snipped away at the hair under his ears until it matched mine. Tucking the hair into my shirt pocket, I said, 'Now we're just the same.'

'You're a strange one today.'

'You're not in love with any actress in Paris are you?'

'God no,' he laughed.

'Violinist?'

'No one.'

'And you'll stay with me always?'

'What is it, Kitty? Tell me.'

I met his eyes then. 'I'm going to have a baby.'

'Now?' The alarm registered immediately.

'In the fall.'

'Please tell me it's not true.'

'But it is. Be happy, Tiny. I want this.'

He sighed. 'How long have you known?'

'Not long. A week, maybe.'

'I'm not ready for this, not nearly.'

'You might be by then. You might even be glad for it.'

'It's been a hell of a few months.'

'You'll work again. I know it's coming.'

'Something's coming,' he said darkly.

The next few days were tense and difficult for us. Some part of me had hoped that Ernest's arguments against a baby only went so deep, and that as soon as he knew one was really coming, he'd be happy, or at least happy for *me*. But he didn't seem to be budging an inch in my direction. Our days looked very much the same as before, but I felt the distance between us and wondered how we'd bridge it to find each other again.

Then, in the midst of my brooding, a new guest arrived at the Pound's villa. His name was Edward O'Brien, and he was a writer and editor staying in the hills above the town, near the Albergo Montallegro monastery. Ezra had heard he was there and invited him down for lunch.

'O'Brien edits a collection of the year's best stories,' Pound said, making the introductions out on the terrace near the tennis courts. 'He's been doing it since the war.' Turning to Ernest, he said, 'Hemingway here writes a damned good story. He's really very good.'

'I'm gathering material for the 1923 edition now,' O'Brien said to Ernest. 'Do you have anything on hand?'

It was only luck that he did. Out of his satchel, he pulled a ragged copy of the jockey story, 'My Old Man,' which Lincoln Steffens had since sent back. He handed it over to O'Brien, and then told an abbreviated story of how his work had been lost. 'So this piece,' he said dramatically, 'is all I have left. Just this last thing, like a small piece of the prow of a ship that's rotting at the bottom of the sea.'

'Well, that's very poetic,' O'Brien said, and he took the story up the hill to consider it.

When he'd left, I said to Ernest, as quietly as I could, 'I wish you hadn't talked that way to O'Brien. It makes me sick to my stomach.'

'Maybe that's the baby, then.'

'Are you angry with me?'

'Why would I be?'

'You don't think I've done this on purpose?'

'What, lost the manuscripts?'

I felt as if he'd slapped me. 'No. Fallen pregnant.'

'It's the same in the end, isn't it?'

By that point, our whispering had gotten fierce, and it was clear to the other two couples that we were in the middle of a serious argument. They began to drift discreetly toward the house.

'I can't believe you really mean that,' I said, my eyes hot with tears.

'I'll tell you what Strater says. He says no other writer or even painter — no one who makes something with all their soul could ever have left that valise on the train. Because they'd have known what it meant.'

'That's cruel. I suffered for those pieces too.'

He sighed loudly and shut his eyes. When he opened them again he said, 'I'm sorry. I've promised myself not to talk about it. It won't do any good anyway.'

I stormed off in one direction and he went in another, and though by the time dinner was served everyone in our party seemed intent on pretending they'd overheard nothing, I knew perfectly well they had and thought it best to just come clean.

'We wanted you very fine people to be the first to know we're having a baby,' I said, reaching for Ernest's hand. He didn't pull away.

'Well done,' Shakespear said, rising to embrace me warmly. 'I thought you seemed more substantial,' she whispered into my ear.

'Damned good show,' Mike said.

'Yes, yes,' Pound said. 'It's the happy fate of the monkey.'

'Ezra!' Shakespear said sharply.

'Do I lie?'

'Congratulations,' Maggie Strater said and hugged me. 'We monkeys have to stick together.'

The next afternoon, we watched the three men play tennis. Ernest was a terrible player, but this didn't stop him from doing it with force. He swung his racket wide and hard around, like a golfer. Mike hit a lovely shot that skimmed the net and fell nearly at Ernest's feet. He missed it anyway, and then cursed loudly and foully and threw his racket to the ground.

Maggie cringed. 'He'll get used to the idea of the baby eventually,' she said. 'Mike did.'

'Of course he will,' Shakespear agreed. 'His pride will take over at some point, and then he'll believe it was all his idea.'

'I'm not so sure,' I said.

I actually had a terrible feeling about the way Ernest was tangling up the lost manuscripts with the coming baby in his mind. If he felt — even in his darkest, most remote recesses — that I was capable of trying to sabotage his work and his ambition, how would we ever recover? Broken trust could rarely be repaired, I knew, particularly for Ernest. Once you were tarnished for him, he could never see you any other way.

I felt very low indeed until Edward O'Brien drove down the hill full of extravagant praise for Ernest's story. It was splendid and he wanted to publish it, even though it would break with the series' tradition of selecting from pieces that had already been published in magazines. Not only that, he wanted to lead the edition with the story and include it in his introduction; he felt that strongly about it.

O'Brien's timing couldn't have been more perfect; he answered my prayers and Ernest's too. His confidence, which had been sorely lacking, had a new boost and there was something solid to aim for and look forward to. Everyone who mattered would read his story when the collection was published. His name would mean something. He hadn't, in fact, been toiling for nothing.

The next morning when I woke, Ernest was at the desk by the window and he was writing.

We had two more weeks in Rapallo and they passed fruitfully for both of us. Ernest seemed to be less threatened by the baby, probably because the words had come back, and he felt the pulse of them. I wasn't as anxious about the future because Ernest was himself again, buoyed up by all he wanted to accomplish. I could finally be happy about the baby. The only thing that marred the experience at all was Ezra's taking me to one side as we were leaving. 'You know I've never been keen on children. That's another matter. But in this case, with Hem, I think it would be a terrible mistake if you tried to utterly domesticate him.'

'I like him the way he is. Surely you believe me.'

'Of course. That's how you feel now. But mark my words, this baby will change everything. They always do. Just bear that in mind and be very careful.'

'All right, Ezra, I promise,' I said, and moved away toward Ernest and our train. Pound was Pound and given to speech-making, and I didn't take him seriously that day. I was far too optimistic about everything to heed any warnings, but years later his parting remarks would come back to me sharply. Pound was Pound, but about this one thing he had been dead right.

TWENTY-FOUR

When we returned to Paris in early April, I was very ready to be home. The trees were newly flowering, the streets were washed clean and hung with fresh laundry; children ran along the gravel paths in the Luxembourg Gardens. Ernest was working with intensity, and though I missed him when he was away, I was happier to be on my own than before.

It sounds funny to say it, but for the first time I had my own project. I took long walks every day for my health and tried to eat well and get plenty of rest. I bought yards and yards of soft white cotton and spent hours sitting in the sun and hand-stitching baby clothes. In the evenings I read the letters of Abélard and Héloïse, a love story that suited me far more than Fitzgerald's disintegrating Jazz Age couple. I felt hopeful about absolutely everything as spring passed into early summer. My middle thickened and my breasts grew fuller. I was tan and strong and content – more *substantial*, as Shakespear had said – and began to believe that I'd finally discovered my purpose.

When he wasn't toiling away in his room on the rue Descartes, Ernest spent a lot of time with Gertrude. She had commiserated when he told her about the lost manuscripts, of course, but was less sympathetic about his concerns over the coming baby.

'You'll do it anyway. You'll push through.'

'I'm not near ready,' he said.

Gertrude had narrowed her eyes at him and said, 'I've never known a man who was. You'll do just fine.'

'What were you hoping she'd say?' I asked when he relayed the story to me.

'I don't know. I thought she might have some advice.'

'And did she?'

'No, actually. Nothing beyond "Do it anyway."'

'That's perfect advice for you. You *will* do it anyway.'

'Easy for you to say. All you have to do is cut and sew baby clothes.'

'That and *make* the baby, thank you very much. It's not coming out of the sky.'

'Right,' he said distractedly, and went back to work.

Not long after we returned to Paris, Jane Heap, the editor of *The Little Review*, wrote asking Ernest to contribute something to the next issue. Among the lost sketches in the valise was a series of vignettes he was collectively calling *Paris, 1922*. They all began with the phrase, 'I have seen' and painted memorable and often violent moments he'd witnessed or read about in the past year. One depicted Chèvre d'Or's ruinous collapse at Auteuil. Another described how Peggy Joyce's Chilean lover had shot himself in the head because she wouldn't marry him. Everyone had followed the actress's desperate story in the headlines, but Ernest's take on it was more vivid and alive than anything you could find in a newspaper. Whether he'd gotten the knowledge secondhand or not, each piece was graphic and brutal and completely convincing. Ernest believed he'd never done anything sharper or stronger and Gertrude agreed. He was writing knockout punches.

'You might not want to hear it,' Gertrude said, 'but I think your losing everything has been a blessing. You needed to be free. To start with nothing and make something truly new.'

Ernest nodded solemnly, but I knew he was tremendously relieved. So was I.

'I want to take another shot at the Paris vignettes for Jane Heap. But I don't want to simply revive their corpses. New is new. I'm thinking of pushing them out into paragraphs, so they really begin to move.' He was watching her face carefully as he spoke, feeding off of her encouragement. 'Each would be less a sketch than a miniature; wound up and let go.'

'By all means,' she said, and in a very short time, he was ready to show her a draft that captured the goring of a matador with ferocious intensity. He was particularly anxious to get her take on it because the scene was based on a story she herself had told him about the bullfights in Pamplona. You wouldn't have known, reading the passage, that he'd never been.

'This is exceptional,' Gertrude said. 'You've reproduced it exactly.'

'That was the point,' he said, clearly pleased to hear it. 'But I want to know how bullfighting works first-hand. If I went myself, I could gather material for more sketches. Mike Strater's keen to go and so is Bob McAlmon. Bob's got plenty of money. He could front the whole trip.'

'Go,' Gertrude said.

'You should,' I agreed. 'Everything's pointing that way.'

When we got home that night, I asked Ernest if I could read all of the miniatures he'd done so far and was stopped cold by one about his time in Turkey. It was set on the

Karagatch Road and described, among other things, a woman giving birth like an animal in the rain.

I handed the pieces back, praising them to high heaven, as they deserved, but also couldn't help saying, 'You don't have to hide how scared you are about this baby coming. Not from me.'

'Sure I'm scared. How will I work? What will happen to our good time?'

'Not just that. I know you're worried about me.'

'A little.'

'Please don't. Nothing bad will happen.'

'How could you possibly know that? Something could always go wrong. I've seen it myself.'

'It's going to be fine. I can feel it.'

'Just the same, I've been wondering if we shouldn't have the baby in Toronto. I could get full time work at the *Star*. The hospitals are supposed to be very fine there, and I would have a steady job. We'll need the money for sure.'

'Aren't you a good papa already,' I said, and kissed him softly on the mouth.

'I'm trying to want this. To ward off all the troubling thoughts too.'

'And stuff in as much living as you can before the baby comes?'

'That too, yes.'

The coming weeks brought a flurry of plans about Spain. He met often with Strater and Bob McAlmon in cafés, planning the itinerary, but for whatever reason Ernest always came back from these meetings peevish and irritated with the other men. McAlmon was a poet and friend of both Ezra and Sylvia. He was married to the British writer Annie Ellerman, who wrote under the pseudonym Bryher. It was very widely known that Annie was a lesbian and that Bob was keener on men than women. The marriage was one of convenience. On and off, Annie had been very involved with the poet H.D., another of Pound's 'pupils,' and although none of this seemed to trouble Bob in the least, it got under Ernest's skin. I wasn't exactly sure why. We were surrounded by every combination of sexual pairing and triangulation, so I didn't think it was the homosexuality that got to Ernest per se. It was more likely the distribution of power. Annie was an heiress. Her father was a shipping magnate who happened to be the wealthiest man in England. Although Bob had money of his own, it wasn't anywhere near what Annie had, and there was the impression that she kept him on a leash and that he needed her if he was going to go on running his brand-new press, Contact Editions. Bob was dependent on Annie and Ernest might someday be dependent on Bob, if he wanted to be published. Contact Editions was new but earmarked for greatness, and actively looking for the sharpest, freshest writing possible.

Knowing that he *should* impress Bob meant that Ernest was ineluctably drawn to offend him. By the time Bob, Ernest and Mike Strater had left for Spain, Ernest and Bob were barely even speaking. The trip became an awkward one in many ways. Bob (with help from Annie) was footing all the bills and this brought out the very worst in Ernest. He was always critical of the rich and hated to feel obligated. I learned later from Mike that Ernest had also immediately taken over as the 'expert' on the trip, lecturing the other men incessantly. He loved bullfighting from the very first moment. In his letters to me, he talked only of the courage of the toreros and the bulls too. The whole thing was a great and moving tragedy that you could see and feel, close enough to raise the hair on your neck.

When he came back a week later, he was brimming with enthusiasm. He practiced the dramatically flared passes he'd learned in Ronda and Madrid with a tablecloth in our apartment.

He turned parallel to our table, the only bull available for the moment. 'There's an incredible calm as the matador watches the animal come, only thinking of what he has to do to bring him in correctly and not about the danger. That's where the grace is. And the difficulty, of course.'

'I'd love to see it,' I said.

'You might find it hard to watch,' he said.

'Maybe, but it sounds like something I wouldn't want to miss. The fights might even be a good influence on the baby,' I said.

'Yes, he'll be a real man before he's even born.'

'What makes you so sure it's a boy?'

'What else would it be?'

We made plans to go back together in July, to the Fiesta de San Fermin in Pamplona, where Gertrude and Alice had gone the summer before. It was supposed to be the very best arena for bullfighting, drawing the most murderous bulls and highest-skilled toreros. Although I'd only expressed excitement at the prospect, Ernest was determined to prepare me for the violence.

'Not everyone can stomach it,' he said. 'McAlmon drank brandy all through his first bullfight. Every time the bull rushed the horses, it made him go green. He said he couldn't imagine anyone ever finding anything to love about it, and if they did, they were deranged.'

'I don't think the two of you are meant to be friends.'

'Maybe not, but it's looking like he and Annie want to do a book of stories for me. Or maybe stories and poems.'

'Really? If you hate him so much, why would you want him to do the book?'

'Someone's got to. Now I only have to write the damned thing.'

All of Pamplona was awake when our bus lumbered into the walled city in the middle of the night. The streets were so crowded with bodies that I wondered how the bus could budge at all, but the dancers moved in a ripple away from the rumbling engine, and then filled in again once we'd passed. We continued to climb the narrow streets toward the public square, and when we reached it there was such a blur of noise and motion – dancers whirling, musicians drumming and blasting reed pipes, fireworks exploding in loud bursts of white smoke – we nearly lost our luggage. Once we had it securely in hand and found our hotel, our reservations, which Ernest had made weeks before, had been given away.

Back on the street again, Ernest told me to stay and wait for him while he looked for lodging. I watched him borne away by the crowd without feeling much hope that he'd find a room, much less make his way back to me. The streets themselves seemed to be shifting. I backed against a thick stone wall and tried to stand my ground as dancers spun by in blue and white. The women wore flaring full skirts. They circled each other, snapping their fingers and stamping their black-heeled shoes on the cobblestones. Their hair was loose and beautiful. Some carried tambourines or bells, and though the music sounded chaotic to me, with shrill fifing and drumming that shook the bones of my knees, the women seemed to hear a clear rhythm and move to it perfectly, their legs lifting in time, their arms arcing out from their sides. The men wore blue shirts and trousers, with red kerchiefs at their necks, and danced together in large groups. They called out to one another with happy yelps that were instantly absorbed. It was all like nothing I'd ever seen.

Somehow Ernest navigated the madness. He returned to collect me, and though all the hotels were booked and had been for weeks, he'd managed to secure us a room in a private house nearby, six nights for twice what we paid in rent each month in Paris.

'So much?' I said, feeling a bit ill at the amount. 'How can we possibly afford it?'

'Chin up, Tiny. We'll be paid back in sketches. I need to be here. I feel that so powerfully.'

I couldn't argue with his instinct, and was dead on my feet besides. We took the room and were grateful for it, but in the end we might as well have stayed on the streets all night like everyone else. The whole city had been waiting all year for this week, this joyful night. They could dance forever, it seemed, and it struck me as funny that we'd been keen to come here to escape the chaos of Bastille Day in Paris, when this was as frenetic if not worse.

I finally got out of bed near 6 a.m. knowing there would be no rest for me, and walked out onto the balcony. On the street beneath me, there were as many people about as the night before, but they seemed more focused and directed. It was nearly time for the running of the bulls, but I didn't know that. I only knew something was happening. I went inside and dressed quietly, but Ernest woke anyway from his very light sleep, and by the time we were back at the balcony together, a cannon had sounded with a crack. We saw its white smoke scatter above the public square, and then the crowd gathered there began to sing. Our room was perfectly situated. We could see and hear everything from where we stood at the railing.

A group of men and boys sang a passionate song in Spanish. I understood nothing, but didn't really need to.

'I think it's about danger,' I said to Ernest over the din.

'Happy danger,' he said. 'They're excited to test themselves. To see if they can outrun their fear.'

He knew the bulls would be released soon. Gertrude and Alice had relayed in great detail all they'd seen at the fiesta the year before, and so had Mike Strater. But Ernest wasn't content to hear what it was like; he wanted to know it firsthand. And if I hadn't been there with him, I knew he wouldn't be standing on the balcony at all. He really wanted to be down in the square, preparing himself to run.

'*Viva San Fermin,*' the crowd shouted. '*Gora San Fermin!*'

The cannon sounded again as the bulls were set loose, and we saw the runners coming very fast along the cobbled streets below. Everyone wore white shirts and pants with bright red scarves around their waists and necks. Some carried newspapers to wave the bulls away and all wore an expression that seemed ecstatic. After the runners, six bulls thundered past with such power the house shook under our feet. Their hooves rang on the cobblestones and their thick dark heads ducked low, looking murderous. Some of the men were overcome and had to scramble up the side of the barricades lining the street. Onlookers reached to help them escape, but there was also a palpable anticipation as the crowd waited to see if some unlucky one wouldn't be fast or limber enough.

There was no goring that day, at least not that we saw, and I was very relieved when the bulls were safely in the arena. The entire ritual took only a few minutes, but I realized I'd been holding my breath.

We breakfasted on wonderfully sweet *café con leche* and dense rolls, and then I tried to nap in our room while Ernest walked

194

the streets of Pamplona taking notes on everything he saw. It was all poetry to him, the heavily lined faces of the old Basque men, each one with the same blue cap. The young men wore wide-brimmed straw hats instead and carried hand-sewn wine skins over their shoulders, their arms and backs well muscled from hard labor. Ernest came back to the room excited by it all, and talking about the lunch he'd just eaten, perfectly crisped river trout stuffed with fried ham and onions.

'The best fish I've ever eaten. Get dressed. You have to try it.'

'You really want to go back to the same café and watch me eat?'

'Watch nothing. I'm going to have it again.'

Later that afternoon when the first fight began, we sat in good *barrera* seats right up next to the action. Ernest had paid a premium to make sure we had an excellent view of the action, but he was also protective of me.

'Look away now,' he said when the first horseman set the long, barbed *banderilla* into the withers of the bull and the blood ran freely. He said it again when the first horse was gored badly, and again when the fine young torero, Nicanor Villalta, killed his bull with deft precision. But I didn't look away.

We sat in the *barrera* seats all that afternoon and saw six bulls die, and the whole while I watched and listened and felt swept up by it all. Between fights, I cross-stitched a white cotton blanket for the baby.

'You've surprised me,' Ernest said, near the end of the day. 'Have I?'

'You weren't brought up to know how to watch something like this. I guessed you'd go weak. I'm sorry, but I did.'

'I wasn't sure how I'd feel, but I can tell you now. Safe and strong.' I'd come to the end of a row of stitches and tied a neat, flat knot, the way my mother had taught me to do when I was a girl. As I smoothed the floss with my fingertips, satisfied with my work, I couldn't help but think how shocked she would be to see me in this passionate, violent place and not cringing the least, but weathering it like a natural.

'When I was very young, I used to be fearless. I've told you.'

He nodded.

'When I lost that, I think my family was happy.'

'I don't know that you ever really lost it. I see it in you now.'

'I'm stronger because of the baby. I can feel him moving when the pipes sound and the crowd roars. He seems to like it.'

Ernest smiled with obvious pride, and then said, 'Families can be vicious, but ours won't be.'

'Our baby will know everything we know. We'll be very honest and not hold anything back.'

'And we won't underestimate him.'

'Or make him feel terrified of life.'

'This is getting to be a very tall order, isn't it?' Ernest said, and we laughed happily, buoyed by our wishing.

Late that same night, when again we weren't sleeping for the fireworks and the drumming and the riau-riau dancing, Ernest said, 'What about Nicanor as a name for the baby?'

'He'll be a fine torero with that name. He can't help it.'

'We've had some fun haven't we?' He squeezed me tightly in his arms.

'It's not all over.'

'No, but I figure I have to be steady when the baby comes. I'll earn the bread and be the papa and there won't be time to think about what I want.'

'For the first year, maybe, but not forever.'

'A year of sacrifice, then. And then he'll have to take his chances with the rest of us.'

'Nicanor,' I repeated. 'It rings, doesn't it?'

'It does, but that doesn't mean the little bugger gets more than a year.'

Twenty-Five

I wanted muskmelons and a really nice piece of cheese, coffee and good jam and waffles. I was so hungry thinking about this I couldn't sleep.

'Waffles,' I said to Ernest's curled back, near dawn. 'Wouldn't that be lovely?'

When he didn't rouse, I said it again, louder, and put my hand on his back, giving him a friendly little shove.

'Oh, for crying out loud,' he said, rolling out of bed. 'It's gone now.'

'What's gone?'

He sat on the edge of the thick mattress, scratching one knee. 'The right words for the sketch.'

'Oh, sorry then,' I said.

I watched him dress and then move toward the kitchen. Within minutes I could hear the coffee boiling and smell it and it made me hungrier. I heard him get his coffee and then heard the chair squeak back as he sat at the table. Silence.

'Tiny?' I said, still in bed. 'What do you think about the waffles?'

He groaned and then pushed his chair back. 'There it all goes again.'

The months were closing in on us. Our baby was due at the end of October and we were set to sail for Canada in late August. That would give us six or seven weeks to find an apartment and prepare. As the time grew closer, Ernest worked hard and worried harder. He was panicked he'd never have time to set down the rest of the miniatures for Jane Heap and the *Little Review*. He was working on five new ones simultaneously, each describing some aspect of bullfighting. When he came home from his studio, he often needed several drinks back to back before he could tell me about his work, which was going well, but seemed to be taking everything he had.

'I'm trying to keep it alive,' he said. 'To stay with the action, and not try to put in what I'm feeling about it. Not think about myself at all, but what really happened. That's where the real emotion is.'

This was one of his newest ideas about writing and because the miniatures would test it, he was killing himself to get them right. I had no doubt they would hit and be perfect, but in the meantime, it was hard to see him so overworked.

He was also slaving over proofs for Bob McAlmon. Even after their prickly time in Spain, Bob had made good on his offer to do a book for Ernest through Contact Editions. The volume would be titled *Three Stories and Ten Poems*, and although Ernest was crowing with excitement at the prospect, he was worried he'd never get the proofs corrected on time. He worked by candle late into the night, and when he'd finally finished his notes and mailed everything back to McAlmon, it was time for goodbyes.

In a series of sad dinners, we saw the Straters, the Pounds,

Sylvia, Gertrude and Alice — each time saying we'd be back in a year's time, when the baby was ready to travel.

'Mind it's not longer,' Pound said ominously. 'Exile weighs on the mind.'

'It's not quite exile, is it?' Ernest said.

'Limbo then,' Pound said, retreating slightly.

'A softer word only if you don't bring in the Old Testament,' Ernest said with a grumble.

Ten days later, we sailed.

It was early September when we arrived in Quebec, and by the time we got to Toronto, there was an enthusiastic note waiting from John Bone, and another from Greg Clark, a reporter friend from Ernest's past, welcoming us warmly to town. All seemed to be boding well, but when Ernest reported for work on 10 September, he learned that Bone wouldn't be his immediate supervisor, as he expected, but Harry Hindmarsh, who was the *Star*'s assistant managing editor. After one meeting, Ernest knew the relationship would be a troubled one. Hindmarsh was heavy physically and also in word and deed; he liked to throw his weight around.

'Right off, he sized me up,' Ernest said when he returned to our room at the Hotel Selby. 'I hadn't said three words before he decided I was too big for my britches.' He paced the room, scowling. 'What about *him*? If he weren't married to the publisher's daughter, he'd be sweeping sidewalks.'

'I'm sorry, Tiny. I'm sure he'll come around to your wonderfulness,' I said.

'Fat chance. He seems bent on treating me like some cub reporter. I won't be getting a byline, and he's sending me out of town.'

'When?'

'Tonight. To Kingston to cover some escaped convict. It's only five or six hours on the train, but I don't know how long the story will keep me there.'

'Does Hindmarsh know this baby could turn up anytime?'

'I don't think he cares.'

I sent Ernest off with a kiss and repeated assurance that all would be well. He made me swear to find reinforcements, and I did. Greg Clark had a lovely wife, Helen, who warmly agreed when I asked her for help in finding an apartment. Money was as much of a concern for us as it had always been; even more so because we were putting away every possible dime for the baby. We couldn't afford some of the nicer neighborhoods she recommended, but we did find something that would do on Bathurst Street. It was a railroad flat on the fourth floor, with a claw-foot tub and a pull-down Murphy bed in the bedroom, which was oddly squeezed between the kitchen and living room. Although the apartment itself lacked warmth and charm, it looked down on one corner of a ravine on the Connable's estate.

Ernest had known Ralph and Harriet Connable since just after the war, when he'd come to Toronto to try and find newspaper work. Ralph owned the Canadian chain of Woolworth five-and-dime stores and was as wealthy as a god as far as we were concerned. He and his wife were both very kind to me as soon as they learned we were neighbors, and I was happy to have someone, anyone, close by as I neared my due date.

Ernest came home from Kingston looking tired and irritable, and then left again, just days later, to do a mining story in Sudbury Basin, easily twice as far from Toronto as Kingston. He barely had time to visit and approve of the apartment.

'Oh, Cat. I feel terrible I won't be here to help you get settled.'

'There's not much to do. I'll hire someone to do the lifting.'

'I can't help but think we were foolish to come here. You're alone all the time. I'm working like a slave for what? Spotty bits of news in nowhere locations? What a bust.'

'I know you're overworked, Tiny. But everything will make sense once the baby comes.'

'I hope to Christ you're right.'

'I am. You'll see,' I said. And kissed him goodbye.

I was doing far too much of that for my comfort, it was true, but I did believe coming to very cold and lonely Toronto would be worth it once our baby was born healthy and well. In the meantime, I tried to make the new space as homey as I could. We'd brought crates from Paris with our clothes and dishes and pictures packed inside. I hired a cleaning woman and an ancient-looking janitor to cart our things up the four flights. We didn't have much in the way of furniture and for the first weeks, as Ernest criss-crossed Ontario like some kind of traveling salesman, I camped out on the Murphy bed, wrapped in blankets against the dropping temperatures and finishing the letters of Abélard and Héloïse.

I was keen for any distraction, and it was easy to lose myself in their words and their story. Some days I only got up to make tea or stuff blankets under the doors and windowsills where the chill crept in. I also wrote letters to Paris, to the friends we were missing there, and home to the States. Fonnie had been trying to muster happiness for me about the coming baby, but she was close to the breaking point on many fronts. Roland had recently suffered a nervous breakdown and was recuperating in a mental hospital in Massachusetts. *It's a highly regarded facility*, Fonnie said in a letter, *as those places go. But the chil-*

dren are confused and ask if he'll ever come home again. I don't know what to tell them. I felt very sorry for them all, but not surprised that such a thing could happen. There had always been too much unrest between them, as with my own parents. And when tensions are that high for so long, something *has* to snap. How could it not?

I also wrote to Ernest's parents. He was too busy to answer his own letters, but his stinginess with his parents was more complicated than that. He'd never wanted them over-involved in his life, particularly Grace. When he left for Paris, I think he felt he had freedom for the first time to completely reinvent himself. His parents reminded him of his beginnings, which he would rather have thrown off altogether. I understood his need for independence, but here we were a few weeks away from the baby's arrival, and Ernest hadn't said a thing to them. I felt they had a right to know and I continued to tell him so when he came home ever so briefly between assignments.

'I'll do it if you insist,' he finally agreed. 'But it's a mistake. They'll just come sniffing around the way wolves always do.'

'You don't really mean that.'

'The hell I don't. Can you imagine my mother *not* forcing her way into everything with this baby, pummeling us with her opinions and advice? We don't need her. We don't need anyone.'

'She and Ed would love any small opportunity to help.'

'So let them, but I'm not asking for a hot dime.'

'Fair enough,' I said, but was grateful when they responded to Ernest's cable quickly and extravagantly, sending trunks full of wedding gifts we'd been storing with them and furniture, too, from our long-ago apartment on Dearborn Street. None of it was especially nice, but having our own things around us made our lot on Bathurst Street seem less provisional. And it all arrived just in time.

Hindmarsh sent Ernest off again, the first week in October, this time to cover the arrival of British Prime Minister David Lloyd George in New York City.

'It's like a personal vendetta,' I said as I watched him pack for his trip.

'I can take it, I guess,' Ernest said. 'But what about you?'

'The doctor said we have until the end of the month, maybe until the first of November. You'll be here.'

'This is the last trip,' he said, snapping shut the new valise. 'I'm going to ask John Bone to talk some sense into Hindmarsh.'

'If it comes directly from Bone, he'll have to lay off, won't he?'

'That's the idea. Take good care of the baby cat.'

'I promise.'

'And the mama cat too.'

'Yes, Tiny, but you'd better hurry. They won't hold your train.'

Several days later, on 9 October, Harriet Connable called on me with a dinner invitation.

'I'd love to,' I said. 'But I'm so very large now nothing fits me. I'll have to wear table linens.'

'I'm sure you'll carry them off beautifully, dear,' she said with a gracious laugh. 'We'll send a car around for you at eight.'

In the end I was very glad she insisted. All afternoon I'd been feeling something I was calling indigestion. Of course it was more than that. My body was readying itself, but I was in denial. I thought if I just stayed calm and didn't over exert myself, the baby would hold off until Ernest returned home.

I spooned up my delicious soup as quietly as a mouse, and then sat on the Connable's rich velvet sofa listening to Harriet play a lively rendition of 'I'll Take You Home Again Kathleen' without so much as tapping my foot. But of course the baby was coming whether I was prepared or not, and this became more and more obvious as the evening passed.

'Hadley, dear, I don't think you're feeling well,' Ralph Connable said when he could no longer politely disregard the strained and serious expression on my face.

'I'm perfectly all right,' I said, stubborn to the last, but then I began to cry as soon as I'd said it, my emotions bursting right through my carefully made dam. The pain was too much now. I bent over with it and began to shake.

'Oh, you poor girl,' Harriet said. 'Don't worry about anything. We'll make sure you're very well cared for.'

They drove me to the hospital, Harriet patting my hand and making soothing noises, while Ralph sped along with determination. The streets glowed faintly under gaslight.

'Can you try and reach someone at the *Star*? There must be a way to let Ernest know.'

'We'll move mountains if we have to,' Harriet assured me. 'There's still a little time, I think.'

But there wasn't. Half an hour later, I was gowned and draped on the surgical table, coached by the doctor and several nurses to begin pushing. This was why we'd come to Toronto – to have these very capable and trained professionals oversee everything. In Paris I would have had a midwife who boiled water on my own cooker top to sterilize her instruments. Even in the States, doctors were only just beginning to perform hospital deliveries. Ernest's father still woke in the middle of the night to answer calls when he was up in Michigan, and though I knew women had been having babies at home forever – my mother, certainly, and Ernest's too – I felt so much safer this way. Particularly when my pushing did nothing at all.

I strained for two hours, until my neck ached and my knees shook with the effort. Finally they gave me ether. I breathed in the fresh-paint smell of it as the mask was drawn over my mouth and nose, the sharpness stinging my eyes. After that, I felt nothing until I woke from my fog and saw the nurse holding out a tightly wrapped bundle. This was my son, swaddled in layers of blue wool. I gazed at him through happy tears. He was perfect, from the pink whorls of his well-made ears and his squeezed-shut eyes, to the dark brown hair with a fuzz of sideburns. I was devastated that Ernest had missed the birth, but here, safe and sound and utterly marvelous, was his son. That was all that mattered.

When Ernest finally did arrive early the next morning, panting and completely beside himself, I was sitting up in bed, nursing the baby.

'Oh, my God,' Ernest said, breaking down. He stood just inside the door and sobbed openly, covering his face with his hands. 'I've been dead worried for you, Tiny. I got a cable in the press car saying the baby had come and was well, but not a single word about you.'

'Dear sweet Tiny. You can see I'm fine. Everything went smoothly, and come look at this fellow. Isn't he wonderful?'

Ernest crossed to me, sitting gently on the edge of the mattress. 'He seems awfully small. Aren't you afraid of doing something wrong?' He put a single finger on the baby's small veined hand.

'I was afraid at first, but he's very solid, actually. I think the bullfights had an effect on him after all. He came barreling out like a good torero.'

'John Hadley Nicanor Hemingway. He's perfectly beautiful. And aren't you something for making it through so well?'

'I feel surprisingly sturdy, but you, Tiny. You look terrible. Didn't you sleep on the train?'

'I tried but I had the most terrible feeling you were in danger.'

'I was in excellent hands. The Connables were so thoughtful and helpful. We owe them so much.'

'Maybe we were right to come to Toronto after all,' Ernest said.

'Of course we were. I told you it would all make perfect sense.'

'I'm so tired I might fall over.'

'Sleep then.' I pointed to a chair in the corner of the room.

'Hindmarsh will be wondering where I am.'

'Let him wonder. You're a new father.'

'Can you believe it?'

I smiled to myself and said nothing as he curled up under a blanket and fell soundly asleep. *Two men, now,* I thought with deep satisfaction. *And both of them mine.*

TWENTY-SIX

Later that morning, Ernest sent out a rash of telegrams saying how well things had gone. He was immoderately proud of the speed with which I delivered the baby, and I was pleased with myself. I had help from the doctors and the ether, true enough, but also braved the whole ordeal like a champion stoic, with Ernest hundreds of miles away.

He left for work, prepared for a dressing down from Hindmarsh, but it was worse than he expected. Hindmarsh didn't wait for Ernest in his office, but humiliated him in front of everyone, saying he should have filed his story before going to the hospital. That was ridiculous, of course, but when Ernest relayed the story to me that evening, after rehashing the whole thing with Greg Clark in a pub over many glasses of bourbon, he was still stung and angry.

'Toronto's dead. We can't stay here.' The drink hadn't calmed him much, and I was worried the charge nurse would come in and evict him before I'd heard the whole story.

'Is everything really beyond repair?'

'Well beyond. We were both furious. He held nothing back, the lout, and I said things they'll probably be talking about for years to come.'

'Oh dear, Tiny. Did he fire you?'

'He transferred me to the *Weekly*. Not that I'll take it. When do you think you can travel again?'

'I'll be fine in a few days, but the baby can't sail for months. We'll have to tough it out.'

'I could kill the bastard. That might solve it.'

'Not for long.'

He grimaced and sat down hard, scraping the chair loudly against the floor. 'Where's the little corker anyway? I want to take another look at him.'

'He's in the nursery sleeping. You should be asleep too. Go home, Tiny. We'll face this in the morning.'

'What's to face? It's dead, I told you.'

'Don't think about it. Just go, and take some bicarbonate too. You're going to wake up with a hell of a headache.'

We didn't immediately bolt for Paris — but only because we couldn't. The baby really was too young for the passage, and we'd also depleted our savings with the move. We were close to broke, with a pile of hospital bills besides. There was nothing to do but dig in and take it — 'like a bitch dog,' as Ernest was fond of saying. He took the transfer and though he wasn't working directly under Hindmarsh any longer, he still felt the man's shadow. Every time he got a lousy assignment, he wondered if Hindmarsh was in on it — like the time he was sent to the Toronto Zoo to welcome the arrival of a white peacock.

'A peacock, Tiny. They're trying to kill me. Death by indignity, the nastiest kind of all.'

'Maybe,' I said. 'But they can't. You're too strong for that.'

'I'm not so sure.'

Winter arrived in Toronto with snow that blew sideways and threatened to knock us over. If Paris winter was damp and gray, this was fiercely white and unremitting. The wind easily pierced our coats and blankets, and found its way into every corner of our apartment, where the baby and I stayed camped against the radiator. I boiled water to keep the air moist and took to wearing Ernest's big overcoat when I nursed. I didn't take the baby out at all and hired a maid to mind him when I had to do the shopping. Ernest limped home in the evening, after dark had fallen, and looked more exhausted and run down all the time. He was good about exclaiming over the baby's new accomplishments as I reported them — he'd smiled at me in the bath; he was lifting his head like a champ — but it was hard for Ernest to take any pleasure just then.

'I can't see how I'll make it a year this way,' he said.

'It seems impossible, I know. But when we're old and doddering, this year will seem like a blink.'

'It's not even the embarrassment of slogging away at stories well beneath me. That's nothing. But not working on my own stuff at all, when that's all I've ever wanted. I feel the material going bad in me. If I don't write it soon I'm going to lose it for good.'

'Stay up and write now. I'll make some strong coffee for you.'

'I can't. I'm too tired to think. It does come in the morning sometimes, but as soon as I try to get anything down, the baby will cry or I'll have to get to work. At the end of the day, there aren't words left. We're so far away from everything here, too. I don't know who's writing what, or what matters.'

'Yes, but you've made some good friends. You like Greg Clark. That's lucky.'

'I do like Greg, but he doesn't box and he doesn't know anything about horse racing. I've also never seen him drunk.'

'Not everyone drinks as well as you do, Tiny.'

'Still, I don't trust a man I haven't seen tight.'

As November passed into December, Ernest's mood grew worrisomely low. He wasn't sleeping well, and the baby's night waking only made this worse. The copies of *Three Stories and Ten Poems* had arrived and Ernest sent some off to Ezra and Gertrude and Sylvia, and several home to his family in Oak Park – and then he waited for praise. He combed the papers and magazines daily, anxious for a review, but there wasn't so much as a hint of the book's existence. If the world didn't know about the book, had it happened? He had a copy of Jane Heap's *Little Review* with the bullfighting miniatures, and sometimes he thumbed through them and frowned. 'I'm not sure I'm the same writer who produced these. Hell, I'm not writing at all.'

I couldn't tell him I thought he was being overly dramatic, because he really did feel the loss of his writing life profoundly. He needed me to keep him warm and loved, solidly tethered to earth; he needed his work to keep him sane. I couldn't help him with that part. I could only look on and feel troubled that our life was burdened by worry at a time when we should be so happy.

'It was a terrible mistake to come,' he said after arriving home in a particularly dire state of mind one night.

I couldn't take his suffering any longer. 'You're right,' I said. 'It was a mistake. We'll go back to Paris and you can give everything to your writing.'

'How will we afford it?'

'I don't know. We just will.'

'Your trust fund pays only two thousand a year. Without my income, I can't see how we'll manage.'

'If you can't write, the baby and I will be a burden to you. You'll resent us. How can we live like that?'

'We're in a bind. That's for sure.'

'Let's not think of it in that light. It can be an adventure. Our great gamble. Maybe we'll come out on top after all.'

'I don't know what I'd do without you, Tiny.'

'Buy the tickets. I'll wire your parents for money. They want to help.'

'They want to obligate me. I won't take it.'

'Don't then. I will, for the baby.'

'What if I did one last series for the *Weekly*? I could kill myself for seven or ten pieces and then resign. With that and some from Oak Park, we'd have maybe a thousand to carry us. A thousand and a prayer.'

'That should just about do it.'

Just after the first of January 1924, as soon as we thought the baby could safely travel, we boarded the train for New York and then the *Antonia*, bound for France. We'd begun to call the baby Bumby for his very round and solid feel, like a stuffed bear. I rolled him tightly in blankets in the ship's berth and talked to him and let him play with my hair, while up on deck, Ernest found anyone at all and began to wax nostalgically about Paris. I would have stayed in Toronto for a year or five if it took that to make a good home for Bumby, but it wouldn't have cost me the way it would Ernest. Some men would have been able to choke it back and take it for a while, but he might have lost himself completely there. Ahead in Paris, it was anyone's guess how we'd make it, but I couldn't worry about that. Ernest needed me to be strong for us both now, and I would be. I would scrimp and make do and not resent it at all because it was my choice in the end. I was choosing him, the writer, in Paris. We would never again live a conventional life.

TWENTY-SEVEN

'I know we are meant to be gone a year,' Ernest said to Gertrude on our first visit to their flat after we returned, 'but four months *is* a year in Canada.'

'You're finished with journalism, that's the main thing,' Gertrude said. 'Time to go all out, now, and write the thing you're meant to.'

'I'm ready, by God,' he said, and helped himself to another glass of pear liqueur.

I watched Alice as the two of them went on this way, feeding off of one another's certainty and enthusiasm. She seemed to tighten and turn inward, and I wondered if she wasn't happy to see Ernest back; if she'd gotten used to having Gertrude to herself when we were away. Granted, there was always someone circling Gertrude, wanting her attention and good opinion, but she and Ernest had a special intensity together – almost as if they were twin siblings with a private language, zeroing in on and hearing the other almost exclusively. I felt it too, and though I had been hurt by their connection at times, I could hardly remember what it felt like to be lonely. The baby needed and responded to me completely. It was my voice he turned toward, the rhythms of my rocking arms that felt most right, the way I patted and rubbed his back when he woke in the night. I was essential to him, and to Ernest too. I made everything run, now.

Motherhood could be exhausting, to be sure. I was forever under-slept, and sometimes didn't have the energy to wash my hair or eat anything more elaborate than bread and butter. But when Bumby nursed, his fist clutching the fabric of my robe, his eyes soft and bottomless and locked on mine, as if I were the very heart of his universe, I couldn't help but melt into him. And when Ernest came home from a long day of work and had that look that told me he'd been too much alone and in his head, I felt just as necessary. He needed me, and Bumby too; without us, he couldn't climb back out of himself and feel whole again.

Family life worked most clearly for us when we were alone, at the end of the day, reconnecting and shoring each other up. But it was very much at odds with bohemian Paris. Gertrude and Alice could be lovely with Bumby. They gave him a shiny silver rattle and knitted booties. When it came time for his christening, they brought some very nice champagne, which we had with teacake, dried fruit and sugared almonds, and Gertrude even agreed to be his godmother. But not all our friends seemed to know what to do with us now that we had a baby in tow. Pound and Shakespear would come to our apartment for a late-night drink or meet us at the café if we found someone to watch Bumby, but Pound made it very clear that babies weren't welcome in his studio. It wasn't because of the noise or the potential mess, but on principle. 'I just don't believe in children,' he said. 'No offense, Hadley.'

He did help us find our second apartment in Paris – not an

easy task. The dollar was losing muscle against the franc, which we'd been silly not to anticipate. We'd lived so cheaply before, we thought we'd go on this way, with three mouths to feed instead of two – but rents had skyrocketed. When we finally did find something that would do, it was three times what we'd paid at Cardinal Lemoine. But we had to pay it. We handed over the first month's rent with a gulp, parked Bumby's pram in the yard next to the coal pile, and called it home.

This was the sawmill apartment, on the rue Notre-Dame-des-Champs, the 'Carpenter's Loft' as some of our friends soon took to calling it. The noise and dust from the lumber-yard below was too much to take at times, but it was much better situated than our rooms above the dancehall. It was very near Gertrude and Alice's apartment and the Luxembourg Gardens, and was also a stone's throw from the Boulevard Montparnasse and many of the best cafés.

Although Ernest had once felt disgust for writers working in cafés, saying they were phonies only wanting to be con-spicuous, he began to frequent them himself now. Part of it was practical. He needed peace and quiet and Bumby, who had begun to teethe, was often fussy. But once he started to work at the Closerie des Lilas routinely, he was surprised to find he preferred it to working alone in his room, sweating it out in silence, as he used to say. It was warmer and more pleasant, too. Friends could find him if they wanted, and there was always someone exciting to talk to or drink with when the writing day was done.

Sometimes he talked about starting another novel, but hadn't yet hit on the right idea. More and more he understood that the draft lost in the valise with the other manuscripts wasn't the right novel, either, no matter how much he'd slaved over it and wanted it to be. Still, he was skittish about committing to anything so large and time-consuming again. He would wait, and in the meantime he would write stories. 'One story,' he said, 'for everything I know. Really know, in my bones and in my gut.'

When he said this I wondered what it was *I* really knew in the way he meant, and could only answer with Ernest and Bumby, our life together. It was a shamefully outdated idea, I knew, and if I'd confessed it to any woman in any café in Montparnasse, I would have been laughed out onto the street. I was supposed to have my own ideas and ambitions and be incredibly hungry for experience and newness of every variety. But I wasn't hungry; I was content.

It wasn't just purpose that had come along to fill me. My days were richer and made more sense. Bumby was a beauty and when we walked every day, twice a day, we were often stopped and chatted up by his admirers. My French was as halting as ever, but a happy baby is the perfect impetus for even primarily one-sided conversations. His cooing garnered us many a gift apple or pear at the market, and even when I brought him to the cafés to meet Ernest for an occasional meal, Bumby won everyone over. Some of our friends might have been at a loss, but strangers were invariably charmed.

The Pounds were off to Rapallo as usual that spring, but even from that distance, Ezra managed to get Ernest a job with Ford Madox Ford, as a deputy editor for the *Transatlantic Review*. Ford had a dark and cramped office on the Quai d'Anjou, and it was there Ernest headed in early February in his worn shoes and shabby jacket, with a chip on his shoulder. There was no money to be had, but he wanted the editing experience and the connections. He couldn't let Ford know that, though, because he couldn't stand not to have the upper hand, most particularly when the upper hand would have been impossible to get. Ford's novel *The Good Soldier* had received some very nice attention. He'd written other novels as well and had published Yeats, Thomas Hardy, Joseph Conrad and others in a magazine he'd founded earlier, called the *English Review*. All of this was bad enough, but Ford was also a gentleman with money and a pedigree, a combination Ernest never had any patience for. He came home from the meeting muttering about how Ford's tastes were slanted so far backward the man was about to fall over on his ass.

'So he's not modern. Why should everyone be? I'm not.'

'No, you're not modern, little cat. But you're very beautiful and good, and a bang-up mother besides. This fellow Ford is too full of his own good opinion, and he wheezes when he talks. It's so bad you'd think every last word has to swim through his lungs to reach his mouth.'

'Good gracious, Tiny. Please tell me you took the job anyhow.'

'Of course I did.' He smiled broadly and wickedly, reaching over to tweak one of Bumby's feet. 'Do you think I'm crazy?'

When I met Ford I was inclined to like him, even after all Ernest had said. He and his lover, the painter Stella Bowen, had us over to lunch, and I was delighted to find they had a baby too, a darling little girl named Julie, about the same age as Bumby. I hadn't brought Bumby out of politeness for our hosts, but I told Stella I would the next time. She was warm in her encouragement about this, and about everything – feeding us a beautiful four-course lunch and engaging me graciously with her charming Australian accent. Ford was ruddy and plump, with wispy blond hair and a mustache. I did wonder at first how Ford, well into middle-age, was able to woo such a lovely woman as Stella, but he soon revealed perfect manners and spoke with an appealing conviction for everything he cared about, including Stella, good wine, creamy soup and literature. All through lunch, he emphasized how important it was for him to help young writers like Ernest find their way. I knew Ernest would rather not need Ford's or anyone's help, but the truth was, he did.

'I can bring a lot to this magazine,' Ernest said when we'd said our goodbyes and were headed home. 'He should be grateful to have me.'

'I liked him.'

'Of course you did.'

'What does that mean?'

'Nothing.' He came upon a loose stone and kicked it into the street. 'Don't you think he looks a little like a walrus?'

'A little,' I admitted.

'And the wheezing?'

'That's fairly serious, isn't it? Stella said he got it in a gas attack in the war.'

'I could forgive him that, then, if he wasn't so superior.'

'You don't have to love him. Just do the work.'

'There's plenty of work to do. That's lucky, I suppose.'

'So much *is* lucky, Tatie. You'll see.'

Ford and Stella took to having literary teas on Thursdays at the Quai d'Anjou. I often went for the company and took Bumby too, parking his pram in whatever sun was coming in through the windows. It was at one of these teas I first met Harold Loeb. Harold seemed to be about Ernest's age, and was very good-looking – tall, with a sharp, straight nose and strong chin, and towering waves of dark hair. As soon as Ford introduced us, we began talking easily about the States.

'I don't miss home exactly,' he said. 'But I can't seem to stop dreaming about it. I wonder why that is.'

219

'It's part of you, I guess,' I said. 'It's locked in, isn't it?'

'That's nicely put,' he said, and peered down at me with clear and intense blue eyes. 'Are you a writer too, then?'

'Not hardly,' I laughed. 'Though I don't think I'd be half bad at it. I've always loved books and felt they spoke to me. I've played piano since I was a girl, but not seriously.'

'I'm not sure I write *seriously*,' Harold said. 'I try very hard to be funny, actually.'

'I should think you'd be very funny if you put your mind to it.'

'That's swell of you to say. Here, come tell Kitty. She thinks all my jokes are a bust.'

We crossed the room together to meet his girlfriend, Kitty Cannell, who was truly beautiful; slim and graceful and golden all over.

'Kitty used to be a professional dancer,' he said. 'If she moves to get more wine, you'll see it instantly.'

'Oh, Harold,' she said. 'Please don't try to be charming.'

'See, Hadley. I have to be very dour around Kitty or she gets impatient with me.' He pulled a face and Kitty laughed, showing her nice teeth. 'And sometimes,' Harold went on, 'she surprises me utterly, the dear girl.'

'It's why you keep me around.'

'That and your ankles, sweetheart.'

By the end of the afternoon I was quite taken by Harold and Kitty both, and happily accepted when they invited Ernest and me to dinner the next evening, at the Negre de Toulouse.

'It's a wonderfully secret local place,' Kitty said. 'You won't find it in the guidebooks.'

'I swear not to breathe a word of it,' I said, and then began to wonder what on earth I could wear. I was still at a loss the next evening when it was time to leave for the restaurant. It had been five months since I'd had Bumby. My maternity clothes swam on me, now, but I couldn't yet squeeze into anything from before.

'No one really cares,' Ernest said. 'You could go in sackcloth and still charm everyone.'

'I could not. You might not give a whit about clothes,' I gestured at his patched jacket and sweatshirt, the uniform he wore day and night, without any regard to fashion or even decorum. 'But people generally do take care and want to make a good impression.'

'You've already made one, obviously. But if you like, I'll tell them I've listened too carefully to Gertrude, who's always said to buy pictures instead of clothes.'

'She does say that, but we don't buy pictures, do we?' I frowned at myself in the mirror.

'Don't fret, Tatie,' Ernest said, coming behind me to plant a kiss on the back of my neck. 'No one's as lovely and straight and simple as you.'

I met his eyes in the mirror. 'You're awfully sweet, aren't you?'

He kissed me again, and then pushed me firmly out the door.

In the end the restaurant was so dimly lit, I found I wasn't self-conscious after the first bottle of wine. While the men talked of Princeton, where Harold had gone to school, and scratch starts at first novels (Harold was working on his just then), Kitty and I had a surprisingly intimate conversation about her first marriage, to Skipwith Cannell, a poet who'd apparently made her miserable, then refused to divorce her.

'How terrible for you. How will you marry again?'

'I'd *never* marry again, dear. Thank goodness Harold and I are in agreement about that much. But I'd rather not be chained to Skip forever. It was hard enough to bear when he was nearby. Now he clinks and clanks and bedevils me all the way from London.'

'It's freedom you want then.'

'Good God, yes. Don't you?'

'I don't know. I want to be happy I suppose.'

'Happiness is so awfully complicated, but freedom isn't. You're either tied down or you're not.'

'Blaming marriage doesn't solve it. As soon as you love someone, you're bound up with them. It's unavoidable – unless you swear off love.'

'Even *I'm* not that hard-nosed.' She laughed and raised her glass. 'To love, then.'

Harold turned to us with a quizzical look. 'What's going on here?'

'Hadley's turning me into a romantic,' Kitty said.

Harold chuckled. 'Fat chance, sweetheart, but it's a very nice idea.'

'Only one romantic per table,' Ernest piped in. 'There's a sign at the door.'

After a vast dinner, they came back with us to the sawmill apartment for a nightcap, and though they pretended to be gracious about how dark and tunnel-like our apartment was, I could see they were unaccustomed to common living. The baby was asleep in the next room, so we crowded around the kitchen table.

'I figure I'll be done with this novel within a month,' Harold said, 'and then I'm going for broke. I want an American publisher, an advance and a slew of good notices.'

'You forgot dancing girls,' Ernest said, smirking.

'They'll be in the contract,' Harold said. 'Seriously, though, I'm shooting for Boni and Liveright. Ford says they're the operation to watch in New York.'

'They publish Sherwood Anderson,' Ernest said. 'They've treated him well, and he says they're committed to contemporary American writers.'

'That's me,' Harold said. 'You too.'

'You should send your stories, Tatie. Sherwood would put in a word for you,' I said.

'Maybe,' Ernest said. 'I've thought about it.'

'Now that's settled,' Kitty said, 'please let's talk about something interesting.'

'Like hats, Kitty dear?' Harold said.

'Maybe.' She turned to me. 'I'd love to take you shopping. You could be my pet project.'

'Oh, brother,' Ernest said.

'What? Everyone likes nice things,' Kitty said. 'I promise not to drape her in pearls or meringue.'

'I'd love to go,' I said, 'let's set a date soon.' But after they'd gone, I saw it was a mistake to have accepted Kitty's offer.

'She only wants to humiliate you, don't you see?' Ernest said.

'She's trying to be nice. I won't take any charity, if that's what's worrying you.'

'It's not that. She wants to lure you in and make you think you're being treated badly.'

'I'd never think that.'

'Just wait. If she keeps whispering in your ear, you'll begin to hate me for how shabbily we live.'

'You're being awfully extreme, Tatie. We're talking about shopping for heaven's sake.'

'No we're not,' he said grimly, and went off to pour himself a drink.

TWENTY-EIGHT

While Bumby napped at home under the care of Marie
Cocotte, who'd been enthusiastic about returning to
work for us, even with the additional nanny duties, I took to
meeting Kitty once a week. We'd have tea somewhere or pop
into antiques stores when she had time. I loved to look at
the jewelry, particularly the cloisonné earrings that were
popular just then, and though Ernest and I had no money to
spare for such indulgences, I enjoyed watching Kitty move
through the shops and hearing her appreciative remarks. She
had an eye and seemed to know, instinctively, what would
hold its value and what was lovely but temporary.
Sometimes she tried to press a gift on me, and I would feel
pangs about declining. She really was just being nice, but
Ernest had his pride, and I didn't want to risk stirring anything
up.

Try as I might to convince Ernest of Kitty's virtues, he
was intent on disliking her. She was too decorative, he said,
and bent on her own comfort, but I wondered if he was actually threatened by her independence. She had a job as a fashion

and dance correspondent for several magazines in the States, and though Harold paid for her charming apartment on the rue de Monttessuy, it was because he insisted on their having separate living quarters, and he was dripping with family money on both sides. Kitty had inherited money, too, and could have supported herself. She was also incredibly confident, with a way of moving and talking that said she didn't need anyone to tell her she was beautiful or worthwhile. She knew it for herself, and that kind of self-possession unsettled Ernest.

I fought for my afternoons with Kitty, even though this created tension at home, because it was the first time since St Louis that I'd gained a friend who was exclusively mine. Gertrude and Sylvia had always belonged to Ernest. He was unapologetically territorial about them. With Alice and Maggie Strater and even Shakespear, I couldn't quite seem to move beyond the realm of artist's wife. Kitty was connected to Harold, whom Ernest now saw often, but she also very much had her own life. And she had sought me out.

'You're a very *American* girl, aren't you?' she had said on one of our first outings.

'What? You're American too,' I said.

'Not like you. It's in everything you say, how direct and simple you are.'

'Egads,' I said. 'You're just finding a polite way to notice how I don't fit here in Paris.'

'You don't,' she said. 'But that's good. We need your sort around to tell us the truth about ourselves.'

Besides Ernest's grumbling, the only continuing difficulty in my friendship with Kitty was the way she continued to offer me gifts, even after I tried, at length, to explain the complexities of Ernest's pride.

'It's just a trifle,' she pressed. 'Why would he mind?'

'He simply would. I'm sorry.'

'It sounds like caveman stuff to me. If he keeps you in animal skins, tending the cook fire, no other man will see you, let alone want you.'

'It's nothing so brutish as all that. We have to economize. It's not such a great sacrifice.'

'All right, I understand. But that's my beef with marriage. You suffer for *his* career. What do you get in the end?'

'The satisfaction of knowing he couldn't do it without me.'

She turned from the beaded handbag she was admiring and fixed her pale blue eyes on me. 'I adore you, you know. Don't change a whit.'

It was shockingly unmodern – and likely naïve too – but I did believe any sacrifices and difficulties in our life were worth it for Ernest's career. It was why we'd come to Paris after all. But it wasn't easy to watch my clothes falling to threads and not feel embarrassed particularly since women were dressed so chicly just then. But I honestly don't think I could have kept up with them, even if we hadn't been so strapped.

Our apartment was so cold I often had a dull ache in my sinuses. We kept Bumby's crib in the warmest corner, but he fell ill even so. We passed a crouping cough back and forth for weeks that spring, which troubled his sleep. He woke crying, wanting to nurse. Feeding him could be a joy in the daylight when I was well rested, but at night it drained my energy away. It was at these times I most needed my outings with Kitty, or walks in the thin sunshine with Stella Bowen and Julie, who were also becoming good companions.

I also tried to slip out of the house for at least an hour each day to practice piano. Money was so tight we couldn't afford to buy or even rent one as we had before, so I played a badly tuned upright in the damp cellar of a music shop nearby. I had to light a candle to see the sheet music, and my fingers often cramped with cold. Sometimes it didn't seem worth the effort, but I kept it up anyway, because I wasn't ready to let this part of myself go.

In the meantime, Ernest was working better than ever. The pressure he felt after escaping Toronto for Paris seemed to have been absolutely essential in stirring him, because he was writing strongly and fluidly, with almost no second guessing. The stories were coming so well he could barely keep up with them.

He continued to do editing work at the *Transatlantic*, and though he was still full of criticism for his boss, Ford went on championing Ernest's work just the same. When Ernest told Ford he was worried it would take years and years to get his name established, Ford told him that was nonsense.

'It will happen for you very quickly. When Pound showed me your work, I knew immediately I'd publish anything of yours. Everything.'

Ernest took the compliment rather abashedly and tried to be kinder about Ford, particularly since he was trying to get him to publish *The Making of Americans*, a novel of Gertrude's, which had been languishing in her desk since 1911. Ford finally agreed to publish the thing serially, and Gertrude was ecstatic. *Transatlantic Review* was gradually becoming more important and widely read among their set, and it would be her first major publication. In the April issue, her work would appear alongside a selection from Joyce's new work in progress, the book that would later become *Finnegans Wake*, several pieces from Tristan Tzara, and a new story of Ernest's called 'Indian Camp', which gruesomely detailed a woman giving birth and her coward husband slitting his own throat because he couldn't stand hearing her cries. He was very pleased with it because he'd been able to take a memory from his childhood – watching his father deliver an Indian woman's baby – and stitch it to another thing he'd seen – the refugee couple on the Karagatch Road – and make a single powerful story.

'Joyce knows this trick,' he said to me late one afternoon after returning from work on the issue. 'He made Bloom up, and Bloom's the best there is. You have to digest life. You have to chew it up and love it all through. You have to live it with your eyes, really.'

'You talk about it so well.'

'Yes, but you can talk and talk and not get it right. You have to do it.'

The April issue also contained the first important reviews of his *Three Stories and Ten Poems*, which were generally rapturous about Ernest's talent and style. He was inventing something new, they said, and was a writer to watch. I was so happy to see his reputation growing finally. Everywhere we went it seemed people wanted to be near him. Walking the boulevard with him at night, past the thrum of talk and tinny music, someone would call out his name and we'd have to stop and have a friendly drink before moving on to another café where the same thing would happen. Everyone had a joke for him or some bit of news, and our circle of acquaintances was increasing day by day.

John Dos Passos, who Ernest had met just after he began working for the Red Cross in Italy, was back in Paris, riding the wave of his literary success and always ready for a good time. Donald Stewart showed up around this time too. He was a humorist who would one day go on to be famous for screenplays like *The Philadelphia Story*, but for the time being, he was just a funny guy standing near the bar in a very smart cream-colored suit. Ernest was proud of his slovenly writer's uniform, but I could occasionally be caught admiring crisply pressed trousers. Don's were perfect. He was also nice looking in a boyish, clean-shaven way, with clear blue eyes that became very animated when he laughed.

When Ernest introduced us, Don was wonderfully familiar with me right away. 'You have beautiful hair,' he said. 'What an unusual color.'

'Thank you. You have beautiful clothes.'

'My mother liked clothes. And etiquette.'

'And ironing boards?'

'I have a mean way with an iron, I must admit.'

We talked a bit more, and I was having such a pleasant time, it took me a good half an hour to realize that Ernest had set-tled himself at a table nearby. I didn't recognize anyone he was with, including the beautiful woman sitting by his side. She was slender and lovely, with very close-cropped dark-blond hair. Her body seemed slim and boyish under a long sweater, but somehow her hair passed her *beyond* boyishness, making her all the more feminine. The instant I saw her, I felt a sharp chill run through me — even before Ernest leaned over and whis-pered something to her. She laughed throatily, arching her long pale neck.

'Are you quite all right?' Don said. 'You've gone white.'

'Oh. Quite fine, thanks.'

He'd followed my eyes to Ernest and the woman. I'm sure everything was quite plain to him, but he smoothly deflected the moment. 'That's Duff Twysden,' he said. 'Lady Twysden, actually. They say she married some British count. Count or viscount or lord twice removed. I can't keep royalty straight.'

'Yes, well. Who can?'

I looked over at Ernest just as his eyes came up. The briefest crackling of suspicion passed between us, and then he got up and came over.

''Scuse me, Don. I see you've met my wife.'

'Charmed,' Don said, before Ernest took my elbow and led me to the table where Duff sat expectantly.

'Lady Twysden,' he said, making the introductions. 'Or do you prefer Smurthwaite these days?'

'Doesn't matter as long as it's Duff.' She half-stood, extending a hand. 'How d'you do?'

I was just collecting myself to say something pleasant when Kitty appeared out of the crowd. 'God, I'm glad to see you,' she said. 'Come let's get a drink.'

Harold was just behind her and looking not at all well. He was pale and his upper lip was damp.

'Has something happened?' I asked, when we were nearer the bar.

'Harold's leaving me.'

'You're joking.'

'I wish I were.' She lit a cigarette and stared at the tip for a moment before inhaling with short stabs of breath. 'Some restlessness has come in and taken him over. We always said we'd give each other every freedom. Funny, though, when it comes you don't want it.'

'Is it someone else?'

'Isn't it always?' She sighed. 'It's probably the new book, too. He wants to reinvent everything.'

'I'm going to London soon. I wanted you to know.'

'Oh, Kitty, really? Is it as bad as all that?'

'Looks like it,' she said. 'I have some things for you I can't bear to pack. I'll come over to the house.'

'I don't care about the dresses. I don't need them.'

'Nonsense.'

'You know what Ernest will say.'

She huffed, blowing out smoke. 'Yes, but he hasn't a clue

how hard it is to be a woman.' She tossed her head in Duff's direction. 'It's brutal out here, isn't it? The competition isn't just younger. They care more. They throw everything they've got into it.'

I didn't quite know what to say. Kitty was one of the most poised and self-confident women I'd ever known, and here she was knocked off her feet and set spinning. It made me want to break Harold's neck.

'Do you want to go home?' I asked.

'I can't wither like a schoolgirl and have everyone feeling sorry for me. I'd die first. Let's have champagne,' she said, putting on her bravest face. 'Lots and lots of champagne.'

I stayed by Kitty's side for the rest of the evening, but kept one eye on Ernest too. This Duff character was just too lovely and too familiar. She and Ernest talked so freely you'd think they'd known each other for years, and I felt newly vulnerable after hearing Kitty's news. The worst events always have the thrust of accidents, as if they come out of nowhere. But that's just lack of perspective. Kitty was blindsided, but Harold had likely been plotting his escape for months. I couldn't help but wonder if this could happen to me too. Just how long had Duff been in the picture, anyway?

Sometime after midnight, when I just couldn't stay awake another moment, I excused myself from Kitty and got Ernest's attention. 'It's time to get your poor wife to bed,' I said. 'I'm nearly falling over.'

'Poor Cat,' he said. 'Go on home, then. Do you want me to find someone to walk with you?'

'You want to stay?' I asked sharply. Duff turned politely away.

'Of course. What's the matter? I'm not the one who's beat, right?'

My voice left me altogether, then, but Kitty appeared, to save me. 'I'll mind your wife, Hem. You stay and have a good time.' She gave him a steely, challenging look, but he didn't bite.

'That's a good chap, Kitty. Thanks.' He stood and gave me a brotherly squeeze on the arm. 'Get some rest.'

I nodded in a kind of trance while Kitty grabbed me firmly by the arm and led me away. When we were outside, I started to cry quietly. 'I'm so embarrassed,' I said.

Kitty gave me a firm, buck-up sort of embrace. 'He's the one who should be embarrassed, darling. Her too. They say she has to keep scores of men around because she can't pay her own bills.'

'Duff,' I said. 'Who calls themselves such a thing?'

'Exactly. I'd bet good money that even someone with as little sense as Hem wouldn't leave a woman like you for that number. C'mon. Chin up.'

'You've been so good to me, Kitty. I can't tell you how much I'll miss you.'

'I know. I'm going to miss you too, but what choice do I have? All I can do is run off to London and hope Harold chases me.'

'Will he?'

'I honestly don't know.'

When I got home, Bumby was awake and gumming tearfully on a small rubber ring.

Marie looked at me apologetically. 'He had a terrible dream, I think. Poor dear. He wouldn't let me soothe him.'

'Thank you for staying so late, Marie.' When she'd gone I tried to settle Bumby, but he was whiny and fitful. It took me over an hour to get him back to sleep, and by the time I fell into bed myself, I was so tired I felt delirious – but I couldn't rest. I'd been feeling so strong and content with our life, but Kitty was right: the competition was getting fiercer all the time. Paris was filled with enticing women. They sat in the cafés with their fresh faces and long lovely legs and waited for something outrageous to happen. Meanwhile, my body had changed with motherhood. Ernest claimed to love my fleshier hips and breasts, but with so much else to look at, he could easily lose interest in me. Maybe he had already – and what could I do about it? What did anyone do?

When Ernest came home sometime later, I was still awake and so tired I began to cry. I couldn't help myself.

'Poor Mummy,' he said, climbing into bed beside me and holding me close. 'I didn't know you were so worn down. Let's get you a nice long break.'

'God yes,' I said, feeling a flood of relief. 'Someplace very far from here.'

TWENTY-NINE

Our 'someplace very far,' was the little village of Schruns in the Austrian Vorarlberg. We arrived just before Christmas, 1924, and from our first day, we felt more at home there than we could have imagined. For less than half of what we spent each week in Paris, we had two comfortable rooms at the Taube Hotel and a nanny, Tiddy, to take Bumby around. There were thirty-eight kinds of beer and red wine and brandy and kirsch and champagne. The air was champagne. Bumby could breathe better at Schruns; we all could. Tiddy would pull him through the village on his wooden sleigh while Ernest worked, or tried to, in our room when the breakfast was done, and I practiced downstairs at the piano, which was there all for my having in the warm room. In the afternoons, after hard cheese and sausages and heavy bread and sometimes oranges, we'd ski.

We did a lot of skiing. A retired professional skier, Walther Lent, had opened a school and we were his students. For weeks on end, there was only the pure white predictable crispness of snow. We'd hike for hours, up and up, because what good was it if we weren't at the very top of something, with no one else around and no tracks or memory of anyone else, anywhere? Skiing this way took strength — incredible strength and stamina. There weren't any lifts or trams. We carried our skis on our shoulders and anything else we'd need in rucksacks. To my great surprise, I could actually do it. Leaving Paris had been the best thing for me. I was sleeping well, I had help with the baby, and the fresh air and exercise had made me feel stronger and more fit than ever. On our slow climb up the long valley we'd see ptarmigan and deer and marten, sometimes a white Alpine fox. On the way down, we were aware only of virgin snow; the plunge and flight of glacier runs, great clouds of powder rising from our skis. I was the better skier but Ernest was the better devourer of anything new — new air, new mantle of eggshell snow. We dropped and dropped. We flew.

If you leaned from our second-story window at the Taube, pushing the top of your body out and holding onto the stucco walls with your fingertips, you could see no fewer than ten Alps dipped in snow.

'How do you like that?' Ernest said the first time he tried this trick and then stood aside for me.

'I like it very much,' I said. By then he'd come and pressed himself against me, his arms coming full around until it was really him holding me there in case I should want to fall. 'I like it very much,' I said again, because I had two strong arms and ten Alps in sight. He pulled me into the room and we lay down on the featherbed and made love. And I was reminded of what was best about us. How very easy and natural we could be as bodies, with no sharp angles or missteps and no need for talking. How in bed, as nowhere else, he was my favorite animal and I was his.

Behind the hotel there was a low hill where I practised my skiing in the new snow while Ernest tried to work without much success. For the work alone he was missing Paris, the busyness of the city and his routine. Generally, if the work wasn't good, nothing was, but at Schruns there was a softer bunting around the day. I could ski on the hill and know that he was looking out over the pasture, the farms and fields and feeling tight in his head but not unhappy. And sometimes he was watching me race straight down the hill, low on my skis, coming fast at the hotel and turning sharply at the last minute.

Ernest grew a fierce black beard that winter and looked magnificent in it. The work wasn't coming, but there were rounds of bowling and poker in the evenings, by the fire, and Schnapps made from mountain gentians that felt hot and tonicy and blue on your tongue and in your throat, just what you'd think drinking violets might be like. The hotel's dining room was thick with smoke in the evenings. After dinner, I'd play the Bach or Haydn I'd practiced earlier in the day. Ernest would read Turgenev in his chair by the fire, or play poker and smoke or talk about the war with Herr Nels, our proprietor. The woodsmoke and the wool, the snow and the lovemaking — all of it warm and winding about us, building the good winter.

The only thing that wasn't perfect during this time was Ernest's worrying about his career. It didn't reassure him that all his friends were convinced of his talent, or that the reviews of *Three Stories and Ten Poems* had been nearly ecstatic. It was a little book, not at all on scale with his big dreaming. He'd sent his family several copies hot off the press, and they'd been returned with a chilly letter from Ernest's father saying he and Grace weren't comfortable having such material in the house. It was vulgar and profane at best. They wanted great things for him and hoped he would someday find a way to use his God-given talent to write something with strong morals and virtues. Until he did, he shouldn't feel compelled to send anything he published home. The letter stung Ernest to the core. No matter what he said, he still deeply wanted his family's approval.

'To hell with them, anyway,' he said, but he kept the letter, folding it carefully and putting it in the drawer where he stored all of his important correspondence. *Families can be vicious*, he was fond of saying, and I could see what he meant clearly now. I could also see how he used the damage, pushing against it, redoubling his efforts to show them he didn't need their love or endorsement. He would keep fighting until he had *Vanity Fair* and the *Saturday Evening Post*. Until an American editor took a chance on him and he had a book, a real one, published the way he'd always dreamed.

It didn't help his mood that things were taking off for Harold. He'd finished his novel when he said he would, sent it directly off to Boni and Liveright. And they'd taken it. We got the news just before we left for Schruns. Harold had come to the apartment fairly bursting with excitement. 'What do you know, Hem. Did you ever think it would hit for me?'

'Sure, why not?' Ernest had said. He was seething with professional jealousy, of course, but he held his tongue and behaved, opening a bottle of brandy and bringing the siphon over. 'Anderson's been trying to get me to go with Liveright too. I have a handful of good stories, and I'm thinking of setting them off with the sketches I've been doing, the miniatures.'

'They're just the place to do it,' Harold said. 'What are you waiting for?'

'I don't know. There are other fish in the sea, right? What about Scribner's? Or Henry Doran?'

'Wherever you land, you'll do what's best. It's all going to happen for you too. You'll see.'

I knew with a certainty that Ernest would have leaped at the chance to have any major publisher do the book, but with a lot of cajoling from me and Harold and Sherwood too, Ernest finally mailed the manuscript off to Boni and Liveright just before Christmas. He'd settled on the title, *In Our Time*, because he'd tried to get to the heart of life at this very moment, with all its violence and chaos and strange beauty. It was the best work he'd done, and he felt good about having sent it off into the world, but the wait for a response was torturing him. When forwarded mail arrived for us at the Taube, Ernest raked through it impatiently looking for one thing; an acceptance letter. It was all he'd ever wanted.

At the end of February, Herr Lent led us up the valley to the Madlenerhaus, an Alpine station that stayed open even in the late winter. It had a good simple kitchen and a dormitory that rocked, in high winds, like the berth of a great ship. From there, we could hike five hundred meters up the slope and plunge down again along the Silvretta, a pristine glacier, our skis kicking up untouched powder. After skiing all day we'd drop into bed at night exhausted.

'Let's not ever go back,' I said to Ernest one night as we lay in our bunk in the dormitory listening to snow and wind and nothing else.

'All right,' he said, holding me more tightly. 'Aren't we lucky to be so in love? No one thought we'd make it this far. No one was on our side at all, do you remember that?'

'Yes,' I said, and felt a small chill. We couldn't hide from the world forever.

After three days, we came back down the mountain to find two telegrams waiting for Ernest. One was from Sherwood and the other was from Horace Liveright and both said the same thing: *In Our Time* would be a book. They were offering a two-hundred-dollar advance against royalties and were sending a contract soon.

It was an epic moment, one we'd never forget — and somehow the skiing seemed ineluctably part of it, as if we *had* to trek up nearly to the sky and fly down again to get this news. It was the end of Ernest's struggle with apprenticeship, and an end to other things as well. He would never again be unknown. We would never again be this happy.

The next day we boarded a train back to Paris.

THIRTY

It rained non stop that spring, but even in the rain, Paris was Ernest's smorgasbord. He knew it all and loved to walk through it, at night especially, dropping into cafés to see who was there and who wasn't. He was recognizable everywhere with his long, unruly hair and tennis shoes and patched jacket, the quintessential Left Bank writer. It was ironic to see him become the very sort of artist that had made him cringe two years before, and a little painful for me too. I missed him and I wasn't sure I *recognized* him all the time, but I didn't want to hold him back. Not when things were finally beginning to hit for him.

If Ernest was changing, Montparnasse was too. American tourists flooded the scene hoping to get a glimpse of a real bohemian while the usual suspects grew wilder and stranger for the new audience. Kiki was one of the most famous artist's models around, and Man Ray's lover and muse. She could often be seen at the Dôme or Rotonde with her pet mouse. It was small and white, and she wore it attached to her wrist with a delicate silver chain. The fleshy redhead Flossie Martin held court in front of the Select shouting obscenities to locals and tourists alike. Bob McAlmon vomited neatly in the flowerbeds of all the best cafés and then ordered another absinthe. That absinthe was illegal deterred no one, and the same held true for opium and cocaine. Ernest and I had always been more than happy enough with alcohol, but there was the very real feeling, for many, of needing to up the ante – to feel more and risk more. It grew harder and harder to shock anyone.

Duff Twysden was one of the wilder girls on the café scene. She drank like a man and told a good, filthy joke and could talk to absolutely anyone. She made her own rules and didn't give a damn who knew it. When we returned from Austria, Ernest began to see more of her than ever. Sometimes they were joined by her fiancé, Pat Guthrie. Pat was a famous drunk and often wasn't well enough to leave their flat without causing a scene. I felt some relief knowing Duff was attached and, ostensibly, in love – but then again that didn't always mean what it should.

Duff was very keen for company at night and so was Ernest, and so they naturally gravitated toward each other. I worried about her a lot, but when he finally brought her by the sawmill to spend time with all of us, she crouched right down on the floor in front of Bumby.

'Hullo there. You're very handsome, aren't you?'

Bumby laughed and toddled behind me; he'd just learned to walk over the winter, and when he ran, he held his chubby legs so stiffly you thought he'd fall headlong into something.

'How very classic,' Duff said watching him with a laugh. 'Why do all the men run away from me? I must be terrifying indeed.'

'You don't know the half of it,' Ernest said.

For the rest of the visit, she sat at my table and made no pretensions about anything. She was well-bred but not fussy, and had a broad, raw laugh that moved everything with it. I liked her. I didn't want to, but I did.

Around this same time, Kitty returned from London and wrote to invite me to tea.

'What's she doing back?' Ernest said. 'I thought we were free of that gold-plated bitch.'

'Be fair!' I snapped.

'I am. I know a bitch when I see one.'

I tried to ignore him. He was never going to change his mind about Kitty, no matter what I said or did. It was one of his qualities that most frustrated me, how once you had a black cross in his book, you were pretty much done for. I'd have much rather not had to fight with him about her, but I was going to see Kitty anyway.

Unfortunately, the only nice dresses I owned were ones she herself had given me, and since I wouldn't turn up in her castoffs, I went in a shabby skirt and sweater. As soon as I entered her apartment, I regretted the choice. She'd also invited two sisters from the Midwest, Pauline and Jinny Pfeiffer, and they were dressed to perfection. Pauline, I quickly learned, had come to Paris to work for *Vogue*. She was impossibly chic, and wore a coat made of hundreds of chipmunk skins sewn painfully together, and a pair of champagne-colored shoes that might have been the finest I'd ever seen. Jinny was the prettier of the two with these incredible almond-shaped eyes, but Pauline had something else, an almost boyish exuberance. She was slim through the hips and shoulders, with sharply cut dark bangs falling nearly to her eyebrows.

The two sisters were the daughters of a wealthy landowner from Arkansas, but they'd grown up in St Louis. Kitty was just beginning to tell me about how close Pauline and Kate Smith had been at one time when Harold and Ernest came in from a boxing workout, sweaty and laughing.

I was surprised to see Harold – were he and Kitty on again? – but she quickly shot me a look that said, *don't ask*. Meanwhile, why had Ernest come if not to harass Kitty? You'd think he would have tried to avoid her. I'd wanted an intimate reunion with my good friend, not tension and awkwardness, and definitely not Ernest and Harold sniffing around these striking new women as if they were exotic animals in a zoo exhibit.

As the afternoon wore on, Harold and Ernest both drank with vigor. I followed Kitty into the kitchen for more tea just as Ernest began to flirt with Jinny.

'I say,' Ernest said loudly to Harold. 'I think I'd like to take this girl out on the town.'

'I wouldn't give that a thought,' Kitty said to me in a low voice. 'Jinny doesn't go in for boys.'

'Really?' I said. From where I stood, Jinny was doing a pretty good imitation of a vamp. She'd turned her almond eyes on Ernest and batted them expertly.

'She just likes to hone her skills occasionally. She finds men amusing, I think.'

'It must be nice to be in such control,' I said. 'And what about you? What's happened with Harold?'

'Well, he did follow me to London, after a fashion. I'd all but given up. He says he's not sure what he wants.'

'But he missed you.'

'Sure he missed me. They always do when you go running. How long can it last, though, now I'm here?'

'Why does everything have to be so complicated?' I said.

'I have no earthly idea,' Kitty said. 'But clearly it does.'

Back out in the living room, Harold sat on the davenport alone with his feet up, lighting a thick cigar, while Jinny and Ernest and Pauline stood on the rug in front of him.

'I could take you both out,' Ernest said to the girls. 'I've two arms after all.'

'Not really,' Harold said noticing me. 'Your wife owns one.'

'All right then. I'll take Jinny — as long as she wears her sister's coat.'

Everyone laughed, and it was one of those domino moments. That laugh would eventually set off an entire series of events, but not yet. It just stood there in the room, tipping and tipping, but not falling.

Not falling yet. Not quite.

Over the coming months, in the spring of 1925, our circle of friends continued to shift. The change was subtle at first, and each instance seemed to have little to do with the others, but our old set was being replaced with richer and wilder specimens. Pound and Shakespear had begun spending more and more time at Rapallo, and were living there nearly all year round now. Gertrude and Ernest had begun to quarrel about things small and large. He seemed flummoxed about why, but I think he was changing too fast for her comfort.

'Alice has never liked me,' he said one evening when we were leaving their salon. 'And now she's trying to turn Stein around to her thinking.'

'Nonsense. Alice loves you.'

'Then she has a fine way of showing it. She all but called me a careerist tonight. My head's growing too fast apparently.'

'Gertrude loves you too. She's just worried.'

'I don't need her chastising, and why is she the great teacher anyway? She's a tastemaker more than anything. I mean, what has she done really?'

It made me sad to think about the professional wedge growing between these two very good friends, and I wasn't sure what it meant for me. The new set was made up of very wealthy artists who were utterly focused on living well, having the very best of everything. We were still squeezing by on less than three thousand a year, and although it seemed to me we had nothing in common with these people, they were interested in us, or in Ernest at least.

Pauline Pfeiffer was one of these. She was a working girl, ostensibly, drawing a paycheck from *Vogue* – but she had a trust fund on top of this, and it no doubt helped to keep her in the clothes she wore so well. This was Chanel's heyday and Pauline had written about her new collection for *Vogue* with a fervency that bordered on obsession.

'Chanel has changed the silhouette for good, you know,' she said to a group of us one night at the Deux Magots. 'We'll never be the same.'

All the other women at the table nodded as if Pauline had predicted the second coming, but I was left cold by fashion. My clothes never behaved, and I felt that no one could change my silhouette unless I stopped eating altogether.

Kitty had known Pauline for ages, and was very keen for us to be friends. I didn't think we'd have the slightest thing in common, but the first time Kitty brought her over to our apartment, I was pleasantly surprised to find that she was awfully bright and funny. She also seemed eager for me to like her.

'Kate Smith has said lovely things about you for years,' she said. 'It's so good to finally meet you.'

'When did you and Kate meet?'

'At the University of Missouri. We both majored in journalism.'

'I'm afraid Kate had her hooks into me far earlier,' I said. 'When we were nine she got me sick to the gills on stolen cigarettes.'

'Sounds like my girl. She would have been hard pressed to find ways to corrupt me. I was pretty far gone already.'

As we laughed I heard Ernest clear his throat from the bedroom. I was embarrassed that he wouldn't join us and tried to make excuses for him.

Pauline frowned a little at the door. It was only slightly ajar, but he was visible on the bed – not indisposed at all, just not interested in joining our party. 'I know all about husbands,' she said. 'I've studied them from afar for years.'

'No near brushes yourself?' I said.

'Very near, actually,' Kitty piped in.

'It doesn't matter. I'm free now,' she said. 'Swimmingly free, and it's lovely.'

'Don't talk to Hadley about freedom,' Kitty laughed. 'She has all sorts of theories and lectures prepared.'

I flushed and tried to explain myself, but Pauline changed the subject quickly and easily. 'Kitty says you're a whiz on the piano,' she said. 'Don't you have one here you could play for us?'

'Sadly no,' I said. 'I'm not a professional.'

'What does professional mean except that you play for others instead of yourself? Have you given concerts?'

'Not since I was in my twenties, and I didn't have the stomach for it even then.'

'It's important to test your nerve occasionally,' she said. 'It keeps you young.'

'You should play a concert,' Kitty said. 'It would be awfully good for you. Everyone would come.'

'I could get ill just thinking about it,' I said, laughing the idea off. But later that night, when we were lying in bed just before sleep, I told Ernest that I wanted a piano of my own. 'I didn't think I'd miss it so much,' I said. 'But I do.'

'I know, Cat. I'd love for you to have one. Maybe when the advance comes.'

'That's such a fine word, isn't it?'

'Yes, and "royalty" is another one, but don't go spending either just yet.'

'No, Tatie, I won't.' But I went to sleep happy just the same.

On a night in early May, Ernest and I were having a night out on our own at the Dingo when Scott Fitzgerald came over from the bar and introduced himself to us.

'You're Hemingway,' Fitzgerald said. 'Ford showed me a story of yours a few weeks back and I said, "Well there it is, isn't it? He's the real article."'

'I'm sorry I haven't read any of your books,' Ernest said.

'That's all right. I'm not sure I write them any more. Since my wife and I have come to Paris it's been a thousand parties and no work at all.'

Ernest squinted at him through the dim light. 'You can't finish anything that way.'

'Don't I know it? But Zelda loves to dance. You should meet her. She's spectacular.' His eyes turned to the dancefloor where several couples were in the midst of a sinuous-looking tango. 'I do have a novel just out. *The Great Gatsby.*'

'I'll look for it,' Ernest said. 'How are you holding up, waiting for the notices?'

'That's not so difficult for me. Not near as tricky as getting it down in the first place. And once I have it all, I can't seem to move on. Like this Gatsby. I know him so well, it's as if he's my child. He's dead and I'm still worried about him. Isn't that funny?'

'You're not working on anything now?' I asked, wondering if I could drum up the nerve to tell him I'd read one of his books. 'Apart from the dancing?'

He flashed his lovely teeth at me. 'No, but I will if you promise to admire every word extravagantly. Tell me, what do you think of me so far?'

An hour or so later, Ernest and I poured Scott into a taxi.

'I don't like a man who can't hold his liquor,' Ernest said when the car had pulled away. 'I thought he might pass out on the table.'

'He did look very green, didn't he? And he asked the most alarming personal questions. Did you hear him ask if I'd ever been in love with my father?'

'He asked me that too, and whether or not I was afraid of water, and if we'd slept together before the wedding. He's very odd, isn't he?'

He was odd, and that might have been our last meeting with Fitzgerald if he hadn't thought to hunt down our address and send a copy of *The Great Gatsby* as a gift. Ernest simply stowed it on a shelf after opening the package, and it might have been forgotten there if I hadn't been so curious to read it. It wasn't too bleak, at least not at first. And when things did get dire very quickly, I was already completely absorbed by the story.

After I devoured it, awfully impressed, I told Ernest to read it too. He finished it in one afternoon, declaring it a damned fine novel, then sent a note saying as much to Fitzgerald. We all met up a few nights later, at the Negre de Toulouse. Fitzgerald and Zelda were there when we arrived, and were well into a second bottle of champagne. Her edges were already blurred when she stood to shake our hands, and she looked as if she cultivated that – a fine blurriness. Her dress was a pale sheath of filmy layers, one over the next and it shifted dreamily around her as she sat. Her skin was fair and so was her waved hair, and all of her seemed to be the same color except for her mouth, which was painted very dark red, and cut a straight hard line.

Scott stood up as we approached their table and Zelda smiled strangely, narrowing her eyes. She wasn't beautiful, exactly, but her voice was – low and cultivated.

'How do you do?' she said, and then quickly turned to Ernest. 'Scott says you're the real thing.'

'Oh? He says you're spectacular.'

'Aren't you just darling, my darling?' she said, running her hand along the side of Scott's sculpted head. With this gesture, which could have been extravagantly silly, she and Scott slipped behind a private net into their own little world. Their eyes locked and they weren't with us any more, or with anyone in the café at all, but only with each other, awash in a long secret look.

Later we watched them dance the Charleston and the effect was the same. They didn't bounce wildly like the other couples; they were smooth as glass, their arms arcing back and forth as if on strings. Zelda's dress bubbled up as she moved and every so often she reached to pull it higher, past the tops of her garters. It was sort of shocking, but it didn't look as if she meant to shock anyone. She danced for herself and for Scott. They moved in one another's orbit, incredibly self-possessed, their eyes locked on each other.

'What do you think of her?' I asked Ernest.

'She's not beautiful.'

'No, but she has something, doesn't she?'

'I think she's crazy.'

'Not really?'

'Really,' he said. 'Have you looked into her eyes?'

At the end of the evening, they invited us to their flat in a fashionable Right Bank neighborhood off the Étoile. It was a rich building, you could see that right away, but when we got inside, the apartment itself was all chaos, with clothes and books and paper and baby things strewn everywhere. We pushed a great heap aside to make a place for ourselves on the sofa, but Scott and Zelda didn't seem embarrassed at all. They went on entertaining each other just as they had in the café, but more loudly. Things got so noisy, in fact, that we heard a child's crying from deep in the apartment, and then an English nanny came out bearing Scotty, their plump daughter. She was dressed in an elaborate bedtime costume with a fat bow listing to the side of her fine blond hair. Her face was prettily rumpled from her pillow.

'Oh, here's my precious,' Zelda said, rising to scoop the girl up. 'Aren't you just a little lamb stew?' The girl smiled sleepily and seemed pleased, but the moment Zelda sat with her in a gilded but shabby wing chair, she became so preoccupied with trying to catch whiffs of Scott and Ernest's conversation that the girl plopped right off her lap and onto the floor. Zelda didn't even seem to notice it happen. The nanny swooped in and spirited the now wailing Scotty off, and Zelda turned to me and said, 'What were you saying?' Her eyes were scattered-looking and strange, as if her mind were on another plane entirely. 'I'm dying for my Scotty to be a flapper, you know. Decorative and unfathomable and all made of silver.'

'She's adorable,' I said.

'Isn't she? She'll never be helpless. You can see that, can't you?' Her intensity was sudden and alarming.

'Yes,' I agreed and wondered if Ernest had been right. But who could separate real madness out from the champagne, which was ongoing and everywhere?

As near as I could tell, the party never stopped for those two. Less than a week later, they showed up at the sawmill apartment at six o'clock in the morning, still drunk from their night out. We were sound asleep when they started banging on the door and singing our names loudly. They didn't seem to care that we were in our pajamas. We made coffee but they didn't drink it. They laughed, and swore allegiance to some ballet artist they'd met in the café the night before but that we'd never heard of.

'Zelda's very sensitive to art, you know,' Scott said. 'She's not really of the earth at all, my girl.'

Zelda's face grew dramatically stricken. 'You're not going to tell them, are you?'

'Maybe we should, darling. They'll guess anyway.'

'Well, then.' Her eyes widened. 'A short time ago, I fell very much in love with another man. It nearly killed me and Scott too.'

Scott stood over her and a made a motion as if he was smoothing her hair without actually touching it. 'It nearly killed us but it *did* kill the fellow. So horrible. It was in all the papers. You must have read something of it.'

I shook my head and said, 'I'm so sorry you had to go through all of that. It does sound awful.'

'Yes, well,' Zelda said, snapping out of the moment as if an invisible director had called *Scene*. 'The man did want to die for me. And it's made Scott and me so much closer.'

Ernest flinched and stared into his coffee cup, saying nothing. I could tell that he hadn't quite made up his mind about these two. They certainly didn't seem our sort, but I wasn't sure I knew what our sort was any more. The rules seemed to be changing all the time.

'I knew she was off her cracker,' Ernest said once they'd gone, 'but now I wonder about him too. She's sucking him in. As if she's some sort of vampire.'

'She does seem to have Scott on a very short leash,' I said.

'I wouldn't stand for it.'

'You wouldn't have to,' I flared defensively.

'Now, Tatie. I didn't mean anything. You're not at all like Zelda. She's so jealous of Scott's work I think she'd be happy if he never wrote another word.'

'They couldn't afford it if he stopped writing.'

'He told me they spent 30,000 dollars last year, just swam through it all.'

'They live on 30,000 and we live on three. It's absurd.'

'I think we live better, don't you?'

'Yes,' I said emphatically.

From the other room, Bumby began to make stirring noises. I put down my coffee cup and stood to go and fetch him when Ernest said, 'I wouldn't want their life, but it's hard to see so much money simply wasted when we haven't got any. What if I borrowed from Scott for our trip to Pamplona in July?'

'Do you think we know them well enough for that?'

'Maybe not. We've got to get there somehow. Maybe Don Stewart?'

'He's a good egg.'

'Yes,' he said. 'I'll tell you what, though. Everyone seems to want in on this trip. It's getting very complicated.'

'It's still weeks away. How complicated could it be?'

'You don't want to know.'

THIRTY-ONE

In the railroad yard, the bulls came off the cars lowing and twisting and panicked, their eyes rolling back in their heads. They didn't know where to go, and it was hard to watch because we knew that by the end of the day they'd be dead. It was morning and quite cool for July. The dust rose up from their hooves and into the air, stinging our eyes as Ernest pointed out the hunched and muscled place between the shoulder blades where the sword had to hit just right.

'Yes, sir,' said Harold Loeb. 'That's the moment of truth.'

Ernest's face turned sour. 'What would you know about it?'

'Enough, I guess,' Harold said.

Just then Duff came up and put her hand in the crook of Ernest's arm. 'It's all wonderful, isn't it?' She looked at him like a child about to get everything her own way, her eyes crinkling and her smile wide. 'It makes a chap hungry, though. Who's going to feed me anyway?'

'Oh, all right. Sure,' Ernest said, still sour, and the two of them led the way to the café. Ernest wore his beret and a navy sweater and white pants, a dark scarf knotted at his throat.

Duff was perfect as ever with her long cotton sweater and Eton collar in pale green silk. Her hair was brushed back from her forehead and she walked straight and tall. Ernest matched her stride, his chin set in a proud way. He was probably still fuming at Harold, though trying to swallow it. From the back, the two of them together looked as if they belonged in a fashion magazine, and I saw Duff's fiancé, Pat Guthrie, noticing this too. Everyone noticed and poor Pat had been looking pained for days.

I felt sorry for Pat, though I wouldn't have wanted to live with him. He drank too much and could be a terrible bother when he did. Each afternoon he would start out sunny and pleased with everything. He liked to talk about popular music and could sing and dance with great energy and enthusiasm, but after three or four cocktails, something turned in him and he became snide and superior. If he kept on with it and Duff didn't send him away, he changed again, growing sullen and morose. I wondered how she kept up with his moods – or how he himself did. When he woke up, did he feel disgusted for the way he'd twisted one way and then another? Did he remember any of it?

'What do you say we drink through till dark?' Harold said, coming up beside me.

I smiled and took his arm, wanting to make him feel better, if only for a moment. Maybe if we stuck together, he'd try to make me feel better too. God knows I needed it.

The trip had started badly in Burguete, the week before, when we went to fish in the Irati – one of Ernest's favorite rivers in the world – and found it all ruined. The landlady at our hotel had tried to warn us that the good fishing was gone, but Ernest had laughed her off. The loggers had been there for the beech and pine, and when we got to the river we found it full of trash and floating debris. Dams had been broken through. Dead fish littered the banks and clogged the small pools. It was almost too much to take in, but we stuck it out, anyway, for several days, trying to go further out to the smaller streams. No one took a single fish.

Bill Smith, one of our old friends from Chicago was with us, having been lured over by Ernest's reports of world-class fishing, and for the bullfights that would follow. We hadn't seen him at all since the days of the Domicile. When Kenley and Ernest had their falling-out, tension trickled through all of our connections to the Smith clan, but we'd since picked up a fairly regular correspondence with Kate, who was back in Chicago, working as a journalist. And when Bill arrived to meet us in Paris, we were happy to find that he was the same as ever, full of lively stories and game for anything. He'd brought along every sure-fire fly he owned for the trip to Spain – all the old winners from summers fishing the Sturgeon or the Black up in Michigan, and I thought Ernest was going to cry when Bill opened his tackle box to show Ernest the flies, because they were useless.

In Pamplona, we still felt the wrongness. We had lots of friends around and it should have been jolly, but it wasn't. In Paris, Ernest and Duff had done their dance around each other, but it had been harmless for the most part. Something had come in to change it, and that something was Harold. He'd fallen hard for Duff and swept her off for a week at St Jean-de-Luz. When Kitty told me about the affair, she said Harold had been so strange of late she'd suspected something like this was coming. Now they were on the outs again. I'd never understood the arrangement Harold and Kitty made of love. I felt equally baffled and more than a little upset by the way Ernest had reacted so extremely to Harold's play for Duff.

He had no rights to her – none of this should have mattered at all to Ernest, but it did, and suddenly everyone knew it.

The morning the fights began, we all woke up at dawn to see the running of the bulls through the streets. The first time I'd watched, the summer I was pregnant with Bumby, it seemed to pass so quickly I couldn't remember what I'd seen. Now Bumby was safe in Paris with Marie Cocotte, and though I had wanted and needed a break from constant mothering, I didn't know quite how to feel as a free agent.

The streets were slick that morning. A light rain had fallen before dawn, and you could see the bulls struggle for traction against the cobblestones. One went down and struggled, craning its thick neck, its eyes rolling to white, and the whole thing seemed to pass in slow motion.

We were standing just behind a low wall, close enough to smell the animal sweat of the bulls and the excitement of everyone watching. Though some didn't watch, or couldn't.

'The bulls are almost prehistoric,' Ernest had told Bill in the café the night before. 'They've been bred for six hundred years to do what they do, to make this run to the arena, to gore what they can on the way to their own certain death. It's goddamned beautiful is what it is. Just wait till you see it for yourself.'

'I'm ready for it,' Bill said, but on the street with a clear view of everything, his conviction seemed to waver. While we watched, one of the young men ran too close to a thick bull and was shoved into the wall, just twenty feet away from where we stood. We could hear his arm snap at an angle behind his back. He cried out and tried to scramble up the wall, and the fear on his face was ugly to see.

'Too much for you, old boy?' Ernest said when he saw Bill look away.

'Maybe,' Bill said.

Ernest was standing near Duff and his color was very high. 'See there, now?' He pointed to the way the bull was coming at the young man, its square head ducked low. 'The bull's sight is very bad, but it smells him, and it's taking its time. Look at him now. He's coming, by God.'

'I can't believe this is sport for you,' Bill said to Ernest very quietly.

'What else would it be? It's life and death, brother, same as every day.'

The bull came forward, leading with the right horn, his thick head swung to one side so he looked like the devil, really, barreling at the scrambling caballero. But then a hand appeared from the other side of the wall. We couldn't see who had offered help, but it was enough. The caballero got enough traction to run up the wall and over, and then he was free. A small cheer went up in the crowd when he was safe.

'I suppose you're disappointed,' Bill said, looking at Ernest pointedly.

'Not at all.'

'Would he have gotten it very bad?' Duff asked.

'Maybe he would have. It can happen. I've seen it.'

'It's terribly exciting, isn't it?' she said.

'The best damned show there is.'

The last bull ran by us and then the *pastores* came behind the bulls with sticks, and then the rocket went off which meant all the bulls were safely in the ring.

'Beautiful,' Duff said.

I tried to remember if I thought them beautiful the first time, when Ernest had taught me the way he was teaching Duff now. My life had changed so much in the two short years since, but I remembered being excited and also strangely calm, because I was pregnant and felt safe, buffered from everything in the best way. My body was doing what it was meant to do, and these animals, they were living out their destinies, too. I could watch and not feel mauled or traumatized, but just sit next to Ernest and sew the clothes and blankets I was working on for the baby who would come in three months, no matter what happened on that day. And I remembered feeling very good about everything in the night, with the riau-riau dancing and the fireworks, though it was impossible to sleep for the noise.

We seemed to be the only Americans in Pamplona that first year. Ernest called it the Garden of Eden – but that had certainly changed now. Limousines brought society over from Biarritz. Uniformed chauffeurs opened doors all night and then waited near their cars for the revelers to tire and spill back into the leather cocoon stinking of champagne. But even with the rich coming in to spoil everything, it was spoiled already.

Harold was still crazy for Duff. You could see it at lunch when he went pale and Victorian with her one minute, and then began to fuss with the waiter to make sure she had her drink.

'Oh, it's all fine, darling,' she said. 'I'm still alive over here, at least for now.'

We were all crowded around an outdoor table, with Duff, Ernest and Harold on one side, and Pat, Bill and myself on the other. Pat had on a beautiful summer suit with a navy linen jacket. He'd gone out and found a beret just like Ernest's and wore it high on his forehead at an optimistic angle. And yet for all of Pat's civilized trimmings, the moment Harold became too conspicuously attentive to Duff, he snapped and grew belligerent.

'Give it a rest, Harold,' he barked. 'Go take a walk around the block.'

'Why don't you shut it,' Harold said. 'Or I'll tell you what, just have another drink.' He turned and shouted loudly behind him to no one, 'Bring this man a drink!'

Just then Don Stewart walked up looking cool and clean in gray flannels and a fresh white shirt. He glanced around the table, instantly sensing tension. 'Who died, men?'

'No one of consequence,' Ernest said.

'I suddenly have a terrible headache,' I said. 'I hope you'll all excuse me.'

I scooted around my side of the table and stood next to Don.

'Why don't you walk the poor kid home, Donald?' Ernest said.

'I'm fine,' I said. 'I'll be fine.'

'Nonsense,' Don said. 'You're pale as a ghost.'

Before we'd even gotten to the door, the gap had closed around the table and you couldn't even tell I'd been there. Ernest was sitting closer to Duff now, and Pat had squeezed around to be nearer too. Duff sat at the middle of it all like a floating island of meringue. She didn't even seem to notice.

I was grateful that Don had offered to shepherd me home. I was feeling terribly lonely, actually, and Don was easy to be with. Ever since we'd met the summer before, he sought my company when we were out in groups together. I felt he was a kindred spirit because he didn't quite fit in Paris either. He was a smart and savvy writer who'd gone to Yale, but in many ways he was still the boy who grew up on a farm outside of Columbus, Ohio. In Paris, everyone was so drastic and dramatic, flinging themselves into ditches for each other.

'I get why no one bothers with the usual rules,' he said to me once. 'I was in the war too, you know. Nothing looks or feels the same any more, so what's the point?' His face grew serious. 'Still, I miss good old-fashioned honorable people just trying to make something of life. Simply, without hurting anyone else. I know that makes me a sap.'

'You'd like to find a girl like your mother, I'll bet.'

'Maybe. I want things to make sense again. They haven't in a long time.'

I believed I'd understood him at the time, but now as Don walked me back to the hotel, I felt our connection even more strongly. I wanted things to make sense, too. More than anything.

'How are you holding up, pal?' he asked.

'Better than some, I expect. Poor Harold.'

'Poor Harold? What about Pat? He's the one with the claim to Duff.'

'Seems like they have a pretty loose arrangement to me,' I said. 'She drags Harold off to the Riviera for two weeks and then seems surprised that he's mooning over her like a sad calf, and even more that Pat's off his head about it. It's cruel.'

'I don't think she means to be cruel. She seems awfully sad under it all to me,' he said.

We'd come to a corner where the Mercado was breaking apart for the day. A woman was stacking baskets and another scooped blood-colored dried chilies into a canvas sack. Nearby, a little girl sat in the dirt, holding a chicken and singing to it. I slowed so we could watch her longer. Wonderfully black hair framed her heart-shaped face. She petted the chicken as she sang, and seemed to have it in a trance.

'You're looking at her like you want to gobble her up,' Don said. 'You must miss your Bumby.'

'Like crazy. It's easier when I don't think about him.

Sometimes I tell myself I'm two people. I'm his mother when I'm with him and someone else when I'm here, away.'

'Hem's Hadley.'

'Maybe. Or maybe I'm my own Hadley.' We could see the stippled arch of the Hotel La Perla and the tangled wall of bougainvillea. I stopped and turned to him. 'Why aren't you all bound up with Duff too? Everyone else is.'

'She's a dish, all right, and it would be easy enough to give in. She's asked me to take care of her bill at the hotel, you know, since she can't ask Harold now. Maybe she's asked Hem too.'

'I wouldn't be surprised.'

'Are you and Hem all right? He wouldn't be stupid enough to throw you over for that title in a nice fitting sweater, would he?'

I flinched. 'Maybe we should have a drink.'

'I'm sorry, I shouldn't have said it. I think the world of you two. If you guys can't make it, what chance do the rest of us have?'

'You really are a peach, Don,' I said, and moved forward to kiss him on the cheek. His skin was shaved clean as a baby's and he smelled clean, like tonic.

'You might be the best girl there is,' he said with feeling, and returned the kiss. His lips were dry and chaste on my cheek, but then he moved ever so slightly and kissed me on the lips. When he pulled away, his eyes were moist and questioning. 'I don't suppose you love me, too, just a little?'

'I wish I did. It might balance things out.' I put my arms around his neck and held him close for a moment, feeling the sadness and confusion, all mixed up together in him. 'This place has us all going crazy.'

'You're not angry with me?'

'No,' I said. 'We're better friends now, I think.'

'Isn't that a nice way to say it? I knew I wasn't wrong about you.' He pulled away and brushed the hair out of my eyes. 'I hope Hem knows what he has.'

'Me too,' I said, and went into the hotel. Inside, the proprietress was placing a cloth over her songbird's cage.

'He doesn't like the rockets,' she said as she settled the blanket more closely around the bars. 'They make him tear at his own feathers. Have you seen this?'

'I have, Señora.' I passed her on my way to the staircase. 'Can you please send brandy up?'

She looked behind me to see who might be coming along, so I added, 'Just one glass.'

'Is the señora well?

'Not very,' I said. 'But the brandy will help.'

THIRTY-TWO

When I woke the next morning, Ernest was already up and gone. I'd heard him come in late in the night but I didn't stir and didn't speak to him. By seven I was washed and dressed and down in the hotel's small café where Ernest was finishing his coffee.

'I've ordered you *oeufs au jambon*,' he said. 'Are you hungry?'

'Starved,' I said. 'How'd it end last night?'

'Good and tight,' he said.

'Good and tight, or just tight?'

'What are you getting at?'

'Nothing.'

'Like hell,' he said. 'Why don't you say it?'

'I haven't even had coffee,' I said. 'Do we really need to quarrel?'

'We needn't do anything. There isn't time anyway.'

Bill came downstairs then and pulled up a chair. 'I'm starved,' he said.

'That's going around,' Ernest said. He signaled the waiter over and asked for another plate for Bill and café au lait, and then signed the bill. 'I'm going to arrange for our tickets. I'll see you up there.'

When he was gone, Bill looked sheepish.

'What really happened last night?'

'Nothing I want to remember,' he said.

'Don't tell me then.'

'I don't know all of it, anyway. Harold said something to Pat and then Hem flared, and called Harold something terrible. It wasn't pretty.'

'I would guess not.'

'Don showed up and tried to straighten things out, but it was too late. Harold had called Ernest out in the street to settle it.'

'Harold did? It wasn't the other way around?'

'No. And that was something, really.'

'Is Harold all right?'

'Right as rain. They never touched each other.'

'Thank God.'

'Apparently Hem offered to hold Harold's glasses for him and that broke the spell. They both laughed and felt like stupid bastards for even starting it up.'

'What's wrong with all of us, Bill? Can you tell me that?'

'Hell if I know,' he said. 'We drink too much for starters. And we want too much, don't we?'

'What is it we want exactly?' I said, feeling a stir of melancholy and confusion. I wondered how Bill was making sense of the way Ernest was throwing himself so obviously at Duff. What *could* he think? What could he say?

'Everything, of course. Everything and then some.' He scratched his chin and then tried a joke: 'My headache today proves it.'

I studied him for a moment. 'If this is a festival, why aren't we happy?'

He cleared his throat and looked away. 'We shouldn't miss the amateurs, right? Hem says it's the best show for your money and that I should get right in.'

I sighed. 'You don't have to prove anything to him. You didn't seem to go in for the running.'

'No,' he said, seeming slightly ashamed. 'But I'm ready to give it another go. I'm not dead yet.'

'Why does everyone keep saying that?'

'I don't know,' he said. 'It's just one of those things.'

The amateurs had long been Ernest's favorite element of the fiesta. For years he'd been practicing veronicas with everything from the curtains to my old coat, and getting good at them. Now he could bulldog the bulls, spinning away at the last moment. Afterward he'd be high and happy, and practice some more in our room at the hotel with the cape he'd bought from a shop well off the square that didn't cater to tourists. The cape was heavy red serge with simple black braid as a border all the way around. He had started collecting corks for the bottom of it, because it was the corks that allowed the matador to really control the cape, and swing it well and wide.

When it was time for the amateurs that morning, he took the cape with him as he climbed down into the ring with several dozen eager men and boys all ready to test their wits. Bill went too, but Harold stayed put for the moment, a few seats down from Duff.

'Pat's still pretty green this morning,' Duff said when I took my seat beside her. 'It was a long night.'

'So I heard.'

'We missed you, you know. Everything's more fun with you along.'

I gave her a sharp look, thinking she was likely putting me

on, but her face was open and warm. That was the thing about Duff, she was a wreck with men, but a good chap all the way around, and she had her own code. I didn't believe she'd actually sleep with Ernest even if he'd wanted to — because she liked me and knew being a wife was hard business. She'd been married twice already and was set to marry Pat if they ever pulled together the money for it. She told me once that she'd never been very good at marriage but that she didn't seem to be able to stop giving it a go.

Down in the ring, the picadors had pretty good control of things, so the action seemed light and fairly harmless. There was only one bull in the ring at a time, and this first was caramel colored and slow moving. It came along and shoved its foreleg against Bill's rump, and he fell to one side like a character in a cartoon. It had everyone laughing. Ernest was just getting into the spirit of things when Harold climbed past us and got down into the ring too.

'Oh, Harold,' Duff said to no one in particular because he looked like a caricature of a rich and helpless American in his pale yellow Fair Isle sweater and snow-white sneakers. We both watched him. 'I've told him there's nothing between us, you know.'

'I'm not sure he hears it,' I said, trying to be as delicate as possible.

'Men hear what they like and invent the rest,' she said.

Once Harold had reached the ring, he looked up to where we were and smiled broadly. The caramel bull was near him and getting nearer, and Harold dodged to one side to avoid the horns, as everyone did. The bull trotted past and then whirled to come again, and that's when Harold grabbed onto the horns and let the bull carry him for a few paces. It was like watching a well-rehearsed circus act. Harold had to be as surprised by his success as anyone, but when the bull set him down again, light as a feather, he turned back to us, looking jubilant.

'Hem doesn't like this one bit,' Duff said. My eyes followed hers to where Ernest stood in the ring watching Harold. His expression was grim. A picador passed within a foot of him, but he didn't even seem to notice.

'He can't stand another man besting him,' I said, but Duff and I both knew that Ernest had been angry with Harold all week, ever since he found out about the lover's tryst in St Jean-de-Luz.

The next bull in the ring was slimmer and quicker. He moved like a cat, loping first toward one wall then another, changing direction on a dime. One local with a dark shirt got too close and was shoved to his knees. The bull reared his head around and the man fell further and was trampled. Everyone came around to distract the bull. Ernest had him for a moment by swinging his cape wide to one side. Other men waved their arms and called out, but the bull returned to the man who hadn't yet risen and pushed him with his head. The man's legs came over his own head just as the bull jerked to one side, his right horn moving into the man's thigh just under his buttock and zipping down to the knee. He cried out sharply, and we saw his thigh bone flash white, and then blood running freely before the picadors rushed the bull and forced him first to the wall and then behind the fence where he would wait nine hours and then be killed.

That was the end of the amateurs. The ring emptied quickly, and Duff and I climbed down to meet the boys. We hadn't spoken a word to each other since we saw the goring. When we got to them we saw they were silent too.

Out on the street, we made our way to a café.

'I'll be damned,' Bill said as he walked beside me. His face was flat and white. His shoes were covered with dust. We found a table and had just ordered a round of the thick beer we liked to have with lunch when the gored man was taken past us on the street on a stretcher. A bloodied sheet covered him from the waist down.

'*Toro, toro!*' someone in the café yelled drunkenly and the man sat up. Everyone cheered, and then a young boy ran over with a glass of whiskey, which the man drank and then threw back empty to the boy, who caught it well with one hand. Then everyone cheered again.

'It's a hell of a way to live, isn't it?' Duff said.

'I can think of worse,' Ernest replied.

Our beer had come and we got to it. The waiter brought gazpacho and good hard bread and some nice fish poached in lime, and though I didn't think I would be able to eat after the sight of the goring, I found I was hungry and that it all tasted very good to me.

Harold stayed to one side of the table, well out of Ernest's way, but when Pat finally showed up, pale and irritable, Harold seemed not to know where to move or whom he could speak to safely. And for the rest of the lunch our table was like an intricate game of emotional chess, with Duff looking to Ernest, who kept one eye on Pat, who was glaring at Harold, who was glancing furtively at Duff. Everyone was drinking too much and was wrung out and working hard to pretend they were jollier and less affected than everyone else.

'I can take the bulls and the blood,' Don said to me quietly. 'It's this human business that turns my stomach.'

I looked from him to Ernest, who hadn't spoken to me or so much as glanced at me since breakfast. 'Yes,' I said to Don. 'But what's the trick for it?'

'I wish to hell I knew. Maybe there is no trick.' He drained the last of his beer and signaled the waiter for more.

'Sometimes I wish we could rub out all of our mistakes and start fresh, from the beginning,' I said. 'And sometimes I think there isn't anything to us but our mistakes.'

He laughed grimly, solemnly, while on the other side of the table, Duff was whispering something in Ernest's ear while he cackled roughly, like a sailor. I turned my chair at an angle away from them where I didn't have to see them at all and as soon as I did, I thought of Fonnie and Roland a hundred years ago in St Louis. She couldn't stand to look at Roland because she thought he was weak and detestable. Their story had always been full of sadness and misery. Roland had since returned home from the sanitarium, but hadn't recovered any sense of peace. He and Fonnie led utterly separtate lives now, though they stayed in the same house on Cates Avenue, for the sake of the children. What was happening between Ernest and me was nowhere near as dire, I hoped, but he was hurting me with every whisper and look in Duff's direction. And I found myself feeling differently about marriage, about the damage lovers could do to one another, irreparable damage, sometimes, and almost without thinking.

'How sad and strange we all are,' I said to Don.

'That's what had me so maudlin yesterday. I'm sorry about that, by the way.'

'There's nothing to be sorry for. Let's just be good friends who know these things but don't have to say them.'

'All right,' he said, and looked at his hands, then drank nearly all of the glass of beer the waiter had just delivered, and the afternoon wore on this way until it was time for the corrida.

The young matador, Cayetano Ordóñez, was a boy, really, but he moved so naturally and with such grace it seemed as if he were dancing. The deep red serge of his cape was alive with even the slightest flick of his arms. He had a way of planting his feet and leaning forward slightly, facing whatever came and urging the bull to charge him with the slightest gesture or glance.

Ernest had been in a foul mood when we entered the ring for the corrida, but was starting to come awake as Ordóñez moved. Duff got up to sit nearer to him, seeing the change.

'My God, but that's a fine man,' Duff said.

'He's the real article all right,' Ernest said. 'Watch this.'

Ordóñez was leading his bull in, turning one veronica and then another, tighter one with his cape, drawing the bull magnetically. The picadors had backed off because they knew Ordóñez had him and was in complete control. It was a dance, and it was also great art. His knowledge was primal and ancient and he carried it so naturally and easily for one so young.

'Some are just going through the motions. It's pretty, all right, but it doesn't mean anything. This *hombre*, he knows you have to get near enough to die. You have to already be dead in order to really live and to conquer the animal.'

Duff nodded, taken over by his enthusiasm and God help me, I was too. Ernest's eyes, as he spoke, were suddenly nearly as alive as Ordóñez's cape. The intensity bubbled up from a deep place in him and came into his face and his throat, and I saw the way he was connected to Ordóñez and the bullfight, and to life as it was happening, and I knew that I could hate him all I wanted for the way he was hurting me, but I couldn't ever stop loving him, absolutely, for what he was.

'Now look,' he said. The bull came in low, his left horn pushed forward, his neck twisting. Ordóñez's thigh was inches from the bull's powerful legs, and he leaned nearer, so that when the bull's head came up, searching for the cape, he just grazed Ordóñez's belly. A gasp went up in the crowd, because this is what they had come to see.

'You'll never see it done better than that,' Ernest said, throwing his hat to his feet in respect.

'Goddamned beautiful,' Duff said.

We all sighed, and when the bull had been broken and was on its knees, bowing, Ordóñez ran the sword in clean. Everyone stood, cheering, the whole crowd moved and taken over by the spectacle and the mastery. I stood too and applauded like crazy, and I must have been standing in a particularly bright ray of sun because Ordóñez looked up at me then, and his eyes took in my hair.

'He thinks you're *muy linda*,' Ernest said, following Ordóñez's eyes to me. 'He's honoring you.'

The young matador bent over the bull, slicing off its ear with a small knife. He called a boy over from the stands and sent him to me with the ear cupped in his palms. He delivered it shyly, barely daring to look at me, but I could tell he felt it was a very great privilege to carry it for Ordóñez. I didn't quite know how to accept it, what the rules were for such things, and so simply held out my hands. It was black and triangular and still warm, with only the faintest trace of blood – the strangest thing I'd ever held.

'I'll be damned,' Ernest said, clearly very proud.

'What will you do with it?' Duff asked.

'Keep it, of course,' Don said, and handed me his handkerchief so I could wrap it inside and also wipe my hands.

Still standing, I held the ear in the handkerchief and looked down into the ring where Ordóñez was being buried in flowers. He glanced up at me, bowed low and deeply, and then returned to being adored.

'I'll be damned,' Ernest said again.

There were five more bullfights that day, but none matched the beauty of the first. When we went to the café after, we were all still thrumming with it, even Bill, who couldn't stomach most of the day, particularly the way two of the horses were gored and went down and had to be killed quickly while everyone watched. It was all terrible and terribly intense, and I was ready for a drink.

I passed the ear around the table so everyone could admire it and be horrified in turn. Duff got drunk very quickly and began to flirt openly with Harold, who was too surprised and pleased to be discreet about it. The two disappeared at one point, which had Pat furious. When an hour or more had passed, they wandered back in a very jolly mood, as if nothing was amiss.

'You little bastard,' Pat said to Harold. He stood and immediately lurched to one side.

'Oh, put a lid on it, darling,' Duff said blithely. But Pat wouldn't be chided.

'Just get the hell away from us, would you?' he said to Harold.

'I don't think Duff would like that. You want me here, don't you?'

'Of course, darling, I want everyone.' She reached for Ernest's glass. 'Be a pal, would you?'

Ernest nodded; she could have the glass, could have every drink on the table as far as he was concerned. It was Harold who disgusted him. 'Running to a woman,' he said under his breath. 'What's lower than that?'

The waiter came around with more drinks and food, but the evening wouldn't be set right. A canker boiled up and tainted everything that had been so powerful and fine.

Ernest sensed this too and tried to bring the talk around to Ordóñez and his posture, his veronicas.

'Which is the veronica, again?' Duff said.

'It's when the matador stands turned to the bull with his feet fixed and swings the cape away from the bull very slowly.'

'Yes, of course,' Duff said. 'It was marvelous, wasn't it?'

'Don't believe her, Hem,' Pat said meanly. 'She doesn't remember any of it.'

'Give a girl a break, Pat.' She turned back to Ernest. 'I'm just a little tight now. I'll remember more tomorrow. I swear I'll be good then.'

Ernest looked at her sadly. 'All right,' he said, but he was clearly disappointed in her and with the whole group. The air had gone out of everything.

Back at the hotel that night, I took the ear, folded it into several more handkerchiefs and put it in my bureau drawer.

'The thing will stink before long,' Ernest said, watching me do it.

'I don't care.'

'No, I wouldn't either.' He started to undress slowly and thoughtfully. 'When this is all over,' he said finally, 'let's follow Ordóñez to Madrid and then Valencia.'

'Will it ever be over?'

'Of course it will.' He turned to face me. 'Ordóñez was wonderful, wasn't he? He makes all of this seem very ugly and very stupid.'

I closed the bureau drawer, then took off my clothes and climbed into bed. 'I'm ready to forget Pamplona. Why don't we try now? Help me, will you?'

At the end of that very long week, we disbanded and everyone went off separately. Don left for the Riviera looking sad and exhausted. Bill and Harold were headed back to Paris, but took Pat and Duff as far as Bayonne. Ernest and I boarded a train to Madrid where we took rooms at the Pensione Aguilar, an unfashionable hotel in the Calle San Jeronimo that was small and very quiet with no tourists. It was like heaven after Pamplona. We went to the bullfights every day and were there the afternoon Juan Belmonte, arguably the best torero of all time, was badly gored in the belly and carried off to the hospital. We'd followed his fights for some time, and Ernest had always admired his bow-legged and hard-jawed determination, but we began to see, even before Belmonte was injured, that Ordóñez was nearly as great as the master, if not better. His movements were perfection and his bravery never wavered, and we watched him, both of us, in awe.

One afternoon Ordóñez paid me the very great honor of letting me hold his cape before the corrida began. He came very close and I saw the utter smoothness of his boy's face and the depth and clarity of his eyes. He said nothing when he handed the cape to me but was very serious.

'I think he's in love with you,' Ernest said, when Ordóñez had walked away to build energy in the crowd.

'How could he be? He's a child,' I said, but I was proud and felt changed by the honor.

Back at the hotel that night when we were dressing for dinner, Ernest said, 'I'm working out a new novel. Or it's working itself out, really, in my head. About the bullfights. The hero will be Ordóñez, and the whole thing will take place in Pamplona.' His eyes were bright and the enthusiasm in his voice was unmistakable.

'That sounds awfully good.'

'It does, doesn't it? I'm calling the young torero Romero. It starts at a hotel, at three in the afternoon. Two Americans are staying there, in rooms across the hall, and when they go to meet Romero, it's a great honor and they notice how alone he is, and how he's thinking about the bulls he'll face that day. He can't share that with anyone.'

'He would feel that way, wouldn't he?' I said. 'You have to write it.'

'Yes,' he said, and although we left and had a long and delicious dinner with several bottles of wine between us, he was already with the book, inside of it. Over the coming days, his thinking grew deeper. He began to write in intense spurts, in the cafés early in the mornings, and in the hotel very late at night, when I could hear the aggressive scratching of his pencil. When we left Madrid for the fiesta at Valencia, he'd filled two thick notebooks, two hundred handwritten pages in less than ten days, but he wasn't happy with the opening any more.

'I'm thinking it should start in Paris and then move. It's what happens in Paris that fuels the fire. You can't have the rest without it.'

'You always said you couldn't write about Paris because you were too close to it.'

'Yes, I know, but for some reason it's coming easily. We were in Pamplona two weeks ago, but I can write that too. I don't know why. Maybe all of my thoughts and rules about writing are just waiting to be proven wrong.'

'It's good to be on fire, isn't it?'

'I hope it goes on like this forever.'

It did go on. In Valencia, the excitement over the fiesta had pitched everything into a fever and we could just enjoy it. We sat at a street café and ate prawns sprinkled with fresh lime and cracked pepper, and beautiful paella in a dish nearly as wide as our table. In the afternoons we went to the bullfights where Ordóñez swept his veronicas with absolute perfection.

'There it was. Did you see it?' Ernest said pointing into the ring.

'What?'

'His death. The bull was so close. That's what makes the dance of it. The torero has to know he's dying and the bull has to know it, so when it's pulled away at the last second, it's like a kind of magic. That's really living.'

One afternoon while he was napping and I was feeling restless, I thumbed through his notebooks, reading here and there admiringly. Quite by accident I came upon pages of sayings and turns of phrases that were recognizably Duff's. I felt a shock at first, reading them. He had listened so closely to her, getting everything down, capturing her perfectly. And now it was all coming through, changed only slightly, in his heroine. It made me feel terribly jealous of her all over again until I was able to make sense of it. Ernest was a writer, not Duff's lover. He'd seen her as a character, maybe even from the beginning. And now that he was living in the book, not in the street cafés in Pamplona, the tension and ugliness could be useful. The whole time had been constructive and necessary for the work. That's why the words were coming so strongly now, with such heat.

From Valencia we went to Madrid again, and then to San Sebastian to escape the rising summer temperatures. In San Sebastian and then in Hendaye, Ernest wrote with great intensity in the mornings, and then we spent the rest of the day swimming and sunning ourselves on the beach. The sand was hot and sugary, and there were long purple mountains in the distance, and the crashing of the surf filled our ears and lulled us into a happy stupor. But by the end of the first week in

August, I was missing Bumby too much to enjoy any more of it. I went back to Paris and Ernest returned to Madrid alone. There he worked better and harder than ever before. It was as though he was inventing the book and inventing himself as a writer at the same time. He wrote to say he'd stopped sleeping except for an hour here and there. *But when I wake again,* he wrote, *the sentences are there waiting for me, shouting to be set down. It's extraordinary, Tatie. I can see the end from here and it's something.*

THIRTY-THREE

At the tail end of August, Paris was virtually deserted. Anyone who could be anywhere else was, but Pauline Pfeiffer and Kitty had both remained in town for work. The three of us often met for dinner, sometimes with Bumby in tow and sometimes only after he was tucked into bed with Marie Cocotte to watch him. Although I initially felt uneasy around Pauline and Kitty as a pair — these fashionable, independent and decidedly modern girls — at bottom they were both wonderfully frank and unfussy. That was why they liked me too, they insisted, and I began to trust it.

Occasionally Pauline's sister Jinny met us out in the cafés, and I found the two sisters quite funny together, as if they were a very chic vaudeville act with a shorthand of dark little jokes. They held their liquor well and didn't embarrass themselves, or others, and always had interesting things to say. Jinny was unattached, but if Kitty was right about her preferring women, that made sense. It was harder to see why Pauline hadn't yet married.

'It was all but settled with my cousin, Matt Herold,' she said one day when I pressed her for more details. 'I'd even modeled dresses and tasted half a dozen cakes.' She shuddered. 'They all tasted like cake, of course.'

'Did something terrible happen between you?'

'No. That might have made some things easier, actually. I just didn't think I loved him enough. I liked him. He would have been a wonderful provider, and a good father too. I could see the whole thing, but never felt it. Not really. I wanted something grand and sweeping.'

'The kind of love you find in novels?'

'Maybe. That makes me incredibly stupid, I suppose.'

'Not at all. I love romance. Women these days seem too advanced for it.'

'It's very confusing, knowing what you want when there are so many choices. Sometimes I think I'd just as soon ditch marriage and work. I want to be *useful*.' She paused and laughed at herself. 'I think I read that in a novel somewhere too.'

'Maybe you can have everything you want. You seem very clever to me.'

'We'll see,' she said. 'And in the meantime we'll be two bachelor girls.'

'Swimmingly free?'

'Why not?'

It was funny to think of myself this way. Ernest most certainly wouldn't have approved, and I couldn't help but wonder what he'd say about my spending so much time with Pauline. If Kitty was too decorative, Pauline would be as well. She was the type of professional beauty he generally despised. Not only did she talk endlessly about fashion, she was always maneuvering her way toward the most interesting people and sizing them up to see how they might be of use to her, her dark eyes snapping, her mind's wheels turning shrewdly. There never seemed to be any spontaneity with Pauline. If she saw you, she meant to. If she spoke to you, she'd already planned what to say so it came out sharply and perfectly. I admired her confidence and was a little in awe of it, maybe. She had that sense of effortlessness that took, in the end, a great deal of effort. And though I never knew quite what to say around other women *like* her – Zelda, for instance – under Pauline's fine clothes and good haircut, she was candid and sensible, too. I knew she wouldn't unravel on me at any moment and quickly came to feel I could count on her.

In the middle of September, Ernest came home from Madrid looking exhausted and triumphant all at once. I watched him unpacking his cases and couldn't help but feel astonished at what he'd accomplished. There were seven full notebooks, hundreds and hundreds of pages, all done in six weeks.

'Are you finished then, Tatie?'

'Nearly. I'm so close I almost can't make myself write the end of it. Does that make sense?'

'Can I read it now?'

'Soon,' he said. He drew me toward him in a long, crushing embrace. 'I feel like I could sleep forever.'

'Sleep then,' I said, but he pulled me toward the bed and began to tug at my clothes, his hands everywhere at once.

'I thought you were tired,' I said, but he kissed me roughly, and I didn't say anything more.

A week later, he'd completed the first draft, and we went to the quarter to celebrate with friends. We met at the Negre de Toulouse, and everyone was in high spirits. Scott and Zelda turned up, as did Ford and Stella, Don Stewart and Harold and Kitty. There were a few moments of awkwardness as everyone waited to see what was what. Pamplona had ended so painfully, but after the drinks came and several glasses were downed quickly, medicinally, the party loosened up. Ernest had more whiskey than he should have, but behaved himself until the very end of the evening when we met Kitty on the way out the door.

'Good show on your book, Hem.'

'Thanks,' he said. 'It's full of action and drama and everyone's in it.' He gestured toward Bill and Harold. 'I'm ripping those bastards all to hell, but not you, Kitty. You're a swell girl.'

His voice was so cold and cutting, Kitty's face went white. I pulled him out the door by his arm, feeling mortified.

'What?' he said. 'What did I do?'

'You're drunk,' I said, 'let's talk about it tomorrow.'

'I plan on getting drunk tomorrow, too,' he said.

I simply kept marching him toward home, knowing there would be remorse in the morning, along with a titanic headache.

I was right.

'Don't be hurt by what I told Kitty,' he said when he finally woke near lunchtime, looking green. 'I'm an ass.'

'It was a big night. You should get some dispensation.'

'Whatever I said, the book's the book. It's not life.'

'I know,' I said, but when he gave me the pages to read, it took me no time at all to realize that everything was just as it had happened in Spain, every sordid conversation and tense encounter. It was all nearly verbatim, except for one thing – I wasn't in it at all. Duff was the heroine. I'd known and expected this, but it was troubling just the same to see her name over and over. He hadn't changed it yet to Lady Brett. Duff was Duff and Harold was Harold and Pat was a drunken sot, and everyone was in bad form except the bullfighters. Kitty was in the book, too — he'd lied about that — in a very unflattering role. Ernest had made himself into Jake Barnes and made Jake impotent, and what was I supposed to think of that? Was that how he saw his own morality or cowardice or good sense or whatever it was that had kept him from sleeping with Duff — impotence?

But if I could step away from these doubts and questions even slightly, I could see how remarkable the work was; more exciting and alive than anything he'd ever written. He'd seen the good story in Pamplona when I'd felt only disaster and human messiness. He'd shaped it and made it something more; something that would last forever. I was incredibly proud of him and also felt hurt and shut out by the book. These feelings existed in a difficult tangle, but neither was truer than the other.

I read the pages in a state of anticipation and dread, and often had to stop and set down the manuscript to right myself again. Ernest had been working so intently and in such solitude that any delay in getting an opinion was killing him.

'Is it any good?' he asked when I'd finally finished. 'I have to know.'

'It's more than good, Tatie. There's nothing like it anywhere.'

He smiled with relief and elation, and then let out a small whoop. 'I'll be damned,' he said. Bumby was on the floor nearby, chewing on a hand-carved toy locomotive that Alice and Gertrude had given him. Ernest swooped him up and lifted him toward the ceiling, and Bumby squealed happily, his apple cheeks filling with air.

'Papa,' he said. It had been his first word, and he loved to say it as often as possible. Ernest liked this too.

'Papa has written an awfully good book,' Ernest said, smiling up at Bumby, who was growing pinker by the moment.

'Give Papa a kiss,' I said, and Bumby, who was now down in Ernest's arms squirming happily, slathered his papa's face.

It was such a fine moment, the three of us perfectly aligned, gazing at the same bright star, but later that night, when I was lying in bed trying desperately to sleep, my worries circled around again and wouldn't let me rest. I'd been edited out of the book from page one, word one. Why didn't Ernest seem concerned that I'd be hurt or made jealous? Did he assume I understood the story needed a compelling heroine, and that wasn't me? He certainly didn't follow me around with a notebook, jotting down every clever thing I said the way he did with Duff. Art was art, but what did Ernest tell himself? I needed to know.

'Tatie,' I said in the dark, half hoping he was sound asleep. 'Was I ever in the book?'

Several seconds passed in silence and then, ever so quietly, he said, 'No, Tatie. I'm sorry if that hurts you.'

'Can you tell me why?'

'Not exactly. The ideas come to me, not the other way around. But I think it might be that you were never down in the muck. You weren't really there in the story, if that makes sense, but above it somehow, better and finer than the rest of us.'

'That's not how it felt to me, but it's a nice thought. I want to believe it.'

'Then do.' He turned over on his side, his open eyes searching mine. 'I love you, Tatie. You're what's best about me.'

I sighed into his words, feeling only the smallest sting of doubt. 'I love you too.'

Over the coming weeks, Ernest continued to work on the novel, tightening the language, scratching whole scenes out. It was all he thought about, and because he was so distracted, I was very happy to have friends around to keep me company. In the end, he didn't seem to mind Pauline, and I was grateful for that.

'She chatters on about Chanel too much,' he admitted, 'but she's smart about books. She knows what she likes and more than that, she knows *why*. That's very rare, particularly these days, when everyone's more and more full of hot air. You never know who to trust.'

With Ernest's endorsement, Pauline began coming by the sawmill in the afternoons to keep me company. We'd have tea while Bumby played or napped, and sometimes she went with me to the music shop when I practiced at my borrowed piano.

'You really do play beautifully,' she said one day when I'd finished. 'Especially the Busoni. I thought I was going to cry. Why is it you never played really?'

'I couldn't break through. I just wasn't good enough.'

'You could still. You should.'

'You're very dear, but it's not true.' I stretched my fingers and then closed my music book. 'This is my life now, anyway. I wouldn't want another.'

'No, I wouldn't either if I were you,' she said, but later, when we were walking home from the shop, the scheme was still on her mind. 'You might not have to give anything up to take music more seriously,' she said. 'A concert wouldn't have to be terribly traumatic. Everyone loves you. They want to see you succeed.'

'It would take so much more time and effort,' I said. 'And I'd need my own piano.'

'You should have your own anyway. Surely Hem knows that. I can talk to him if you'd like.'

'We'll see,' I said. 'I'll give it some thought.'

The rush of anxiety about performing in front of others never diminished much, but more and more I began to wonder if a concert might be good for me after all – particularly now, when Ernest was so absorbed by his novel. The book blotted out every other thought and crept in even when we were making love. I could feel him there one moment, with me, inside me, but then gone the next, simply vanished into the world he was making.

My playing wouldn't change anything about his habits – I wasn't naïve enough to think that – but I thought it might give me my own focus and outlet, beyond the details of Bumby's feeding schedule and exercise regimen. I loved being his mother, but that didn't mean I couldn't have other interests. Stella managed it beautifully. In fact, she was the new model of a wife, and I was the outdated, provincial variety.

It was ironic to think that nearly all of the women I knew now were direct benefactors of the suffragette work my mother did decades ago, right in our own parlor, while I curled up with a book and tried to be invisible. It was possible that I was never going to catch up with the truly modern woman, but did I have to hide my head so wilfully? Couldn't I experiment just a little to see what else might feel right, especially when I had good friends who loved me, as Pauline had pointed out, and wanted me to succeed?

In time, Pauline introduced us to many of her finer, Right Bank crowd, like Gerald and Sara Murphy. Gerald was a painter, but more than this, he was an icon of good taste and the good life. He and Sara had come to Paris in 1921, and though they had a beautiful apartment on the quai des Grands-Augustins, they were gradually migrating to the South of France, where they were building an estate on the Riviera, at Antibes. Gerald had studied architecture and the estate, Villa America, would be the Murphys' joint opus, the most beautiful thing they could imagine and afford — and they could afford a great deal. Pauline also introduced us to the poet Archibald MacLeish and his lovely wife, Ada, who sang well, professionally even, and wore the most beautifully beaded dresses I'd ever seen.

I was surprised at how tolerant Ernest seemed of these new acquaintances. In private he snidely called them 'the rich,' but he couldn't help but respond to the attention he got from them just the same. *In Our Time* came out in the States in early October, and not long after, copies could be found at bookshops all over town. The reviews were all tremendously positive, calling Ernest *the* young writer to watch. His prospects seemed brighter and brighter, but these new friends weren't simply hangers-on. They wouldn't be content warming their hands at the edge of Ernest's success; they wanted to fan the fire.

In the meantime, Pauline began coming to the sawmill for dinner several nights a week, and sometimes Ernest would meet her in one or other of the cafés. I was so relieved that the relationship felt natural and mutual. I'd never liked fighting with Ernest about Kitty, but he wouldn't budge. She was and would always be 'that gold-plated bitch' to him, but Pauline brought out his kinder, more fraternal side. He began to call her 'Pfife,' and so did I. To Bumby, she was Tante Pfife and she had nicknames for us too. Ernest was Papa or Drum, and I was Hash or Dulla. Together we were her adorables, her cherishables.

As fall turned to winter, and the Paris damp seeped in through the windows and under the doors, Ernest made a decision to put the Pamplona novel away.

'I can't see it at all any more. I don't know what's good or where I'm failing. It has to simmer on its own awhile.' He sighed and scratched his mustache, which had gotten thick and unruly lately, handsomely uncivilized. 'I've been thinking about starting something wholly different. Something funny.'

'Funny seems to suit Don and Harold, but I'm not sure it's the thing for you.'

'The first thing you ever saw of mine was funny. You're saying that wasn't any good?'

'Not at all. Only that your work has more of a spark when it's dramatic.'

'I don't know about that,' he said, and began working immediately. I had no idea what he really had in mind, or how quickly he would cast it off. Within two weeks he had an entire draft of *The Torrents of Spring*, a parody-satire of Sherwood Anderson's latest book, *Dark Laughter*. But having written the thing didn't make the next step any easier. He wasn't sure what he had or who to let in on it. They might get the wrong idea and think it mean-spirited.

'I'd love to read it,' I said. 'I can keep an open mind.'

'Sorry, Tatie. I'm not sure you can.'

'Is it that bad?'

'I can't say. I'm going to show it to Scott and maybe Dos, too.'

Unfortunately, they weren't at all keen on the project and told him to leave well enough alone. Anderson's book might well be silly and sentimental, they agreed, but he was a great talent and had done so much to secure Ernest's future, it wouldn't be fair to lambaste the man. What would be the point?

'The point,' Ernest said, 'is that his book is rotten and deserves to be harpooned and if someone's going to do it, why not a friend?'

'That's a damned funny way to see it,' Scott said. 'I tell you, lay off.'

Undeterred, Ernest had taken the manuscript over to the Murphys' apartment and read it aloud while Gerald tried very hard not to be shocked, and Sara fell asleep sitting straight up on the sofa in a pale silk dressing gown. I listened with slow-growing dread. When Ernest finished, Gerald cleared his throat several times and, ever the diplomat, said, 'It's not for me, but someone might think it's just the thing.'

'You're killing me,' Ernest said.

Gerald turned to me. 'What do you think, Hadley? You've a good head on your shoulders.'

'Well,' I hedged. 'It's not entirely kind.'

'Right,' Gerald said.

'It's not meant to be kind. It's meant to be funny.'

'Right,' Gerald said again.

I had a secret theory that Ernest had really written the book to distance himself from Sherwood and come out from under his shadow. Friends and reviewers both were often comparing Ernest's prose to Anderson's, and this made Ernest crazy. He didn't want to be lined up to anyone, especially not a good friend and champion of his work. He was grateful for Sherwood's help, he swore he was, but not indebted to him. Not indentured. His work was his own and he would prove it once and for all.

Desperate to get someone to agree with him about *The Torrents of Spring*, Ernest finally went to Gertrude, but things hadn't been good with those two for some time and this was the last straw. When he told me how it had gone, I felt heart-broken. She nearly threw him out of her flat, saying, 'It's detestable, Hem, and you should know better.'

'Should I?' he tried to laugh it off.

'I thought so once. You used to be committed to your craft. Now you're mean and hard and only care about positioning yourself and about money.'

'Don't be such a hypocrite. You'd love to be rich.'

'I'd love to be rich,' she agreed. 'But I won't do all the things it takes to get that way.'

'Like cutting down your friends, you mean?'

She was silent then.

'I get it. You've painted a real nice picture of me here.'

He stormed out, and when he came home he wouldn't even talk about it at first. But he put the book away in a drawer and I was relieved to see him done with it.

It was nearly Christmas by this time. We were preparing to return to Schruns and stay through until spring, and Ernest put all his energy into making plans.

'Why don't we ask Pauline to join us,' he suggested. 'It will be so much nicer for you if she's there.'

'I'd love that. Aren't you sweet to think of me?'

We invited Jinny too, because the two sisters often came as a matched set, but Pauline assured us that Jinny would go to Nîmes with other friends. She herself was delighted to come. She couldn't wait.

THIRTY-FOUR

Pfife came off the train looking pink and well. There had been two feet of snow the week before but the weather had grown steadily warmer and it was all soft now, impossible for skiing. Ernest had promised to teach her to ski, and she carried her skis awkwardly when we met her on the platform, but didn't seem disappointed when we pointed out the thaw.

'It's enough to be near you two pets,' she said. 'And Bumby, of course.'

Bumby stood holding my hand. He wore his winter togs and looked like a proper Austrian baby, and was very brave about the train, which thrilled and terrified him.

'Say hello to Tante Pfife,' Ernest said to Bumby, who hid behind my skirt and peeked curiously out again, making us all laugh.

Pauline seemed charmed by Schruns and by her room at the Taube, which stood at the end of the long hall, just next door to where Ernest worked. 'It's smaller than yours,' she said when she saw it, 'but I'm not so big really.'

I sat on the bed to watch her unpack while Bumby played

with the fringe of the bed quilt on his hands and knees, singing a little Austrian folksong Tiddy had taught him. Pauline opened her bag and began to take out long wool skirts and well-made stockings. She picked up a butter-colored cashmere sweater, held it against her and folded it into thirds.

'You have the loveliest things,' I said, looking down at my own trousers and thick wool sweater. 'But you'll embarrass all of us if you actually wear any of this.'

'Embarrass myself is more like it,' she said. 'I guess I have overdone it. Hem said there was the best society ever here.'

'He must have meant the chamois. Or maybe the fat Austrian butchers and woodsmen he plays cards with, each one holding a bigger cigar. You might find yourself a husband in that lot if you're not careful.'

'The goats would fall easier than the woodsmen, I'd wager,' Ernest said from the doorway. He filled the frame and the hall was dark behind him.

Pauline smiled. 'I'll try not to set my cap too high then.'

We all laughed and Ernest went back to work, locking his door with a click. I was relieved to see him writing again. He'd spent our first two weeks at Schruns in bed, nursing a sore throat and harsh cough, so it was very good that he seemed ready to get to it now, and better that I had a friend to entertain and talk with while he was occupied.

After Pauline was well moved into her room, we dressed Bumby warmly and then pulled him through the town on his little sled so I could show her everything – the small square with its shops and *Gasthäuser*, the bowling alley and the sawmills and the stream, Die Litz, which split the town several times and was covered over with sturdy wooden bridges.

'I just love it so absolutely already,' Pauline said with a sigh.

Right then Bumby's sled hit an iced-over trough and dipped low to one side, tumbling him out in the snow. He squealed with delight, stood and quickly climbed onto the sled again. 'Again, again, Mama!'

'Again, again!' Pauline echoed, and stamped the snow around her happily with her pretty, impractical boots.

Back at the hotel, she followed me into my room while I changed.

'Nothing I've brought will do here,' she said. 'Do you mind lending me some of your things?'

'You can't be serious. I'm twice your size.'

She frowned. 'Not twice, surely. What about shops? Is there anything nearby?'

'If you're not too choosy. There's nothing like a Right Bank boutique for several hundred miles.'

'That's just what I came to get away from. I intend on being only practical the whole while, with sensible, no-nonsense trousers and men's shirts, just like yours.'

I couldn't help laughing. 'Are you sure you know what you're getting into?'

'Absolutely. And I want slippers just like yours too. They simply have to be the same.'

'You're a funny one. You can have these,' I said, taking off my own and handing them to her. 'I'll wear Ernest's. That's what marriage does to you, by the way. Somewhere along the line you discover you have your husband's feet.'

She smiled. 'I wouldn't mind that.'

'Don't tell me you're getting soft on marriage. Is there some-one new?'

'No, no. I'm just in love with the way you and Drum are together. There are things I didn't see before, like how nice it is to have someone around. Not the white knight whisking you away, but the fellow who sits at your table every night and tells you what he's thinking.'

'They don't *always* do that, you know. They don't always talk, even.'

She smiled again and said she didn't care, and then put my slippers on her feet. They were standard Alpine fare, bulky and warm, lined with fleece, but she swore she loved them anyway. 'I want to die in these,' she said. 'You won't be able to pry them off me.'

The conditions stayed too warm and wet for skiing, but we fell into a lovely routine anyway. Pauline was my shadow and because I'd never had one before, I enjoyed the attention and her company. She took to watching me play the piano every afternoon, filling the space in between pieces with encouragement and praise. She'd become my most important collaborator since she'd begun to push me toward the idea of a concert, and I was surprised to find I liked having her champion my cause with Ernest, who now had earmarked a portion of his advance for a rental piano when we returned to Paris. I didn't know I'd needed her help until it was there, and I could rely on it – and then I wondered how I'd done without it.

Maybe it was the proximity, the way we three were thrown together so much, but at Schruns, Pauline began to take on a crusading role for Ernest's work too. She'd always admired it and thought him a great talent, but now that took a more personal turn. He'd just begun working on the Pamplona novel again, and one afternoon when Pauline and I were lunching, he came down from his studio with a clear and buoyant look in his eyes.

'Your work went well,' I said. 'I'm so glad.'

'Very well. I've moved them on to Burguete.'

'I don't suppose you'd let me read a little,' Pauline said.

'It's not in any state. You're just being polite, anyway.'

'Not at all. I just know it's brilliant. It is, isn't it Hadley?'

'Of course it is,' I said. And it was. But I didn't feel I could share, at least not yet, the breadth of my complicated feelings about the book. Even hearing her ask to read it brought a flaring of discomfort. She was a shrewd girl. What would she think when she saw I wasn't even the smallest character? Would she believe Ernest and I were on shaky ground? Would she see something I didn't or couldn't?

'The Pamplona novel will wait,' he said. 'It's got more cooking to do.' He dug heartily into his plate of sausage and nice potatoes, pausing to say, 'I have something else you can see if you're really serious.'

'I'm *only* serious,' she said. 'Didn't you know?'

After lunch, when Ernest brought the pages down and handed them to Pauline, she said, 'This is such an honor.'

'We'll see if you feel that way when you've read the damned thing,' he said, and then readied himself for billiards with Herr Lent.

It was only when I walked around to read over her shoulder that I realized the manuscript he'd given her was *The Torrents of Spring*. I felt a small wave of nausea as I realized he'd never really stopped considering the project. He'd only been biding his time, waiting for the right reader.

After Ernest went off to his game, Pauline curled up in the nice red chair by the fire, and I went back to my piano. It was hard to concentrate because she was laughing out loud as she read. I finally decided I needed a long walk and it wasn't until dinner, many hours later, that we all met up again.

'It's all so hilarious,' she said to Ernest before he'd even gotten comfortable at the table. 'Damned smart and very funny. You have my vote.'

'I thought it was funny too,' he said. 'But my very good friends seem to see it differently.' He looked at me pointedly.

'I just think it's nasty to Sherwood,' I said.

Pauline could clearly see her cause now. 'If the book is good, isn't it kind of a tribute to Anderson?' she said. 'No press is bad press, right?'

'That's just what I thought,' Ernest said again, and the two kept egging each other on, growing more emphatic in their agreement.

'There's no other way to see it, is there? Mightn't he be flattered after all?' she said.

'No one with any stuff could be wounded by satire,' he said.

'Well I think it's great. It's a damn fine book and you should submit it right away.'

It wasn't until that moment that I fully understood how hurt he'd been when everyone, including me, had disparaged the book and shut it down. He loved and needed praise. He loved and needed to be loved, and even adored. But it worried me to have Pauline bolster him this way just now. With her encouragement, he would send *Torrents* to Boni and Liveright and nothing good would likely happen then. Anderson was their most important author, and because it was his encouragement that had gotten Ernest a contract in the first place, I couldn't imagine the book wouldn't offend them. When Anderson heard, he'd be more than offended. My guess was we'd lose his friendship for good, the way we were clearly losing Gertrude's. It was so hard to watch Ernest pushing these mentors away, as if striking deep blows was the only way to prove to himself (and everyone else) that he'd never really needed them in the first place. But I felt my hands were tied with this book. I couldn't say anything else against it.

The next afternoon, Ernest arranged the typescript and put it in a bundle with a letter to Horace Liveright saying they could have the book for an advance of 500 dollars and that his new bullfighting novel, which he had every reason to feel excited about, was very near completed. Off the parcel went.

As we waited to hear, a fresh storm came in with more rain. We bided our time in the hotel, reading and eating better than ever. In the afternoons, Ernest and Pauline began taking long walks along the slopes behind the hotel, or winding through the town slowly, deep in conversation.

'She's read so much,' he said to me one night when we were getting ready for bed. 'And she can talk about books beauti-fully.'

'About more than Henry James, you mean?'

'Yes,' he said, smirking. Henry James had never stopped being our private joke, the writer that stood as the line between us, showing how stuck in the past I was, no matter what else I was introduced to or had found on my own.

'She's a smart girl all right,' I said, feeling a twinge of jeal-ousy about their growing affinity. She *was* smart, and seemed to find pleasure in matching Ernest intellectually. I could be a cheerleader for him, and had been ever since that night in Chicago when he'd first handed me clutched and creased pages. But I wasn't a critic. I couldn't tell him *why* his work was good and why it mattered to literature, that age-old conversation among writers and lovers of books. Pauline could do that and he was responding, as he would. He had a new energy, par-ticularly in the evenings when he came downstairs after a day's work, because there was someone interesting to talk to and talk *with*. What was more exciting than that? I could love him like crazy and work very hard to understand and support him, but I couldn't be fresh eyes and a fresh smile after five years. I couldn't be *new*.

Two days after Christmas, the reply came from Boni and Liveright. They were rejecting *Torrents*. Aside from being an unnecessarily vicious piece of satire targeting Anderson, they didn't think it would sell well. It was too cerebral and not as funny as it intended to be. They were very interested in the novel about the Spanish fiesta, however, and eagerly awaited its completion.

'I'm a free man then,' Ernest said sourly when he'd read the cable aloud to us. 'Scott's talked to Max Perkins at Scribner's about me, and there's always Harcourt. I could go anywhere.'

'Someone has to see the genius here,' Pauline said, pounding one of her small fists on the arm of her chair for effect.

'I don't know,' I said. 'Do you really want to cut ties with Liveright? They've done right by you with *In Our Time*.'

'Why do you always have to be so damned sensible? I don't want to play it safe any more. Besides, they should be grateful to *me*. I've made them good money.'

'They're certainly not the only publishers around,' Pauline said. 'Scott's had great good luck with Scribner's. Maybe that's the thing.'

'Something good's bound to come for it,' he said. 'It's a damned fine book.'

'Oh, it is!' she said. 'I'll go to New York myself and tell Max Perkins just what funny is if he doesn't know.'

Ernest laughed and then sat quietly for a moment. 'You know,' he said. 'It might not be a bad idea to go to New York and meet with Perkins myself. Scott tells me he's the best, but it would be good to have a face-to-face and make the deal that way, if it's going to happen at all.'

'Aren't you good to know it?' Pauline said, and I was struck by how quickly this scheme, too, had become a fait accompli. She fit so well inside his ear. She told him what he most wanted to hear, and it was obviously a powerful tonic for both of them, to be united in their thinking. Meanwhile I was on my own now, against *Torrents* and the whole scenario.

'Surely you can do all of this by mail,' I said. 'Or go in the spring, when you've finished the changes on the new book, and then you'll have more to show Perkins.'

'But *Torrents* is finished. I know you hate the book, but I'm going to strike while the iron is hot.'

'I don't hate it,' I said. But he was already up and refilling his drink, his head thick with plans.

'It's the right thing, you'll see,' Pauline said.

'I hope that's true,' I said.

Later that night, as we were readying ourselves for bed, I said, 'I'm not *just* sensible, you know. You used to like my forthrightness.'

'Yes,' he said, with a small sigh. 'You're very good and very true. But I'm going to do this. Are you on my side?'

How many times had he asked me that in our married life? A hundred? A thousand?

'I'm always on your side,' I said, and wondered if I was the only one who felt the complicated truth of that hovering over us in the dark room.

THIRTY-FIVE

February in Schruns was a small kind of hell. Outside, the weather raged or flailed. Inside, things weren't much better because the stuffing of life had gone to Paris and then to New York, and I was alone with my doubts.

The night before Ernest left, I had helped him pack, but the mood was tense.

'You could come as far as Le Havre if you like, and see me off there.'

'It's too hard with the baby on the train.'

'So leave him here with Tiddy. It's only for a few days.'

'Maybe,' I said, but I already knew I wouldn't do it because it wouldn't solve anything. It wouldn't dispel my worries that a wedge was growing between us, that he'd stopped listening to and trusting my voice, and it couldn't soothe my anxieties about the way he was turning toward Pauline. He was attracted to her, that was obvious, but I didn't really believe he would act on it. He hadn't with Duff, and she hadn't been anywhere near as ingrained in our life. Pauline was my friend. He wouldn't ruin that and neither would she. Her letters had arrived nearly every day since we put her on the train back to Paris. They were always addressed to us both, her two great pets, as she liked to say, her cherishables. Her tone was exuberant and inclusive and untroubled – like Pauline herself – and reading them made me feel better. It also helped to remind myself that she wanted sweeping romance, the kind in great literature. She wouldn't settle for tawdry. It wasn't her style.

'You'll see Pauline in Paris, of course,' I said as Ernest put the last of his things into the suitcase.

'If there's time. She's very busy now with the spring fashion shows and there are lots of other friends to see. You won't come then?'

'No, I think I'm better off here.'

'Suit yourself,' he said, and closed the case with a click.

Ernest was on the high seas for ten days, out of reach. During that time, Bumby and I kept to our routine as much as possible because it made me feel more grounded and stable. We ate the very same things at the same times. We went to bed early and rose early. In the afternoons I walked in the village or wrote letters while Tiddy cared for him. Most mornings I rehearsed a Bach-Busoni chaconne until I thought my fingers would fall off. It was for the concert, which I'd finally decided to act on. Ernest's absence and my growing fears helped me see that I needed it more than ever. I wrote a letter to the house manager of the Salle Pleyel, a small concert hall on the rue Rochechouart, expressing my interest in performing there, as well as giving details of my background and connections. I waited for a response with trepidation, but I needn't have. He wrote back quickly and graciously, setting a date for the 30th of May. The details would be settled when I returned to Paris in early April.

When Ernest finally wrote, I learned he'd headed right for Horace Liveright's office on landing in New York. The meeting had gone well. Liveright had been civil and everything had ended on a pleasant enough note. They were holding no grudges and, what was more, Maxwell Perkins thought *Torrents* was 'a grand book.' He'd offered a 1,500 dollar advance against the royalties of it and the new book, which Ernest had newly titled *The Sun Also Rises*, as a package, which was more money than we'd ever heard of anyone getting. He was set to leave New York at the end of the week, but changed his mind at the last minute to extend his stay. He was on top of the world, after all, and there were so many interesting people around. He met Robert Benchley and Dorothy Parker and Elinor Wylie, and everything was as good as could be. Why would he rush back?

Meanwhile, the weather in Schruns had evened out. We had three feet of new snow, and in an effort to keep myself from going crazy with waiting, I skied and hiked until my legs felt stronger than ever, and my lungs hardly burned with the altitude. Up above the town, I could look down and see the hotel, in miniature. From that distance, I could cup it in my palm, but it also seemed solid and reliable. Of all the places Ernest and I had been together, this was where I felt safest and strongest. If I had to brave out weeks of uncertainty, I was glad it was here.

Ernest stayed in New York for three weeks altogether, and then there were ten more days at sea. His ship landed at Le Havre in early March, but he didn't come back to Schruns immediately. There were friends to see in Paris, after all. He was able to catch Scott and Zelda for a very nice lunch before they headed off to Nice for the spring. He saw Gerald and Sara Murphy and the MacLeishes and Pauline, too, of course.

He took care of the banking that needed to be done and saw to the apartment, and the days passed. When he finally arrived, on an afternoon shot through with bright sunlight, Bumby and I met him at the train.

'Look at you, wife,' he said when he met us on the platform. 'You're so fine and tan and lovely.'

I smiled and kissed him.

'And look at those woodchuck cheeks, Mr Bumby,' he said. 'I must say I have the most beautiful family. What great luck.'

All through dinner he was full of exciting stories about New York. It wasn't until we were in bed that I told him about the concert at Salle Pleyel, and he was nearly as excited for me as I had been for myself.

'I've always wanted this for you, Tatie. To have music in your life just like you did back home. For it to matter that much.' He ran his hands through my hair, which was growing out wildly and had become quite blond with all the sunshine. 'I didn't know how much I missed you until I saw you today.'

'Didn't you?'

'There's something about coming home that reminds you of what you have.'

'I missed you the whole while.'

'That's nice too,' he said. 'It's all nice.'

I kissed him, and then lay down in the featherbed and watched him fall asleep. His eyes relaxed completely and showed no lines around them and no tiredness. He was like a boy when he slept well. I could see the child he used to be under the man, and I loved them both, simply and completely and irreversibly. I crept into the place beneath his arm that felt so right, and felt his breath moving in and out, and let myself sleep.

*

In March, the avalanches came disastrously to Schruns. Herr Lent was leading a party of Germans when the first loss came. There'd been so much sun, conditions were dangerous, and although Lent had told the Germans not to come, they came anyway and insisted on skiing whether he led them or not. So he took them to the soundest slope he knew and crossed it himself, first, to be sure. They came across as a group, thirteen of them reaching the center of the slope just as the hillside came crushing down, burying all thirteen. By the time a rescue party arrived to dig them out, nine were dead.

When Lent and his pretty assistant Fraulein Glaser came to spend an evening with us at the Taube, we heard the whole thing first hand.

'One man got caught in heavy snow, old snow, especially wet and deep,' Lent said. 'We didn't find him for two days. The rescuers dug and dug, and when he finally turned up it was his blood that had made an easy trail for us to follow. He'd nearly twisted his head off trying to find a way to breathe.'

'Right to the bone,' Fraulein Glaser added. She was so fresh and lovely with her tightly knotted hair and a tanned brown face that it was almost a shock to hear such horrible details coming from her. 'There was another man, years ago, killed in a powder snow avalanche. He'd been turning to wave to his friend, and both of them died while waving, smiling.'

'I can't believe the part about them smiling,' I said.

'I can,' Ernest said. The fire crackled and snapped and we all went quiet for a time. 'Maybe it's like bullfighting or anything else,' he finally said, staring into his cup of mulled wine. 'Maybe you can learn the avalanche, versing yourself on the conditions and what sets them off and how to survive in one if you're taken away.'

'Perhaps,' Lent said. 'You might improve your chances, in any case, but it would never stop being dangerous.'

'Do you think we'll get up again this season?' Ernest asked.

'Unlikely,' Lent said. 'And if you could talk someone into taking you up the mountain, it wouldn't be me. I couldn't live with myself if something happened a second time.'

Fraulein Glaser nodded compassionately, but Ernest didn't seem the least bit chastened by Lent's experience. He was still thinking about how it might be done. I could tell by the spark in his eyes that any challenge set off. He wanted to test his skill and his fear, too, just as I was thinking, *Men have died. We shouldn't be here at all.*

Because Lent remained adamant about our not skiing, we were happy to get a letter from Dos Passos, near the end of March, saying he was coming by for a visit with the Murphys. When they arrived, being at Schruns was like being anywhere with the very rich. It was an incomparable party at all hours of the day, and everyone was jolly.

'I love your little hideaway,' Sara Murphy said when she came to breakfast in new and absolutely pristine ski clothes even though the skiing was nil.

'It's the best place around,' I agreed.

'But not hidden any longer,' Ernest said with a snide smile.

Ernest was often quick to complain about the Murphys' unending good taste and loads of ready cash. He had more patience with Sara, because she was so beautiful and gave us all something nice to look at. Gerald was trickier. He was too polished for Ernest, too refined. His clothes were beautiful and he spoke so well, one couldn't help but feel he'd built himself from the ground up into a creature that was only elegance, only charm. But he also seemed strangely determined to do whatever it took to impress Ernest and gain his friendship and approval. We couldn't reach the slopes, but Ernest gave Gerald skiing lessons on the hill behind the Taube, and it was here Gerald began to call Ernest 'Papa' because he was the seasoned teacher and loved that role. He said, 'Show me again how to cut that turn at the bottom of the slope, Papa. That was a beauty.'

Ernest remained wary. 'They could buy the whole stinking Riviera if they chose,' he said in bed one night. 'And they'd people it with lots of interesting specimens to entertain them at all hours, like us. We're all monkeys for the organ grinder and Dos is the worst. He hasn't got any spleen left at all, he works so hard to keep them.'

'But some of it's nice, and they're very generous, aren't they?'

'Here's my good and true wife again. Would it kill you to agree with me once?'

'Would it kill you to see the good in them? They admire you to no end.'

'The very rich only admire themselves.'

We lay still for some moments and in the silence I could hear Bumby's dry cough in the next room. The older he grew, the less often he woke in the night, and we didn't bother employing Tiddy now except by day. But as I listened to the cough build, I thought that it might be nice to have her there, for moments like this one.

'Are you going to get that?' Ernest said. 'You wouldn't want him to wake our good and generous guests.'

'Do you have to be such a perfect ass?' I said, getting up tiredly and reaching for my robe.

'I do, yes. It keeps me in shape.' He rolled over and made a big show of getting comfortable for sleep while I went in to mind the baby, who wasn't really even awake. He coughed with his eyes closed, still dreaming, and when the spell finally settled, he seemed perfectly well and breathed deeply. When I went back to bed, I crawled in quietly thinking Ernest would already be asleep, but he wasn't.

'I'm sorry I'm such a crotchety shit,' he said in the dark. 'You've always been the better guy.'

'I'm not,' I said and turned to face him. 'We're the same guy, aren't we?'

'Sure,' he said, and he tousled my hair and kissed me on the nose. 'Goodnight, Tatie.'

'Goodnight, Tatie,' I said back.

Thirty-Six

At Chenonceaux the château stood, reflected perfectly in the Cher River. It looked as if it was there because I'd imagined it, that it had come out of my dream to hover until I turned away and it dissolved. My eyes were drawn over and over to the doubled string of arches until I couldn't tell which was the real and which was the still mirror.

'It's called the Ladies Castle,' Pauline said, reading from her guidebook.

'Why?' Jinny asked.

'It doesn't say why. Maybe because it's the grandest lady around.'

'Maybe it's where the ladies were corseted up and kept quiet,' Jinny said. 'While the men were over in their castle entertaining whores and chewing on great sides of beef.'

I laughed. 'One would think you didn't like men at all.'

'Oh, they have their uses.'

'I should say so,' Pauline said.

We were traveling in the Loire Valley, in château country. I'd never been before, but Jinny and Pauline knew just where to stay and which restaurants to visit and what to order. We'd had potted minced pork in Tours; wild boar and quail and buttery veal cutlets; white asparagus and mushrooms that melted on your tongue and seven kinds of *chèvre*. Everywhere we went there was a different regional wine to try, and at night we slept awfully well in the best inns. At first I felt strange about letting the girls foot the bill for everything, but they kept insisting that I was their guest, and that the whole trip had been invented because they wanted to treat me.

Ernest generally hated for me to accept charity, but when Pauline and Jinny proposed the Loire scheme, not long after we returned to Paris in April, he'd surprised me by encouraging me to go.

'Marie Cocotte will come around every day and feed us,' he said. 'The book's done. I'll take Mr Bumby to the bicycle races every day and park him in the sun for long naps. We'll be a fine team, and you've earned your break.'

I had, I thought. In the last few weeks at Schruns I'd spent every spare moment preparing my concert pieces, afraid I wouldn't be ready. We'd told everyone we knew, and the hall was already nearly sold out. That alone was a maddening thought, but I stuck to the work at hand, each piece, phrase and nuance, trusting that when the time came, I could rely on habit if everything else failed. Meanwhile, Ernest had been throwing everything he had into finishing up *Sun*, which he'd been rewriting at a clip of several chapters a day. Now he was preparing to mail the manuscript to Maxwell Perkins.

'I'm thinking of dedicating it to Mr Bumby,' he said, 'and including something about the book being full of instructive anecdotes.'

'Are you serious?'

'Of course not. It's meant to be ironic. Scott says I shouldn't do it, but I think it's fine. Bumby will know that I really mean don't ever live this way, like these poor lost savages.'

'When he can read, you mean,' I said, laughing.

'Yes, of course.'

'It's not easy to know how to live, is it? He's lucky to have you as a papa and someday he'll be so proud.'

'I hope you mean it.'

'Of course, Tatie. Why wouldn't I?'

'Because it's not always easy to know how to live.'

As I packed for my trip, I had to admit that I was relieved to have our Paris routine back and Pauline well in it. As soon as we'd returned, she had come around to the sawmill immediately and was wonderfully herself, laughing and joking with both of us, calling us her 'two dearest men'.

'God, I've missed you, Pfife,' I said, and meant it all through.

As we started our trip, both sisters were in the merriest of spirits. For two days, we stopped at every château starred on the map, each of which seemed grander and more exquisite than the last. But as time passed, Pauline's mood seemed to shift.

At the Château d'Azay-le-Rideau, a stronghold of white stone that appeared to be floating up out of the lily pond that bounded it, she looked at everything with eyes darkened and sad. 'Please let's go,' she said. 'I don't want to see anything.'

'You're just hungry, ducks,' Jinny said. 'We'll have lunch right after.'

'The carpets are supposed to be Persian splendor,' I said, looking at the guidebook Pauline had passed to me.

'Oh, shut up, will you, Hadley?'

'Pauline!' Jinny said sharply.

Pauline looked shocked that she'd actually said what she'd said, and she walked quickly toward the car. For my part, I was so stung I felt the blood leave my face.

'Please don't mind her,' Jinny said. 'I don't think she's sleeping well. She's always been sensitive that way.'

'What is it really? Does she not want me here?'

'Don't be silly. It was all her idea. Just give her a little space and she'll come around.'

Jinny and I spent the better part of an hour walking through the park around the château, and when we got back to the car, Pauline was more than halfway through a bottle of white wine that had been chilling on ice in the boot. 'Please forgive me, Hadley. I'm such a daft ass.'

'That a girl,' Jinny said.

'It's all right,' I said. 'We all have our moods.'

But all that day she drank too much and seemed to be simmering just under the surface of our good time, no matter what we ate or saw or did, no matter what I or anyone else said.

Late in the afternoon we had stopped and were walking through the Jardin de Villandry on the Loire River. The whole thing was perfection and splendor. The garden stood on three levels, with the first level rising out of the river plateau and surrounded by flowering linden trees. The other levels were terraced in pleasing geometries, curving around paths of small pink stones. There was a herb garden, a music garden, and then one called the Garden of Love, where Pauline walked ever more slowly. She finally stopped still near a patch of love-lies-bleeding, and then, inexplicably, started to cry.

'Please stop, darling,' Jinny said. 'Please be happy.'

'I don't know what's gotten into me.' She wiped her tears

with a pressed linen handkerchief, but couldn't stop them coming. 'I'm sorry,' she said, with a small choke in her voice, and then ran, her good shoes tripping on the pink stones.

THIRTY-SEVEN

When he saw Pfife on the street in her good-looking coat, she was always so fresh and full of life. She cocked her head to one side when he talked to her and squinted her eyes and listened. She listened with everything she had and talked that way too. When she said things about his work, he had the feeling that she understood what he was trying to do and why it mattered. He liked all of this, but hadn't meant to do anything about it. Then one night she'd been at the sawmill until very late. Hadley had gone to bed with a raw throat and they'd stayed up talking. When it came time for her to go, instead of putting her in a taxi, he walked her home. It was three miles at least, but they covered the distance in a kind of trance, smiling strangely at one another, their steps ringing on the cobblestones. They walked ever more slowly as they approached her door, but finally there was nowhere else to go.

She turned to him and said, 'You can kiss me.'

'All right,' he said, and kissed her deeply on the lips. Then he walked home alone, desire buzzing through him, wondering if Hadley would suspect anything.

A few days later they met by chance at the Dingo. It had been chance for him in any case. They'd each had a glass of Pernod and then she said, 'If we *stay here some of our friends will eventually turn up and then we'll have to stay for good.'*

'Where should we go?'

She'd given him a serious look and paid the check herself, and then they'd walked quickly to her apartment on the rue Picot. Her sister was out for the evening and they hadn't even turned on the lights or pretended they were there for anything else. He'd been surprised by her intensity — she was very Catholic, after all, and he'd guessed she'd be timid and full of guilt. But the guilt came much later. For the moment, there was only the totally convincing and wonderful strangeness of her. Her narrow hips and very long white legs were nothing like his wife's. Her breasts were like the small tight halves of peaches and she was a new country, and he was very happy to be with her as long as he didn't think about what it stood for.

When he went home to his wife, he'd felt like a terrible shit for doing it and swore to himself that it wouldn't happen again. And then, when it did, over and over, more and more planned and deliberate all the time, he wondered how he'd ever get out of the mess he'd made. If Hadley knew it would kill her twice, once for each of them betraying her. But if she didn't, well, that was almost worse. It wasn't even quite true, that way, because she was his life and nothing meant anything if she didn't know it.

He loved them both and that's where the pain came in. He carried it in his head like a fever and made himself sick thinking about it. And sometimes, after hours lying awake, it came to him clearly that he only had to change his life to match his circumstances. Pound had managed it. He had Shakespear and Olga both and no one doubted he loved them. He didn't have to lie; everyone knew everything and it all worked because he'd kept pushing and hadn't compromised or become someone else.

That was the trick, wasn't it? Ford was almost as old as his own father, but he had done it too. When his first wife wouldn't divorce him, he simply changed his name and married Stella, who was very beautiful and true and also never enough. He took up with Jean Rhys, moving her right into the house where Stella painted in one room and the baby cried in another, and in yet another he edited Jean's books and bedded her too. Everyone called Jean 'Ford's girl' and Stella 'Ford's wife,' and that made everything plain enough, apparently.

Why couldn't Pfife be his girl? The arrangement might be deadly, but couldn't marriage also be, if it banked the coals in you? You could grow very quiet in marriage. A new girl got you talking and telling her everything made it fresh again. She called you out of your head and stopped the feeling that the best part of you was being shaved away, inch by inch. You owed her for that. No matter what else happened, however terrible, you wouldn't forget it.

Thirty-Eight

'Let me just go and see about her,' Jinny said, and followed Pauline to the edge of the garden, where a small green berm stood surrounded by willow trees. I couldn't hear anything they said, but saw Pauline burying her head in her hands and shaking it back and forth. That's when it struck me that Pauline was being very brave about me, about inviting me to be near her for days on end when she was very much in love with my husband. As soon as the thought formed in my mind I knew I wasn't being a jealous wife. It was true and couldn't be managed or changed. She had walked through the garden and felt it speaking to her of all she couldn't have of happiness. Ernest and I were the garden, and we could only destroy her, and it was already happening.

On the berm, Jinny bent near her and whispered something tender, and Pauline seemed calmer. But when Jinny tried to lead her back to where I stood, she resisted. Finally, Jinny came back alone.

'I don't know what to say. She's a Pandora's box of moodiness, always has been really. Ever since we were girls.'

'Jinny, please be straight with me. Is Ernest involved in this? Has Pauline fallen in love with him?'

Jinny looked at me with surprise. Her eyes were very brown and very clear under the sharp fringe of her dark bangs. 'I think they care for each other.'

That's when I saw the part I hadn't seen before and I felt very strange and stupid for missing it. 'Oh,' I said, and then could think of nothing more to say.

The rest of the trip was a blur for me. There was another interminable day, and I passed it painfully. I couldn't rally and pretend things were fine. I could barely speak to Pauline and Jinny civilly. It was too striking that once Pauline's secret was out, both of the women were easier and seemed to enjoy themselves. I began to think that they had engineered the trip specifically to let me know, in one way or another, about the affair.

Driving back the way we'd come, we saw many of the same châteaux in the distance, struck by sunlight or floating in mists as if they were made of helium. But I couldn't feel the beauty of any of it now. My head was floating also, well above my body as I wondered how far had things gotten between Ernest and Pauline and how far things might yet go for all of us. Had they become lovers in Paris, as Ernest was coming and going from New York, or even before, at Schruns? It made me sick to think of them together there. That was our garden. Our best and favorite place. But maybe nothing was safe any more.

Back in Paris, Jinny and Pauline drove me to the sawmill and dropped me there. They didn't ask to come up and I didn't offer. If Pauline wanted to look up at the windows on the second floor to see if Ernest was looking down at her, she resisted. She sat and stared straight ahead in a very pale gray hat, and we said our goodbyes like near strangers.

Upstairs, Ernest was reading in bed, and the baby was out with Marie. He put his book down when I came in and watched with growing recognition as I stood there shaking, unable to take off my hat and coat.

'You're in love with Pauline.' I made myself meet his eyes as I said it.

His shoulders stiffened and then fell. He clenched his hands and then unclenched them, but stayed silent.

'Well?'

'Well what? I can't answer you. I won't.'

'Why not, if it's true?' My breath was shallow, and it was getting harder and harder to look at him, to stare him down and pretend that I was in control of anything.

'Who gives a damn what's true? There are things you shouldn't say.'

'What about the things you shouldn't do?' My voice was arch and very high. 'What about the promises you've made?'

'Guilt won't do it, you know. If you think you can make me feel worse than I've made myself feel, you'll have to try much harder.'

'Goddamn you.'

'Yes, well. That much is guaranteed, I'd wager.' And then, as I watched him, my face fallen, my mouth open like an idiot's, he grabbed his coat and hat and went off to walk the streets in the rain.

I was stunned. All the long drive back to Paris I'd thought of what to say that would draw Ernest out and make him tell me plainly what was going on. If there was something terrible to know, I wanted it straight out and clean with no waffling or evasion. But what on earth was I supposed to do with this? His

317

silence was as much as an admission that he was in love with her, but somehow he'd turned it all back on me so that the affair wasn't the worst thing, but that I'd had the very bad taste to mention it.

When Marie came in with Bumby, I was crying so hard they were both alarmed. She stayed and helped me feed the baby and put him to bed, as I was clearly useless. As she left, she said, 'Please, Madame, is there something I can do?'

I shook my head.

'Try not to be so sad, yes?'

'I'll try.'

Outside, the gray rain fell and fell. Where had spring gone? When I'd left, the leaves had been out on the trees and the flowers were beginning to bloom, but now everything was drenched and drowned. It had been a false spring, a lie like all the other lies, and I found myself wondering if it would ever really come.

It was well past midnight when Ernest came home, drunk. I was still awake and had moved from sad to angry many times over.

'I don't want you here,' I said when he sat down on the bed to remove his shoes. 'Go home to your lover if that's what you want.'

'She's headed to Bologna,' he said. 'And how would you know what I want?'

I sat up quickly and slapped him as hard as I could, and then did it again.

He barely flinched. 'Play the victim if you want, but no one's a victim here. You should have kept your goddamned mouth shut. Now it's all shot to hell.'

'Are you telling me you would have been perfectly happy to just go on this way, in love with her, saying nothing about it?'

'Something like that,' he said.

'I can't believe you,' I said, and began to cry. 'I can't believe any of this.'

Just then, the baby woke in the next room and whimpered.

'Perfect,' he said, staring at the wall. 'Now I guess he'll start wailing too.'

He left the room and went into the kitchen, and a few minutes later when I came out in my robe to check on Bumby, he had already poured himself a whiskey and was reaching for the siphon.

Ernest never came to bed that night, and in the morning, when I got up to make breakfast, he had already left the apartment. Late in the afternoon he came home and when he took off his coat and emptied his notebook and pencils from his pocket, I was surprised to see them, on this of all days.

'You worked today?'

'Like the devil,' he said. 'I got a draft of a new story. It came out whole as a fish.'

I could only shake my head as I put some cold meat, cheese and bread on a plate. Bumby came over as Ernest ate and sat on his knee and shared nibbles of his bread. I watched them for a time and then said, 'What happens now?'

'I don't know. I haven't written this. I haven't any idea what comes next.'

'Will you still go to Spain?'

'Why not? The plans are all made. I'm leaving on the twelfth. Not a day later if I don't want to miss the corrida in Madrid. I'll be back for your concert, of course. That won't be a problem.'

'I can't do it now,' I said. I'd all but forgotten about the performance. How could I possibly give it without dissolving into tears in front of everyone we knew?

'Why the hell not? The theater's booked. You can't back out.'

'I can and I will.'

'Everyone will talk, you know.'

'They're probably doing that now. I wouldn't be surprised if the cafés aren't burning with this gossip.'

'To hell with them. Nothing hurts if you don't let it.'

'You don't really believe that?'

'I have to,' he said.

'Have you told Pauline?'

'That you know? Not yet.'

'Well, let's ask her how we go on from here. I'm sure she has some brilliant plan.'

'Careful there.'

'Why? Are you afraid I'm becoming a bitch? If I am, we know who's to blame.' He got up and came back with a bottle of brandy and two glasses. 'Drink this,' he said, filling the tumbler and passing it across the table. 'You could use it.'

'Yes, let's get stinking drunk.'

'All right. We've always been good at that.'

Thirty-Nine

The next few days were so strained and so full of quarrels, even in daylight, on the street, that Ernest packed a bag and left for Madrid early. It was easier to have him gone. I didn't know what the future held, but I knew I needed some rest and time to think.

I'd felt like a coward doing it, but I had followed through and cancelled my performance. Now I had to deal with the awkwardness of making excuses to everyone. It felt terrible lying, blaming my nerves and lack of preparation – but not as terrible as going through with it, I thought. Particularly since news of the affair had spread, just as I'd suspected.

It was Kitty who told me. She came around just after Ernest left for Madrid and listened to everything in her stalwart way, letting me fall to pieces around her. Once I'd finished and only had tears left in me, she quietly said, 'I'd like to say I'm surprised, but I'm not. I saw Pauline on the street just before she headed to Schruns. She had her skis on her shoulders and was all loaded down with packages, and though she didn't say anything really, there was something about the way she talked about you two. An authority in her voice, as if you both belonged to her.'

'She has nerve. I'll give her that.'

'Zelda said she and Scott were at the Rotonde when Pauline came in and started to go on about a letter she'd gotten from Hem, and how funny it was that he knew so much about women's perfume, and did anyone else find that funny? She was obviously baiting. Luring suspicion.'

'Or maybe she couldn't help herself. She's in love with him.'

'Are you saying you have sympathy for her?' Kitty asked incredulously.

'Not at all. But love is love. It makes you do terribly stupid things.'

'I still love Pauline, God help me, but she's very wrong in this. Freedom is one thing, but you draw the line at a friend's husband. You have to.'

The weather turned glorious; creamy white horse-chestnut blossoms choking the air with their sweetness – but I couldn't get out and enjoy it. Bumby had fallen ill. It began with sniffles, but soon turned to fever. Now he was pale and listless, and fighting a terrible cough that only descended fully at night, waking us both. We kept to the apartment. I read him books and made up silly songs to distract him, but it was very difficult, for even several minutes together, to forget that my life was falling apart.

Every few days there would be a cable from Ernest. He was miserable in Madrid. The city was too cold and dusty and the good corridas were far and few. The bulls were mysteriously weak and sick; he felt like a sick bull too. There was no one to drink with. All his good friends were elsewhere, and he was very lonely. He was writing, though. In one Sunday afternoon, he'd finished three stories that he'd only had broken up drafts of before, and the good energy seemed not to be slowing. He'd keep writing there and play it out. Were Bumby and I coming? If so, we should hurry up. He needed the company to keep from going crazy.

I wrote back saying that Bumby wasn't well enough to travel. I wasn't in any state either. I didn't know where Ernest and I stood, and didn't think I could bear waiting things out in a hotel room in Spain, particularly if I had to see cables arriving from Pauline every day. No, it was better to have this distance, and his writing was going all the stronger for it anyway. He always worked well during difficult times, as if pain helped him get to the bottom of something in himself and got the real machinery turning.

It also didn't surprise me that he was feeling sorry for himself. There are men who love to be alone, but Ernest was not one of them. Solitude made him drink too much, and drinking kept him from sleeping, and not sleeping brought the bad voices and bad thoughts up from their depths, and then he drank more to try and silence them. And even if he didn't admit it to me, I knew he was suffering because he'd hurt me badly with the affair. Knowing he was suffering pained me. That's the way love tangles you up. I couldn't stop loving him, and couldn't shut off the feelings of wanting to care for him – but I also didn't have to run to answer his letters. I was hurting too, and no one was running to me.

Near the end of May, Bumby's cough had rallied slightly, and I packed our bags and we went to Cap d'Antibes, to Gerald and Sara Murphy's Villa America, where we had been invited to stay at the guesthouse. Many of our set were already there. Scott and Zelda were nearby at the Villa Paquita, in Juan-les-Pins, and Archie and Ada MacLeish were staying on a little cove a few miles up the beach. There would be plenty of sun and swimming and good food, and even though I knew it might be awkward for me, given that whispers had been circling for some time, I also wasn't so provincial as to think our story would interest this group for long. Zelda had men dying for her, after all, and was proud to brag about it. Ours was barely a mouthful of gossip when you thought of it that way. Whatever the risks, I needed the break. Ernest would join us when he was through in Madrid, and by that time, I was hoping I felt enough like myself that I could face him.

Gerald met our train and drove us back to Villa America in a shockingly fast lemon-yellow roadster. I couldn't help but be impressed by it all. The Murphys had been sculpting and perfecting the villa for more than a year while they lived in a hotel in town. Before they arrived on the scene in Antibes, there wasn't really a scene. The town was small and sleepy, with a narrow spring season. No one ever went to the Riviera in summer, but the Murphys loved the summer and they loved Antibes; they would find a way to make the place suit them. They paid a hotelier in town to stay open all year for them alone, and soon enough, other hotels were staying open and more were being built. The beach had once been buried in seaweed, but Gerald had cleared it himself, a few yards at a time, and now it was pristine. Before the Murphys came along and made it fashionable, no one ever thought to sun on the beach. They invented sunbathing, and to be around them for any time at all made you think they'd invented everything that was good and pleasurable and civilized.

Their estate sat on seven acres of terraced gardens, with

heliotrope running everywhere. There were lemon and date and olive and pepper trees. Black and white figs grew and an exotic Arabian maple with sheer white leaves. Aside from the guesthouse, there was also a small farm and stable, a gardener's cottage, a chauffeur's cottage, a playhouse for the Murphys' three children and a private painting studio for Gerald. Before we headed to the main house, he walked us to the end of a rocky path and onto the white, white sand of their private beach. Scott and Zelda were there, reclining on wide cane beach mats and drinking sherry from dainty crystal glasses. Scotty played nearby in the surf with the Murphy children, all of them very blond and dark-skinned from the sun.

'Come have a drink, Hadley,' Zelda said, rising to kiss me on both cheeks. 'You must need one after Gerald's driving.'

'It is rather paralyzing coming over the coast road,' I said.

'Scott's cocktails are paralyzing too, but that's what's nice about them,' she said, and everyone laughed.

'How's Hem getting on?' Scott asked, shading his eyes and squinting up at me.

'Well enough, I think. The writing's been good.'

'Damn him anyway,' Scott said cheerfully. 'It's always good for him, isn't it?'

'Is that what he says? Don't believe it.'

'See there,' Zelda said, as if settling something between them.

'Yes, darling. I heard her.' Then both of them handed their glasses to Gerald for refreshing.

The main house had black marble flooring, black satin furniture and bright white walls. The severity of the color scheme was offset, everywhere, by flowers from the garden – just-picked jasmine, gardenia, oleander, roses and camellias. The whole operation was stunning and I felt conspicuous even standing in the entry with my worn summer jacket. None of my clothes would do, in fact.

'Sara's up in bed with a bit of a cold,' Gerald explained. 'I'm sure she'll rally and come down shortly.'

Bumby and I changed into our beach things and went down to the beach to wait for Sara, but she didn't come down all that day. I was beginning to wonder if I should feel slighted when the Murphys' physician arrived in the evening to check on her.

'He might as well take a look at Bumby too,' Gerald said. 'Sara can hear his cough from all the way upstairs. It really is worrisome.'

'It is, isn't it? I was hoping the Mediterranean air would do him some good.'

'It might yet, but why not consult the doctor? Just to be safe.'

I agreed, and after a very thorough examination with Bumby being a perfect lamb, undressed to his skivvies on the bed in the guesthouse, the doctor diagnosed whooping cough.

'Whooping cough?' I said with mounting alarm. 'That's serious, isn't it?' The word that came to mind was *fatal*, but I couldn't bear to say it out loud.

'Please calm down, Mrs Hemingway,' the doctor said. 'Based on his symptoms, the boy's likely had the disease for months. The worst has passed, but he'll need plenty of rest to recover fully, and he mustn't be let near other children. We'll have to quarantine him for at least two weeks.'

He prescribed a dose of special cough medicine, and a eucalyptus rub for his chest and back, to aid breathing, but even with tonics and reassurances on hand, I was worried about Bumby. I also felt terrible for not knowing he should have seen a doctor in Paris.

As soon as we got the diagnosis, Sara grew agitated and

began making plans for us to be moved to a hotel in town. 'You'll still be our guests,' she insisted. 'We just can't have him here. You understand, don't you?'

I did, of course. In fact, I felt dreadful that we were such a source of concern for everyone. I couldn't stop apologizing as I packed our things.

The Murphys called their chauffer to deliver us to our new lodgings, and the next morning sent him back with groceries and fresh fruit and vegetables from their garden. It was all very generous. I don't know what we would have done without someone to look out for us there. But they couldn't help with the nursing or the isolation, and I knew I couldn't bear it alone. I sent a cable to Marie Cocotte in Paris, asking her to come and help care for Bumby, and one to Ernest in Madrid, explaining the situation. I didn't ask him to come, though; I wanted him to arrive on his own or not at all.

Very shortly after it was clear we'd need to be quarantined, Scott and Zelda stepped in and volunteered the lease on their villa at Juan-les-Pins. They would move to a larger villa near the casino that had its own beach. This was a godsend, really. The place was lovely, with pretty hand-painted tile everywhere. There was a small garden with poppies and orange trees, and Bumby could play there safely, without infecting any other children. But I felt very low and separate and worried that Bumby would have a relapse. I spent my days rubbing eucalyptus oil on his chest and back, and trying to bribe him into taking his bitter medicine. At night I woke every few hours to feel his forehead for returning fever. The doctor came every day, and so did telegrams from Paris and Madrid. Pauline wrote to say how sorry she felt for me but also for Ernest, who was still lonely in Spain and feeling very desperate about it. I was so angry to read this I very nearly wrote back saying she could have him, but in the end I just folded the telegram in thirds, and then tore it into pieces.

One evening as I sat reading in the little garden, I heard a honking car horn, and there, coming up the drive, were the Murphys and the Fitzgeralds and the MacLeishes, all in separate cars. They stopped just in front of the terrace behind the iron fence and the women glided out in their long beautiful dresses looking like works of art. The men were beautiful in their suits, and everyone was in high spirits. Gerald held a pitcher of very cold martinis, and as I walked up to the fence, he handed me a glass.

'Reinforcements have arrived,' he said, clearly pleased that he'd had the idea. Everyone gathered around to lift a glass, except for Scott.

'I'm on the wagon and trying very hard to be good,' he said.

Zelda frowned. 'It's so very boring to hear you say it, darling.'

'It's true,' he said. 'But just the same, I'm a good boy today. Smile for me will you, Hadley?'

We all stood at the fence and chatted for some minutes, and then they glided back into the cars, followed by laughter, and headed off to the casino in town. I watched them go, wondering if I'd dreamed them, and then went inside to an early bedtime and a book.

When Ernest finally came in from Madrid, ten days after our quarantine was imposed, the Murphys threw him a champagne and caviar party at the casino. Marie had arrived to care for Bumby and I felt tremendously relieved and free to leave the villa for the first time.

Ernest looked pale and tired when he arrived at the house.

It had been cold in Madrid and he'd worked hard most days, late into the night. I was still exhausted from worry over Bumby, and also didn't know at all how Ernest was feeling about me, but he greeted me with a nice long kiss and told me he'd missed me. I let myself be kissed, and didn't ask what he'd decided to do about Pauline. I didn't think it was safe to mention her name at all, and because I didn't, and because that was the principal thing at stake in our lives, I felt absolutely powerless. 'I missed you too,' I said, and then went to dress for the party.

Gerald had spared no expense in welcoming Ernest to town, and why should he? The Murphys had inherited their money and had never once been without. There were camellias floating in glass bowls and mounds of oysters and fresh corn dotted with sprigs of basil. It seemed possible that the Murphys had specially ordered the deep purple Mediterranean sky and the nightingales thick in the hedges, trilling and whistling a series of crescendos. It began to grate on me. Did everything have to be so choreographed and civilized? Who could trust it anyway?

As we waited for Scott and Zelda to arrive, Ernest began telling the table about his recent correspondence with Sherwood Anderson over *The Torrents of Spring*, which had just been published in the States.

'I had to write him,' he said. 'The thing was going to be out any day and I felt inclined to tell him how it happened and why I would be such a son of a bitch after he'd done so much to help me.'

'Good man, Hem,' Gerald said.

'Right, yes. You'd think so, wouldn't you?'

'Didn't he take it well?' Sara asked.

'He said it was the most insulting and patronizing letter he'd ever gotten, and that the book itself was rot.'

'He didn't really say that,' I said.

'No, he said that it might have been funny if it had been a dozen pages instead of a hundred.'

'I thought it was awfully funny, Hem,' Gerald said.

'You haven't read the book, Gerald.'

'Yes, but from everything you've said, it's obviously very, very funny.'

Ernest turned away with a sour expression and began to apply himself to his glass of whiskey. 'Stein let me have it too,' he said, coming up for air. 'She says I've been a shit and a very bad Hemingstein indeed, and that I can go to hell.'

'Oh dear,' Sara said. 'I'm sorry to hear it.'

'Damn her anyway.'

'Come on now, Tatie,' I said. 'You don't mean that. She's Bumby's godmother after all.'

'Then he's bitched, isn't he?'

I knew Ernest's bravado was almost entirely invented, but I hated to think of all the good friends we'd lost because of his pride and volatile temper, starting in Chicago with Kenley. Lewis Galantière, our first friend in Paris, had stopped speaking to Ernest when he'd called Lewis's fiancée a despicable shrew. Bob McAlmon had finally had enough of Ernest's bragging and rudeness and now crossed the street to avoid us in Paris. Harold Loeb had never recovered from Pamplona, and Sherwood and Gertrude, two of Ernest's biggest champions, now topped the long and painful list. Just how many others would fall, I wondered as I looked around the candle lit table.

'Hemmy, my boy!' Scott shouted as he and Zelda crested the steps up from the beach. Scott had his socks and shoes off and his trousers rolled up. His tie was loose, and his jacket was rumpled. He looked several sheets to the wind.

'Have you been for a swim, Scott?' Ernest said.

330

'No, no. I'm dry as a bone.'

Zelda laughed at this with a small snort. 'Yes, yes, Scott. You're very dry, and that's why you just recited all of Longfellow to that poor man on the pier.' She'd drawn her hair severely back from her face and pinned a giant white peony behind her ear. Her make-up was impeccable, but her eyes looked strained and tired.

'Who doesn't like Longfellow?' Scott said as he landed in his chair with some aplomb, and we all laughed thinly. 'Come dear,' he said to Zelda, who was still standing. 'Let's have a drink with all these marvelously affected people. There's caviar. What the blazes would we do without caviar?'

'Please shut up, darling,' she said, taking her seat. She smiled broadly and falsely at all of us. 'He'll be good now, I promise.'

The waiter came and brought more drinks, and then came again to serve the table next to us, where a beautiful young girl was sitting down to dinner with what looked like her father.

'Now that's a pretty arrangement,' Scott said, staring at the girl hungrily. Ernest elbowed him to stop, but he wouldn't stop.

'You are not a gentleman,' the father finally said to Scott in French, and then escorted the girl inside, well away from us.

'A gentleman is only *one* of the things I am not,' Scott said. 'I'm also not well and not smart and not nearly drunk enough to spend any kind of time with your lot.'

Gerald paled and turned to whisper something to Sara.

'I say Gerald, old chap. How about you chuck an oyster at a fellow? I'm famished.'

Gerald looked at him coldly and turned away to speak to Sara again.

'Sara,' Scott said, trying to draw her attention away from her husband. 'Sara, please look at me. Please.'

But she wouldn't, and that's when Scott picked up a cut-glass ashtray from the table and pitched it well over Gerald's shoulder at an empty table behind. Sara flinched. Gerald ducked and barked at Scott to stop. Scott grabbed another ashtray, which hit the table dead center and then ricocheted off with a loud clang.

Zelda seemed set on ignoring him entirely, but the rest of us were appalled and embarrassed.

'C'mon Prince Charming,' Ernest finally said flatly. He went over to Scott and took his elbow, helping him up. 'Let's have a dance,' he said, and then led Scott right off the terrace and down the steps to the beach. Everyone stared after them except for Zelda, who was looking intensely at the hedges.

'Nightingale,' she said. 'Was it a vision, or a waking dream?'

Archie MacLeish coughed and said, 'Yes. Well.' Ada touched her marcelled hair lightly, as if it were glass, and I looked out to sea, which was black as the sky and invisible. Years and years later, the waiter brought the check.

I slept late the next morning, knowing Bumby was in Marie's capable care. When I came downstairs, Scott and Ernest sat at the long table in the dining room with a sheaf of carbon pages laid out before them.

'Scott's just had a momentous idea,' Ernest said.

'Good morning, Hadley,' Scott said. 'Very sorry for last night and all that. I'm a proper ass, aren't I?'

'Yes,' I said, and then laughed lightly, with the affection I truly felt. When he was sober, as now, he was sane and sound — as refined as anyone you'd ever want to meet. I went to get some coffee and came back to the table to hear about the scheme.

Ernest said, 'In the first fifteen pages of *Sun*, we get Jake's autobiography, and Brett and Mike's back story, but all of that we also get later, or it's explained enough anyhow. Scott says we lop it all off, right at the head.'

'I think it will work,' Scott said very seriously, nodding into his café crème.

'It's what I've always said about the stories, that you get by with as little explanation as possible. It's all there already or it's not. The exposition slows it and ruins it. Now's my chance to see if it will work for something as long as a novel. What do you think, Tatie?' His eyes were very bright and he looked so young and like the boy I'd met nearly six years before in Chicago that I had to smile, no matter what else I felt.

'I think it sounds brilliant. You'll make it work beautifully. Get the knife.'

'That's my girl.'

Don't forget that, I wanted to say. *I'm still your best girl.*

I took my coffee to the terrace and looked out past the rooftops of the little town to where the sea stood bright blue and uncompromised by anything. Not a seagull, not a cloud. Behind me, the men had bowed their heads again and were back at work, talking it through meticulously because it was heart surgery and they were the surgeons, and it was as important as anything they'd ever done. Scott could be a terrible, painful drunk. Ernest could shove cruelly against everyone who'd ever helped him up and loved him well – but none of that mattered when the patient was at hand. In the end, for both of them, there was really only the body on the table and the work, the work, the work.

For a solid week after Ernest arrived from Madrid, we followed a routine that seemed very nearly sustainable. Every morning, we had sherry and biscuits on our terrace at Juan-les-Pins, just like they did at Villa America. At two o'clock, we went over to have lunch with the Murphys or the MacLeishes, while Bumby napped or played with Marie. At cocktail time, our driveway would fill with three cars and much laughter as we went back on the quarantine and tried to make it stick, passing good food and liquor through the grillwork of the fence.

Ernest wrote very hard for the first few days, but then realized it was impossible to be really alone – and that maybe he didn't really *want* to be alone. Scott tried to get back on the wagon but failed miserably. He and Ernest spent a great deal of time talking about work, but they didn't do any of it. They sunned on the beach and soaked up praise from the Murphys as if they could never get enough.

Sara was a natural beauty, with a thick, tawny bob and clear, piercing eyes. Scott and Ernest both longed for her attention, and Zelda couldn't stand the competition. She grew edgier and bolder by the day, but she wouldn't direct any ire at Sara. They were friends and confederates after all – so she reserved her sharpest barbs for Ernest.

Zelda and Ernest had never liked each other. He thought she had too much power over Scott, that she was a destructive force and probably half-mad to boot. She thought he was a phony, putting on macho airs to hide an effeminate center.

'I think you're in love with my husband,' she said to Ernest one night when we were down at the beach and everyone had had too much to drink.

'Scott and I are fairies? That's rich,' he said.

Zelda's eyes were hard and dark. 'No,' she said. 'Just you.'

I thought Ernest might hit her, but she'd laughed shrilly and turned away, beginning to take off her clothes. Scott had been talking intently to Sara, but he came to full attention then. 'What on earth are you doing, dear heart?'

'Testing your nerve,' she said.

To the right of the small beach was a towering cluster of stones. The highest point was thirty feet or more above the waves, and the current below was always choppy, swirling over hidden jagged points. This is where Zelda headed at a steady swim while we all watched with a horrible curiosity. What would she do? What wouldn't she do?

When she reached the base, she scaled the rocks easily. Scott stripped and followed her, but he'd barely reached the outcropping when she let out an Indian cry and plunged off. There was a terrible moment when we wondered if she'd killed herself, but she bobbed to the surface and gave an exhilarated laugh. The moon was very bright that night and we could easily see the shapes their bodies made. We could also hear more wild laughter as Zelda clambered up to do it again. Scott had a go at it too, both of them drunk enough to drown.

'I've seen enough,' Ernest said, and we went home.

The next afternoon at lunch on the terrace, things were quietly strained until Sara finally said, 'Please don't scare us like that again, Zelda. It's so dangerous.'

'But Sara,' Zelda said, batting her eyes as innocently as a schoolgirl, 'didn't you know, we don't believe in conservation.'

Over the coming string of days, as Pauline lobbed her letters at us first from Bologna and then from Paris, I started to wonder if Ernest and I believed in conservation – if we had it in us to fight for what we had. Maybe Pauline was tougher than we were. She wheedled her way in, complaining that she felt so very far away from all the good action and couldn't something be done to fix that? She wrote that she wasn't afraid of the whooping cough because she'd had it as a child, and couldn't she come and share our quarantine? She sent this in a letter to me and not to Ernest and I was struck, as I often was with Pauline, at her intensity and single-mindedness. She never ever dropped her pretense that she and I were still friends. She never gave up an inch of her position.

Pauline arrived in Antibes on a blindingly clear afternoon. She wore a white dress and a white straw hat, and seemed impossibly fresh and clean, a dish of ice cream. A widening sunspot. Another woman might have felt self-conscious arriving on the scene this way, when everyone knew or at least suspected her role as mistress – but Pauline didn't have an ounce of self-consciousness about her. She was like Zelda that way. They both knew what they wanted and found a way to get it or take it. They were frighteningly shrewd and modern and I was anything but that.

'Isn't it nice for Hem,' Zelda said one evening, 'that you're so agreeable all the time? I mean, Hem really runs the show, doesn't he?'

I'd flinched and said nothing, assuming she'd said it out of jealousy over the boys' closeness, but she was right, too. Ernest did run the show and ran me over more than occasionally, and that wasn't by chance. He and I had both grown up in households where the women ruled with iron fists, turning their husbands and their children into quivering messes. I knew I would never be that way, not at any price. I'd chosen my role as supporter for Ernest, but lately the world had tipped and my choices had vanished. When Ernest looked around lately, he saw a different kind of life and liked what he saw. The rich had better days and freer nights. They brought the sun with them and made the tides move. Pauline was a new model of woman and why couldn't he have her? Why couldn't he reach out and claim everything he wanted? Wasn't that the way things were done?

For my part, I felt utterly stuck and conspired against. This was not my world. These were not my kind of people and they were drawing Ernest in and in with every passing day. What could I do or say? He might ultimately fall out of love with Pauline and come fully back to me – that was still possible – but nothing was in my control. If I gave him an ultimatum and said she couldn't stay, I would lose him. If I got hysterical and made public scenes, it would just give him an excuse to leave me. All that was left for me was a terrible kind of paralysis, this waiting game, this heartbreak game.

FORTY

He didn't know how love managed to be a garden one moment and war the next. He was at war now, his loyalty tested at every turn. And the way it had been, the aching and delirious happiness of being newly in love had passed out of his reach until he wasn't certain he'd ever had it. Now, there were only lies and compromises. He lied to everyone, beginning with himself, because it was war and you did what you had to do to stay upright. But he was losing control, if he ever had it. The lies grew tighter and more difficult all the time. And because there was sometimes more pain than he could properly cope with, he had a black buckram notebook, thick with creamy rag paper, where he put down the ways he'd thought to kill himself if it ever came to that.

You could turn on the gas and wait for the slow fog and the blue and strangled half-sleep. You could slash your wrists, the razors were always there, and there were other places on the body that were even quicker, the neck below the ear, the inner thigh. He'd seen knives in the gut and that wasn't for him. It reminded him of gored horses in Spain, the purplish coil of entrails unzipped. Not that, then, not unless there wasn't an alternative. There was out the window of a skyscraper. He'd thought of that in New York when he was drunk and happy after meeting Max Perkins and saw the Woolworth Building. Even happy he thought it. There was the deep middle of the sea, off an ocean liner at night, with only the stars as witness. But this was terribly romantic and you had to arrange the ocean liner in advance. There was any swim anywhere if you meant to do it. You could dive down deep and stay there, way down, letting the air slip out of you and just stay, and if anyone wanted you there, well, they could come and get you. But as soon as he hit on it, he knew that the only way he would really do it was with a gun.

The first time he'd seriously looked at a gun and thought about pulling the trigger he was eighteen and had just been wounded at Fossalta. He'd felt a lightning rod of pure pain take him over, more pain than he knew was possible. He'd lost consciousness and when he came to again his legs were mush and didn't belong to him at all. His head didn't either, but there he was on a stretcher, waiting to be carried away by the medics, surrounded by the dead and the dying. Overhead the sky went white, a stuttering of light and heat. Screaming. Blood everywhere. He lay there for two hours, and every time he heard the shelling, he couldn't help himself, he started to pray. He didn't know where the words came from, even, because he never prayed.

He was blood-soaked, open to the sky, and the sky was open to death. Suddenly he saw the gun, an officer's pistol very near his foot. If he could just reach it. Everyone was dying, and it was so much more normal and natural than this pain. This hideous openness. With his mind, he reached for the pistol. He reached again and failed. And then the medics came and they bore him away alive.

He'd always thought of himself as brave, but he didn't have a chance to find out that night of the shelling. He wasn't any closer to knowing now. In the fall, he'd promised himself he'd do it if the situation with Pfife wasn't resolved by Christmas, and it hadn't been and he still hadn't done it. He told himself then it was because he loved her too much and Hadley, too, and he couldn't cause suffering for either of them — but they all suffered badly anyway.

Now it was summer and things were more and more impossible. He couldn't imagine living without Hadley and didn't want to, but Pfife was winding herself more firmly around his heart. She used the word 'marriage' and meant it more all the time.

He wanted them both, but there was no having everything, and love couldn't help him now. Nothing could help him but bravery, and what was that anyhow? Was it reaching for the gun or sitting with the pain and the shaking and the terrible fear? He couldn't know for sure, but since that first gun, he'd reached for many. When the time came, he knew it would be a gun and that he'd simply trip the trigger with a bare toe. He didn't want to do it, but if things got too bad — if they got very bad indeed, then suicide was always permissible. It had to be.

FORTY-ONE

Along the Golfe-Juan a white road cut into the cliff side. You could ride a bicycle there for five or ten or fifteen miles, looking out at the bright boats in the quays, the rocky beaches and pebbled beaches and sometimes a shoal of impossibly soft-looking sand. Bathers napped beneath gaily striped red and white umbrellas looking as if they belonged in a painting. Everything did, the fishermen in dark caps releasing their nets, the stone ramparts that sheltered Antibes from the weather, and the red rooftops of the village stacked one on the other in terraced clusters.

Pauline and I often bicycled together after breakfast while Ernest worked. It hadn't been my idea, but we were there in paradise, after all, and had to do something. The lease at Villa Paquita ran out in early June, and so we rented two rooms at the Hôtel de la Pinède in Juan-les-Pins. Bumby and Marie Cocotte were nearby, in a small bungalow surrounded by pine trees. The cure for his whooping cough had at last begun to work, and he felt a little better every day. His color had returned and he was sleeping well, and our worrying about him was almost entirely gone. The quarantine was over, but we kept to ourselves in the daylight anyway, forming our own island, while just a few miles across the peninsula at Villa America, the Murphys and the Fitzgeralds and the MacLeishes carried on as before, drinking sherry with biscuits at 10:30 sharp and Tavel with caviar and toast points at 1:30 and playing bridge at a gorgeous blue and green mosaic table that had been set up on the beach for this. The image on the tabletop was of a siren with flowing hair. She balanced on a rock and gazed into the distance. At Villa America, everyone loved the siren because she seemed to be a symbol of something. They loved her the way they loved their sherry and their toast points and every moment of every ritual that wound around them like clock springs.

At the Hôtel de la Pinède, we had our own rituals. We breakfasted late, and then Ernest went off to work in a small studio off the terrace while Pauline and I rode bicycles or swam and sunned at our little beach with Bumby. After lunch we had siesta, then bathed and dressed for cocktail hour either at Villa America, in one of the terraced gardens, or at the Casino in town, and no one raised even an eyebrow in our presence or said anything that wasn't in good taste because that was the contract.

Anyone looking on from nearly any vantage point would have believed that Pauline and I were friends. She might have believed it herself. I never really knew. She certainly worked hard to stay cheerful, inventing errands for us in the village to secure freshly picked figs or the very best tinned sardines.

'Wait until you try this olive,' she would say, or whatever it was — strong coffee or pastry or nice jam. 'It's heaven.'

I must have heard her say, 'It's heaven' a thousand times over that summer, until I wanted to scream. I didn't scream, though, and that became one of the things I grew to regret.

We had two rooms at the hotel, each with a double bed and heavy bureau and shuttered windows that opened onto the coastline. Ernest and I occupied one and Pauline kept to herself in the other — at least at first. For a week or ten days, when Pauline and I came back from bicycling or swimming, she'd excuse herself to change for lunch, but then went to Ernest's studio instead, passing through the hotel to where a second entrance lay unmarked, as inconspicuous as a broom closet. They likely had a secret knock. I imagined that and so much more, though it made me sick to do it. When she came to lunch an hour or so later, she was always freshly showered and impeccably dressed. She'd sit down, smiling, and begin to praise the lunch or the day extravagantly. It was all so modulated and discreet I wondered if she took a certain pleasure playing her role, as if in her mind a film reel was spinning and she was a great actress who never fumbled a single line.

I wasn't nearly so clever. More and more I found myself at a loss for words, and didn't want to hear other people talking either. Their conversations seemed false and empty. I preferred to look at the sea, which said nothing and never made you feel alone. From my bicycle, I could watch the boats moving in blue chop, or focus on the bright green scrub growing out of the ramparts with great tenacity. Somehow it stayed rooted, no matter how the wind or waves attacked, immovable as the dark moss on the rocks below.

One morning after a storm had raged for hours the night before, Pauline was intent on pointing out every sign of demolition — overturned dinghies and fallen pine boughs, the tangle of umbrellas on the beach. I tried to escape her chatter by pedaling faster until I could only hear the rush of momentum, the purr of my wheels on the road. But she wouldn't be thrown off.

'I've been trying to talk Drum into going stateside in the fall. You know my parents have land in Arkansas. The living is so cheap there, you'd save a fortune.'

How I hated her using nicknames for him so casually. That was our language. Our dance. 'You can save your breath,' I said. 'He'd rather cut off his arm than go home.'

'Actually, he thinks it's a fine idea.'

'Arkansas?'

'Piggott. It's rustic, of course, but you like rustic.'

'I like our life here. What are you trying to do?'

'I'm sorry. I'm only thinking of you. You're bound to run out of money soon in Paris. He should be starting a second novel and worrying about nothing but that. You can afford nice new things in Piggott. Surely that means something to you.'

'No,' I said. 'It doesn't.'

For the rest of our ride, I fought back both incredulity and tears. I didn't want to let Pauline see either, and so stayed well ahead, riding faster and faster. Some of the turns were perilous. If I had lost my balance even for a moment, I might have pitched out over the stone precipice and onto the jagged boulders below. I wobbled at times but kept my course, and it was a kind of sharply edged euphoria I felt, heading back to confront Ernest. My heart was flooded with adrenaline and my mind raced. What would I say? What could he say to defend himself?

When I reached the hotel I was in such a state I left my bicycle sprawled in the gravel and hurried inside, breathless and covered with a fine film of sweat. I planned to burst into his studio, but of course the door was locked.

'Who is it?' he said when I knocked.

'Your wife,' I said, my voice thick with anger.

When he opened the door I could see he was very surprised to find me there. This was Pauline's time, or nearly so. He'd probably begun to anticipate her with growing desire.

'You can't think I'd go to Arkansas,' I spat out before he'd even closed the door.

'Oh,' he said. 'I was going to tell you soon. If you could think reasonably, you'd see it's not a bad scheme at all.'

'We'd live with her parents?' I laughed shrilly.

'No, she'd find us all a house together, maybe in town.'

I could scarcely believe what I was hearing. 'You want us to live all together.'

'We're doing that now, aren't we?'

'Yes, and it's awful. It makes me sick to my stomach to know you're making love to her.'

'I'm sorry, Tatie. But maybe that's because the situation is new and we don't know how to do it well.'

'Do you really think it *can* be done well?'

'I don't know. I don't want to lose you.'

'And if I don't agree?'

'Please, Tatie,' he said, his voice low and anguished. 'Just try. If it works and we all start to feel good about it, we'll head for Piggott in September. If it doesn't, we'll go back to Paris.'

'Alone?'

'Yes,' he said, though I could hear some kind of hesitancy or hedging in his voice. He wasn't sure about any of this.

'I think it's a mistake. All of it.'

'Maybe, but it's too late to go back. There's only what's ahead now.'

'Yes,' I said sadly, and left the way I came.

Over the next few days, I began to wonder if Ernest's proposal was a new idea, an attempt at some solution out of the mess

345

at our feet, or if he'd intended it all along. For years we'd been surrounded by triangles — freethinking, free-living lovers willing to bend every convention to find something right or risky or liberating enough. I couldn't say what Ernest felt watching their antics, but they seemed sad and even tortured to me. When we last heard from Pound, his mistress Olga Rudge had given birth to a daughter, though they agreed not to raise her. Nothing in Pound's life invited a child and neither one of them wanted to feel compromised, apparently. They gave the baby to a peasant woman in the maternity ward where Olga had delivered. The woman had miscarried and was only too happy to take her.

I was stunned that anyone could hand over a child so easily, but doubly surprised when we heard in another letter that Shakespear was pregnant. It wasn't Pound's child; in fact, she wasn't saying a word about who the father was, only that she was keeping the baby. Her behavior was obviously retaliatory. That's what terrible, sordid situations did to you, made you act crazily, against your own truths, against your self.

One afternoon when Ernest and I were napping in our room, Pauline came in on cat feet, making no noise whatsoever. I'd been having a dream in which I was being buried under tons of sand. It was an image of suffocation, and yet strangely not a nightmare. The sand felt warm and sugary, and as it crushed me slowly, I kept thinking, *This is heaven. This is heaven.* I was feeling so languid and so drugged, I didn't even know Pauline was in the room until she'd slipped under the sheets on Ernest's side of the bed. The afternoons were hot, and we slept naked. I knew what was happening, and I also didn't want to come awake enough to feel it. I never opened my eyes. My body wasn't mine exactly. No one spoke or made any noise that would shake me out of my trance. The bed was sand, I told myself. The sheets were sand. I was still in the dream.

FORTY-TWO

In the morning, when the sun pried its way through the slats of the plantation shutters and fell on my face, I knew the day had come whether I wanted it or not and I opened my eyes. A breeze pushed the cream linen curtains so they swayed. Light fell in oblong swatches along the dark wood floor, and I yawned and stretched and pushed the sheets back. Across from the bed was a long mirror and I saw myself in it, brown as can be and solid and firm from all the swimming and bicycling. My hair had lightened in the sun until the only red left was just a hint of ginger, and my eyes were clear and bright and I looked very well. I'd already stopped being surprised by this – how I could look strong and healthy when I was dying, really.

At our hotel, there were three of everything – three break-fast trays, three wet bathing suits on the line. On the crushed rock path along the windward side of the hotel, three bicycles stood on their stands. If you looked at the bicycles one way, they looked very sound, almost like sculpture, with afternoon light glinting cleanly off the chrome handlebars – one, two, three, all in a row. If you looked at them another way, you could

348

see just how thin each kickstand was under the weight of the heavy frame, and how they were poised to fall like dominoes or the skeletons of elephants or like love itself. But when I noticed this, I kept it to myself because that, too, was part of the unwritten contract. Everything could be snarled all to hell under the surface as long as you didn't let it crack through and didn't speak its name, particularly not at cocktail hour, when everyone was very jolly and working hard to be that way and to show how perfectly good life could be if you were lucky, as we were. Just have your drink, then, and another and don't spoil it.

After I dressed and bathed, I went downstairs to the little garden terrace and there was our breakfast on the table in the sun. Three *œufs au jambon* with lots of butter and pepper, three steaming brioches, three glasses of juice. Ernest came out from where he had been working, in the little room off the terrace.

'Good morning, Tatie. You're looking very well.'

'Yes,' I said. 'And so are you.'

He wore tan canvas shorts and a black and white striped fisherman's sweater from Grau-du-Roi and his feet were bare. I was dressed similarly, and when Pauline came out onto the terrace, she was freshly washed with her dark hair combed back straight from her face and she, too, wore the striped fisherman's sweater. We all looked just the same as we said good morning to one another and ate our breakfasts hungrily, as if we'd never eaten before.

The sun was already very bright on the beach, and it struck everything evenly. The sand was almost white with it. The water flashed it back blindingly.

'Our swim will be good today,' Pauline said.

'Yes,' Ernest said, breaking his brioche in half so that the steam rose prettily. 'And then we'll have Madame bring the

Bollinger, very chilled, and some of the sardines with capers. You'd like that, wouldn't you?' he said turning to me.

'It sounds perfect.'

After breakfast, I went to tell Madame what we'd planned for lunch and then packed a small bag for the beach. I found my shoes and then walked down the lane to the bungalow, where Bumby was playing in the yard.

'Hello little boy-bear,' I said, scooping him up to nibble his ears. 'I think you're taller today. You seem very large to Mama.'

He was pleased to hear this, pushing his shoulders back and jutting his round chin.

Marie said, 'No coughing at all last night, Madame.'

'Aren't you very good?' And when he nodded proudly I said, 'Come then, boy-bear, we'll go for our swim.'

At the small moon of beach at the other end of the road, Ernest and Pauline had already set up the blankets and umbrellas and were lying in the sand like tortoises with their eyes closed. We sunned on the beach all in a row while Bumby and Marie played in the shallows and made little patterns with shells in the sand. When the sun grew too hot, I went into the water, which always hit you cold and was wonderful that way. I ducked my head and then surfaced, and swam out several hundred yards, where things were still. I treaded water and let the swells buoy me. At the top of one, I could look back at the beach and see them small and perfect, my husband and child and the woman who was now more to us than we could manage. From that distance, they all looked equal and serene and I couldn't hear them or feel them. At the bottom, in the trough of the wave, I could see only the sky, that high white place that seemed not to change much for all of our suffering.

As a kind of experiment, I stopped swimming and let my arms and legs fall, my whole weight fall as deep as it would. I kept my eyes open as I sank down, and looked up at the surface. My lungs began to sting, first, and then burn, as if I'd swallowed some small piece of volcano.

I knew if I stayed there and let the water come in, come through every door of me, some things would be easier. I wouldn't have to watch my life disappear, bead by bead, away from me and toward Pauline.

The little volcano in me burned, and then something popped, and I knew that even if I didn't want to live this way anymore, I also didn't want to die. I closed my eyes and kicked hard for the surface.

Back on the beach, Pauline rose and greeted me. 'Let's try and dive, shall we?'

'I don't think I'd be very good at it.'

'I'll teach you. I'll be the diving instructor today and Hem will watch and give you your marks.'

'Please not that,' I said, trying to laugh.

'Some practicing first then.' She turned and led the way up the little path along the beach where the brown stones were piled higher and higher. They were very dark and riddled with crevices, and looked as if they'd been made by some god with clay and then baked in the sun over the millennia. The rocks were hot under our bare feet and we climbed them quickly until we stood at the top.

Pauline looked over the edge to gauge the tide pushing and falling back fifteen feet below. 'When you hear the rushing sound, that's when you jump,' she said. Then she straightened, and pointed her arms very gracefully over her head and long neck. She waited, and then, with the scalloped whoosh of the tide, she pushed from her lean legs and was out, hanging in space, and then rocketing down very straight and tall. The water closed over the place where she'd been and there was nothing, just water like the flat skin of a drum. Then she surfaced, pushing her hair back and squinting. 'Good, then,' she shouted up. 'Now you.'

'It looks too easy to be easy,' I called back, and she laughed.

Ernest had gone into the water, and swum over, around the little cornice of rocks to where Pauline bobbed and waited for me.

'Let's see you go, then,' he said, sweeping his arms back and forth.

'No marks and no corrections, or I won't do it at all,' I said.

'Don't you want to get it right?' Ernest asked, squinting.

'No, actually. If I get it at all without smashing myself to hell on the rocks, it'll be good enough.'

'Suit yourself then.'

I stood at the edge and felt the hotness under my toes and closed my eyes.

'Your arms should be straight up, touching your ears,' Pauline said.

'No corrections,' I said without opening my eyes. I stood up tall, and then arced my arms over my head. I listened for the shushing sound, but when I heard it, I found I couldn't move. I was fixed there.

'C'mon then, you've missed it,' Ernest said.

I didn't answer him and still didn't open my eyes, and there was a moment of perfect vertigo, when I heard the whooshing of the surf again and felt I was part of it, swirling with it and also standing still, swept up and sewn into the sea and into the universe, but also very, very alone. I opened my eyes and here were these two wet heads in the slow-moving waves. They looked playful and natural as seals there, and suddenly I knew I wouldn't jump and it had nothing to do with fear or embarrassment.

I wouldn't jump because I didn't want to join them. I felt the stones under my feet, smooth and hot, as I turned and climbed down slowly, undramatically.

'Hadley,' Ernest shouted after me, but I kept walking away from the beach, then down the road and toward the hotel. When I got to our room, I showered away all the sand and climbed into bed still wet and very clean and tired. The sheet was white and stiff and smelled like salt against my face. And as I closed my eyes, I made a wish that I would wake up feeling as strong and clear about things as I did just then.

When I woke up much later, I realized that Ernest hadn't come to the room at all for siesta and that he must have gone to Pauline's room instead. This was the first time he had gone to her in the daylight. Madame and Monsieur, the proprietors of the hotel would know and everyone would know. When everything was out in the daylight, it couldn't ever go back to the way it was before. *All right, then*, I thought to myself. *Maybe it's better this way.*

Just then the door to the room opened and Ernest came in. Pauline was just behind him and they walked in together.

'We've been very worried about you,' Pauline said.

'You didn't have any lunch. Are you feverish?' Ernest said. He came over and sat beside me on the bed, and then Pauline sat on the other side and they looked at me as if they were my parents. It was all so very strange and even absurd that I laughed.

'What's funny?' Pauline said.

'Nothing at all,' I said, still smiling.

'She can be very mysterious, can't she?' Pauline said to Ernest.

'Not usually, no,' Ernest said. 'But she is now. What are you thinking, Cat? Are you well?'

'Maybe not,' I said. 'I think I should rest through the evening. Do you mind?'

Pauline looked stricken and I realized she was truly worried about me, and that for whatever reason, maybe because her good Catholic upbringing urged kindness on her in the oddest moments, she needed me to be well and be her friend and approve of all of this. Approve of her taking my husband.

'Please go away,' I said to both of them.

Their eyes met over me.

'Really. Please.'

'Let me have Madame bring you something to eat,' Ernest said. 'You'll be sick if you don't eat.'

'Fine. I don't care.'

'Let me get it. I'd like to,' Pauline said, and she left to make arrangements about the meal the way a wife would.

'Everything's handed over then,' I said, once the door had closed behind her.

'What?'

'She can do everything now. She'll take care of you just fine.'

'You're not well. Just get some rest.'

'I'm not well, you're right. You're killing me, both of you.'

His eyes dropped to the sheet. 'This isn't easy for me either.'

'I know. We're a sorry, sordid lot, the three of us. If we're not careful, we'll none of us get through it without terrible big chunks missing.'

'I've thought the same. What do you want? What will help?'

'I think it's too late, don't you?' I looked to the window where the light was fading rapidly. 'You'd better leave soon or you'll miss cocktails with the Murphys.'

'I don't give a damn.'

'You do, though, and so does she. Just go. She'll be the wife for tonight.'

'I hate to hear you talk this way. It makes me think we've ruined everything.'

'We have, Tatie,' I said sadly, and closed my eyes.

FORTY-THREE

I'd like to say that that was the last of it; that what was made plain to us that afternoon forced us out of the arrangement altogether. We were in the death throes, truly, but something made us each go on for weeks afterward, the way the body of an animal goes on moving after its head is gone.

The next week was the beginning of fiesta in Pamplona. We'd made a plan very early that summer to take Gerald and Sara Murphy with us, and we followed through with all of it, while Bumby went off to Brittany with Marie Cocotte for several weeks, his cough having dried up and vanished into nothing.

We stayed at the Hotel Quintana that year, in rooms that were right across the hall from the rooms of the toreros. Every afternoon we sat in the best possible ringside seats that Gerald had paid for. Every evening we sat round the same table at the Café Iruna in dark wicker chairs and drank ourselves into a stupor. Ernest was as much of an *aficiónado* as always, and took on Gerald and Pauline's education as he had mine and Duff's and Bill Smith's and Harold Loeb's and Mike Strater's and anyone else's who would listen. Gerald was very serious about learning about the corrida. Ernest took him to the amateurs and they both went down in the ring to test their nerve with the yearling bulls, Ernest barehanded that year, and Gerald holding onto his raincoat with white knuckles. When a bull rushed Gerald at top speed, he managed to turn him off at the last moment by twitching his coat to one side.

'That was a perfect veronica, old boy,' Ernest said to Gerald later at the Iruna, but Gerald knew he wasn't a tough or strong enough man to suit Ernest. He didn't believe him and wouldn't take the praise.

'I promise to do it better next year, Papa,' he said. 'It matters to me that I truly do it well.'

I smiled at Gerald across the table, because I hadn't done anything really well or truly for months. I was sad to my bones and Ernest was too, and across the table Pauline looked as if she might burst into tears at any moment. We none of us were on our game. We none of us were living by our own standards.

At the end of that chaotic week, Pauline boarded the train for Bayonne with the Murphys. She was headed back to Paris, to work. We were off to San Sebastian because that was what we'd always planned to do. But at a certain point, I knew the plans wouldn't hold any more. The bottom would drop out of every day.

In San Sebastian there was a measure of peace with Pauline gone, but all that really meant was we could quarrel more freely, without interruption. We said nothing new to one another, but the old material still worked if we were loud and ugly enough with it.

'She's a whore,' I told him. 'And you're selfish and a coward.'

'You don't love me. You don't love anything,' he said.

'I hate you both.'

'What do you want from me?'

'Nothing,' I said. 'I wish you'd die.'

We embarrassed ourselves in cafés and taxicabs. We couldn't sleep unless we drank too much, but if we crossed some line with the drinking, we couldn't sleep at all, and then would just lie there beside one another, our eyes dry and red from crying, our throats clenched.

Pauline continued to write every day and her voice was like a wasp in my ear: *I'm missing my cherishables beyond reason. Please write to me, Hadley. I know we can all take care of each other and be happy. I just know it.*

'We can't go on like this, can we?' Ernest said, picking up one of Pauline's letters and then putting it down again. 'Do you think we can?'

'I hope not.'

'The world's gone to hell in every direction.'

'Yes,' I said.

'You make your life with someone and you love that person and you think it's enough. But it's never enough, is it?'

'I couldn't say. I don't know anything about love any more. I just want to stop feeling for a while. Can we do that?'

'That's what the whiskey's for.'

'It's letting me down, then,' I said. 'I'm raw all over.'

'Let's go home.'

'Yes, it's time we do. But not together. That's done.'

'I know it is,' he said.

We looked at each other across the room and saw everything plainly and couldn't say anything more for a long time.

On our way back to Paris, we stopped overnight at Villa America, but we'd given up trying to fool anyone, not even ourselves. Over cocktails at the beach, we told Gerald and Sara that we were splitting up.

'It can't be,' Gerald said.

'It can. It is,' Ernest said, draining his glass. 'But keep that coming, will you?'

Sara gave me a tender look — as tender as she was capable of — and then got up to mix another shaker of martinis.

'How will it work? Where will you live?' Gerald said.

'We haven't quite worked all that out yet,' I said. 'It's all very new.'

Gerald looked thoughtfully out to sea for several minutes and then said to Ernest, 'I've got the studio, you know, at rue Froidevaux. It's yours if you want it. As long as you need.'

'That's damned good of you.'

'You have to count on your friends, right?'

When Sara came back, Don Stewart and his pretty new bride, Beatrice Ames, trailed her. They were honeymooning at a hotel in town.

'Donald,' I said, and embraced him warmly, but his face was pale and he looked uneasy, and so did Beatrice. Sara had obviously whispered our news on the way down to the beach. She'd made very good time.

More chairs were brought round the little mosaic table in the sand, and we all drank pointedly and watched the dusk come.

'I don't mind saying I thought you two were indestructible,' Donald said.

'I know it,' Gerald said. He turned to Sara. 'Haven't I always said the Hemingways did marriage like no one else? That they seemed lassoed to some higher thing?'

'All right then,' Ernest broke in. 'Let's cut the post-mortem, shall we? We're sick enough as it is.'

'Let's have something happy,' I said. 'Tell us about the wedding, Don.'

Don flushed and looked to Beatrice. She was a very pretty Gibson-girl type, with a high forehead and red bow-shaped mouth, but just then she'd lost her composure. 'I don't think we should talk about it,' she said. 'It doesn't feel right.'

'Oh, that,' Ernest said. 'You'll get used to it.' His lips were tight and dry and his eyes were resigned. I could tell that all of this was going too fast for him but that he was playing through it anyway, following the gin and the blithe talk. The end had been coming for months and months, ever since our time at Schruns, but now that it was on us, we didn't know what to do with it.

It wasn't until the next afternoon, when we were on the train back to Paris, that the full weight of what was happening hit us both. The day was airless and oppressively hot, and the train was too full. We shared a sleeping compartment with an American woman who carried an intricately scrolled birdcage with a small yellow canary inside. Before we'd said more than hello to her, the woman launched into an elaborate story of how the bird was a present for her daughter who had been engaged to marry a Swiss engineer before she stepped in to break up the match. 'I immediately saw how I needed to send him packing,' the woman said. 'You know how the Swiss are.'

'Yes, of course,' Ernest said, tightening his lips around the words. He knew no such thing. 'You'll excuse me,' he said. 'I think I'll go and look for the porter.' When he came back, he was carrying a bottle of brandy and we drank it straight out of the water glasses on hand.

We were near Marseilles by then, and out the window everything seemed very dusty and white-gray – the olive trees, the farmhouses and fieldstone walls and hills in the distance. All of it looked strangely bleached out and the woman was somehow still talking about marriage and how she hoped her daughter would forgive her. I drank my brandy and had another, and tried not to hear the woman at all. The bird chirped prettily, but I found I didn't want to hear that either.

As evening fell, the woman finally closed her eyes and began to snore, her thick head nodding on her shoulders. We were coming into Avignon, where a farmhouse was on fire in a dry field. We could see the flames rising dramatically into the darkening sky, and sheep running back and forth behind sagging fencing looking wild and panicked. The blaze must have announced itself early on, because much of the furniture was spread out in the field well away from the house while men worked to save what they could. I saw a pink enamel washtub and a rocking chair and a baby buggy on its side, and it was all utterly heartbreaking. This was someone's life, a pile of furniture like matchsticks. It didn't look rescued but abandoned — while smoke billowed in great plumes.

When we approached Paris, it was very near morning. Ernest and I had both slept very little all night, and we had talked very little as well. What we did was drink and look out the window, where it seemed the signs of destruction were unending. On the outskirts of the city, near Choisy-le-Roi, a wrecked baggage car steamed in a crush to one side of the tracks.

'Are we really going through with this?' I said to Ernest.

'I don't know, are we?'

Just then, the American woman woke and stretched loudly and then took the velvet cape off of the birdcage to wake the canary. Somehow it was morning and we were home, though it was hard to feel anything. I'd drunk so much brandy, my hands twitched with it and my heart thudded dully in my chest.

When we arrived at the train station, Ernest handed the porter our bags through the window and we walked out onto the platform. It was nearly September, and the morning air was cool and dewy.

'Sixty-nine rue Froidevaux,' Ernest told the taxi driver, and my breath caught in my throat. He was going to Gerald's studio, not home with me. Not back to anything. It really was over.

'Why not just go to Pauline's apartment directly?' I said.

'Please don't start. This is painful enough.'

'What would you know about pain? You're doing this, you bastard.'

I didn't know what I was saying. The brandy was still clogging my bloodstream and moving my thoughts. For the moment, all I really knew was that I couldn't be alone. I started to hyperventilate, and when Ernest moved closer, worried for me, I lashed out at him with the flat of my palm, hitting his chest, his shoulder, his jaw. Everything landed strangely, the way it does it dreams. My hand felt elastic and so did his body. I started to cry then and couldn't stop.

'Pardon my wife,' Ernest said to the driver in French. 'She's not well.'

When the cab finally stopped, Ernest got out and came over to my side and opened the door for me. 'C'mon then,' he said. 'You need to sleep.'

I let him lead me up the stairs like a mannequin. Inside the studio, there was a cold concrete floor, a single table and two chairs, a low sink with a pitcher and stand. He walked me over to a narrow platform bed and tucked me into it, pulling a red wool blanket up to my chin. Then he climbed behind me and brought his arms around and tucked his knees against the backs of mine, hugging me as tightly as possible.

'There's a good Cat,' he said to the back of my neck. 'Please sleep now.'

I started to shake. 'Let's not do this. I can't.'

'Yes you can. It's already done, my love.' And he rocked us back and forth as we both cried, and when I slept finally, I didn't give into it as much as was taken over by it, like a sickness or like death.

When I woke up hours later, he was already gone. My head swam from the brandy and there was another level of nausea that came from a deep and unanswerable place. My life was in shambles; how would I right myself? How would I get through this? Picking up a piece of charcoal from a low table, I wrote him a note on sketchbook paper that was much calmer and more collected than I felt or even believed I could feel: *So sorry for the scene in the cab. I've lost my mind, but I'll do my best to be as good as I can about everything. I'll want to see you, I will, but I won't search you out.*

I left the studio, locking the door behind me, and walked out into a little courtyard, where a stone bench sat flanked by coppery mums. The walls to each side were hung with ivy. This was what Ernest would see when he gazed out the studio's windows – a new view that had nothing whatever to do with me. I tried not to let this terrible thought chink away at my thin resolve as I climbed into a cab bound for the Hôtel Beauvoir on the avenue de l'Observatoire. This was the first place I thought of because it was right across the street from the Closerie des Lilas and I'd looked up at it a thousand times and admired its simple and well-made wrought-iron grille and its pots of geraniums. I would find a way to live through this. I would rent two rooms, one for me and one for

Bumby. Marie Cocotte would return from Brittany with him the following week, and I'd write to tell her to bring him there. We could breakfast every morning at the Lilas. He could see his father often there, and other friends, and it would all be very familiar, and that would be important now.

As the cab moved slowly against traffic, I closed my eyes and tried not to think of anything except the café crème I would have very soon. I would make that last and then do what came next, whatever that was. All of my things were at the sawmill and that would have to be dealt with. I would ask Ernest to do it or hire someone, because I knew I couldn't go back there. I wouldn't. I didn't. I never did again.

Forty-Four

Ernest once told me that the word *paradise* was a Persian word that meant *walled garden*. I knew then that he understood how necessary the promises we made to each other were to our happiness. You couldn't have real freedom unless you knew where the walls were and tended them. We could lean on the walls because they existed; they existed because we leaned on them. With Pauline's coming, everything had begun to tumble. Nothing at all seemed permanent to me now except what was already behind me, what we'd already done and lived together.

I said all of this to Don Stewart one night at the Deux Magots. He and Beatrice were back in Paris and he had looked me up, worried for me and sick about our breakup.

'I hate to be morbid,' I said, 'but next week is our fifth anniversary. Or would be. His timing stinks.'

'You could fight for him, you know.'

'It's much too late for that. Pauline's pushing him to ask for a divorce.'

'Even so, what will you do later if you do nothing now?'

365

I shrugged and looked out the window where a very pretty woman in Chanel was waiting for someone or something on the corner. She was a slender black rectangle with a button of a hat, and she didn't look fragile at all. 'I don't know that I can actually compete.'

'Why should you have to compete? You're the wife. He rightfully belongs to you.'

'People belong to each other only as long as they both believe. He's stopped believing.'

'Maybe he's just terribly confused.'

He walked me back to my hotel and kissed me gently on the cheek, and it reminded me of that dangerous summer in Pamplona with Duff and Pat and Harold, when everything boiled over and grew ugly. But even then, there were small stabs of happiness.

'You've always been good to me, Don,' I said. 'That sticks more than you know.'

'Forget what I said in the café if you want. I don't mean to tell you what to do with your marriage. Hell, I'm only just married myself. But there must be something. Some answer.'

I said goodnight and walked slowly up the stairs to the third floor, where Bumby was well asleep and Marie was folding his clothes in perfect stacks with her very sure hands. I sent her home and finished the folding myself, thinking about what I still might do to make any kind of difference with Ernest. And the thing I kept coming back to was how if Pauline weren't nearby and he couldn't see her, he might come out of his fog and return to me. He still loved me; I knew it. But the real presence of the girl was like a siren's call and he couldn't fight it.

The next day, feeling very resolved about a new decision, I walked to Gerald's studio at the rue de Froidevaux, through the

366

little courtyard, which was still a battlefield of plaster body parts, and found Ernest working at the stiff little table. I didn't sit down. I couldn't.

'I want you and Pauline to agree not to see each other for a hundred days.'

He was silent and surprised. I'd definitely gotten his attention.

'I don't care where she goes – she can board a ferry for hell, for all I care – but she has to go away. You can't see her and you can't write her and if you stick to this and are still in love with her after the hundred days, I'll give you a divorce.'

'I see. And how did you come up with this brilliant scheme?'

'I don't know. Something Don Stewart said.'

'Don? He's always been after you, you know.'

'You're hardly in a position to judge.'

'Yes, all right. So one hundred days? And then you'll give me the divorce?'

'If that's what you still want.'

'What do you want, Tatie?'

'To feel better.' My eyes were wet and I struggled to keep more tears from coming. I handed him the piece of paper where I'd written out the agreement and signed it. 'You sign it too. I want this to be clear and straight.'

He took it solemnly. 'You're not trying to punish me, are you?'

'I don't know. I don't know anything any more.'

He took the agreement to Pauline and told her the scheme and, strangely, she agreed right away. I guessed it was her very strong Catholicism that brought out the martyr in her. She might have thought my asking for three months was a reasonable request for a jilted wife, but she also might have felt she hadn't yet suffered enough for the relationship. The separation would help with that. She wrote to me that she admired and trusted my decision, and then she took a leave of absence from the magazine, and booked a passage on the *Pennland* for the States.

Within eleven days of my writing out the agreement, Pauline was out of Paris, if not out of the picture.

'Can I write her while she's still on board her ship?' he asked. 'Is that allowed?'

'All right, but then the hundred days don't really start until she arrives in New York.'

'You're like some sort of queen, aren't you? Handing down the rules.'

'You didn't have to agree.'

'No, I guess that's true.'

'I'm not trying to be nasty,' I told him gently. 'I'm trying to save my life.'

Ernest hated to be alone and always had – but Pauline's absence had left him more than alone and very vulnerable. Within a very few days, he showed up at my hotel room at the dinner hour. He'd just finished writing for the day and had that look behind his eyes he always got when he'd been in his head for too long and needed talk.

'How'd the work go today, Tatie?' I asked, inviting him in.

'A little like busting through granite,' he said. 'Can a fellow get a drink here?'

He came into the dining room, where Bumby was eating bread and bananas. He sat down and I could feel each of us, even Bumby, exhaling into that space. Just to be at the same table.

I brought out a bottle of wine and we had that, and then shared a very simple dinner.

'*Scribner's Magazine* is paying me a hundred and fifty dollars for a story,' he said.

'That's a lot of money, isn't it?'

'I should say. Maybe you ought not read it, though. It's about our train ride back from Antibes with the canary woman. It won't be very pleasant for you.'

'All right, I won't,' I said, wondering to myself if he'd put the burning Avignon farmhouse in the story, as well, and the caved-in smoldering train cars. 'Do you want to do the baby's bath?'

He rolled up his sleeves and got out the washtub, then squatted on the floor beside it while Bumby played and splashed.

'He's almost too big for the tub, isn't he?'

'He'll be three in a few weeks. We should give him a party with hats and strawberry ice cream.'

'And balloons,' Bumby said. 'And a little monkey.'

'You're a little monkey, Schatz,' Ernest said, and scooped him up in the big towel.

Afterward, I put him to bed and when I came out of his room and closed the door, Ernest was still at the table.

'I don't want to ask if I can stay,' he said.

'So don't ask,' I said. I flicked off the lamp and then went over to the table and knelt in front of him. He cupped the back of my head in his hand tenderly and I buried my face in his lap, breathing in the coarse fabric of his new trousers — ones he'd bought with Pauline's help, no doubt, so she wouldn't be embarrassed to parade him in front of her Right Bank friends. I pushed harder, and then flexed my fingertips along the backs of his calves.

'Come on,' he said, trying to stand, but I didn't rise. I suppose it was perverse, but I wanted to have him right there, on

369

my terms, and keep him there until the hot, sick feeling in my stomach went away. He was still my husband.

When I woke the next morning, he was asleep next to me and the bedding was warm around us. I pressed my body against his back, grazing his stomach with my palms until he was awake enough and we made love again. In some ways, it was as if nothing had changed. Our bodies knew each other so well we didn't have to think about how to move. But when it was over and we lay still, I felt a terrible sadness come down because I loved him as much as I ever had. *We're the same guy*, I thought, but it wasn't really true. He'd always been emphatic over the years that we were essentially alike. We did grow to look like one another, with our hair short, our faces tan and healthy and round. But looking alike didn't mean we weren't alone, each of us.

'Does this mean anything?' I asked, careful not to look at him when I said it.

'Everything means something.' He was silent for several minutes and then said, 'She's ripping herself apart, you know.'

'We all are. Did you see Schatz's face last night? He was so happy to have you here. He must be very confused.'

'We're all bitched for sure.' He sighed and rolled over and started to dress. 'You know, Pfife thinks you're very wise to do all of this and to try to make some order out of the mess we've all made, but she's falling to pieces over it and so am I.'

'Why are you telling me any of this? What am I supposed to feel?'

'I don't know. But if I can't tell you, who should I tell?'

FORTY-FIVE

As soon as he mentioned the split to the Murphys, Gerald had become so accommodating. Why was that? He'd pulled the studio out of a hat and money, too. He could draw on Murphy's bank.

'This isn't just about marriage,' Gerald had said when he made the offer, just the two of them sharing a drink in private. 'I don't know what I'd do without Sara, but you're different and so the rules are different too. You can have a place in history. You do already. Your name's there on a card, and you only have to turn one way and not the other.'

'What do you have against Hadley?'

'Nothing. How could I? She runs at a different speed is all. She's more cautious.'

'And I'll have to be cut throat. Is that what you mean?'

'No. Just determined.'

'She's seen me through this whole while.'

'Yes, and she's done it beautifully. But what comes next, that's all new. You need to be looking forward now. I know you see that.'

He had often felt that Gerald over-flattered him, but now with *Sun* behind him and so much ahead, he did feel as if there was so much more required. He didn't know what, exactly, only that it would take everything he had.

Pfife was full of ideas for the future. She'd already organized the marriage ceremony and had likely been planning it from the beginning. That was how she made a deal with God or her own conscience.

'Tell me you love me,' she said the first time, when he was still inside her.

'I love you.' She was muscular and strong and it was interesting to have her in bed, strangely adversarial, with a wildness and a toughness that was nothing like Hadley.

'More than you love her? Even if it's not true, I want you to say it.'

'I love you more,' he said.

She pushed him over with her long firm legs and straddled him. Her hands on his chest. Her dark eyes boring into his intently. 'Tell me you wish you'd met me first,' she said driving hard against him.

'Yes,' he said.

'I would be your wife now. Your only wife.'

Her expression was utterly removed and fierce all at once, and it unnerved him a little. Maybe she had to invent a life for them in her head, or else how could she live with herself and be Hadley's friend? At Schruns, he had watched them side by side in front of the fire, talking and laughing. They had their legs crossed in the same direction, wearing the same socks and the same Alpine slippers. They weren't sisters, they were nothing alike. He was the only thing that really joined them.

He wasn't sleeping well and his nightmares were back. Sometimes, in the still middle of the night, he thought about the women he'd loved. He remembered trying to please his mother, and how awful that was. He called her Fweetee and invented songs for her, and when she took him to Boston on the train, alone, when he was ten years old, he remembered how proud he was to sit with her in the dining car and eat crab salad with a three-pronged silver fork, hushed white linens all around. But shortly after they returned home, another baby had come and then another, and he was too old to be so desperate for her anyway. He killed the desperation off slowly and deliberately by remembering how changeable and critical she was, under the tenderness, and how he couldn't trust her.

372

This trick didn't always work. Sometimes a woman stayed mysterious and unmanageable, like Kate, and sometimes she got down into the core of you and stayed there, no matter what. Hadley was the best woman he knew, and far too good for him. He'd always thought it and kept thinking it even when she lost the valise with his manuscripts. He tried never to let himself dwell on that day. It had been the most terrible thing he'd ever lived through. Being wounded was one thing. That had broken up his body and awakened him to fear and terror. It was still with him, like the shrapnel buried deep in the tissue of his muscles. But his work, that was him. When it was gone, he'd felt entirely empty, like he might simply recede and become air — a hurt place and a feeling around nothingness.

He still loved Hadley afterwards. He couldn't and wouldn't stop loving her, maybe ever, but she'd killed something in him too. He'd once felt so anchored and solid and safe with her, but now he wondered if he could ever trust anyone. That was the real question and he didn't have an answer. Sometimes it felt as if there was a flawed keystone at the center of him, threatening everything invisibly. Pauline was his future. He'd made his promises and was committed to giving her all he had. But if he was honest with himself, he knew he didn't trust her either. That part of love might be lost to him forever.

FORTY-SIX

In the middle of October, Ernest came around with a copy of *The Sun Also Rises*, which had just been published in the States. He made a great ceremony of unwrapping it from the brown paper and string and handing it to me shyly. Just inside the flyleaf, the book was dedicated to Bumby and to me. He'd changed it since we separated to include my name.

'Oh, Tatie. It really is a beautiful book and I'm so proud.'

'You like the dedication then?'

'I love it. It's just perfect.'

'Good, then. I wanted to do this much for you at least. I've made such a wreck of everything and there's so much damage, now, all around.'

'Yes,' I said, very moved. 'But look at this.' I held up the book. 'Look what you can do. You made this.'

'It's us. It's our life.'

'No, it was you from the beginning. You must have known that, writing it.'

'Maybe so.' He looked at the book in my hands, and then turned away to the window.

I did my best to try to break out of old habits and see friends. There were a few people from the old days who wanted to help. Ada MacLeish called round to take me to dinner and get my mind off of things. Gertrude and Alice invited me to tea, but I thought it would be a bad idea to rekindle that friendship and risk Ernest believing I was choosing Gertrude over him. Loyalty was a dicey game, and it was tough to know whom I could safely turn to. Kitty was torn. Pauline was her friend but so was I; she'd never liked Ernest at all and didn't trust him. She came to the apartment a few times but asked me not to pass on to Ernest that I'd seen her.

'Caught behind enemy lines and all that,' she said.

'How is it I'm the enemy when she's the other woman? That seems very unfair doesn't it?'

'When Harold and I split, you'd think I'd fallen into the *pissoir* for all people cared for me. It takes time. Things will shift back your way after a while. Just breathe through it, darling.'

One afternoon I thought Bumby was napping, but he must have heard me crying at the dining table, my head in my arms. I didn't know he was in the room until I heard him ask, 'What are you worrying about, Mama?'

'Oh, Schatz, I'm fine,' I said, drying my eyes on my sweater.

But I wasn't fine. I was lower than I'd ever been, and finding it harder and harder to rally. It was early November and less than sixty days into the hundred when I asked Ernest if he'd watch Bumby so I could go away for a bit to think. He agreed to give me the time and at the eleventh hour, I asked Kitty to go with me. I had chosen Chartres, and told her that without her good company, I wouldn't be able to appreciate the châteaux and the lovely countryside, but in truth I was afraid to be alone.

We checked into the Grand Hôtel de France just before

sunset, and though it was a little chilly, Kitty suggested we take a walk around the lake before dinner. The air was crisp and all the trees seemed sharply etched.

'I've been thinking a lot about my wedding vows,' I said to Kitty when we were halfway around. 'I promised to love him for better or worse, didn't I?'

'Worse has definitely arrived.' She frowned. 'Honestly, I had a hard time choking down my own vows. The way I see it, how can you really say you'll love a person longer than love lasts? And as for the obeying part, well, I just wouldn't say it.'

'I didn't say that part either, but strangely I've managed it anyway.'

'When I met Harold, he'd lost his faith in marriage too, and so we made our own private pact. We would be partners and equals as long as things were good, but when love ended, we'd end too.'

'It's an admirable idea, but I can't believe it can ever be that civilized. It wasn't for you two.'

'No,' she said. 'Lately I've wondered if maybe I'm not meant to have love – the lasting kind, I mean.'

'I'm not sure what I'm meant to have. Or *be*, for that matter.'

'Maybe this break from Ernest will give you a chance to find out.'

'Maybe it will.' I looked up to find we'd made it all around the lake while we talked and now were back, exactly, at where we'd started.

After a week at Chartres, my head finally began to clear. One morning, I sent Kitty off to explore alone and wrote:

Dearest Tatie,

I love you now more than I ever have in some ways and though different people view their marriage vows differently, I meant mine to the death. I'm ready to be yours forever if you must know it, but since you've fallen in love and want to marry someone else, I feel I have no choice but to move aside and let you do that. The one hundred days are officially off. It was a terrible idea and it embarrasses me now. Tell Pauline whatever you choose. You can see Bumby as much as ever you like. He's very much yours and loves and misses you. But please let's only write about the divorce and not talk about it. I can't quarrel with you any more and live through it, and I can't see you much either, because it hurts too much. We'll always be friends — delicate friends, and I'll love you till I die, you know.

Ever yours, the Cat.

I was crying hard when I mailed the letter, but felt lighter for it. I spent the rest of the morning staring into the fire in my room, and when Kitty came back from sightseeing alone, I was still in my pajamas and robe.

'You look different,' she said, and there was a great deal of kindness in her eyes. 'Are you through with it, then?'

'I'm trying to be. Will you help me by opening us a very good Château Margaux?'

'I'm sure Hem's been just as miserable waiting for a decision from you,' she said, uncorking the wine. 'Although I don't know how I could still have a stitch of sympathy for him after that damned novel of his. He was even crueler to Harold. He's going to lose all his friends, you know.'

'He might very well,' I said. 'I still don't know why he needed to write it that way, stepping on bodies as he went, but you have to admit it's a brilliant book.'

'Do I? You're not in it at all. How do you forgive him that?'

'The same as always.'

'Right,' she said, and we lifted our glasses silently.

Kitty and I drove back to Paris several days later and it was there I received Ernest's reply.

My Dearest Hadley — I don't know how to thank you for your very brave letter. I've been worried for you and for all of us because of this terrible deadlock. We've drawn things out so painfully, neither of us knowing how to move ahead without causing more damage. But if divorce is the next necessary step, then I trust that once we start, we'll begin to feel stronger and better and more like ourselves again.

He went on to say he wanted me to have all the royalties from *Sun* and that he had already written Max Perkins telling him this, and finished by saying:

I think you're a wonderful mother, and that Bumby couldn't be better off than in your very lovely and capable hands. You are everything good and straight and fine and true — and I see that so clearly now, in the way you've carried yourself and listened to your own heart. You've changed me more than you know, and will always be a part of everything I am. That's one thing I've learned from this. No one you love is ever truly lost.
Ernest

FORTY-SEVEN

We called Paris the great good place, then, and it was. We invented it after all. We made it with our longing and cigarettes and Rhum St James; we made it with smoke, and smart and savage conversation and we dared anyone to say it wasn't ours. Together we made everything and then we busted it apart again.

There are some who said I should have fought harder or longer than I did for my marriage, but in the end fighting for a love that was already gone felt like trying to live in the ruins of a lost city. I couldn't bear it, and so I backed away – and the reason I could do it at all, the reason I was strong enough and had the legs and the heart to do it is because Ernest had come along and changed me. He helped me see what I really was and what I could do. Now that I knew what I could bear, I would have to bear losing him.

In the spring of 1927, Bumby and I sailed for the States for a nice long break from Paris and all that still could drag on us there. We lived in New York for several months, and then got on a long slow train across the country that dropped us, finally, in Carmel, California. I rented us a house close to the beach in a grove of pines. The sky went on forever there, and cypresses stood twisted by the wind, and the sunshine made me feel stronger. It was there I learned that Ernest and Pauline had married, in a small Catholic ceremony in Paris. Somehow he'd managed to convince the priest that he was Catholic, and as such, since his first marriage had been presided over by a Methodist minister, it didn't count. I read this news on a rare cloudy day in May, while Bumby dug a trench in the sand with his shovel. Seawater spilled over the sides, dissolving the sand walls even as they were being built. It made me want to cry just watching, so I took the letter and walked to the water's edge. Beyond the breakers, the waves bled from gray to white and the horizon was white too, everything melting into everything else. Out past all that water, Ernest and Pauline were building a life together. He and I had already had our time, and though it was still very close and real to me, as beautiful and poignant as any place on the map, it was, in truth, another time – another country.

Bumby came over to where I stood and pressed his damp salty face into my skirt.

'Should we make a boat?' I asked.

He nodded yes, and I folded Ernest's letter, creasing and squaring the edges until it seemed sturdy. I gave it to Bumby and together we waded out into the surf and let the boat go. It bobbed and dipped, words on water, and when the waves gradually took it, I only cried a very little, and then it was gone.

Epilogue

Bumby and I returned to Paris after our summer in Carmel. He missed his father terribly and honestly, I didn't know where else I should go.

After a few months there, I became involved with Paul Mowrer, an old journalist-acquaintance of Ernest's. Paul was the foreign editor of the *Chicago Daily News*, and a good poet in private as well. He and Ernest had worked together in Genoa, and I'd met him a few times back then. Not long after Ernest and I separated, I ran into Paul at a tennis club and he invited me out after my game, for a beer at the Café de l'Observatoire. He was interested in me, and made that gently clear, but I needed time to think. So much of me still belonged to Ernest, I wasn't sure I could ever really love anyone else. But Paul was incredibly kind and patient too, and he had these wonderfully clear Mediterranean blue eyes. The longer I looked into them, the longer I wanted to go on looking into them. There was nothing complicated about Paul. He was solid and even and had that wonderful stillness all the time. I knew he would love me forever and not ruin me, not even a little. I just had to let it happen.

In the spring of 1928, Ernest and Pauline left Paris for the States. Pauline was five months pregnant at the time, and they were headed to Piggott and then to Key West, where Dos Passos had promised the best tarpon fishing in the world. Pauline would buy a house for them and make everything wonderful because she knew how to do all of that – where to buy the best furniture and how to get pictures framed the right way and which friends to cultivate. She could care for him better than I had, maybe. Or maybe not.

In the end, Ernest didn't have the luck I did in love. He had two more sons, both with Pauline, and then left her for another. And left that one for another, too. He had four wives altogether and many lovers as well. It was sometimes painful for me to think that to those who followed his life with interest, I was just the early wife, the Paris wife. But that was probably vanity, wanting to stand out in a long line of women. In truth it didn't matter what others saw. We knew what we had and what it meant, and though so much had happened since for both of us, there was nothing like those years in Paris, after the war. Life was painfully pure and simple and good, and I believe Ernest was his best self then. I got the very best of him. We got the best of each other.

After he left for the States, I saw him just twice more in my very long life, but I watched from a distance as he became, very quickly, the most important writer of his generation and also a kind of hero of his own making. I saw him on the cover of *Life Magazine*, and heard about the wars he covered bravely and the other feats – the world-class fishing, the big-game hunting in Africa, the drinking enough to embalm a man twice his size. The myth he was creating out of his own life was big enough to take it for a time – but under this, I knew he was still lost. That he slept with the light on or couldn't sleep at all, that he feared death so much he sought it out wherever and however he could. He was such an enigma, really – fine and strong and weak and cruel. An incomparable friend and a son of a bitch. In the end, there wasn't one thing about him that was truer than the rest. It was all true.

The last time we ever spoke was in May of 1961. He called out of the blue around lunchtime on a cool afternoon when Paul and I were in Arizona, vacationing at a ranch we returned to every few years for the fine fishing and the views. I took the call alone while Paul invented an errand because he knew I needed this. I didn't have to ask. We'd been married thirty-five years and Paul knew me better than anyone. Almost.

'Hello, Tatie,' Ernest said when I picked up the receiver.

'Hello, Tatie,' I said back, smiling to hear our forty-year-old nickname again.

'Your housekeeper told me how to find you. I hope you don't mind.'

'No, I'm happy you called. I'm happy it's you.'

I told him quickly about the ranch Paul and I were staying at, because I knew he would approve of it. It wasn't prissy or too comfortable. There were dark silky places on the wood paneling in the cabin from eighty years of good fires, and all the furniture was rugged and plain and felt real under you. The days were long and open. The nights were full of stars.

It had been ages since I'd heard from him, and now he was calling to talk about a new book, a memoir. He wanted to share stories about our time in Paris.

'Do you remember the whores at the *bal musette*, and the accordion music and the smoke and the smells?'

I told him I did.

'Do you remember that Bastille Day when musicians played under our windows for nights on end?'

'I remember it all.'

'You're everywhere in the book,' he said, and his voice dipped. He was working hard to stay cheerful, but I knew he was sad and low and haunted. 'It's been something, writing that time and living it all again. Tell me, do you think we wanted too much from each other?'

'Oh, I don't know, Tatie. It's possible.'

'Maybe that's it. We were too hooked into each other. We loved each other too much.'

'Can you love someone too much?'

He was quiet for a moment and I could hear static coming through the line, a low crackle that seemed to stand for every sharp thing that had come between us. 'No,' he finally said, his voice very soft and sober. 'That's not it at all. I ruined it.'

I felt a hot clench in the muscles of my throat, but I tried to rally. We both did. We talked about Paris a while longer and then about Bumby and his new wife Puck, and then stayed on the phone though everything had been said.

'Take care of the Cat,' he said when he rang off, meaning me. I hung up and sat down hard on the sofa, and then surprised myself by bursting into tears.

Later that afternoon, Paul and I took the long way to the stream and dropped our lines in just as the insects began to swarm and the light began to change. It was our favorite part of day, this in-between time, and it always held and seemed to last longer than it should – a magic and lavender space unpinned from the hours around it, between worlds. I held my reel and felt the line list, and was back in Cologne with Ernest and Chink. Back at my first fish, knowing there

384

wouldn't be any fish without this one, and no love without this first one either.

It was a Sunday in July when we got the call from Ernest's wife Mary that he had shot himself. He'd woken early and put on his favorite red robe and gone into the front foyer with one of his most loved guns. He'd stood in a pool of light, and leaned into the barrel and tripped both triggers.

The irony wasn't lost on me that this is exactly the way my father had killed himself, and Ernest's father, too, in 1928, when Ernest was just twenty-nine. Maybe it wasn't irony at all, but the purest and saddest sort of history. Ernest's father used a Civil War pistol. Later, his brother Leicester would use a pistol too. His sister Ursula would take pills. With this much loss, you begin to think it's in the blood, as if there's a dark magnet pulling the body in that direction – pulling, maybe, from the beginning.

I couldn't pretend to be surprised by Ernest's death. I'd heard from various friends about the sanitarium in Rochester and the shock treatments. Death was always there for him, sometimes only barely balanced out.

'Can I get you anything?' Paul said after a while, stepping back from me and cupping my shoulders with his hands.

'No,' I said, and my own voice sounded strange and separate in the room. Tatie was dead. There was nothing Paul could possibly do for me except let me go – back to Paris and Pamplona and San Sebastian, back to Chicago when I was Hadley Richardson, a girl stepping off a train about to meet the man who would change her life. That girl, that impossibly lucky girl, needed nothing.

ACKNOWLEDGMENTS

First and foremost, I need to thank my agent, Julie Barer, whose absolute investment in this project was obvious (and so very crucial) from word one. The completely brilliant Susanna Porter was vital in bringing the book to its final form and nothing less than my dream editor. I'm deeply appreciative for the support and assistance of so many at Ballantine Books and Random House, including Libby McGuire, Kim Hovey, Theresa Zoro, Kristin Fassler, Quinne Rogers, Deborah Foley, Steve Messina, Jillian Quint and Sophie Epstein. William Boggess at Barer Literary fielded every desperate phone call with aplomb and has been indispensable to the process. Many thanks to Ursula Doyle, Victoria Pepe and Virago, Kristen Cochrane and Doubleday Canada, as well as Caspian Dennis of Abner Stein, and Niki Kennedy, Sam Edenborough and all at ILA.

Special appreciation goes to friends and early readers, Glori Simmons, Lori Keene, Brian Groh, Anne Ursu, Alice D'Alessio, Sarah Willis, Terry Dubow, Toni Thayer and the East Side Writers, Denise Machado and John Sargent, Paul Cox and

Kristen Docter, Pam and Doug O'Hara, Tawny Ratner and the Cedar Hill Walking Club, William Joson, Becky Gaylord, Heather Greene, Amy Weinfurtner, Margaret Cohen and Patricia Kao, Suzannah Hagan and Karen Rosenberg. Also to Karen Long of the *Cleveland Plain Dealer*, Judith Mansour at the LIT, Jim Harms and Jacqueline Gens of the MFA Program in Poetry at New England College, and many dear colleagues and students over the years.

I owe my family much for their unending patience and encouragement – Greg D'Alessio, Connor, Fiona and Beckett, D'Alessios far and wide, Julie Hayward, Rita Hinken and, finally, my wonderful, unflappable sisters, Teresa Reller and Penny Pennington. Many thanks and much love to all.

A Note on Sources

Although Hadley Richardson, Ernest Hemingway and other people who actually lived appear in this book as fictional characters, it was important for me to render the particulars of their lives as accurately as possible, and to follow the very well documented historical record. The true story of the Hemingways' marriage is so dramatic and compelling, and has been so beautifully treated by Ernest Hemingway himself, in *A Moveable Feast*, that my intention became to push deeper into the emotional lives of the characters and bring new insight to historical events, while staying faithful to the facts. Along the way, I've been very grateful for a number of sources, including *Hadley: The First Mrs Hemingway*, by Alice Hunt Sokoloff, *Hadley*, by Gioia Diliberto, *The Hemingway Women*, by Bernice Kert, *Ernest Hemingway: A Life Story*, and *Ernest Hemingway Selected Letters: 1917–1961*, by Carlos Baker, *Hemingway: The Paris Years* and *Hemingway: The American Homecoming*, by Michael Reynolds, and *The True Gen*, by Denis Brian. Enormously useful to my understanding of Paris in the twenties and other details of place and time were *The Crazy Years*, by William Wiser, *Paris was Yesterday* by Janet Flanner, *Living Well is the Best Revenge*, by Calvin Tomkins, *Zelda*, by Nancy Milford, *The Great War in Modern Memory*, by Paul Fussell, and *The Selected Writings of Gertrude Stein*. Susan Wrynn and Sam Smallidge of the Hemingway Collection at the John F. Kennedy Memorial Library in Boston were very helpful as I navigated a wealth of materials, including correspondence between Hadley Richardson and Ernest Hemingway, and Hemingway's writings in manuscript form. Finally I'm indebted to many of Ernest Hemingway's works in addition to *A Moveable Feast*, most notably *In Our Time*, *The Sun Also Rises*, *The Garden of Eden*, *Death in the Afternoon*, and *The Complete Short Stories*.

PERMISSIONS ACKNOWLEDGMENTS

Paula McLain received an MFA in poetry from the University of Michigan and has been awarded fellowships from Yaddo, the MacDowell Colony, and the National Endowment for the Arts. She is the author of two collections of poetry as well as a memoir, *Like Family: Growing Up in Other People's Houses*, and a first novel, *A Ticket to Ride*. She lives in Cleveland, Ohio with her family.